NOB

Dids Hall

Text copyright © 2012 David M. Hall
All rights reserved. No part of this publication may be reproduced or transmitted in any form or by any means, electronic or mechanical, including photocopy, or any information storage device and retrieval system, without permission in writing from the author.

This book is a work of fiction. Names, characters and businesses, organizations, places and events are either the product of the author's imagination or are used fictitiously. Any resemblance to actual persons, living or dead, events or locales is entirely coincidental.

**To my parents Michael and Valerie Hall
for their continuing belief and support.**

For Sandra Kane RIP.

Acknowledgements

My thanks go to Jodie for all her help and also to my 'proof-readers' Penny and Nick Evans. I used to think I was quite good at grammar. Thank you to all of my friends for their encouragement.

Revised April 2014

If you have any comments or want to know more about forthcoming stories you can follow me on: Twitter @DidsHall
Facebook Dids Hall
e-mail dids@didshall.co.uk
www.didshall.com

A selection of reviews from Amazon:

***** An excellent book with lots of twists and turns. 19 Jun 2012 By A. D. Siddall Kindle Edition| Amazon Verified Purchase
Just finished 'Nobody Special' by Dids Hall and thoroughly enjoyed it. I really liked the building of characters and the pace of action, watch out for Hollywood buying the film rights, as it lends itself to the big screen.
The plot develops in different directions and in different countries, growing tension and a genuine fondness for the lead cast.
Looking forward to the sequel as I'm sure there will be one.

***** Utterly Fantastic 6 Aug 2012 By Maureen Kindle Edition
Since starting this book, I have hardly been able to put it down. It is a ripping yarn and not at all what I expected. This book is good for all ages of reader and I cannot wait for the next book to be published. An almost real empathy can be created with the characters. Overall I would thoroughly recommend this book, especially if you like action and adventure.

***** Gripping Story with Real Emotion, A Must Read! 30 Jun 2012 By Elaine Curran Kindle Edition
I had lost my reading mojo for several reasons but i think i may have found it again with this book! :) I found myself reading late into the night....right from the first chapter i was hooked. The attention to detail and the evocative images are praiseworthy, but most of all the real emotions which are so well captured make you care about these characters in a way which only the best authors can achieve imho. I really want to hear more about these people...there must be a second book to follow. Dids Hall is a name to watch I think.

***** Review of Nobody Special by Dids Hall, 28 Jun 2012 By COLIN RANCE Kindle Edition Amazon Verified Purchase
I flew through this one really quickly, just didn't want to put it down. It is nice and easy to read with likeable characters and idyllic settings. You don't get bogged down with long descriptions or character detail, it has just the right blend. The plot unfolds at a good pace with some twists and unexpected turns. I thought it got a little drawn out in the middle but then the action comes fast furious.
If this is his first book can't wait for a second. I am sure these characters could use a second outing

Chapter One

She knew before the muffled voice of the captain came through the speakers, that the plane had started its descent. It was always the same, slight pressure on the eardrums, partial loss of hearing and a feeling of light-headedness.

God, she hated to fly. Thinking back on it she hadn't flown for nearly five years. In fact, she would not be flying now if she had not received the devastating news just a few hours ago. Joseph was dead; her only brother had been murdered.

Up until roughly 12 hours ago Davina Stanton thought that she had it all. At thirty years of age, she was fit and well-toned; she was the managing partner in a club in Miami. She had worked diligently for the last five years with minimal help from her brother and their third partner Stephen Lawrence. Of course they regularly came over, ostensibly to see how the club was doing, but in reality, just for a holiday.

She could remember the feeling of pride she felt when Joseph had told her that he thought she would make a good manager and that the job was hers if she wanted it, as if it were yesterday. The pride was tinged with a touch of guilt as she thought of how Stephen would feel about being passed over. That fear was soon put to rest as Stephen told her that he had suggested the move and not to feel bad.

Deep down she had known that, in reality, neither Stephen nor Joseph would have been happy separated by the Atlantic Ocean. Although Joseph was more than capable of running the English club, he did rely heavily on Stephen's incredible business acumen. That coupled with the fact that they had been best friends since they were young.

Once the plane had touched down and taxied to the terminal, Davina waited for the rest of the passengers to disembark before making her way through to Passport Control.

There always seemed to be long queues for Passport Control. Then, of course, she would have to run the gauntlet of Customs. As a lone female travelling with hand luggage only, she was sure that she would be turned over.

As it turned out, she breezed through both Passport Control and Customs. Although there were Customs Officers present they seemed completely disinterested in her.

As Davina went through the doors into the packed arrivals hall she looked around for Stephen. She found him immediately. Whenever Stephen was in a crowded place, he seemed to exude an aura that said, "Give me space." This still held true and she saw him standing like a lone island in a sea of expectant faces, somehow untouchable.

He made his way towards her and the sea of people just seemed to part of their own volition.

They embraced like the old friends that they were and finally she started to cry.

"Hey, sweetheart, it's okay now! You'll be fine." He said this as he held her close in to his chest, just being there for her.

She didn't say anything for a long time. They just stayed where they were. Nobody seemed impatient or asked them to move. It was as though they were the only people in the arrivals hall. Then she started to marshal her thoughts.

"What happened?"

"Not here." Stephen said as he guided her through the arrivals hall towards the exit. "I'll tell you on the way."

They looked good together as they crossed the arrivals hall, his six foot four frame leading her five feet six inches easily towards the exit. They were both blond haired and could almost have been related, but that was just a quirk of nature. People stared at them as they walked, but she was used to that. It was probably because Stephen was stunningly handsome and attracted glances from both men and women and although she was no supermodel, her own looks might have something to do with it.

Stephen stopped at the ticket machine in the car park and then guided her over to his Land Cruiser Colorado. She had long ago stopped being amazed at how easily he found parking spaces in busy car parks. Stephen always said that confidence was the answer. Just be confident that you will find a space and there would be one.

Yeah. Right! It never works for me, she thought as she climbed into the car and Stephen shut her door. The car was immaculate. Both the boys had always been fanatical about their cars. As Stephen climbed into the driver's seat she relaxed back into her own seat and thought that it felt like an old glove.

She waited until they had negotiated their way onto the road out of the airport before she asked what had happened again.

"To be honest, I don't really know," he said. "It's like I told you on the phone. To all intents and purposes it was just a fight that kicked off and got out of hand. Joseph went to help and got shot. Having said that, there are other issues that need to be taken into account. There have been a few incidents in the last few months."

"What incidents? Neither of you said anything when you last came over." She was looking at him curiously from the side of her seat. He concentrated on his driving and thought how best to answer her question.

"It started when we came back. Joseph had had an offer to buy the club, which he refused. Then various things started happening, which on their own could have been nothing, but happening in sequence seemed to have darker implications."

"What things? Why didn't you tell me?" Davina looked accusingly at Stephen.

"Joseph didn't want to worry you and to be fair, up until now Joseph has succeeded in everything he does, sorry, did. Nothing was ever a problem so it should not have been an issue. You know how many offers we get for the club, you get hundreds in Miami."

They were on the motorway now and heading in the familiar direction of their home. It was funny but she still thought of it as her home, even though she had been away for five years.

"What do the Police say?" she was still looking at him. "I take it they have been told?"

"They're not sure what to make of it. They are being very helpful and seem to be taking it seriously."

"I should bloody hope so, Joseph has been shot." She closed her eyes and drifted off to sleep.

Stephen let her sleep for a while. There would be time enough to explain it all. She would be surprised about some of the details but he would hold nothing back.

They had reached the end of the boundary wall of Joseph's property when Davina awoke. Although Joseph was technically the owner, they had all lived there together for many years before Davina moved to Miami. It was funny but none of them had ever thought of living separately even though they could afford to.

After a few minutes they reached the gate and turned onto the driveway. The property was set back into the countryside in about ten hectares of land. The building itself was only about ten years old but it was designed to appear much older. In fact it was a showpiece to modern living. In the private river there was an Archimedes screw that powered the property and special rainwater collection and recycling tanks for watering the grounds. The list of alternative and energy efficient features that the house boasted was very impressive.

Stephen got out of the car and walked around to Davina's door. "There is someone here who has been waiting for you," Stephen said, as he took her bag and turned away.

"Oh, Stephen, I can't see anyone now. I'm jet lagged and I must look awful." She was still looking at Stephen as she spoke and did not see the dark shape that launched itself at her from behind the rear of the car until it was too late.

She screamed as one hundred and eighty pounds of Rottweiler landed on her chest. She fell back onto the side of the car and then finally lowered herself onto her bottom. "Get off of me you stupid mutt," she managed to get the words out even though it felt like the skin was being licked from her face.

"He's just pleased to see you," Stephen said laughing as he walked back towards her. "And to be fair it has been five years since he last saw you." He watched as the dog that Davina had last seen as a puppy jumped all over her. She hugged the dog hard and strangely he calmed down. "You haven't lost your touch then sweetheart!"

"Basic dog psychology," she laughed. "It works on most males. Alright Vincent, let me up!" The big dog sat back on his haunches and watched as Davina stood up. Then he walked at her knee all the way into the house. The full horror of the situation returned and she looked sadly around. Everything was different now.

"Mrs. Hoon has left you a sandwich," Stephen indicated the pile of food on the sideboard, "she thought you might need fattening up." Davina groaned as she looked at the food. She knew that she would have to eat something but had forgotten about her brother's housekeeper and her only goal in life, which was to force as much food into each of them as was humanly possible.

"Where is she? How is she coping?" Mrs. Hoon adored her brother. She thought the older woman must be really hurting inside with his death.

"She had to get back to her grandchildren, but she promised to be around bright and early tomorrow. She says you can have a cuppa and a chat then. She is happier now that you are here for a while though." Stephen looked knowingly at Davina as he remembered how Davina and Mrs. Hoon had always been as thick as thieves when Davina had lived here.

Davina ate the sandwiches and started yawning. Stephen told her that her old room had been made up, aired and was ready when she was. She wandered up the stairs and fell asleep face down on her duvet, still fully clothed and slept for nearly ten hours. When she woke up at five o'clock in the morning, she looked over to see Stephen sleeping in a high backed chair at the end of her bed. Vincent was asleep at his feet.

"My bodyguards," she mumbled, but as she spoke Vincent lifted his head and stared at her. She smiled and closed her eyes as she turned over. She felt safe here, she always had.

Chapter Two

On the deck of the motor yacht 'Jodast' Johnny Miller felt the deck vibrate slightly and reached under his towel. He had been staying on the boat for the last six months and had become accustomed to the various sounds she made at her mooring in the small Spanish marina. Joseph had been very generous letting them stay there and use his car. The Miller brothers could not hope to repay the help that they had been given.

He listened as the footsteps came forward around the cabin and his brother Terry called across to him. "It's alright Boy, it's only me."

Terry watched as his brother physically relaxed and heard the click of the Sig Sauer being made safe. It was only a basic precaution but Terry was glad that he had announced his presence. It did not pay to sneak up on Johnny at the moment, not if you valued your health anyway.

Johnny rolled over and Terry saw the pistol shaped lump under the towel. As his brother looked up at him and before any questions could be asked, he threw the English newspaper over to his brother.

As Johnny read the paper, Terry walked into the main saloon towards the small galley. He put his purchases away but doubted that they would be enjoying the Spaghetti Bolognese that they had planned for that night.

He opened the fridge and got a bottle of chilled water for himself. As his younger brother walked in he reached in for another without being asked. Johnny took the bottle in silence and unscrewed the cap.

"It's started then," he sighed, putting the paper on the counter so the headline showed face up. 'Night club owner and Entrepreneur shot dead at club.' Tilting the bottle to his lips and draining the contents in one swallow. He crushed the bottle and replaced the top to save space in the recycling bag that hung on the back of the galley chair. "When do we leave?"

"Are you sure you are up for this?" Terry asked.

"I can't believe you're even asking me that…." Johnny started to speak but stopped when his brother held up two tickets.

"We have a couple for hours before the flight. That should give you time to sort things with your girlfriend." As he spoke he looked at the scars on his brother's back. They were healing nicely but it was the internal scars that Terry was more worried about.

"You know she's not my girlfriend." Johnny headed to the shower as he spoke. "Anyway I'll talk to her when I've had my shower."

Terry smiled as he thought of the blonde German teenager on the next boat along. Since they had arrived she had been a constant visitor to the boat. It was obvious that she had a crush on Johnny but it was never going to go anywhere. He looked through the porthole that overlooked the neighbouring boat. As usual she was cleaning the deck of her parent's Sunseeker, just hoping to catch a glimpse of his brother. The boat was the cleanest in the marina because of the amount of time she spent cleaning it. Her parents had initially been a bit dubious when they had first seen Johnny. His scars made him seem dangerous.

Once her parents had actually spoken to Johnny and he had explained away his scars as an outboard motor accident, they realized that their little baby was safe and they all got on famously. In truth, meeting them had been good therapy for Johnny. His recuperation had come on exponentially.

Johnny had always been honest with Alsina. He told her that he was not looking for a relationship, but she was happy to continue with things the way they were. She was determined to be there when he was looking for a relationship. As such, she came in for a lot of teasing from her parents, Terry and a few of the waiters in the marina cafes.

Johnny came out of his cabin, freshly showered and changed. His faded jeans and polo shirt would be ideal for when they got back to England. As he walked past Terry, he pointed to Alsina's boat and walked off down the boarding rail.

Alsina Hauffman smiled happily as he asked permission to come aboard. She gestured for him to come ahead, standing unselfconsciously in her bikini and asked if he wanted something to drink. He shook his head and asked if her parents were aboard. On finding out that her parents were in town for the afternoon he asked if they could sit down and he explained that he had to leave for a while.

The crushed look on her face disappeared slightly as he asked her to keep an eye on the boat and to let them know if anyone came around. Her eyes lit up when he gave her his mobile number and a U.K. number that she could reach him on. He also explained that he may not be able to answer straight away but he would get back to her if she left a message.

He thanked her and kissed her lightly on the cheek as he left her Sunseeker and returned to the 'Jodast'. He smiled as he approached the back of the boat. The boat was named from the first two letters of each of the owners' names, unfortunately it spelt a word that sounded very rude in Spanish, especially if you did not pronounce the last two letters very loudly, which the local dialect seemed to encourage.

He thought back over the last few months here when they had been asked where they were staying, the looks of surprise and shock when he said the name if he was talking to Spanish people, or even if they were anywhere near when he said it.

It was a source of constant conversation when he went into the marina office to deal with anything concerning the boat. The staff always had a smile when they asked, "What is the name of the boat again?" Of course they knew the name but it never stopped them asking. They were nice people here and he would miss them.

Terry was coming out of his cabin, freshly showered and changed as Johnny walked back into the main saloon. They packed in silence and walked out to the black Range Rover. Putting their bags on the back seat, they drove towards the marina exit.

As they got to the exit, they met Alsina's parents and told them that they had to go away due to the death of a friend and that Alsina had graciously accepted the task of keeping an eye on things. They all shook hands and Alsina's mum teased Johnny about not being away for too long as their daughter would pine. Johnny smiled and waved as Terry eased the Range Rover through the barrier.

They arrived at the airport about an hour later and left the car in its long-term parking space. Then they checked in and walked through to the boarding gate. After that it was just a waiting game.

Chapter Three

When Davina next woke up, Stephen was gone but Vincent was still there. He looked up at her with his intelligent eyes. She smiled at him as she walked into the en-suite shower. When she emerged about twenty minutes later, Vincent was gone. The smell of eggs and bacon frying was wafting up the stairs invading her room. She went to the wardrobe and took her old tracksuit off of the rail. She thought about wearing shorts but decided that a good sweat was just what was needed.

She saw Mrs. Hoon as she walked into the kitchen and was greeted by a bone-crushing hug. Apart from dark bags under her eyes, she looked the same as she had when Davina had left for the States.

"Stupid question but how are you child?" The housekeeper stared at Davina as she asked the question. "It must have been a shock. I know it was for all of us here."

"Oh my God!" Davina held her hand to her mouth as she realized that she had not asked Stephen how he was coping. "Stephen must have been crushed."

"As it happens, I am coping quite well but thanks for thinking of me." The answer came as Stephen walked in through the back door followed closely by Vincent. The tracksuit told Davina that Stephen had been on his morning run. He had the healthy flush that most athletes have after a good session. "Do you want some company on your run?"

"That would be good but I thought that you had just come back?"

"I cut it short when Vincent caught me up. I guessed you were up or he would still be here."

"Clever boy." Davina mumbled as she grabbed Vincent's jowls and started stroking him. As she played with his head she stared into Vincent's eyes and was struck again by how intelligent they were. "You coming?" she asked the dog. Then she addressed Mrs. Hoon as she asked, "Is that food good to wait for a while?"

"Of course child. It will be ready when you come back, say forty minutes?"

Davina nodded as she followed Stephen and Vincent out of the back door and headed for the fields behind the house and garden. Stephen was glad that Davina was staying in shape. He started into his long loping gait and she matched him easily, just like before when they ran, many years ago.

As they ran, Davina glanced around the place that meant so much to her. She loved it almost as much as her brother had. Thinking of her brother made her smile, she always did when she thought about him. Even news of his death had not been able to take her smile away completely, as she thought of everything Joseph had been doing with his life. He was always so positive and full of life. The more she thought about the situation the more she was enveloped by a feeling of sadness. She tried not to dwell on things as they started back.

Nearing the house, she saw a midnight blue 4x4 heading up the drive. Vincent was already off to investigate it and Stephen changed direction from the back door to the front. As they came around the front the occupant of the car was just opening the rear door.

The man must have been about forty, with deep black hair. He gave the impression of being extremely fit. He had a good physique under his black t-shirt. Davina thought as she studied him that ten years ago, perhaps even five years ago, this guy must have been like Adonis.

Hearing them walking on the gravel driveway, he looked up and smiled. Extending his hand to Stephen, he clasped his hand and then hugged Stephen to him and slapped him on the back.

"Good to see you, Terry. The Boy with you?" Stephen looked in the passenger side of the car as he spoke. It was obvious that someone had been in the car but there was nobody in sight. Terry inclined his head towards the boundary wall and Stephen realized that Vincent was already heading towards a lone figure walking across the grass.

"As we drove past we thought that someone was in the tree overhanging the wall. I dropped Johnny off at the gate and he went to have a look."

"Don't!" Davina shouted out as the young man walking towards them put his hand out towards Vincent. She knew that very few people could get away with being so familiar with the big dog. The young man seemed not to hear her as he continued to extend his hand.

Davina wanted to close her eyes to block out the image of Vincent taking a bite out of the young man's hand but found that she couldn't. Instead she saw that not only did Vincent not bite the man but that he also lay down on his back for his belly to be rubbed. She couldn't believe it.

The young man spent a little while fussing Vincent before he stood up and continued on to greet them.

Stephen greeted him with the same warmth that he had greeted the man's companion, before turning to Davina to introduce them.

"Davina, may I present Terry and Johnny Miller. Likewise you two, may I present Davina Stanton."

Terry extended his hand and Davina took it, before taking Johnny's outstretched hand. She compared the two men and realized that they were indeed brothers. In fact, Johnny was a younger version of Terry. They had the same height and build, but although Johnny's hair was still black, she thought that she could just see the first silver or grey hairs. Impossible, she thought, he is far too young for that surely.

"Sorry for your loss, Miss Stanton. We'll miss Joseph." Davina looked down as Terry spoke.

"Call me Davina," she mumbled.

"Thanks for the warning. You never quite know when a dog will change." Johnny nodded at Vincent, "I think he is okay with me though." Then as he looked at his brother, "No one about now but there is definite sign that someone has been."

Terry took charge of the situation and suggested that they all talk inside. Strangely Stephen agreed readily and they all went indoors. Davina heard the double blip of the car alarm as Terry tapped the fob.

As they entered the hallway, Davina noticed that Johnny had taken two large hold-alls out of the car before Terry set the alarm. He set them down on the floor and they made a heavy 'thunk' as they touched down.

Noticing that Davina was interested, Terry explained what was in the bags. "Updates for the security system."

"Security for what?" She looked confused. Directing her gaze towards Stephen, she arched her eyebrows questioningly. "And who would be watching the place?"

"I never finished explaining, there have been a few threats directed at the club and possibly us too. Let's go into the kitchen and have a coffee while we talk."

As they entered the kitchen Mrs. Hoon took in the two newcomers with silent attention. They gave the appearance of some sort of security personnel, or she very much missed her guess. She looked at the older of the two men and wished that she was a few years younger. Then she took in the younger man and got the impression of a wounded soul, wounded but functioning, barely. She looked at Davina who smiled at her before gazing at the young men in her kitchen. "Hmmm" she thought, then seemed to wake up and started bustling around the stove.

As it happened, the first lot of food went straight down the throats of the two newcomers. Davina had disappeared for a shower realizing that she had just had a heavy work out. She knew that whatever Stephen had to say could wait ten more minutes. Stephen came back in wearing his worn black jeans and a shirt.

Both Terry and Johnny stood when Davina walked in and she was reminded of Joseph again. Good manners seemed to abound in his friends. She waved them back to their seats but Johnny remained standing.

"You can sit too, Johnny."

"Thanks Miss Stanton but I need to do a quick recce. Oh, and by the way you can either call me Johnny or 'The Boy'. Terry can fill you in with what's been happening." With that he left the kitchen and Davina heard him carefully closing the front door as he went out. She shivered. She knew some very hard men but none of them seemed to be as focused as Johnny or as confident.

"Will he be okay on his own? I mean if people are watching the house it might be a bit dangerous."

"Trust me, you don't have to worry about that boy!" Terry answered.

Davina shivered and thought again how he had unnerved her just now.

Davina stared at the two men in the kitchen. Stephen gestured to the table. Mrs. Hoon was just dishing up fresh plates of food and was pleasantly surprised when Terry accepted seconds.

"It is definitely a hostile takeover of the local drugs trade." Terry broke the silence. "We've been told that we're here for the foreseeable future. Is that alright with you two?"

Davina looked to Stephen for guidance and saw that he was more than happy. She nodded too but said nothing.

"Why us?" asked Stephen. "We aren't in the drugs trade!"

"Believe me, we know that. However, the club is a prime site for distribution. The new guys must have thought Joseph had no choice but to sell."

"What do we do now? Obviously we won't sell!" said Stephen, just before Davina.

"First we fortify this place and then we will take a look at the club. Can I have a look around now to see what needs doing?"

"Of course you can. Are you staying here as well? Mrs. Hoon can soon ready a room for you"

"If it's not too much trouble," Terry looked apologetically at Mrs. Hoon. The Boy and I can share if it makes it any easier."

Stephen looked across to Davina who nodded. It made sense to have protection on site, even if she didn't know them very well. Obviously Stephen did, which meant that she would need yet another heart to heart with him in the not too very distant future.

"How is the Boy now? Is he up for this sort of thing again?" Stephen asked with such sincerity that Davina looked at him and frowned. He obviously knew them both very well, if he knew that Johnny had been ill.

Terry shook his head as he answered. "I'm not really sure. He says he is and physically he looks well but I'm more worried about the psychological damage. He's restless at night and I think he still has flash backs."

Stephen nodded as he took in this information. Davina was puzzled and realized that now would be a good time to ask a few questions.

"So what exactly do you two do then? How do you know Joseph and Stephen?" As she asked the question Davina realized that she was still referring to her brother in the present tense. She supposed that eventually it would sink in. So far no one had corrected her.

Stephen looked at Terry and received a nod before he answered. He took a deep breath and slowly blew out before he continued.

"Terry and the Boy work for the government. They're involved with stopping human trafficking and also with the drugs multi-group task force. We met a few months ago when we started getting the threats. We think that the people behind all the problems are into people smuggling and drug trafficking. The Boy was working undercover in their organization with his partner but his partner was bent. He literally stabbed him in the back and left him for dead outside the club. Joseph found him and called Terry."

"I owe your brother more than I can ever repay, not only for saving Johnny's life but also for allowing me and the Boy to stay on your boat for his convalescence. Johnny was in hospital for nearly a month before he was well enough to leave." As the memories came back, Terry's voice drifted almost to a whisper.

"Why do you call him 'The Boy'?" Davina too, spoke in a whisper.

"Johnny has always been the youngest at what he does and as such his instructors have mostly been a lot older. John is a popular name and it made it easier to differentiate on some of the courses. I have to say I'm surprised he let you call him 'The Boy' so quickly; he generally only lets people call him that if he knows and respects them. He's not quick to take offence but you can generally tell if he doesn't like you."

"So, why am I special, we've only just met? Does he normally let women that he's just met call him that?"

"He's a strange kid sometimes. It's probably because your brother spoke so highly of you. He spoke about you all the time, in fact. He seemed very proud of you and Johnny definitely respected Joseph!"

Just then Vincent walked into the kitchen followed by Johnny. Johnny was smiling and Davina thought that it made him look even younger than normal.

"All good, from what I can see, you can have a double check if you're not sure, Terry. The only dodgy bit is that tree we spoke about. That will need to come down but I wouldn't worry about it too much." The innocent way that Johnny spoke started warning bells ringing in Terry's head.

"What've you done, Boy?"

"Let's just say that if they come back it should be an illuminating experience for them and we'll definitely know about it."

"So, what do you reckon then? Just a few cameras and sensors should do it and then the house itself?" Terry gave up his interrogation as he guessed that Johnny had booby-trapped the tree, based largely on what he had seen Johnny take from the bag in the car. Flash bangs could be very useful in his experience.

"Yeah, sounds about right. I'll see what other goodies we have in the bags, maybe there are some secure comm's too, just to be on the safe side. The fitters should be here soon."

Chapter Four

Edward Chesney walked into his office with a step that belied his age. At fifty-nine he seemed much older, a fact which he used to his advantage on many occasions to get what he wanted. He was five feet eight inches tall, but slightly bowed over. Prematurely grey but his body had a whipcord strength about it. He had one son who, depending on the day, could be his pride and joy or a millstone around his neck.

Today was a millstone day. As the day wore on, Edward thought that there seemed to be more and more millstone days. Edward thought that if it carried on it would be the death of him.

Adrian Bull watched his boss enter the office before him. Adrian was what he appeared to be, a bodyguard. A minder was par for the course in his boss' line of work. Six feet tall and eighteen stone of solid muscle helped in his own line of work.

They had worked together for over forty years, but his boss was starting to look old and it worried him. He wasn't worried about his job, as he knew that if his boss retired he would still have a job, if he wanted one. He was financially secure and he certainly didn't need to work. He worked because he enjoyed it.

He knew the cause of his boss' agitation. He had seen this day approaching for a long time. Tony Chesney was a head case. It was true that all the crew liked a bit of ruck but Tony enjoyed it far too much and used violence as a first, not a last resort. And now he had gone and shot someone. Worse, not just anyone but Joseph fucking Stanton.

"Do you want me to send the idiot in?" He knew that if anyone else in the crew had called Tony that, they would be in deep shit. But being the boy's godfather had its privileges.

Edward nodded and sat down. Tony swaggered in and sat in the chair in front of his father's desk. The chair creaked under his large frame. He was naturally strong but his body was running to fat after such a spoilt upbringing. He took after his mother, tall and large boned. Only his eyes matched his father's.

"You wanted to see me, Dad?"

"What do you think? In fact, what were you fucking thinking? You knew the game we were playing, now the club is untouchable!"

"You're getting soft in your old age, Dad. We needed to make a statement and show that nobody fucks with us. You should retire. We don't really need the club anyway."

"Oi! Shit head, show some fucking respect." Tony looked at Adrian and smiled as the older man spoke. He had a lot of respect for Adrian. It was rumoured that he could kill a man without showing any emotion. That was in the good old days but hard men still backed down if Adrian paid them a visit. Tony held up his hands in submission.

"What do you want me to say? Sorry? Okay, I'm sorry. There, are you happy now?"

Edward shook his head sadly. If it went to rat shit and Tony did time he would be protected. What was more worrying was the rumour about Tony ripping off the competition. If the report was true, then he would not be able to protect his son in prison.

Edward thought again about chucking it all in and buggering off to Spain. His holiday villa was bought and paid for and he could have an easy life, totally stress free. So long as this current business didn't come back and bite them in the arse.

He walked around the desk and slapped his son around the head. Tony's mouth went into a thin, tight line and for one moment Edward thought that his son might actually retaliate. Outwardly Adrian had not moved but Edward could sense that he was ready to intervene. Tony sensed it too and knew that even being his godson would not prevent a beating if he struck his father in front of Adrian.

Edward turned his back on his son and walked out of the office. Tony just sat there as Adrian followed his boss and realized that he had been holding his breath. He let it out in a long, slow sigh.

He'd been lucky and he knew it. If his father even suspected what was happening, he knew that he was dead. He sat in the chair for nearly half an hour, thinking over what he had done and what he was trying to do, before he finally got up and left the office.

In the car park, he got into his Ford Sapphire Cosworth and wheel spun out of the gate. He headed for the south side of town. He needed a stiff drink.

Chapter Five

After breakfast, Davina realized that she would need to get some transport. She asked Stephen if he had any ideas and was stunned when he suggested Joseph's Porsche. She hadn't given it a thought. She could count on the fingers of one hand how many times she had driven the classic 911. Not because she wasn't allowed to but more because Joseph loved driving it. Stephen dug out the keys and threw them to her. She caught them in her left hand and put them in her pocket.

When she had asked what the plan was, Stephen had said that they should drive into town and get some lunch while colleagues of Terry and Johnny upgraded the house security. They got into the black mirror finish Porsche and drove into town, followed by the brothers in their midnight blue Range Rover. It was a lower specification of what they'd been driving in Spain. They would definitely miss some of the accessories. Stephen smiled when he saw it.

Returning after an uneventful lunch and small shopping excursion, they all went into the house to shower and get changed. There were a couple of hours to kill before leaving for the club, so the brothers inspected the work done by the fitters and synchronised communication units and remote cameras.

Stephen wandered into the control room that had been created out of a spare room and whistled when he saw the equipment. They had reviewed some of the latest, state of the art security systems for the club and he knew that some of the stuff he was looking at was worth a pretty penny. Indeed, some of it did not even look as though it was on the market yet, if it ever would be.

Davina walked into the kitchen for a chat with Mrs. Hoon. It had been a long time since they'd seen each other and although they talked on the phone from time to time, there was nothing like a face-to-face, hand on hand conversation.

Davina wanted to know if Mrs. Hoon had any other information on her brother's death and how they had been coping. For the most part, everyone was coping well. Only time would tell. Davina wondered how much time she would have to spend here, her life and business were on another continent. She needed closure here to move on but did she really want to?

She already knew what her brother wanted her to do because it was written in his will. The will was not secret, they had all been friends for so long that they were each equal beneficiaries of each other.

Both Davina and Stephen would be co-owners of the clubs, Davina being majority shareholder in Miami and Stephen in England. There was no legacy expected and Joseph had stated that if they wanted to sell up, they could do so. Although they owned and worked the clubs together, they were Joseph's vision. He would have been happy whatever they wanted to do.

Vincent was a straight 50/50 split and the Porsche went to Davina. Mrs. Hoon got twenty thousand pounds for her service, but would be kept on by Stephen anyway. The only thing left for them to do was to find and punish the killer. The Police seemed to be fairly well clued up and it would appear to be only a matter of time before a suspect was charged.

Although she loved her brother dearly, the five years apart had given her a strength she did not know she had. Of course, they had spoken on the phone and Joseph was always there if she truly needed him but she had grown less dependent on him.

She watched as Mrs. Hoon prepared some sandwiches for the brothers and realized that they were being given royal treatment. She appeared to be spoiling the new houseguests. Thinking of the brothers made Davina's interest in them reawaken.

She knew that Joseph had been acquainted with some interesting characters but she'd never realized exactly what was going on. Joseph was a Ninjutsu Sensei and as such held courses on stick fighting, or in the case of the Police, baton wielding. He held some unarmed combat classes for prison officers and a few foreign Police forces. He was well known for both the Club and his martial arts and respected by his peers and competitors. It just seemed such a waste.

Vincent stirred at her feet and there was a loud bang followed by a whistling sound from the front of the grounds. Vincent flew through the back door and Davina heard Terry and Johnny running through the front door. She started to get up before Stephen walked in and sat down.

"Best we wait here for a few minutes!" He took a cup of coffee from an increasingly curious Mrs. Hoon.

Davina didn't know what to do as neither Stephen nor Joseph had ever just waited patiently if something out of the ordinary happened.

"Terry thinks it best to wait and see if the guy is armed before he puts us at risk," he said by way of an explanation, as if he had read her mind.

"How does he know it's to do with the killer?"

"They think it would be too much of a coincidence for a casual passer-by to have tripped that Flash Bang and who else would be climbing the tree?"

Davina was stunned. She still had her coffee cup in her hand and stood staring at it. The brothers returned a few minutes later. Johnny was laughing at something he had just said and Terry tried hard not to smile. They became serious as they entered the kitchen.

"We're fairly confident it was the same guy as before, we heard his motorbike leaving as we got half way there. By the time we got to the tree, he was long gone. Vincent beat us there which probably made the guy think twice about hanging about or hiding." As he spoke Johnny bent down and affectionately tickled Vincent's head.

Again Davina was amazed at how quickly the dog had befriended the young man. Many things about him intrigued her.

"We'll have to bring in a permanent guard for the house now, if that is alright with you? I'll call the boss and get someone sent over. We weren't sure if the house was still a target. This sort of ups the ante a bit. It's strange though because now that Joseph's dead the club becomes a moot point. Perhaps there is something else going on that we don't know about." Johnny walked to his room to make the call.

"Is he always that…" Davina paused for thought, "…professional?" She asked Terry. "Sometimes he scares me a little bit."

"That boy scares a lot of very hard men. He was always focused but since the stabbing he seems to have become more intense. I hope it's just a phase! I worry about what it's doing to him. You don't need to worry though. You'll never have a problem."

"I appreciate that but he seems so young to be doing what you two are doing."

"Well, speaking as an old man…"

"I didn't mean you were old, but he *is* very young. He must've joined straight from school. Did he consult you?"

"I wouldn't say consulted, more like, informed me. I smiled when he told me and just wished that I could be there when some of the instructors met him. As I said, he's always been focused."

They all laughed at the thought of Johnny as a teenage recruit and couldn't stop as Johnny came back into the room. He asked what they were laughing at and Terry told him it didn't matter. Johnny was never insecure and thought that if it was important, Terry would tell him later.

Johnny sat at the table and accepted a cup of coffee from Mrs. Hoon. Vincent curled up at his feet and Davina felt a small pang of jealousy. Before she left England, she had been part of the dog's everyday life and now felt strangely distanced from him. She put the thought from her mind and watched Johnny start on the fresh sandwiches that had miraculously appeared in front of him. She was right about Johnny and Terry getting special treatment from her housekeeper. She made a mental note to talk to Mrs. Hoon about it a little later but that could wait. First, she needed to get ready for the club.

Chapter Six

Tony Chesney had hooked up with some acquaintances in a local pub and they had well outstayed their welcome. The landlord would not normally have had a problem but their leery behaviour had upset some of the local faces and *that* was a problem.

Not wishing to further antagonise his father today, he piled everyone into his Cosworth and they started cruising around looking for something or someone to vent their anger on.

Driving around the town, Tony spotted a Porsche a couple of cars ahead and gave chase for a bit of fun. He started overtaking the cars in front of him one by one.

Chapter Seven

For the second time that day, Davina fired up the Porsche and listened to the flat roar of the straight six engine. She pulled out of the drive a little ahead of the brothers but she was confident they would catch up.

They were still a few cars behind when she hit the town and she slowed to let them get behind her. As she looked in her mirror, a Ford Cosworth came flying past both the car behind and her Porsche. Without thinking she hit the horn and the Cosworth skidded to a halt. Four big men got out and started walking aggressively towards them.

Stephen reacted first and opened his door. Davina was only seconds behind him. The leader of the group of men looked surprised and then leered at her. Like a red rag to a bull Davina lost her calm and started verbally laying into the man about dangerous driving.

He continued advancing on her before he noticed the true size of the man who was with her. Altering his plans, all four of the men converged on Stephen just as a Range Rover drove straight towards them. The four men jumped out of the way and two men got out of the big car. The younger one headed straight up to Tony and asked in a chillingly quiet voice "Is there a problem?"

Still getting over the sudden appearance of the Range Rover, Tony was caught out for a second and did nothing. Johnny looked at the other men who were obviously the worse for wear and asked them the same question. As Johnny turned his head, Tony launched a head butt at his unsuspecting victim. Fighting fair was never one of Tony's strong points.

Unfortunately for Tony his head connected with Johnny's rapidly moving elbow. Not used to this defence and certainly not expecting it, Tony followed through with his full force to be met with excruciating pain. Tony was not used to being hit and found out for the first time what a broken nose felt like. He collapsed in pain on the ground with his hands covering his bloody face.

In the meantime, Terry blocked the approach of Tony's friends.

Stephen stepped forward and Davina, calming down now, backed him up.

"Pick up your friend and leave, we don't want any trouble." Davina spoke in a calm authoritative manner. The men looked at Tony and decided that a bit of discretion was in order. They hauled him to his feet and got back into the car. Looking back to see if they were still being observed, they saw Davina, Stephen and Terry turning away from them. Any thoughts of returning to the fight left them as they noticed the cold, mocking stare on Johnny's face. All hope that they harboured of instant revenge left them immediately.

Johnny watched them drive away before turning his attention to the others. Seeing they were alright, he smiled at them, which made him look even younger, then calmly and silently walked back, got into the passenger seat of the Range Rover and buckled himself in.

The others looked at him and Davina started giggling. Terry shrugged and Stephen chuckled before himself getting back into the Porsche. Five minutes later they were back on their way to the club. Apart from the silence in the cars, it was as if nothing had happened.

Chapter Eight

After his friends left him at his flat Tony looked in the mirror at his broken nose. Ordinarily he would be shifting heaven and earth to find out who had dared to oppose him but he already knew. He sighed as his mind flashed back to the moment he recognized Joseph Stanton's sister. The car should have given it away. Perhaps he should cut down on the coke and the booze for a bit. He wondered if his father would find out what had happened.

He walked into the lounge and picked up his jacket. He found the little baggie and cut himself a line. He needed this to dull the pain of his broken nose. That boy had a beating coming and Tony would make sure that he suffered. Nobody did that to Tony Chesney.

He would ask amongst his friends to find out who the new talent was. Someone would be sure to know.

He paced around his lounge and then returned to his jacket and cut himself another line. That boy would pay dearly.

Chapter Nine

Pulling up to the club, Davina got out and looked around. There was already a queue forming. She watched as Stephen walked up to the front door and chatted to the doormen. She did not recognize them and Davina wondered who she would still know from the old crew. Joseph's employees were loyal but it had been five years.

Stephen opened the door and ushered the group into the foyer. Davina compared the security arrangements with her own place in Miami. There were more men visible on the ground here but she supposed that was to be expected.

A tall, tanned, shaven-headed man of about forty years of age approached her from the entrance to the dance floor. As she watched him come over, Davina suddenly realized that Johnny had moved to a position slightly in front of her but between her and the newcomer. With sudden clarity she realized that he was putting himself in a position to protect her, in harm's way, if you thought about it that way. She was not sure if she liked the direction her life was taking right at this moment.

Stephen hailed the newcomer and introduced him as Bernie Holt, their head of security. He smiled and nodded at her but glanced at Johnny before he offered his hand for her to shake it. Johnny smiled at him and backed away a step.

For his part Bernie was impressed with the newcomer. He had assessed the situation and guessed correctly that Johnny was acting as bodyguard. He respected the man's candour and looked to him for permission to continue his approach. The things he'd heard about this man were true, for once.

After introducing Bernie to Davina, Stephen introduced the brothers and Bernie appraised the pair as he shook hands. Both were dangerous men, of that he was sure. The older man looked to be quite a handful but the younger man looked to be the bigger threat. Not many people unsettled Bernie but this boy did.

Fortunately, he knew he had no reason to be worried. If these two were protecting Stephen and Davina, his job would be a lot easier.

Terry grasped Bernie's hand and felt the strength in the grip. Their boss had briefed them on Bernie. By all accounts, he was a safe pair of hands. Their boss respected him, which said a great deal and he was not known to suffer fools gladly.

"Jack Fairfax says hello." Terry watched Bernie's eyebrows lift as he mentioned his boss' name.

"It has been some time since I last heard that name, how do you come by it?"

"He's our boss. He says to be candid with you and respect your judgement."

Right then Bernie knew that he'd been correct in his assessment of the two brothers. If they worked for Jack Fairfax then they were more than just good. If Jack had told them about him then they had his ear, which told him a lot more about them.

"If you don't mind, we'd like to assess the security with you. We're not here to tell you your job but more to offer some accessories that you may not have access to. Can we talk in your office?"

Terry knew how touchy some security chiefs could be if you assessed the way they worked. He also knew that Bernie would not be territorial about his domain, having been briefed by the Police. Bernie was a professional and knew that there was still a viable threat.

For his part, Bernie liked the direct and diplomatic approach that Terry had employed. This guy was good. He smiled as he directed them to his office.

"I would like to get the feel of the place again." Davina said as she and Stephen walked into the dance area. She looked around as she walked and thought that she recognized a few of the workers. Some of them certainly recognized her and smiled. She could see the new employees being filled in about who she was and looks of awe and curiosity on some of their faces.

As they stopped at the bar, a strikingly beautiful shaven-headed waitress smiled at her. It took her a moment to realize that she knew the girl, for that had been what she was when Davina left for the States, not the beautiful young woman that now stood before her.

"Hello Amelia, I didn't recognize you with the new hairdo."

"I wasn't sure that you'd remember me, Miss Stanton."

"You can stop that right there! Call me Davina like you always used to. Since when did we become all formal?"

"I wasn't really sure how to speak to you, to be honest. In my experience time changes people." Amelia sounded sad as she spoke and Davina made another mental note to find out how things had changed so badly in her friend's life, to make her talk in such a cynical way.

"I haven't changed but you have. What happened to your hair? Don't get me wrong, I love it and it suits you but you loved your hair."

Amelia blushed a little and Stephen smiled at her as he made his excuses and walked off.

"I have alopecia, I tried to resign 'cos I thought that it might put the punters off but your brother said 'Stuff them and just shave it off.' He even offered to make all the others shave their heads too."

Davina laughed at the thought of Joseph and Stephen with bald heads. They had both had short hair in the past but that was a long time ago. Amelia blushed again and Davina realized her error.

"I wasn't laughing at you, Amelia. I just can't imagine Stephen with a shaved head, that's all."

"It made me laugh too, when Joseph said it." Amelia was smiling now and seemed much more relaxed. "What would you like to drink?"

Realizing that no offence had been taken, Davina asked for an orange juice. As Amelia left to fill her order, Davina sat on a stool and watched the people enjoying themselves.

Stephen had been worried about takings dropping off after Joseph's death. He had thought that people would not feel safe. As it turned out, his fears were groundless. The takings had increased since the murder. Mostly regulars but some new faces came just to see where it had happened.

Amelia left the orange juice on the bar and served a few customers before returning. She remained silent until Davina decided to talk again. They had been friends a long time ago, but people moved on. Davina definitely had. Amelia could not believe the change in her friend, for the better, she thought.

"So, have you got a fella in the States?"

Davina smiled as she turned to look at her friend. "Not so as you'd notice. You?"

"I've got a girlfriend!" Amelia looked at Davina with a mixture of fear and defiance. She had not told anyone at the club before. Not that she was embarrassed but she found that people treated her differently. She was fairly confident that Davina would be all right with it but one was never really sure.

With a smile of genuine pleasure, Davina reached across and took her friend's hand in hers. "Good for you, my lovely."

More confident now Amelia went into a bit more detail about her partner. Davina listened with a huge smile on her face. Finally her friend seemed settled. They had both been fairly popular with the boys when they were younger but neither of them had found the love of their life. Davina was focused on starting and running the club and Amelia had been unlucky with some of her choices, leaving her confidence slightly dented. That seemed to be all in the past though.

As more customers came into the bar, Davina let her friend work and walked towards the office. She'd put it off long enough.

Stephen was already in there with Bernie and the brothers but the meeting appeared to be coming to a close. The security needs looked like they'd been agreed upon, helped out in part by the fact that the brothers' employer was paying. Apparently, if it helped to convict human traffickers, it was money well spent.

Davina thought about the changing attitudes of the various governments these days. If there was even a possible chance that a business funded global terrorism, budgets could be set aside.

They left shortly after that and returned to the house. Davina was dead on her feet. It had been an emotional time since she had received the phone call about Joseph's death. Sleep gave her some well-needed peace.

They got in to find a pasta bake in the oven. It smelt delicious but Davina only managed a few mouthfuls before she retired for the night. Vincent followed her up to her room. She smiled at him as he lay next to her bed.

The brothers took some food to the night guard which was received with appreciation. This job wouldn't be such a bad gig. The housekeeper had already kept him supplied with coffee and snacks and he was in danger of gaining weight on this job. After checking to make sure all was quiet the brothers left him to his monitors.

Returning to the kitchen, the three men caught up on what had been happening in both England and Spain. Terry said that they had paid the mooring fee by way of a thank you. Stephen was about to complain but remained silent when Terry looked in the direction of his brother and said it was worth every penny. Stephen took the hint, he knew that Terry cared deeply for Johnny and would have paid a lot more to see him convalescing properly.

They told Stephen about Alsina and her crush on Johnny, well Terry did, as Johnny repeatedly tried to change the subject. Stephen had met Alsina's family briefly when they had first put the boat in the marina. He remembered them and that they had given the impression of being nice people.

As they talked, Stephen thought that a holiday in Spain might be a good thing for him. Perhaps Davina would come too. He'd ask her later for her thoughts on the matter, as it could not be an easy time for her at the moment. Bernie could handle the club, for a week or two, that wouldn't be an issue.

The next week was a blur of activity, they organised a memorial service for Joseph until such time as his body could be released and they could have a private ceremony.

They held the memorial at the club as it made things easier for everyone and with the new security it made perfect sense.

The threats seemed to have stopped. Nobody could make an offer for the club now without becoming a suspect in Joseph's murder. Davina started thinking about returning to the States and Stephen said he would go with her if she wanted a bit of moral support.

Chapter Ten

Davina and Stephen cleared Miami international airport with minimal fuss and were met by Sue, one of the security personnel from the club. They had decided before they left England that security procedures needed to be implemented for Davina's personal protection. Davina knew her well and they had previously been out clubbing together on their nights off. Now, however, Sue was all business.

They went straight to Davina's apartment and Sue told them to call her when they were ready to head to the club, as she would only be in the lobby with the doormen. Sue explained that the doormen were aware of their situation and were happy to help. Davina tried to get Sue to stay in the apartment with them but Sue winked at her and said that she had a better offer. Davina knew that Sue and the young doorman had a history and smiled at her friend.

Davina watched Stephen as he was looking at the view from the balcony. They had a magnificent view of the 'Golden Mile' as the locals called it. The beach was phenomenal and the shops and boutiques were expensive. They had been lucky to buy the apartment when they had as prices had rocketed in recent years.

"Your room is just as you left it."

"What? You haven't cleaned it?" Stephen ducked as Davina threw a cushion at him.

"You know what I mean, Idiot."

"What time are we going to the club?"

"I thought about sevenish, if that is good with you?" Davina replied.

"That suits me. See you in a bit."

When they arrived at the club, they talked to the staff as they wandered around. They finally got to the office and started on the waiting pile of correspondence. The return to America was fortuitous, as another nightclub chain had just put in yet another offer to buy them out. This particular group had been after them to sell for years and it was as if a switch in Davina's head had been thrown. There was no question that the other chain had anything to do with Joseph's death so it was an opportune time to sell.

She hadn't been considering selling but now having Stephen to talk to they decided to sell everything in Miami and concentrate their efforts in England. Stephen counselled against making a rash decision but admitted he would like to work more closely with her again.

All sorts of emotions came flooding into her mind. Her time in England had made her feel homesick and she decided that a return to her native soil was a good idea.

It took about three weeks to finalize the sale and off load the rest of the holdings in Miami. Their initial investment had been just short of five hundred thousand dollars and they sold it for a small fortune. She would be coming home financially secure.

"Well that went more easily than I imagined it would." Stephen was relaxing in their hotel bar, sipping his ice-cold mineral water. "I will miss it in a way, I suppose."

"I know what you mean, I had no intention of selling up when I went back for the funeral but it just seems so right somehow." Davina handed Stephen a rum and coke. "A toast, to us!" she raised her glass and clinked with Stephen, it was done.

Her life was starting again, she was happy now the decision had been made and she was feeling much more settled. Everything just felt right.

Chapter Eleven

"That boy's a fucking liability!" Edward Chesney slammed his crystal tumbler down as he finished his outburst. He looked at Adrian expecting him to try and defend Tony but he remained silent.

"Well say something, for fuck's sake!"

"What do you want me to say mate, he always could be a wanker. We all know that."

"Well thanks for your honesty." Edward sighed.

"I can't defend what he's been doing, it's almost as though he's deliberately trying to bring you down. I've asked him outright and believe him when he says he isn't but I don't know what the hell he's up to."

They had heard what had happened with Davina and Stephen within hours. Since then they'd tried to keep Tony with them as much as possible but short of hand cuffing him, they couldn't keep him with them all the time.

They knew he was trying to find out the identity of the men who were with Stephen and Davina but so far he'd drawn a blank. However, it was only a matter of time and money.

Tony was working in the dark because Davina and Stephen had disappeared. To top it all off, they could no longer watch the house, since their observation post had been compromised. Their look out had said that he thought he recognized the men in the Range Rover but could not place them at the moment.

Edward decided to cut his losses and get Tony out of the way. He'd sent Tony to oversee the French side of the operation but had since found out that he and Frank, his new minder, had buggered off down to Spain.

No one had thought to inform them what was happening because Tony was the boss' son. Now they were playing catch up trying to find out where he was. They weren't worried for his safety, more for what fresh stupidity he could get up to.

The minder was going to get it in the neck too, as he was becoming another liability. He'd only been switched to being Tony's minder because Edward thought that he would be a calming influence.

"Has anyone said anything about what's going on? Any clue whatsoever?"

"Only that Frank thought he had an idea who the blokes were that broke Tony's nose." Adrian sighed.

"Oh, that's just fucking wonderful! Just when, pray tell me, were you going to let me into that little secret?"

"When I knew exactly what he was up to. You've got enough on your plate at the moment."

"What are you, my fucking mother?"

In a fairly good impression of an old lady Adrian said, "Yes, now do as you're told and stop worrying until we find out what he's up to? Oh, and eat your greens, too!"

Edward couldn't help but laugh. He looked over at Adrian and saw him grin and then threw back his head and roared with laughter.

"Wanker!"

"Look mate, as soon as I know something I promise I'll tell you. I've got our best people on it, so it's just a matter of time."

Chapter Twelve

Johnny, Terry and Stephen finally managed to put all of Davina's possessions in the cavernous loft space above the garage.

"Are you sure you really need 2000 pairs of shoes?" Johnny asked and Davina went scarlet at his question.

Before she could answer Stephen said, "I think half of them are handbags actually!"

In fact, most of the boxes contained photographs of her time in Miami. The club was popular with celebrities and she had some good pictures.

Johnny said that he needed a holiday after all that and Stephen thought that now was as good a time as any to suggest that they go to Spain for a few days.

"You know. Sun, Sea and Sangria. Johnny can see his girlfriend again and we will all be happy."

It was Johnny's turn to blush now. Davina raised her eyebrows. She hadn't thought that the brothers would have partners. She'd got used to them always being around.

"She is *not* my girlfriend."

"It's alright Johnny, I didn't realize that you had a partner. I would never have dreamed about taking up so much of your time if I had known." She looked at Stephen and Terry who were falling about with laughter. Johnny seemed to have gone a deeper shade of red. "What have I said?"

Terry tried to speak but couldn't get his breath. Stephen wasn't much better.

"She is *not* my girlfriend, honestly. She lives on the boat next door. These two know full well who she is."

"Are you talking about Alsina? That little German girl?"

"Yes, but she's *not* my girlfriend."

"Okay, I believe you. Actually, I think it's a great idea. The holiday that is."

They locked the garage and went into the kitchen. The 24-hour guard had been dispensed with, as with no more obvious threats the operation was downgraded. There were still security cameras covering the grounds and house, with dedicated senders to an offsite monitoring station. It would only be a matter of time before the brothers were reassigned.

Mrs. Hoon had brewed fresh coffee for them and they drank as they made plans and ate sandwiches from a never diminishing pile. The brothers would miss being waited on.

Vincent sat between Johnny and Davina as Mrs. Hoon agreed to look after him and keep the house together.

The brothers called in to their boss to get clearance and then they booked the tickets. They would leave in the morning.

Chapter Thirteen

The waiter bought the two men an after dinner liqueur which was customary in Spain. They'd been staying in the area for the last three days.

This was the first meal they had eaten in the marina. So far, they'd been working the bars, searching for the man they were after, or at least word of where he was staying.

As they drank their complimentary drinks they caught sight of a pretty blonde girl sitting down to a meal with her parents. They looked Germanic in origin but were speaking faultless Spanish.

"I wouldn't mind some of that", said the shorter of the two men. "It would do me good to clean the pipes, if you know what I mean?"

"After me, you can go first, bit young for me though." Tony laughed but his eyes rarely left the young girl, a fact that did not escape his companion's attention.

Frank Underwood was five feet eight inches tall with short cut blond hair and a stocky frame. He looked fit for his age and gave the impression of having been around the block.

It was risky for him to be here now, as the person they were searching for could recognize him and that was something that he was not prepared for yet. He knew from what he had heard that Johnny was supposed to be somewhere in the south of Spain recovering and that was the only information he had to go on. Frank was not even sure if Johnny was still in Spain. However, you didn't say no to Tony. He mentally cursed himself for mentioning that he thought he had recognized the description of the men who had upset his boss.

If he was honest with himself, he was a little afraid of what would happen if and when they should ever meet again. He should've finished the job properly and then he could have carried on working. As it stood, he could not return to England any time soon. He was sure that the

Spanish Police had him on a list somewhere too. And the Guardia Civil were not his favourite choice of law enforcement agency.

He watched Tony leering at the young girl. Her parents had noticed too and were glaring at him. Frank suggested that it might be a good idea to return to the brothel in the next town. He knew Tony liked exotic women and they didn't need to get into anything in this marina. Not until they found out exactly where Johnny was staying.

As they left Tony blew the young girl a kiss. Her father started to get up but Frank directed Tony to the Mercedes, which they had left double-parked just outside the restaurant.

"What do you think you are fucking playing at, Frank? If the old man wants an argument, I'm happy to give him one."

"We haven't located Johnny yet. I was under the impression that finding him was more important to you." He waited while Tony thought this through.

"You're right, mate, let's find some women. The filthier the better."

Frank sighed as they drove away. This was turning into one hell of a fuck up. He ran through his possessions in his mind just in case he needed to do a runner quickly.

When they got to the brothel that they'd used every night so far, he called the doorman over for a chat. The doorman knew who they were, as they had mutual acquaintances both here and in the U.K. He asked if the doorman knew where they could get some guns and after being told to leave it with him, they went inside.

They had a laugh and a drink with the girls they'd met before and were just about to go into the back rooms when an English guy came and sat at their table uninvited.

"I'm told you are in the market for something?"

"Yeah, who told you that?" Frank replied.

The stranger pointed at the doorman, who had just looked in to check that things were going smoothly.

"We might be able to do some business, what have you got?"

"What do you want? Pump actions, sawn offs, semi auto, fully auto, sniper rifles, you name it, I can get it"

"Can you get us two semi auto pistols with silencers and a couple of pump actions with a box of shells for each?" Frank asked.

"They'll be waiting for you when you've finished with your dates. You want holsters or anything?"

"No mate, we're good. How much?"

"Twelve hundred each for the hand guns and a grand each for the pumps. A hundred for the shells and I'll throw the suppressors in for free."

"Done, we'll take delivery in five hours. You good with that?"

"I'm good, cash on delivery."

Frank peeled off nine five hundred euro notes and handed them over. "We trust you." He smiled as he spoke and the stranger knew that he would be accountable, if there were any problems.

"See you in five." With that he stood up and left the bar.

The doorman looked in to see that everything was still cool and Frank waved him over. He handed him another five hundred euro note from his roll, to show his gratitude. The doorman nodded his thanks and shouted to the bar to get the men anything they wanted on him.

Tony and Frank walked into the back room with a bottle of brandy, a bottle of rum and a girl on each arm. One of the girls slipped a small bag of coke out of her bra. It looked like it was going to be a most successful night.

Chapter Fourteen

Terry waited with Stephen and Davina, while Johnny collected the car. It had been serviced and cleaned in the time that they'd been away.

Johnny pulled up outside departures and the others loaded their bags into the back.

The drive back to the marina took about an hour and they had just finished unloading the bags when Alsina's parents turned up at their Sunseeker.

Johnny went over to say hello and see if anyone had shown an interest in the boat and to catch up on any gossip. Alsina's father, Werner, told him about their meal the previous night and the men who had been ogling his daughter.

Johnny looked around for Alsina but couldn't see her. Werner told him that he'd left her on the beach and that she'd make her own way back. He knew that she would be glad to see him again.

Johnny said to send her over when she got back and returned to the 'Jodast'.

Johnny was starting to feel uneasy as he told the others what had happened. Leaving Stephen and Davina to get settled, Terry and Johnny got back in the car and headed for the beach.

As Johnny and Terry got to the beach car park, they saw Alsina walking towards them. She was facing towards them, passing a Mercedes parked at the side of the road, when the car door opened and a hand reached out and grabbed her. Alsina screamed and tried to pull away but the car started to drive off and she lost her footing. Terry didn't hesitate and drove the Range Rover straight at the Mercedes.

The driver of the Mercedes swerved to avoid the Range Rover, an action that made his passenger lose his grip on the girl. Alsina fell to the ground and the Mercedes shot past them.

Both Johnny and Terry saw the occupants of the car and could hardly believe their eyes. They recognized Tony as the guy whose nose Johnny had broken but sitting next to him in the driver's seat was Frank Underwood, Johnny's ex-partner and the man who had stabbed him in the back.

Jumping out, Johnny shouted at his brother to turn the car around. He ran to Alsina who was rising from the ground, tears streaming down her face. She screamed as she saw a man running towards her and then screamed again and flung herself at Johnny when she recognized him.

By now a group of people had started to gather, blocking Terry's chance to go after the Mercedes. He hit the horn and cursed as Johnny got Alsina into the car but he knew he couldn't just drive through the crowd. He thumped the steering wheel and looked at Johnny.

"Fuck! You saw who that was?" Terry wanted a chance at Underwood, nearly as badly as Johnny but they could not leave Alsina alone.

Johnny nodded at his brother and Alsina shuddered as she saw the look in his eyes and felt him tense. She closed her eyes and sobbed into his shoulder. She did not understand how Johnny knew her attackers. She was just glad they had arrived when they did.

Terry got out of the car and phoned Jack Fairfax. They would require his help now and he needed to know what they had found out. Things had just taken an alarming turn for the worse.

Chapter Fifteen

"Stop the car, you cunt! I said stop the fucking car!" Tony screamed at Frank.

He had turned around in his seat to face the rear windscreen.

"Stop the car! Turn around! That was him! That was *fucking* him!"

Frank floored the accelerator. "Are you mad?" He rapidly drove out of town and headed for the countryside. They needed to sanitize things quickly and regroup.

"The Old Bill will be there by now and those fuckers are armed. You'd be signing our death warrants."

Slowly, very slowly, Tony started to realize what he was doing. He started to understand the wisdom of what his friend was saying.

They had blown any immediate chance of revenge on the boy and it was all the fault of that tart. Strangely, he didn't see his lust for the girl as the cause of his failure, or the fact that if he had just ignored her, they would have found out where the boy lived by now. He started to breathe deeply and tried to focus. Thank fuck Frank was with him and fully focussed.

They drove into the countryside and abandoned the car, setting fire to it before they walked away. It wasn't traceable back to them but their fingerprints and DNA were all over it. Hopefully they would be out of the area before the smoke attracted anyone's attention.

It took more than an hour to get back to the hotel where they were staying. They checked out and Tony phoned his father. He needed help, the kind that only his father could arrange for him. The call lasted twenty minutes and he could hear his father's disappointment in him. He smiled when his father told him that he was sending Adrian over but that in the meantime some of their local contacts would help them.

They went back to the brothel that they'd been frequenting. A new doorman was working but he had been filled in on who they were.

He let them in and they sat around drinking chilled bottles of water. They needed clear heads, at least for a while.

The intention had been to find out where Johnny lived and set a trap for him. Frank had too much respect for Johnny's fighting skills to want a fair fight and Tony knew that he just wasn't good enough to take him on without some sort of edge. Well, they'd blown the element of surprise that was for sure.

Ten minutes later the owner of the club arrived, a stocky guy called Dale, with sun bleached hair and a deep tan. He asked if they needed anything, which in itself was a testament to how much power Tony's father wielded over here.

They could not be sure what they would need until Adrian got there. A secure place to stay and some safe transport was a must to start with. For the rest they would have to wait for Adrian.

Chapter Sixteen

They were finally allowed to leave the Guardia Civil cuartel after five frustrating hours. Even though they all spoke Spanish well, it was still a very trying time for them. It could have been a lot longer but Jack Fairfax had made some calls and matters were expedited.

Alsina's parents had finally calmed down. The appearance of London gangsters was an unwelcome intrusion in their lives and they were extremely worried for the safety of their only child. Alsina on the other hand seemed none the worse for wear now.

She clung to Johnny like a second skin and Davina thought that the girl actually seemed to be happy that the incident had occurred as it gave her an excuse to be close to Johnny. She smiled to herself. Was she like that when she was younger?

Johnny travelled back to the marina with Alsina's family. She did not want to let go of him and her parents didn't want to let her out of their sight.

Terry drove the Range Rover with Davina sat next to him and Stephen stretching out in the back seat. Terry was in constant contact with his boss now and reinforcements had started to arrive. They returned to the boats when Terry received the all clear and Alsina reluctantly let Johnny return to his own boat for a few minutes to shower and change.

They planned to eat together that night, it would be easier to police if they were all together.

Chapter Seventeen

The guard at the barrier watched as several 4x4s and people carriers arrived and booked into the hotel. They were all fit young men and women. This late in the season was generally the time for the more advanced groups of divers to arrive, which he assumed they were. They were not as boisterous as the normal groups and he was thankful for small mercies.

He watched as they unloaded their vehicles. Judging from the amount of equipment they carried, they were certainly serious. It looked like the dive centres would have a good year after all.

He opened the gate to allow entry for the Guardia Civil patrol. Uncharacteristically, they stopped just inside the gate and got out. As the four officers approached his hut, he got an uneasy feeling. These were not the usual bunch that came to check the new arrivals, not if the MP-5 sub machine guns they carried were anything to go by.

They gave him a picture of Frank Underwood and told him to alert them if he tried to gain entry into the marina. The guard told them that he remembered the man from the day before.

One man remained with him while the others got back into their vehicle and drove towards the marina office.

Shortly afterwards they returned and left another picture. Both would be left in the guard hut for the shift change later that night.

Driving away from the guard hut, they approached the 'Jodast' and boarded the boat. After a few minutes they left and the guard guessed that this would be the first of many visits.

He hoped that the owners of the 'Jodast' were not in any trouble. He liked them and the two men who had lived on the boat for the last six months. It was unusual for most English people to try and learn the language but the two men were fluent. The younger one made him uneasy on occasions though, like when he had left the marina that afternoon. He had looked very menacing.

Chapter Eighteen

The evening passed uneventfully for the occupants of the two boats. The restaurants were busier than normal due to the influx of people that afternoon. Although neither Terry nor Johnny acknowledged the newcomers, they knew them very well, having worked with them all at different times over the last few years.

Near the end of the evening, one of the women spilt a drink over Terry. Looking flustered, she ordered a round of drinks for the table to apologize. Terry invited her to join them and they joined the tables together and the talk turned to diving, as invariably happens when there were more than two divers in a group.

Alsina's parents had no idea who the new people were but they accepted them just the same. Now having an excuse to converse, they arranged to meet in the morning for an early morning run.

Alsina asked if she could go but her parents were a little concerned. They relented when Davina offered to run with her. Thinking that nobody would attack her if she ran with a group, they felt a lot better about the situation.

Alsina was ecstatic to be allowed to join the run. Although everyone in the group was a lot older than her, she was accepted without any complaint. As her parents watched her interact with the group, they realized how little she was able to mix with people of her own age. When everything was arranged, they headed off to their various beds. Johnny kissed Alsina on the cheek and she hugged him hard against her and thanked him for saving her.

That night and early into the next morning, Terry and the others discussed the reasons that Frank Underwood might have for being in the area. The only thing they knew for sure was that nothing good would come of it.

Turning in for the night, Davina and Stephen spent a restless night in their respective cabins. It had been nearly a year since Stephen had stayed on the boat and over five years for Davina.

It felt like she had only just closed her eyes, when Davina found herself being gently roused. Johnny had prepared coffee. Davina drank a cup but still felt that she needed at least a gallon more.

They collected Alsina and made their way over to the cafe area where they had arranged to meet the others. Davina had a lot of respect for Alsina, as she had matured so much in the last five years. She had half expected to find her dressed in a sports bra or bikini top with hot pants for Johnny's benefit but she had chosen an oversize t-shirt and running shorts.

They drank more coffee whilst they waited for the others and Davina found herself liking the young girl more and more.

Yes, she was a pretty girl but she wasn't in your face about it. She had a maturity far in advance of her age. She thought about her answers before offering an opinion on anything and was really well mannered. The fact that she adored Johnny was obvious but now she had got some sleep she wasn't as clingy as she had been the day before.

The others arrived and declined the offer of coffee. Stephen settled the bill and they warmed up gently, stretching on the utility supply boxes provided for the boats.

The guard saw them coming and lifted the barrier for them, he was glad that Alsina had found some friends. They waved as they passed him and he lifted his coffee cup in return.

The running party followed the road for a couple of miles and then headed for the beach. There were a few people doing yoga and T'ai Chi on the beach and various street vendors were setting up their stalls.

Alsina reminded Davina of a scene she had once seen on the news, of Madonna running in the middle of her bodyguards. Only five of the people they had talked to the night before had turned out but it made for a fair sized group all the same.

Johnny and Alsina stretched the pace a little and the surrounding group matched them effortlessly. Some of the group were wearing packs on their backs, which reminded her of a group of army runners that she had met years ago, on a charity run.

They got back to the marina a couple of hours later and headed off to the shower blocks after collecting their washing gear from the boat. Davina stayed with Alsina and the boys went off in the other direction.

All seemed quiet and the marina was slowly starting to come alive for the day. Davina asked what Alsina was doing for the rest of the day and on being told nothing special, asked her to act as a local tour guide for her. Alsina was pleased to do it and was happier still when Johnny said that he would come too.

Alsina did not realize that they would try to keep her close to them from now on. As far as she was concerned, she was getting to spend more time with Johnny and Davina seemed worth getting to know as well. She wanted to know more about the clubs in America and for the first time wondered if maybe club work could be a career for her.

They checked in at their boats and organized the day's agenda. Terry and Stephen would stay in the marina, as Stephen wanted to sort out some paperwork with the marina office.

Alsina turned up a few minutes later and slipped her arm through Davina's like they were old friends. Johnny opened the door of the Range Rover and held it open for them with an exaggerated bow. Alsina found this hysterical and laughed loudly. Her parents looked up from their boat and waved at them. They were more than happy that their daughter seemed to show no ill effects from the events of the previous day.

Over the next few days, Alsina spent more and more time in Davina's company. Although she still had a huge crush on Johnny, she was just as happy spending an afternoon shopping or sunbathing with Davina, who was starting to think of her as a younger sister.

Both Stephen and Johnny generally joined them when they went to the huge retail parks and more often than not made up a foursome for dinner or taking in a film. Sometimes they would go ten-pin bowling for the afternoon, occasionally running into some of the divers from the marina. Alsina still had no idea who they really were but enjoyed their company just the same.

Her parents watched her blossom socially and realized that maybe she needed a change from the isolated lifestyle of their powerboat. They started thinking about returning to Germany to give her more of a chance to do the normal things that teenagers do and suggested it to Alsina, who was devastated. She ran off in tears to the 'Jodast' looking for Davina.

About an hour later, Davina followed Alsina onto her parent's boat and they sat down on the rear deck seats. Alsina's parents came out and joined them, apologising if their daughter was becoming a nuisance.

They sat and listened as Davina explained that far from being an inconvenience, she wanted to offer Alsina a job in the club when they returned to England. However, she would respect their wishes if they preferred that their daughter remain with them. Alsina was about to object but her father put up his hand to silence her.

He looked at his wife before he spoke and then said he would be delighted with the opportunity. They had never seen their daughter show so much interest in any job before and were happy to let her gain the experience.

Happy now, Alsina remained to talk to her parents, while Davina returned to the 'Jodast'.

There had been no further sign of Frank Underwood and Davina was not sure if that was a good or bad thing.

Chapter Nineteen

Adrian had arrived in a bad mood and Tony decided that it might be a good move to agree with everything he said. This seemed to piss him off even more, so in the end he just acted normally. It took a while but eventually Adrian calmed down.

Adrian had brought new travel documents with him for both of them and had sourced an escape route out of Spain. Tony was not happy to be leaving without getting his revenge but Adrian was adamant.

On a couple of occasions, Tony had thought that Adrian might actually thump him. He had never seen him so upset. They hired a small fishing boat from Galicia to take them back to the U.K. which made the week seem a lot longer than it was.

The reunion with his father shocked him as, from Adrian's behaviour on the trip back, he had expected his father to murder him. Instead, his father just asked if he was well and then disappeared into his office with Adrian. He had looked awful and Tony suspected that something was going on that he was not privy to.

Looking around, he noticed that there were more minders hanging around than usual. Granted, Adrian hadn't been there for a few days but that didn't warrant the amount of security he was now seeing.

He approached Frank and asked if he had any idea of what was happening.

"A whisper has gone out that your old man's on the ropes. The sharks are circling and someone just hijacked his last shipment."

"What, those Romanian birds?"

"Yeah." Frank replied.

"Do we know who it was yet?"

"No, we're waiting for an update. Now that Adrian's back, things should speed up."

"Bollocks! This is just bollocks."

Tony left Frank at the office and got in his Cosworth. Driving through town, he took a mental inventory of what was in his flat. When he got there, he went to the floor safe and removed all of the plastic wrapped bundles of cash. Then he took a picture down from the wall and twisted the fixing. A secret panel opened, he reached in and took out a Mini Uzi and the boxes of ammunition that he kept there.

Throwing his clothes into a laundry bag, he had a last look around and walked away. The flat was one of many that he kept locally. He drove to a nearby industrial estate and pressed a remote on his key fob. A steel shutter started to rise in a small warehouse. Driving inside he parked the car and climbed the stairs to the mezzanine floor. He opened the door and walked into the office suite, which had been converted into a two bedroom flat a few years ago.

Dumping his clothes on the sofa, he walked into the bathroom and switched on the power shower. Stripping off, he showered for about fifteen minutes and then walked naked into the front room.

He didn't see the men until it was too late. The noise of the pump action shotguns was deafening in the confined space. They literally tore him apart.

Reloading the shotguns they walked over and at point blank range fired into his face.

Walking past the Cosworth, they fired at the fuel tank and the car caught fire, then they slid the shotguns under the car into the burning fuel and calmly walked away.

They did not see the CCTV cameras, high up in the roof beams. In total ignorance, they walked out to their Land Rover *Defender 110* and went back to report to their boss.

They did not know that they themselves had only forty-eight hours left to live.

Chapter Twenty

Edward Chesney collapsed in his chair when Adrian told him the news. He leaned forward, put his head in his hands and did not move for a very long time.

Adrian watched his boss and friend of over forty years crumple before his eyes. He sat on the sofa and waited for what seemed like an eternity before Edward finally looked up.

"Are you sure it's him?" Chesney asked, still hoping that a mistake had been made.

"I saw the body myself, there's no doubt."

"Who did it?"

"Cameron's lot. They didn't know about the CCTV." Adrian said sadly.

"How many men have we got outside?"

"Eighteen."

"All tooled up?" Chesney asked.

Adrian nodded and saw a calm settle over his boss that he hadn't seen for a long time.

"Right, let's wipe them out then!" Getting up, he took a MAC 10 machine pistol out of his desk drawer, followed by a Heckler and Koch MP-5, which he threw to Adrian.

Adrian opened the filing cabinet and took out spare rounds and magazines for both guns. Slipping them into his pockets, he followed his boss out of the room.

They jumped into the VW Minibuses and drove to Cameron's base of operations. On the way Chesney rang Cameron and told him that he needed him to help find his son's killers.

Knowing nothing of the incriminating evidence against him, Willy Cameron agreed and welcomed Edward with a show of friendship. As they opened the warehouse doors, Adrian left the minibus followed by his crew and opened fire on Cameron's minders, annihilating them and wounding Willy in the leg.

Willy Cameron crawled along the warehouse floor, desperately trying to find a weapon, looking around wildly for cover as he went.

Walking up behind him, Edward Chesney emptied his magazine into Cameron's back. With a cyclic rate of over a thousand rounds a minute, it didn't take long to finish off his rival.

As the rest of the gang returned throughout the afternoon, they were despatched without pity. In just over four hours, they had slaughtered fifty men.

Frank Underwood watched as Chesney and Bull changed their magazines, then he opened fire on them with his own MP-5, killing them both instantly. The look of betrayal and understanding as Edward Chesney's eyes finally found his did not give Frank any satisfaction. He had been waiting a long time for this moment, too long in fact.

As he turned around, his men grinned at him. In just under a year he had gone from government agent to crime boss. It had been looking decidedly uncertain when Tony had run into Davina and started his vendetta. By manipulating the situation in Spain, he had expedited his plans. If his training had taught him anything at all, it was to be adaptable. He had proved that, in no uncertain terms.

Now he only had one loose end, Johnny Miller.

Chapter Twenty One

After two weeks without further disturbances, Stephen and Davina decided to return to England. The sun, diving and relaxation had given them both a renewed vigour.

Johnny and Terry were recalled too, nothing had been proven but rumours had been circulating that the human trafficking operation had moved up a gear. Johnny was now fully fit and raring to go back to work. Alsina would be safe at the club and he would try to pop in and see her when he could.

A combined farewell and eighteenth birthday party was held for Alsina and everyone attended, including all her new diver friends. Her parents were sad that she was leaving but accepted that she must be allowed to make her own way in life. They knew how lucky she had been to be given this chance. At least it was something she was interested in and Stephen and Davina would look after her and let her stay with them until she found a place of her own.

Everyone said their goodbyes and a bottle of brandy was dispatched over to the gate guards. The office staff overlooked this breach of regulations because Alsina was very popular.

Alsina cried as she got into the car and Johnny gave her a hug. She smiled shyly at him and he looked away. Her mother leaned in and whispered something into Johnny's ear. Then she kissed him on the cheek and smiled at her daughter. Huge tears were rolling down her face.

Terry drove away and joined a convoy of 4x4s and people carriers. The night guard had come in on his day off and both guards saluted them as they passed through the barrier. Terry touched his fingers to his forehead in return and accelerated out of the marina.

They returned the Range Rover to its space in the airport's long term parking area and hitched a ride in one of the rented people carriers. The divers stayed with them through check-in and sat around them on the plane.

The flight went smoothly and again Davina knew before the captain announced it that the plane was descending. They cleared customs easily and Davina recognized the supervisor as the same one she had seen before. She couldn't be certain but she felt sure that he nodded his head slightly at Terry.

Bernie Holt met them at the airport and Davina introduced Alsina to him. On the way to the house they discussed Alsina's future and Bernie filled them in on what had been happening, reassuring them that the club was still in one piece. Meanwhile, Johnny and Terry got a cab to their headquarters.

Bernie dropped Stephen and the two girls at the house and made a quick exit before Vincent flew out of the door.

Alsina looked around; she had not been able to imagine the house and grounds when Davina had told her about them. It was even lovelier than she could have imagined. She stopped dead in her tracks when Vincent came hurtling out. He was about to chase the car, when he caught sight of Davina. Barking loudly, he launched himself at her, pushing her to the ground. She couldn't stop laughing as she fell backwards. "We have to stop meeting like this."

He jumped up and bounded between Stephen and Davina. Alsina tried not to make eye contact with him as she had been told. The next thing she knew, he came up to her from behind and put his huge head under her hand, raising it gently. She stroked him tenderly and then he was off.

"He'll be as good as gold with you now." Stephen said as he bent down to pick up the bags. He gathered them all up as if they weighed nothing and walked into the house. Mrs. Hoon hugged him as he went by and then she grabbed Davina in a bear hug. She released her after nearly a minute and looked at Alsina.

"My God! She's even more beautiful than you described." Alsina blushed deeply at the remark and found herself swallowed up in the arms of

Mrs. Hoon. Allowing herself to be led by the hand they went into the kitchen where a mountain of sandwiches and cakes were waiting.

"Dig in while I brew some coffee. Do you drink coffee, my lovely, or do you want some juice?"

"Coffee is fine, thank you ma'am."

"Oh dear! Isn't she just perfect? Call me Mrs. Hoon my angel, everyone else does." Alsina blushed again at the compliment and looked at Davina.

"You'll get used to Mrs. Hoon." She said in a stage whisper. "She really is larger than life."

Alsina ate silently as she watched Mrs. Hoon fuss over Stephen and Davina. Mrs. Hoon didn't forget her and kept piling food onto her plate each time she emptied it. It was nice for her to see such an open display of affection. In her experience the British did not show their feelings often enough.

Davina came to her rescue and told Mrs. Hoon that she would show Alsina to her room. She knew if they did not escape now they would never have room for the dinner that was cooking in the oven.

Alsina thought that she had died and gone to heaven. She had lived on the boat for so long that she had forgotten what it was like to live in a proper house, and what a house it was.

Due to the requirements of Joseph's guests, all his guest rooms had en-suite bathrooms. It was not unheard of for most of his students to stay on after a course, so rather than waste time queuing for a shower after training, they each had a private shower unit. There was a bath in Joseph's en-suite if she preferred.

Leaving Alsina to her unpacking Davina walked into her own bedroom and lay down on the bed. Stephen woke her four hours later and she in turn woke Alsina. They showered and got changed before going down to dinner.

Fully refreshed they decided to head off to the club. They took the Land Cruiser as it was more comfortable for the three of them.

They parked in the car park and walked up to the entrance. A few of the regulars nodded to Stephen so he wandered off to speak to them. As Alsina walked into the club, she marvelled at how popular it was.

Davina took her arm and headed for the dance area. She introduced her to Amelia and ordered a couple of fresh orange juices. Then she took her on a guided tour of the club, introducing her to everybody who worked there and some of the regular customers.

They finished the tour in the office and Alsina looked through the one-way glass as Davina and Stephen checked over the paperwork.

Davina told her that Amelia would be responsible for her training and if she had any questions to ask and one of them would help her.

Alsina hugged Davina and thanked her again for the opportunity she was being given.

During the next few months there were no more incidents. No one else had offered to buy them out and with the money from the sale of the Miami club in the bank, they were able to introduce a number of security upgrades with the latest specifications.

Alsina flourished in her job and picked the trade up quickly. All of the staff liked her and were very protective of her. With her first pay packet she invited her new bosses and the brothers out for a celebratory meal.

Terry couldn't make it and the resulting foursome spent an enjoyable evening in a popular Spanish restaurant, as a reminder of the good times they'd had in Spain.

After dinner, they went to the pictures and then on to a bar within walking distance of the cinema. They were just getting ready to leave when a group of five men walked into the bar. They had obviously been drinking and seemed hell bent on getting into a fight. The other customers tried not to make eye contact and kept themselves to themselves as the group collected their drinks.

Stephen tried to get the girls out before it kicked off but as soon as Alsina stood up all eyes turned to her. Johnny was returning from the men's room and watched the situation unfold.

"Hey love, what you hanging about with your grandparents for?"

Stephen ignored the comment and Alsina tried to act as if nothing had been said. He was helping Davina put her jacket on when the man who had spoken grabbed Alsina roughly by the arm.

"What's the matter Bitch? Too good to talk to the likes of us?"

"I do not want any trouble, we were just leaving. I am sorry if you thought that I was being rude." Alsina's command of English was excellent but heavily accented.

"You foreign birds are all alike. Stuck up bitches the lot of you."

Stephen turned to look at the man. Very few people were stupid enough to pick on someone the size of Stephen; unfortunately common sense and alcohol did not go hand in hand.

"I think it would be a good idea to let her go mate. We're just leaving." As he spoke he let his hand rest on the man's arm.

"Fuck off, Grandpa!"

Shrugging him off, the man ignored Stephen and turned back to Alsina, undressing her with his eyes.

"Do yourself a favour and walk away, mate." Though spoken fairly quietly, Johnny's words carried to the surrounding groups of people and a hush descended on the bar.

"Who the fuck do you think you are?" The man was looking at Johnny but still had hold of Alsina's arm.

"Nobody special."

"Well, you can fuck off an' all."

"Do yourself a favour, wind your neck in and walk away." Johnny warned the man.

"Fuck off! What are you gonna do about it?" He threw his bottle of beer at Johnny's head as he spoke, but missed.

Johnny smiled at him as he snapped a punch into the man's throat. The move was explosive and decisive. Nobody watching had realized that he had actually moved until he swung round and squared off against the remaining men, who watched helplessly while their friend collapsed on the floor, fighting for breath. It was one against four but they just stood there. Stephen bent down and checked the man's injury. Though painful and incapacitating, he was lucky this time, it wasn't life threatening.

It was all over in seconds. Johnny extended his arm and put it around Alsina, escorting her past the fallen man and his cohorts. He stared at the men, with a thin smile on his face, as he walked past them.

He walked to the door and held it open for Stephen and Davina. Davina saw the look in his eyes and remembered what Terry had told her about his brother when they had first met. 'That boy scares a lot of very hard men'.

She watched as Alsina put her arm around Johnny. He looked down at her face and smiled, looking almost as young as she did. He let the door swing shut behind them and they walked slowly to the car. He asked how she was and in answer she reached up and kissed him on the cheek.

They got into the Land Cruiser and drove away in silence. Davina found it difficult to reconcile the Johnny she now saw with the Johnny she'd seen five minutes ago.

There is a look that good martial artists develop when they fight, totally devoid of emotion. Stephen could carry it off but what she had just witnessed surpassed anyone she had ever seen, including her late brother, who had been very accomplished at it. She realized that she was holding her breath and as she breathed out she was thankful that Johnny was on their side.

Chapter Twenty Two

Frank Underwood was calling in a lot of favours. Through his connections with bent solicitors and judges he was slowly assuming ownership of all the properties owned by Chesney and Cameron.

It was taking time but he knew where the title deeds were kept and more importantly, he knew where they hid their ready cash. The months of silent observation had paid off. It was amazing what some people thought of their hired help, it was almost as if they were non-existent. Frank had used this arrogant flaw of his former boss to note as much information as possible on where the money went.

He began converting some of the bars and pubs into specialist sex clubs. With his connections in the people trafficking world he was bringing misery to almost two hundred young girls that had been brought over to the United Kingdom. Not that he ever thought of it like that.

His crew loved him. He was not slow in sharing the money around. In under a month he had found or recovered over five million pounds in cash of which, he'd shared about five hundred thousand with them. It was enough to keep them on side but not enough to allow them to draw attention to themselves.

Of the hundred or so properties he had "inherited", nearly half were now in his name. So far, his property portfolio was worth over forty million pounds and growing, though none of his men were aware of this fact.

Using contacts he'd made while working for the government, he replaced all the guns in his organisation with newer, more efficient models. Selling the old stock to some of the street gangs at low prices and using middlemen so that there would be no comeback. He was not overly greedy. He'd acquired everything for free, so he would make a profit at whatever price he sold them for.

He treated the new stock as an investment and, because he was bulk buying, he actually got them for a better price than he was selling the old shit for.

Everything he touched seemed to turn to gold. People called him Midas now, which suited him, as the Frank Underwood name was a liability.

He now had five different identities, with funds spread equally through his various accounts. If he had to leave tomorrow, he could disappear without a trace.

So far, by some fluke, the Police were not aware that anything had happened to either Edward Chesney or Willy Cameron and Frank was using this breathing space to good advantage.

He was rapidly becoming the biggest human trafficker in the country, with the guns and drugs as a profitable side-line. Money was coming in from all directions and this did not include the revenue from the existing businesses that he had acquired.

Still, he couldn't rest, not until the Miller brothers were dead. He had decided that if anything happened to Johnny, Terry would come after whoever killed him and with a lot more than just arresting him in mind.

This had to be sorted soon, the sooner the better.

Chapter Twenty Three

Jack Fairfax's unit had uncovered a sharp rise in human trafficking. To make matters worse, two of the main players had gone to ground.

Although they had not been able to introduce any more people into Edward Chesney's organisation, they did still have two people in Willy Cameron's crew. Nothing had been heard from either man for over a month. They knew that both gangs were still operating and that most of their assets had been sold off.

They had been able to obtain copies of deed transfers but could find nothing dodgy about the new owners. It was as if they had just vanished completely.

Jack sent Terry and Johnny to the club to see if they had been getting any hassle. He decided to station Johnny at the club so that they would know immediately if anything happened.

Alsina was over the moon, spending as much time with Johnny as possible when her work allowed.

Bernie Holt was happy to have Johnny on his crew and he quickly proved to be a big hit with the other doormen, gaining a reputation as a safe pair of hands.

The weeks passed into months and no new leads had come to light. Jack Fairfax knew from his sources that more and more girls and boys were coming into the country but they weren't surfacing.

Fairfax was not happy. He felt like he was sitting on a powder keg and the flames were getting closer. Something had to give soon either way.

Chapter Twenty Four

Davina came into the kitchen one morning after her run, to find Terry tucking into a huge plate of sausage, bacon and eggs. Mrs. Hoon was chatting away and as Davina headed for the tea pot, he started to rise. She waved him down and filled her cup before asking the others if they wanted a refill.

She had not seen much of Terry, as he had been busy hunting for leads. She smiled at him as she blew on her tea to cool it down. Mrs. Hoon stopped talking and made herself busy, putting more food into the pan. Terry asked after Alsina who, as if on cue, walked into the kitchen. She walked over to Terry, kissed him on the cheek and gave him a quick hug. He smiled warmly at her and said that they were just talking about her. She took a cup of coffee from Mrs. Hoon and sat next to Davina.

Terry waited for them all to finish eating before telling them what he had learned so far. The news was good and bad. They were sure that Tony was responsible for Joseph's death but could not locate him. The rumours that were now surfacing were that he had disappeared and was presumed dead.

His bank accounts were untouched and all effort was being made to find his whereabouts. They knew he worked for his father but he too had disappeared.

They were still no nearer to finding Frank Underwood but wouldn't give up looking. They thought he was in the country somewhere but could shed no light on his exact whereabouts.

Johnny would remain at the club for the time being and Terry would liaise between the office and Johnny.

Mrs. Hoon refilled their cups as Stephen came in through the front door. Normally he and the two girls ran together in the mornings but he had been strangely absent this morning.

The doorbell rang and seeing that Mrs. Hoon was busy with breakfast for Stephen, Alsina jumped up saying she would answer it. The post normally came about this time and she wanted to see if there was a letter from her parents.

In the kitchen they listened in silence as they heard the front door open. Ten seconds later Alsina came in screaming hysterically.

"Thank you, thank you, thank you, thank you!"

Davina shrugged and the rest smiled at her as they got up and followed her out of the kitchen, towards the front garden.

Johnny was taking a big red bow off of a shiny black Mini Cooper. He and Stephen had collected it that morning while Davina kept Alsina busy with the run.

"Who wants to come out for a ride?"

"I think just you and your boyfriend." Davina watched as both Johnny and Alsina blushed deeply. She had been watching Alsina closely over the last few weeks and it was obvious that her feelings for Johnny had not changed. What she had noticed, however, was a slight change in Johnny's feelings for Alsina.

Johnny had always liked Alsina, as everyone knew, but recently his behaviour had given away his deeper feelings. Since the incident in the bar, they had spent every moment that they could together.

"Just be honest with each other, it will be a lot easier for you in the end." With that, Davina went back into the house, followed by Stephen and Terry.

"Pot and Kettle," Alsina shouted before looking at Johnny. "Well, that was embarrassing." She couldn't quite look into Johnny's eyes.

"Only if it's not true." he whispered.

Alsina didn't quite understand what he meant at first and it took a few seconds to sink in. She ran into his arms and for the first time kissed him hard on the lips. After a few minutes he gently eased her away from him and led her around to the driver's door. "Take me for a ride," he grinned and walked back to the passenger door.

They drove around for hours and stopped off for lunch at a riverside pub before she dropped him off at his apartment. Then she headed back to the house and got ready for her evening's work.

Stephen and Davina followed her to work in the Porsche. Although she always seemed cheerful, they had never seen her as happy as she was now.

When they got to the club Alsina parked as near to the front doors as she could and ran inside. The doormen looked at her and smiled. Two minutes later she was dragging Amelia out to see her new car.

Seeing Stephen and Davina approaching, Amelia tried to go back inside but Alsina's exuberance was clear to see. Davina told them to go for a spin and get it out of her system but to make sure they were back in time to open.

This was the first time she had done anything but concentrate on work since she started and Davina thought that it was good for her young friend to let off steam. Normally, once they got to work, she was all business and went about her tasks with a vigour that infected everyone.

As the Mini left, Bernie Holt drove in and parked in the newly vacated space. Johnny got out of the passenger seat and they walked into the club.

The girls returned well before opening, having taken a quick circuit around the neighbourhood and Amelia ran in to check on her bar.

Johnny smiled at Alsina and she winked at him as they passed. Now she was the consummate professional. Johnny didn't mind, he was happy enough now that they were together.

Chapter Twenty Five

It was nearly a month before anyone at the club, other than Amelia, found out about Johnny and Alsina. Then it was just a matter of time before Frank Underwood received the news. Finally, he thought he had found a way to tie up all the loose ends.

Frank had someone who worked at the club on his payroll, so he knew Johnny was working there and guessed that it was some sort of a cover.

Security at the club was very good now. The only way to get at Johnny was to go through Alsina and that would work well for Underwood.

He picked up the phone and made a call to his armourer. It would take a few days to get what he wanted but it was not unachievable.

Chapter Twenty Six

When Alsina was not driving Johnny home, she took Amelia. She got on well with both her and her partner, Karen, who did not see Alsina as a threat. Alsina had never had any prejudices about how other people lived their lives, which meant a lot to her new friends.

Now they were officially an item, Alsina spent several nights a week at Johnny's flat. They stayed at the house as well but she wanted to give Davina a bit of breathing space. There was another reason too but she couldn't be sure that she had guessed correctly.

Davina and Stephen missed having Alsina for company and started going bowling and going out for meals together. Sometimes they would make up a foursome with Johnny and Alsina, sometimes, though very rarely, Terry and Mrs. Hoon would join them too.

In less than two months, the Mini clocked up thousands of miles. Alsina loved the car and her new found freedom. It also meant that she could nip out during the day if they needed anything.

Sometimes on Friday nights after work she would go on to a gay club with Amelia and Karen. Occasionally, Johnny would accompany them but Alsina enjoyed herself whether he was there or not. She had a routine to her life now and since her relationship with Johnny had moved up a level, she was also quite self-assured.

Karen arrived on Friday, as usual, just as they were closing and the doorman showed her inside. Amelia was nearly ready. They talked as she finished up and planned the rest of the night. They were making a foursome with Alsina and Johnny.

Davina and Stephen would join them later, maybe, but their work would probably make them an hour or so later than the rest.

Johnny and Bernie were doing the rounds, clearing the toilets and passageways of anyone who was still in the club after hours. Stephen and Davina were in the office with Alsina, discussing the events of the evening.

They still had a security crew at the front entrance and four men situated in the car park, making sure everyone got to their cars or taxis.

Amelia finished first and waited with Karen, while Alsina finished up. The three of them waited for Johnny who was all but finished now and then they all said goodbye to their friends and workmates and headed out of the door.

Bernie called Alsina back and apologized, telling her Stephen needed five minutes of her time before she left. She threw the keys to Amelia and told her to get in and fire the car up.

Johnny went to the office with Alsina, grabbing a quick kiss before she entered. She opened the door to see Stephen holding the phone out to her, silently mouthing the word "Mum".

Alsina smiled, she had promised to ring her mum earlier that day but had forgotten about it. She took the phone and told her mother she was fine and that she was not to worry, before repeating the same conversation with her father. Five minutes later she hung up. They checked that Davina and Stephen were still on for joining them later and walked out arm in arm.

Johnny slid his hand down to her backside and gave it a quick squeeze. Not to be outdone she did the same to him. Smiling at each other they walked into the foyer.

They saw Karen chatting to the doormen and Amelia walking off to the car to start it up. Finishing her cigarette Karen started to follow Amelia. She was just over half way to the car when there was a blinding flash and the Mini exploded. Karen was thrown to the ground by the shockwave.

Alsina stood stunned as Johnny ran out of the door towards the wreckage. The doormen followed his lead but it was too late to save Amelia. There seemed to be nothing left of the car but a burning floor pan.

They checked on Karen but the unnatural angle of her head told them that she too was probably dead, still they attempted CPR but to no avail. Johnny told the doormen to carry on until the paramedics arrived.

Davina was hugging Alsina to her while Stephen ran to what was left of the car to see what he could do. Johnny was already on the phone to Terry explaining what had happened.

Bernie Holt came running with the remaining security men and some fire extinguishers. The best word to describe the scene was carnage.

Alsina slowly started making her way towards the wreckage with Davina. She held her hand as they watched the remains of their friend smouldering, half in, half out of the car.

They went over to Karen but saw there was little they could do. Alsina was still deeply shocked and Davina was not much better. Stephen came and hugged them both as he led them away, back towards the club.

Johnny looked up as Terry entered the car park with the emergency services in front and behind him.

Terry checked that his brother was unhurt and hugged him tight. Thanking the universe for saving his brother once more, he led him towards the club as their boss, Jack Fairfax, tore into the car park.

They entered the club and filed into the office, which, although spacious, was starting to feel extremely cramped.

"It has to be Underwood!" Jack Fairfax spoke with authority. He was a well-built man, usually immaculately dressed in a suit and tie. Now though, his shirt was open and he was tie-less. His greying hair was ruffled and the lines on his face seemed more pronounced.

"Why Underwood and not Chesney?" Terry asked the question.

"Because this appears to be an attack on Alsina, not the club. There's no reason to attack her, unless he thought that Johnny would be in the car as well and we know that Underwood's after Johnny."

"But they *could* be after Alsina again, Chesney tried to grab her once before." Terry was desperately hoping that things did not look the way they seemed. He did not want his brother as a target.

"Tony Chesney didn't have murder on his mind, the last time he grabbed her." Jack looked at Alsina as he spoke "And anyway we're almost certain that he's dead now."

"What are the options? What's the plan of attack?" Johnny spoke quietly and all eyes turned to him. They'd heard that tone in his voice before and it *wasn't* good news.

"Firstly, back to the house. I've had people over there since you first rang me. There will be round the clock security and roving patrols in the grounds. Oh, sorry Davina, Stephen, but we had to use a tranquilliser dart on Vincent. He didn't take kindly to the team turning up without you."

"Oh God! He didn't hurt anyone, did he?" Davina's face was taught. She knew how Vincent would react to a house invasion in the middle of the night."

"We went prepared, dog handlers and marksmen. Sorry but I couldn't take the chance. That is one scary animal!"

"Don't worry about it. He'll be fine when we get there." Davina replied more confidently than she felt.

Davina sat next to Alsina with Johnny on the other side. After making sure she didn't need medical attention, they left the office and made for the cars.

Fortunately, Stephen had his Land Cruiser at the club, which was big enough to take them all. Even without Stephen's vehicle, there would have been enough government cars that they could have made use of.

Leaving Bernie to secure the club, they moved out in convoy as soon as Stephen's Land Cruiser had been given the all clear.

Chapter Twenty Seven

The next morning found Terry in his old room, Johnny and Alsina in her room and Stephen and Davina in Davina's room. Vincent was in with Davina and Stephen, nobody else wanted to be around one hundred and eighty pounds of pissed off Rottweiler when he woke up, although Johnny had offered.

Armed guards were patrolling the grounds and Mrs. Hoon had been stopped and searched as she turned up in her car. After the initial upset, she waded straight in to making sure there was enough coffee and sandwiches for everybody.

Stephen kissed Davina on the cheek and woke her up. Vincent knew there were other people in the house and was trying to get through the door to them. Davina smiled at Stephen, thinking that she would not have coped with half of the events they had endured if he had not been there. She wondered if he knew what he meant to her.

Stephen put Vincent on a lead, which wasn't normal for either of them but he couldn't take the chance of the big dog attacking any of their protectors.

Vincent pulled Stephen into the kitchen; Johnny looked up and called to him. Immediately Vincent calmed down. There was definitely a bond there but Stephen would dare any psychologist to explain it.

Both Johnny and Stephen accompanied Vincent through the grounds for his morning walk. They introduced him to the guards and he seemed to understand that they were friends. The dog handler and the marksman from the previous night had already left, which was probably for the best.

Terry joined them a little later and they discussed their plans. That Johnny was now a target was obvious. Realistically, they had known that anyway. Terry was worried that his brother would be affected by the memories of his last encounter with Underwood but his fears looked to be without foundation.

"You're welcome to stay here until this is cleared up." Stephen wasn't looking at Johnny as he spoke but instead was looking through the window at Davina, who was chatting with Mrs. Hoon in the kitchen.

"I appreciate the offer but it would make your house a target." Johnny continued, "Jack offered to put me in a safe house but I don't think that's such a great idea, either."

"What about Spain? You can use the boat again and Alsina can stay with her parents. At least you can keep an eye on them and the security at the marina will keep an eye out for you."

"I don't know if I want Alsina to be around me for the next few weeks. I nearly lost her last night and I can't accept that."

"I'd like to be a fly on the wall when you try to get that one past her." Stephen chuckled.

"She must see that I'm a liability at the moment. At least if I take her to see her parents they can back me up."

Stephen was sceptical but the conversation dried up as Alsina joined them. Stephen marvelled at her composure. She absently slipped her arm around Johnny's waist and he hugged her. What ever happened, he knew they were safe at the house for a while. She looked at Johnny and opened her mouth to say something but then changed her mind.

"How are you doing, sweetheart?" Johnny asked.

"I do not understand what's going on. Why did Amelia and Karen have to die?"

Johnny remained silent.

"Tell me about this man Underwood. Why is he after you?"

Johnny thought about what he was going to say. Alsina knew a lot about him and his work but he did not know if she was ready to know the whole truth. He didn't know if *he* was ready for her to know the whole truth.

"Did he give you your scars?"

Johnny looked at her in amazement. She smiled at him.

"Oh Johnny, it was obvious they were not propeller wounds. I think that in some small way I wanted you to be a little dangerous."

"Sweetheart, I think that at this moment, I may be *very* dangerous for you. It might be a good idea if you went to Spain for a while, just until things calm down."

"Yes, I think that it is a good idea." Johnny could not believe how easy this conversation was, until she continued, "And you can come with me!"

"I don't think I can sweetheart, not until we catch this guy."

"Terry can catch him!" She said it so matter of factly that he nearly laughed.

"I need to catch him!"

"No, you do not!" Alsina said defiantly.

"I won't be safe until he's caught. *You* won't be safe until he is caught."

"And do you not see? I am safe with you! I have always been safe with you."

"I can't protect you properly if I'm worried about you." Johnny was losing the argument.

"That is not my problem. I want to be with you."

Johnny looked to Terry and Stephen, who held up their hands in surrender. Davina walked over and put her arm around Stephen.

"Davina, tell her that I'm not safe to be around, please."

"I agree with you, Johnny." She looked at Alsina, "I promised your parents I would look after you and look what's happened."

"If it was you, would you go?"

"But it isn't me."

"Tell me honestly, if Stephen was a target, would you leave him?" Alsina pressed.

Davina paused; she knew now that she would never leave Stephen. Alsina recognized that she had won and did not push the point.

"What can we do?" Davina looked at the faces around her. "We are safe here, aren't we?"

"We still have the club to run." Stephen shrugged. "Johnny doesn't have to go back there, but we do."

"They may still target Alsina if they think she's seeing Johnny. I think Spain is still the best option!" Terry spoke slowly.

"I am not going back without Johnny!"

"I didn't mean that you go back alone. Underwood has connections here but I don't think he's got the same pull in Spain. Me and the Boy can go with you."

They all considered this as they returned to the house. Johnny took Alsina to her room and tried to convince her that she was wrong. He tried to tell her that she was being stupid but could not express his feelings sufficiently and she would not be swayed.

He thought that if he did return to Spain, he could leave her in her parents' safe keeping and continue the hunt with Terry. He sighed heavily as he kissed her. She hugged him to her with all her strength.

Terry called his boss, who agreed with the arrangement. At least with a dedicated team in Spain they could concentrate their attentions here.

Davina took Alsina to one side and told her that she would still have her job when she came back. She hoped that she would return as Alsina had become like a sister to her.

Alsina packed and came down the stairs. Terry had collected Johnny's things with his own and they loaded them into a people carrier.

As Davina hugged her one last time, Alsina whispered in her ear. "Tell him how you feel about him!"

Davina looked at the young girl who she had grown to love as Alsina continued, "Just be honest with each other, it will be a lot easier for you in the end."

Alsina kissed her cheek and ran to the car. Looking back she saw Davina and Stephen waving to her. As she watched, they turned and walked back into the house arm in arm. She smiled, then turned back and kissed Johnny.

Chapter Twenty Eight

Her parents were surprised to see them drive into the marina. At first they thought that she and Johnny had had an argument. Their expressions turned to horror as Alsina told them what had happened.

Johnny fully expected them to demand that he leave and stay out of Alsina's life. Strangely, it seemed to him, they didn't.

They could see that their daughter was in love. Equally, from what they saw of Johnny, he loved her too.

Johnny suggested that she move her things onto her parents' boat. Her mother smiled as she watched her daughter tell Johnny that he was mistaken and would he kindly put her things in their room on the 'Jodast'.

Johnny collected her things and left the boat. Their security team was in place and the Guardia Civil would make regular checks on them.

He boarded the 'Jodast' and asked Terry if there was any news. He was in a quandary, they knew who the enemy was but could not take the fight to Underwood until they knew his whereabouts.

He grabbed a bottle of water from the fridge and waited for Alsina to return. The gentle motion of the boat made him want to doze off. He shrugged off the feeling and looked out of the window. He tried to catch sight of the security detail but couldn't. That was good. They were safe enough here at least.

Chapter Twenty Nine

Frank Underwood was not happy. Not only had his plan failed, but also it had tipped Johnny off that he was a target. Now, to cap it all, his sources had told him that Johnny had left the house to destinations unknown.

He thought about his options. If he found Terry and killed him first, that would definitely get Johnny's attention. The major drawback to that was that Johnny would leave no stone unturned until he found him. He wanted to find Johnny, not the other way round. The last thing Frank wanted was the boy coming after him looking to get even.

Frank was sure that Johnny would come. Of that there was no doubt.

He gave himself a deadline of twenty-four hours. If nothing had come to light by then, he would start feeling up his old work connections. Someone, somewhere, knew where Johnny was.

The telephone on the desk rang and he snatched up the receiver. The news was good and bad. He now knew where Johnny was, but Frank did not have the clout in Spain that Edward Chesney had commanded.

He made some calls to Dale, the guy that owned the brothel. Nothing had leaked out about Chesney's demise but word on the street had it that Chesney was on the missing list.

If and when Frank went after Johnny, he would take some of his own muscle with him, people he trusted. Chesney had been well respected in his day and Frank did not want to offer himself up as "Dish of the day" to any Tom, Dick or Harry who fancied making a name for himself by using revenge for Chesney as a reason to attack him.

He checked his new Glock 20, racking back the slide and making sure there was a round in the chamber. Starting off as an unconscious check, it had developed into something of a nervous habit.

He put the weapon back in his shoulder holster. He needed to get out so he grabbed the keys to his Mercedes and walked out. He summoned two of his crew to accompany him and then drove off.

He cruised for hours until finally deciding that a product test was in order. He drove to the halfway house that he was using for his new girls. Choosing one at random he spent the next hour fucking her brains out. None of the girls meant anything to him, they were all basically the same to him.

The more he went at her, the more his mind cleared. The beginnings of an idea started to form in his mind. It was dangerous, but it might work.

Walking out of the bedroom, he called his companions and strode purposefully to his car. Whatever happened he would be a long way from it, so he would be safe enough. He could not leave the country yet, until he was sure of the continued loyalty of his men, but that would work in his favour.

Chapter Thirty

They had been back a week so far and nothing untoward had happened. They set about cleaning the boat again. They were fastidious in this work, because the relentless sun and salt air would destroy a million pounds worth of boat in no time.

Also it was their way of saying thank you. They ran the engines up every few days and took her out on the odd occasion. The 'Jodast' had slipped her moorings this morning with the muted sound of the two huge diesel engines venting under the waterline.

Stopping at the fuel pontoon they passed an elegant Guardia Civil launch as it made one of its frequent visits to the marina. It was a new boat and the paintwork gleamed as only a newly polished hull can.

The sun shimmered on the Mediterranean like the twinkling of thousands of tiny diamonds. Only the three of them were on board, Alsina's parents having declined their offer of a day's sailing.

It was a glorious day with a slight easterly wind but no real waves to speak of. As the 'Jodast' cleared the marina, they surveyed the immediate area before bringing the boat onto the plane.

They looked like any other pleasure boat out that day. A blonde girl in a bikini and two men in swimming shorts and t-shirts was the norm for around here.

They headed out along the coast, waving at the other craft that were lucky enough to be able to go cruising on a weekday.

The setting was idyllic but Johnny was on edge. Progress on the case was slow and although their boss kept them informed, they seemed to be getting nowhere.

Johnny cursed Underwood's training. There was nothing to go on. He knew all the Police procedures, which made it easier to hide his tracks.

Alsina came up to the fly bridge with three large bottles of water. She looked gorgeous. Terry watched her as she touched Johnny's arm lightly and he took his bottle.

He was pleased for his brother. He had been through a lot and deserved to be happy. They would all be much happier when the Underwood situation had been taken care of.

Taking his own bottle of water, Terry took the controls over from Johnny and the two young people went down the stairway and forward to the bow. Alsina had left some towels under the snap down canvas mattresses earlier, which she retrieved and laid on top. She was fighting with the wind, so Johnny had to help her.

They headed for a protected Marine Reserve. Anchoring was illegal but most of the boats just cut their engines and drifted. Terry watched the locals free diving with their spear guns. Most of them now used the surface marker buoys, required by law to show boat traffic that divers were below the surface. Some didn't.

The brothers got on well with the residents of the marina. They never bothered the local fishermen if they could help it and the locals generally left them alone. Speaking the language helped, but the local dialect was far from the Castilian Spanish that they had first learned.

They arrived at the Marine Reserve and drifted, the only sound was the soft lapping of the occasional wave against the hull.

Terry stayed on the fly bridge. It was a better vantage point and it meant he was immediately available if they needed to fire the engines up quickly.

Some of the underground rocks and reefs were not marked on any charts. Knowledge of the dangerous areas was passed on by word of mouth but only if the locals liked you.

Of course that meant quite a few tourists and holidaymakers going aground. Terry remembered something a boat mechanic had once told him, "You can't tell a boat owner anything! They always know better."

The mechanic who told him was usually very busy in tourist season, fixing holes below the waterline and replacing bent propellers.

As they drifted, Terry kept an eye on the radar. He knew exactly where all the other boats were in relation to him and noticed that one had followed them from the marina.

He tagged the boat and started the engines. They headed further down the coast and the little dot disappeared. When they moored up finally, well past the Marine Reserve the little dot reappeared. He marvelled at the technology that showed him the boat was the same one he had tagged earlier.

Getting out a pair of stabilized 12x50 magnification binoculars he scanned the area and looked in the direction of the boat. He saw the sleek and powerful Guardia Civil launch come slowly into view.

As they passed him, they waved at Terry. Evidently his paperwork had been checked and passed in the marina office. He didn't think the details of his brother's situation would have been passed on to the Marine Division of the Guardia Civil, but who knew?

They ate their lunch in a small cove, of which there were hundreds along this coastline. They slept after lunch and then went swimming, exploring some small caves in the rocks. Johnny looked at the caves with interest; you could get a smaller boat than theirs into them, maybe up to seven and a half metres or more.

Little wonder this coast was loved so much by smugglers. In the time they had been here, the waiters in the marina had regaled them with countless stories about the smuggling history.

Speedboats would be found on beaches, empty of everything including engines. Sometimes there would be fuel cans aboard, but not often. Also in the early mornings you could follow the coast and find pateras, the Spanish name for the boats that the people smugglers use, drifting slowly just offshore, again stripped of everything.

They had been warned never to tie an empty boat to theirs, at least not until they had called the Guardia Civil as it was better to tell them in advance that you had found one, than try to explain why you were towing one when you returned to port.

As the afternoon wore on, they steered the boat back in the direction that they had come. Nothing had been resolved and no new information had been phoned through to them but they felt a little more relaxed.

Just after they arrived back in the marina Johnny had asked Alsina what self-defence training she had, if any. On finding out that she had none, he and Terry started teaching her the basics. Werner already knew some moves and Sabine decided that she would benefit from the lessons with her daughter as well, which made it a fair sized group.

The training went well, made more enjoyable because they all had fun. Midway through the second week they took the boat out again. This time Alsina's parents came and they carried on with the training on a secluded beach.

After a quiet word from Terry, Alsina's father bought snorkelling masks and fins from the local dive shop and a couple of divers' knives. Johnny wanted them all to have basic weapons training. As it turned out, Alsina's father had been in the German Army and was already comfortable with using a knife.

Johnny and Terry already had their own dive knives and were more than proficient with their intended use and their alternative uses.

Johnny bought Alsina a two-inch lockable, folding knife that fitted on her key ring, although she would have to remember not to take it back to the U.K. Once she had got used to carrying it, they started her training on pressure points and making oblique references to the fact that a knife blade in the same areas would do considerable damage. They hoped that her subconscious would put two and two together.

Johnny was becoming fonder of Alsina and Terry was extremely happy that his brother had found someone to care about. He worried about the timing but with the security they had on hand, he hoped that they would be safe.

Deciding to treat Alsina with total honesty, Johnny told her about the pistols that he had on board. Stressing that they were not toys, he showed her how to strip, clean and load the matching Sig Sauers that he and Terry had been supplied with.

Both Johnny and Terry were proud of the way she conducted herself. They hoped that if things went pear shaped, she now had more than just a slim chance of defending herself.

Alsina thought that she was being prepared for war but remembering her near abduction, she thought the safety measures a very good idea. She became more aware of her surroundings and for the first time realized how Johnny must have lived his life while working under cover. The realization hit her hard. No one should have to live like that.

Chapter Thirty One

Hanging up the phone, Frank Underwood smiled. If all went to plan, then he would be rid of all his problems before too long.

Both Dale, the owner of the brothel and the guy that had supplied their guns were siding with him. He had also sent a couple of his own men over and, in theory at least, his plan looked like a goer.

He now had a small army of muscle in Spain, enough to carry out his instructions without too much trouble.

Money was continually rolling in and he was still being generous to all of his employees and associates. In addition, he was now a silent partner in the brothel, which had its own rewards and would facilitate his longer-term goals quite nicely.

Many of the criminals on the coast frequented the club and he could use it to extend his influence on the mainland. Still smiling, he walked out of his office and got into his car. He decided that another product test was in order.

Half of his crew were collecting a debt for an acquaintance. He smiled as he realized how great his power base was growing. He was slowly becoming the largest weapons supplier in the U.K. The drugs were a bonus and his connections at the ports were invaluable.

He tried not to get overconfident as that was when mistakes were made. He eventually wanted to retire to distant and exotic lands. This meant that he would have to be extra cautious. He always tried to be careful as it was in his nature but now even more so.

After finishing with the girl, he went back to the office to wait for the call he was expecting that evening. Driving off with his minders, he saw his extra security detail following at a discreet distance. It did not pay to take too many chances.

Chapter Thirty Two

Dale watched as the men filed out of his bar. This was going to be the start of a new way of life for him. With the money that Frank Underwood was throwing around, he would be able to retire soon.

He had faith in his men; the two from England looked especially useful. From what he was hearing, Frank was the man to back. He smiled again as he thought of the last instruction that he had been given. It was like Christmas had come early for him, no hardship at all.

He sat with the barman sipping his brandy coffee, which was more brandy than coffee. He didn't usually suffer from nerves but this was the biggest thing he had ever been involved in. He finished his drink, got up and left the bar. Walking to the adjoining bar, he would strike up a conversation with the owner, Pablo. They had been neighbours a long time and catered for different trades, consequently they never trod on each other's toes.

Two British women were at the bar talking to Pablo and seeing Dale enter, he waved him over. They all drank and chatted aimlessly for the next two hours. Pablo was on a promise and the women agreed to continue their session in more intimate surroundings.

Chapter Thirty Three

Alsina and her mum were sunbathing on the beach. Werner had dropped them off on his way to the bank. Johnny was walking towards them, having just left Terry. The plan was for Terry to grab some food from the local supermarket and then collect them all later.

Johnny could not see the security team but he knew it was there. He stopped at the kiosk to buy some ice creams. There were a couple of girls in the queue that could not make up their minds, so Johnny waited patiently for them to decide.

After he was finally served, he balanced the three small tubs in his hands while he trudged across the sand.

The rusty white Nissan Patrol 4x4 screamed onto the beach followed by a red Nissan Pathfinder. Johnny watched them separate and while one came straight for him, the other headed for Alsina.

There were four men in each car and three from the closest one jumped out firing at Johnny, who dropped the ice creams and dived over a sun bed, drawing his Sig as he went.

Firing from a prone position, he hit the driver of the Patrol and aimed at the three men running towards him.

As he watched, he saw the three men from the Pathfinder grab Alsina and turn back to the car. Johnny found out where Alsina got her composed outlook from, as both she and her mother fought the attackers, using some of the moves they had been taught but also improvising when necessary.

The attackers had not been expecting any resistance, so were forced to release Alsina and try to fend off her mother.

At this moment, the security team made their presence known. Partly made up from Johnny's colleagues and partly from the Guardia Civil, they shouted out in Spanish and English to the attackers to lay down their arms.

Seeing armed men running towards them, the attackers opened fire on the new arrivals. This proved to be a fatal mistake.

Not many criminals have the kind of training to shoot accurately when under pressure and this group proved no exception, as a withering hail of bullets decimated them. The driver of the Pathfinder used this opportunity to escape.

He did not stop to check on the condition of his colleagues but hit the accelerator and flew past Johnny, towards a group of sunbathers, scattering them as he went. Johnny couldn't risk firing through the innocent bystanders, so the driver got away.

Johnny turned to Alsina and her mother. Seeing the men and women with machine guns arrive, they had dived to the sand and stayed down while the bullets flew above them.

Now Sabine was making sure that her daughter was unhurt, while Alsina was also checking her mother for injuries.

Johnny arrived on the run and ignored the security detail, while they checked on the dead men. Reaching Alsina, he quickly made sure both she and her mother were unharmed before hugging Alsina to him as if she would fall apart.

Only when he was sure they were unscathed did he turn his attention to the security detail. He shook their hands, thanked them for their timely arrival and praised their concealment skills.

Sabine gasped as she saw the expression on Johnny's face. She had never seen him look that way before. The cold mask of fury scared her but the murderous look in his eyes chilled her to the core, in a way she had never felt before.

Alsina slipped her arm around Johnny and tucked her head into his shoulder. The homicidal look in his eyes disappeared instantly as he smiled at her.

If she had not seen it with her own eyes, Sabine would not have believed what she had just witnessed. She knew beyond any shadow of a doubt that the boy was a killer. Strangely though, she was reassured, she knew now that he would never harm her daughter. In fact, she got the distinct impression that he would die trying to protect her.

She did not know whether to be happy or sad. She looked at Johnny now with her daughter and saw his genuine love for her. He smiled at her and she thought that he looked like an innocent child. It was only when he glanced at what remained of their attackers that his expression changed again.

Chapter Thirty Four

Frank Underwood cursed as he took the phone call. He was stunned that his immaculately prepared plans had gone to shit again. Why wouldn't that fucking boy die?

Asking to speak to Kevin, the sole survivor of the pair that he had sent to Spain, he waited while his new partner put him on.

Kevin made sure that he was not overheard for the few minutes while they talked.

Frank made Kevin repeat his instructions twice, before he reluctantly hung up, telling him to ring him when it was done.

The phone rang five minutes later, "Underwood" he barked without thinking. He did not realize the possible ramifications of his error.

Chapter Thirty Five

Kevin hung up the phone. He asked for a drink and while Dale was filling his order he walked towards the Gent's. Taking out a silenced Browning 9mm, he took a deep breath and walked back into the bar.

As Dale looked up he shot him in the face, then quickly took care of the doormen who came running in at the noise of the suppressed rounds. 'Silencer' really is a misnomer.

Walking into the back room, he shot the two girls that were there and systematically searched the rest of the building.

Finally, confident that everyone was dead, he walked over to the till and emptied it. Going over to Dale, he emptied his pockets of cash and calmly walked out the front door, placing a call to Underwood on his mobile as he left.

Taking the vehicle that he had used for the afternoon's work, he drove to the rocky peninsular that separated this village from the next.

He stripped the gun, wiped his prints off and then threw it piece by piece into the sea. The saltwater would clean his DNA. Then he drove the car to an industrial estate outside Malaga and making sure nobody was looking, he set fire to it.

He walked into the city and stopped at a restaurant where he ordered a meal. After eating he asked the waiter to call him a taxi to go to the airport.

He bought a ticket at the first desk he came to, checked in and waited for his flight. He was debating whether to return to Britain or not. In the end he decided to go back to Frank and face the consequences of leaving Johnny alive. This was not a meeting he was looking forward to but he hoped that his subsequent actions would show his competence.

Chapter Thirty Six

Frank Underwood held his head in his hands. This was getting old. Three times now, he had attempted to rid himself of Johnny. That boy led a charmed life.

They had been watching Johnny and the girl for days and thought that only Terry was protecting them. That in itself was dangerous, given how well the brothers could look after themselves but with enough firepower, he could succeed.

The plan had been simple. Eight men armed to the teeth should easily have been enough to deal with Johnny and Terry, given the element of surprise. Then they could have snatched the girl and started her on the journey into sex slavery. It had all been arranged. He had even offered the girl as a sweetener to his new partner, until she could be moved on.

Once she had been exposed to enough heroin, she would do anything for a fix. It would have taken a little time but the money he could get for her was phenomenal. In the right continent, she was worth more than her weight in gold.

That was where Tony Chesney had gone wrong. He wanted her for his own personal amusement, whereas Frank was looking at her for purely professional reasons, but it had all gone tits up, *again*.

His new partner's "reliable" men had missed a protection detail and paid the price. He was lucky that one of his own men had survived, sanitizing everything as far as he could, so nothing would point in Frank's direction.

He had thought about disposing of Kevin, but quality of his level was hard to find. After all it was not his fault the locals had screwed up.

No, he thought, a bonus was in order and promotion. For what Kevin had just done for him, he should be encouraged, not killed.

He sent a couple of his top men to meet the plane. It was better to get the good news out in the open before Kevin started doubting his own safety. He also wanted a more thorough debrief. He couldn't get all the details on the phone because it wasn't secure.

Chapter Thirty Seven

Echelon is the multi-government operation that routinely monitors emails, phone calls, faxes and radio transmissions. Since the end of the Cold War, its main task has been to seek out terrorist organisations.

With the right clearance, other government departments could also benefit from its use but you needed to be very high up in the pecking order and Jack Fairfax *was* very high up the pecking order.

The Echelon listening post picks out key words. Therefore, Underwood was flagged immediately and Jack Fairfax was alerted within the hour.

There were many reasons to use the word "Underwood", but not with the parameters that Jack had specified. With what had transpired this afternoon, the name could easily be the start of something special.

He tasked his team to find out where this particular "Underwood" was. When initial enquiries came back with no information, his interest peaked. Did someone have something to hide? Finally they might have a lead. They only needed the inkling of an idea and the rest of the search would take care of itself.

Jack rang Terry and told him the news. He stressed that it could be nothing. Knowing Johnny as he did, he asked the question that had been hanging around in the back of his mind. "How is the Boy taking it?"

"You know him as well as I do, God help Underwood if he gets his hands on him!"

Fairfax was worried though, if Johnny went off the programme on this, the consequences could be fatal.

Telling Terry to keep a close eye on his brother and contact him if he needed anything, he put the phone down.

Shaking his head, he walked out of his office and checked on the progress of their enquiries.

Chapter Thirty Eight

When they had finally finished with the Guardia Civil, Johnny and the others returned to the marina.

The security team melted into the background. The team's rotation would be brought forward, just in case they could be identified. Within twenty-four hours, they would be gone.

They did not think realistically that there would be another attack on Johnny and because of the precautions that had been put in place at the marina, they knew him to be safe enough on the 'Jodast'.

The only change was that Alsina would stay with Johnny as much as possible, now that she too had been identified as a target.

Johnny was trying to remain objective. If he started taking this personally he knew he could be killed. It was hard enough knowing that he was a target but he never really believed until today that Alsina was too.

Terry suggested that they go for a dive in the morning, as he wanted to clear his head. Scuba diving relaxed him. It had something of a Zen like quality for him.

He started talking about the dive and his mind started to clear. He could think better under the water. Terry smiled as his brother visibly started to relax as well.

They talked about the various dive sites available to them, most of them were good and if they were lucky, they would go to a more advanced site.

Alsina was soon caught up with the idea and they talked about their various experiences and favourite dive sites.

They decided to ask the local centre what they had going the next day. It was easier to jump on their fast RIB, than to take the boat out themselves.

Alsina followed Johnny into the cabin when the conversation finally started to quieten down. She mostly spent the night in his cabin but sometimes she had spent the night on her parents' boat. From now on she would stay with Johnny all the time. There was no point splitting the resources of the security team.

The night passed uneventfully and the next morning they walked round to the dive centre to check on availability. They were in luck. They could do a wreck dive.

On the way back to their boats to collect their equipment, Alsina mentioned that she was not qualified to dive wrecks.

Johnny told her not to worry, as it would be a non-penetration dive. The wreck was not that deep and they could just swim around and over it rather than through it. Acting as an artificial reef, the sea life would be phenomenal.

Alsina told her parents what they had planned as she collected her gear and then waited on the quayside for the brothers to return.

They hefted their bags onto their shoulders and walked back to the dive centre, chatting about the dive and making sure that Alsina was comfortable with it. Terry and Johnny were very experienced divers and made it clear that if at any time Alsina was not happy, she could let them know and they would abort the dive.

The brothers had both seen instances where people were persuaded to do dives above their ability due to peer pressure. Diving was supposed to be an enjoyable activity, not a scary one. In their minds it was better to take pleasure in a relaxing dive than to be put off for life.

They presented their qualifications, medicals and insurance at the counter and showed their logbooks to prove their experience; they were then shown into the wet room to collect their cylinders and weights.

While they set up their equipment Alsina noticed that that both brothers had dive lights. Thinking that they had intended to go inside the wreck, she asked if she was holding them back.

Johnny explained that you could see more if you took a torch. Inside the wreck it would be dark and with the torch you could see things that preferred to stay away from humans, hiding in nooks and crannies, especially if you were outside looking in.

They also reminded her about the colour loss as the depth increased and said that they preferred to see the underwater life in full colour.

The guide watched them kit up and smiled. He had dived with the brothers before and wasn't surprised to see them using patched up wet suits and faded BCDs or buoyancy control devices.

They loaded the equipment into the boat and the skipper logged them all on.

There were two others on the dive using the club's rental equipment and Terry had watched them put their gear together.

Neither of them could be mistaken for beginners and the minimal weights on their belts told him what he needed to know. He smiled at them and they nodded an acknowledgement.

They left the marina and were on top of the dive site within 10 minutes. The guide briefed them on the dive plan and told them what to do in the unlikely event of an emergency. He told them how they would enter the water and more importantly for some, how they would get back into the boat.

Each little group did their safety checks and told the skipper the amount of air they had. They spaced out on the tubes and entered the water in opposing pairs.

Giving a final OK signal to the boat, they sank below the surface as the skipper logged the time of entry.

They equalized as they descended and noted that the visibility must have been over twenty metres as they could see the bottom and the wreck quite clearly. There was no current to speak of, so it would be a great dive.

Terry watched his brother slowly sink down towards the wreck, giving the OK sign to Alsina. The others were already on the wreck peering into the dark recesses.

He noticed one of the other group turn away from the wreck and look around. Seeing nothing after a couple of minutes of slowly looking left and right, up and down, he turned his attention back to the wreck.

They slowly circled the wreck and shone their torches into every crevice. After about twenty minutes one of the others signalled that he had used half of his air and the group started the slow ascent, watching their bubbles rise up ahead of them.

Johnny surfaced with a feeling of complete tranquillity and a huge grin on his face. Alsina swam over and kissed him, before handing her weight belt up to the skipper and slipping out of her BCD. She kicked her fins gracefully and exited the water like a dolphin, hardly putting any pressure on the side of the boat.

Some skippers could be fussy about people pulling themselves up and tearing off the hand lines. The others used the ladder at the stern of the boat and then they hauled in the BCDs.

The skipper logged the air levels and exit time and checked that everyone was healthy before detaching the mooring line and smoothly accelerating back towards the marina.

Johnny winked at the other two divers and they smiled back. They were part of the new security team and had arrived the previous night. They spoke only to each other but were aware at all times of their surroundings. Johnny turned to Alsina and took her hand in his, he wished today would never end. He was at peace with the world, if only temporarily.

They showered in the dive centre after thoroughly washing their equipment and asked if they could leave their kit to dry off a little. The guide told them to come back after lunch and not to worry as he would make sure no one touched it.

They met Alsina's parents at the nearest restaurant and had a leisurely lunch. Alsina asked the other divers to join them and they discussed the dive as they ate and filled out their logbooks.

Terry checked his phone for messages and found no updates. He shook his head at Johnny in answer to the silent question.

Having eaten their fill and said their goodbyes, they made their way back to the boats, collecting their dive gear on the way.

Johnny and Alsina took a siesta for a few hours, while Terry busied himself around the boat. There was always something that could be done, checked or cleaned on board.

Finally he could contain himself no longer and called his boss. Jack asked if he had enjoyed the dive, after telling him that there was still nothing new.

They talked for a while and Terry told Jack how relaxed his brother was. He heard Jack breathe a sigh of relief and smiled. Johnny had that effect on most of the people he worked with.

Terry looked out of the window at the bright sunshine being reflected off the brilliant white buildings. He checked the fridge and wondered what to do for dinner. After ten minutes he gave up and decided that they would go back to the restaurant.

He walked over to Alsina's parents and invited them, before finally returning to the 'Jodast' and grabbing his book. He was halfway through Othello, having randomly picked the story from his second edition, complete works by William Shakespeare. After an hour he closed the book, woke the other two and told them about dinner, before taking a short siesta himself.

Chapter Thirty Nine

Stephen was in the office of the club as Davina walked in. They had heard about the incident in Spain and having finally spoken to Terry and Alsina, continued their nightly preparations.

Davina had been out of her mind with worry for her friends. She and Stephen had talked endlessly about what they could do. They finally decided that whatever happened, they would stay in England. Any help they could offer for facilities and money, if it was needed, would be given freely and quickly.

When Davina had first returned to the U.K. she had only had her brother's death on her mind. Now she did not know what was happening.

The questions running through her mind were: Why was her brother killed? Was she a target? Was Stephen a target? Was the club a target?

Jack Fairfax had told her that neither they, nor the club were still targets but he was keeping up security on the house and was now liaising daily with Bernie Holt.

Fresh rumours had surfaced about why her brother had been killed but there were more than one and they contradicted each other. The general consensus was that Joseph's death was actually an accident, if being shot could be classed as an accident. If he had been killed because he wouldn't sell the club, it would have been too obvious to then come along with an offer to buy it.

The seemingly senseless killing of her brother saddened Davina immensely. She thought about him all the time. Scenes from their childhood kept flooding back.

She grew closer to Stephen than before. They had always been close and shared intimate details with one another but now they shared a bed too.

She wondered what Joseph would have thought about that. As she pondered, she realized that he must have known it would happen. Everything in his will made her and Stephen need regular contact.

It had come as a shock to them both when they first slept together, a few nights after Amelia was killed. On the night of the explosion they had shared a bed but nothing more. They shared Davina's bed again when Alsina had left, again platonically. In the end they had just headed to Davina's room every night after that. One thing led to another and within days they were a couple.

They threw themselves into work to keep them busy and showed a strong leadership when it was needed. The employees were shaken up about losing Amelia so soon after Joseph and the manner in which it happened.

They kept the club closed the next night but Davina called the staff and told them that they would open the night after. Amelia would have expected that and the staff had agreed. Slowly they all came to terms with their grief in their own ways.

Everyone was now much more vigilant. There was a near Zero Tolerance policy on any incident in the club. Chances could not afford to be taken.

The security staff were now on patrols twenty-four hours a day. Until this thing, whatever it was, was finished they would remain in place.

They decided to implement some changes, which they had previously discussed with Joseph. For whatever reason they had been shelved at the time but now they seemed to be the way forward.

Again Davina realized that her brother must have known that the changes would not work unless she was here to implement them.

Every day they trained when they got up for up to four hours. She could not believe that she had forgotten how much more energy she had when she was training.

They were both good at Ninjutsu, though neither of them had been quite as good as Joseph. He had been a brilliant and inspiring teacher.

Whenever they could, they asked their acquaintances if they could shed any light on what had happened. In their world, someone was always gossiping. Still they could find nothing concrete.

Life went on, some days were better for her than others but she thought she was coping well. Stephen was her anchor, even Vincent had settled down again, not twitching at every little noise.

Chapter Forty

Fresh from his experiences in Spain, Kevin Daniels now found himself in a position of authority in Frank Underwood's organisation. In fact, far from the punishment he had imagined, he had been showered with praise and more importantly, money.

Although Frank did not ask his advice on matters, he gave him the pick of the jobs that needed doing as well as supervising roles in the day to day running of the operation.

Kevin tried not to let things go to his head, as the younger, more impressionable men and women looked at him in awe. He did not say a word about what had happened but people did watch the news and of course they knew where he had been and how he had been treated since he got back.

He was with Frank now, in his office, checking over the schedule of the latest batch that they had brought over. After an initial debrief, nothing more had been said about Spain.

Kevin knew that the Johnny situation was not over and silently agreed with his boss that Johnny must die and that he must die soon.

Due to his efficiency in Spain, they no longer had eyes and ears on Johnny. Eventually they would go back out there and take over the brothel. For now they were forced to wait and see.

He practised his shooting skills whenever possible. He had seen what happened if you waved a gun at Police officers and couldn't back your play. He liked the fact that his boss had access to so many weapons. It gave him a feeling of security.

Chapter Forty One

They had gone diving for three days running now and Johnny was finally able to focus on the situation objectively.

He knew if he remained here, that nothing would be accomplished. He talked to Terry and Alsina, suggesting that it would be better if he returned to England.

Alsina told him that she would go anywhere that he went. She would brook no argument and that, apparently, was that. Even her parents agreed with her. In their minds the only person, other than them, who would selflessly look after their little girl was Johnny.

Terry had already spoken to Jack Fairfax and informed him of Johnny's relaxed state of mind. Happier now that he was not a loose cannon, Jack had already been entertaining the idea of calling them back.

This time, when they returned to England there was no party. They had a meal in the restaurant, which had become their habit and the next morning they were gone.

Davina welcomed them back with open arms and said nothing when the security detail on the house increased yet again. Johnny would come and go from the house and Alsina would return to work at the club.

When Mrs. Hoon saw Alsina again she cried openly, gave her a hug and then ran into the kitchen to check that she had enough food for the extra mouths.

"We shall have to get you another car." Davina was alone with Alsina in the lounge. "But I don't think you should go out on your own until this is completely over."

"I can't let you get me another car. You are spending too much money on me. I will just get a lift in with you or Stephen, if that is okay?"

"No really, it's fine. The insurance paid out on the last one and you may need transport in an emergency. We will let you pick your own this time though."

Alsina looked at her friend and shook her head in resignation. "Fine, but there is no hurry!"

In fact the insurance had not paid out. All their cars were covered on a small fleet policy and although they had informed the insurance company, they were still arguing over whether they could claim or not. Alsina would never know this and, as it was not her fault, Davina was happy to get her another car.

She still had money in the bank and the club was making a fair amount. So why couldn't she spoil her friend?

Vincent was overjoyed to see Johnny again and was constantly by his side, when he was at the house. Sometimes Johnny trained with them in the mornings, before heading out to work and Davina was again reminded of the similarities between Johnny and Joseph.

Though not adept at Ninjutsu, Johnny was definitely well grounded in martial arts.

Each of them tried to teach Alsina something that she could use, if anything happened to her again.

Alsina spent a lot of time with Davina, when she was not with Johnny. The club was a safe place for her and, if she was in a public area, she was never out of sight of security or Davina and Stephen.

The first breakthrough in the case was phoned through to them a few days after their return. Actually, it was because of their return that any progress was made at all.

It had not taken long for their presence in the country to filter through to Frank Underwood. Again, thanks to Echelon, they plucked a conversation out of the ether.

The lead was not directly to Frank but through one of his employees. On recognising Johnny on the street, one of Frank's doormen had phoned through to his immediate boss and used Underwood's name.

Because of the speed with which the conversation had been reported, Jack Fairfax was able to place men in the club from which the phone call originated.

Jack had no prior knowledge that this particular establishment had any connection to Frank. Surveillance was made on anyone they thought might be a suspect. Lists and time lines were started, documenting all contacts.

Slowly things started to take shape. Jack prioritised this part of the investigation in an effort to shake something loose. They followed the network of calls made to and from the various mobile phones and email accounts.

Johnny realized that he was in with a chance of finding his old partner and his focus intensified.

Having viable proof that Johnny was still a target, it was suggested that Alsina did not travel anywhere with him.

Where possible they wanted to minimise their own exposure and split the resources of Frank Underwood's organisation.

Plans were being thought up as to the best way of bringing Frank out into the open.

As more and more information came in, Frank's criminal empire was starting to become exposed. Also, and as far as Jack was concerned, this was a bonus, names of certain well placed people in the Judiciary, Police, Customs and his own department started coming to light.

Although he wanted Frank found and brought to justice quickly, he realized that the wealth of information he was receiving was little short of a gold mine.

Johnny was happy enough to know that Frank was nearly within his grasp. He agreed with Jack that, the more damage they could do to undermine Frank's operation, the better.

Chapter Forty Two

Frank Underwood sat in his new office, still totally unaware that his personal security had been compromised. As far as he was aware, his men called him "Midas" or just "The Boss."

His "man" in the club was actually a woman. She had been hired initially as agency personnel and then taken on full time. Her references were excellent, not surprising as one of Frank's clubs had supplied them.

Now, after finishing his call to her, Frank thought about the information, or lack of, that she had been giving recently.

He knew that Alsina was in the club most nights, never alone and accompanied only by security personnel or Davina and Stephen. Basically, she was untouchable at the moment. If she was not at the club, then she was with enough manpower to deter a small army.

He still wanted her, not for himself but for what she represented in monetary terms. She would make a nice bonus for him, she might even work as bait for a trap but he had to get at her first.

Now, on top of everything, his woman on the inside wanted out of the club. She was starting to feel paranoid since the disastrous attempt with the car bomb. Feeling at the club was running high, as the girl who died had been very popular, as was Alsina.

He would have to think long and hard about what he was going to do. He needed eyes in the club but not if her behaviour started to trip her up.

She was not stupid enough to own up to what she had been doing. Conspiracy to murder was not something you want hanging over you and if the other club workers found out they would probably give her a beating.

He decided that he would play it safe and pull her out. No one would question her motive for leaving. Either she was too sad or too scared to work there anymore. He toyed with the idea of making some money off of her by selling her overseas but decided against it. He wanted her close, where he could keep an eye on her.

Catching Johnny was not easy to arrange. He knew that Johnny was looking for him and it would be easy to leave a false lead for him to follow. The problem was, that there was no guarantee that Johnny or his brother would be the ones to follow it.

He looked around his new office; everything was temporary until he could sort Johnny out. He took his own security very seriously. Kevin Daniels was to him now, what Adrian Bull had been to Edward Chesney.

He wished that Adrian Bull was still around, as he could have done with the fear his reputation instilled but that would never have happened. Bull had been extremely loyal to Chesney, too loyal.

Though Daniels was good, he wasn't in Bull's class but given the time and encouragement, Frank was sure that the man would shape up. It all boiled down to time and if Frank would get enough of it.

"Was it worth it?" he wondered. He could just cash everything in and move away. His personal fortune now exceeded one hundred million pounds and that did not include his property portfolio.

He was sure he could start anywhere and have a peaceful existence, right up until Johnny Miller found him. And Johnny Miller would find him, of that Frank was under no illusion.

Chapter Forty Three

Johnny was following up a lead when Alsina rang him. He carried on following the paper trail while he talked to her. Finding nothing of real interest on the sheet of paper in front of him, he fully concentrated his attention on Alsina.

"Do you think that we could go out after work tonight? That is, if you are not too tired. I know you are busy but I miss you and before you say it, I know it has only been a couple of days."

Johnny smiled down the phone line. "What do you want to do sweetheart?"

"Well, not go clubbing, that is for certain. Can we find somewhere to eat?"

"I don't see why not. Just us two or are the others coming?"

"I hadn't really thought about it, I just wanted to make sure that you would be available."

"Great, let me know what we are doing, I'm happy either way."

"I will try to make it home a bit earlier tonight. Bernie can close up, if the others do decide to come."

"Whatever you say, babe. Listen I have to go now but you take care, you hear?"

"I love you."

Johnny looked at the phone in his hand. He had never really thought that anyone could make him this happy. It was a new experience for him but he liked it so far.

Chapter Forty Four

The hours flew past for Alsina. The others had declined but said they might see her at the house afterwards. Davina had said that she wanted to see the night through, to test a theory she had about changing music on certain nights.

Alsina waited just inside the foyer talking to Bernie. There was a steady stream of people coming into the club. She looked stunning in a designer business suit with white blouse.

People just stared at her and some of the regulars nodded or smiled. She returned all the salutations but she was thinking of Johnny. This made her smile even more and that made her even more eye catching.

Johnny arrived in a Land Rover Discovery. He was wearing a suit, which was unusual and Alsina thought he looked fantastic.

She had booked a table at a little Italian place, in the commercial park near the cinema. She chose this because she knew that they stayed open late to cater to the cinema trade.

They parked in the communal car park and he put his hand around her waist as they walked into the restaurant.

Terry parked his own Discovery further down the car park, unseen by Alsina but not by Johnny. His partner eased back the passenger seat to get comfortable. It would be a couple of hours. As the man watched Johnny and Alsina enter the restaurant, he mumbled "Lucky Git" to which Terry smiled.

The waiter seated Alsina and Johnny at the table and they ordered a drink while they looked at the menu. Alsina reached out and held Johnny's hand.

He squeezed it in response and they smiled at one another.

"You look more beautiful every time I see you!"

"And you are more handsome every time I see you." Alsina replied smiling.

"You don't have to return the compliment sweetheart, even if it is true."

She laughed when he said that, she was happy with her life. She was happy with her man. She really wanted a normal life, to do things that normal people do, so she told him so.

"Trust me sweetheart, I'm moving heaven and earth to finish this thing."

"I know, my love. I know." Alsina sighed.

They ordered their food when the waiter came back and then they sat in silence just staring at one another.

The bar manager watched them as they sat there. He thought they looked familiar but could not place them. He called the waiter over and asked if he knew them. The waiter shook his head saying that they seemed a nice couple.

The bar manager looked at them for a while longer and then started restocking the shelves and fridges. As he busied himself with his chores, it came to him in a flash. Trying not to act out of the ordinary, he casually walked to the phone and punched in a number. He spoke quietly into the receiver and then hung up.

Johnny and Alsina finished their meal and ordered coffee for desert. When they had finished they paid the bill and walked to the door. The entire exercise, from walking in to walking out, had taken just over an hour and a half. This was more than enough time for the real world to find them.

Holding the door open for Alsina, Johnny looked towards the car park. As he watched a dark BMW saloon car came screaming up to the restaurant. It mounted the kerb and continued on towards them at speed before swerving off at the last minute. The rear door opened and a man jumped out racking a cartridge into the chamber of a pump action shotgun.

The man fired at Johnny as Johnny pushed Alsina to the ground, trying to protect her and draw his own weapon simultaneously. He pushed Alsina's head into the ornamental lawn as he aimed and fired. He felt his hair move as a pellet travelled through it.

The assailant was halfway through reloading when Johnny's bullet caught him in the throat. He spread his arms wide, as he was thrown backwards into the car door. It was a lucky shot, as Johnny had been aiming for his chest but had pulled the gun high as the lead shot passed through his hair

A man was coming around the back of the car, bearing down on Alsina. Too late he realized his folly. So intent had he been on heading for Alsina, that he did not see his accomplice fall.

He ran with his own gun in his hand, pointing at the ground, as Johnny changed his aim and hit him in the chest, destroying his heart and lungs, as the bullet shattered bone and fragmented outwards.

The driver of the car tried to accelerate away but was hit from the side by Terry in the second Land Rover. The airbags went off in the BMW, temporarily disorientating the driver.

Terry's partner was out of the Land Rover and running full speed towards the BMW. Shoving his Glock into the driver's forehead, he screamed at him to raise his hands.

Terry checked the car to make sure there was nobody else in it before he ran over to check on his brother.

Johnny was kneeling in front of Alsina checking her for bullet holes and asking frantically if she was okay.

Finding his brother unhurt, Terry went back to the BMW and helped his partner drag the driver out of the car. They handcuffed him behind his back, pushed him roughly into the back of the Land Rover and then collected the weapons.

The Police Armed Response Unit was on the scene within minutes. Terry stood with his arms outstretched holding his official I.D., just to make sure there were no accidents.

Spectators piled out of the restaurant and surrounding bars to see what was going on. The bar manager and the waiter came out too.

Jack Fairfax arrived twenty minutes later and took control, quickly intervening when he saw the look on Johnny's face as he walked towards the driver of the BMW. He marvelled at how calmly Alsina was taking the events of the evening.

He told Johnny to take Alsina home and that he would debrief him there. Johnny started to argue but Terry put a hand on his arm. They wanted as much distance between Johnny and the driver as they could possibly get.

Alsina saw the look on Johnny's face and felt scared for the driver. She asked Johnny to take her home and he slowly started to calm down. Terry led them to their Discovery and put them in the rear seat, while he got into the driving seat.

They drove off as Jack Fairfax called through to the house to warn Stephen and Davina. With Johnny finally off the scene, he left the Police to finish off and went to book the driver in at their headquarters.

Nobody saw the bar manager return to the bar and make a call. This would be another nail in his coffin and furthermore one for Frank Underwood, although he did not know it yet.

Chapter Forty Five

"In fairness, I think you are wrong to try to capture the girl. Do them both and do it remotely, not up close and personal."

"You're having a fucking laugh, Kev."

"No seriously, if they had gone straight for the kill and not tried to avoid the girl, they might have succeeded."

"Kevin, you are off your fucking head. They did go straight for the kill! It's just that Johnny was too fucking quick for them."

"Will the driver talk?"

"Not if he knows what's good for him!"

"Can we get to him, Frank?"

"In time, I can get to anyone. I've got to Johnny four times now but it didn't do me any fucking good, did it?"

"Will you think about doing it remotely, at least?"

Frank sighed, "Alright, think up some options. I want it spectacular though! I need to start sending a message. We are finally getting some resistance from what's left of the competition."

"Oh yeah, who?"

"Mr. Jonathon Pearce!"

"You're kidding right? Now, you're having a fucking laugh!"

"No, it seems that the righteous Mr. Pearce has decided that he wants to keep his little empire and doesn't need my help."

"Tosser!" Kevin spat the word out.

"Exactly. In fact that would be a good way to kill two birds, as they say. Get one of the M16 grenade launchers and take the fucker out!" He thought for a minute. "Yeah, that will make a statement sure enough."

"Seems like over-kill to me boss. I thought maybe we could do Johnny with one of those instead."

"Use it as a dummy run. They won't be able to tie it to us." Frank replied.

"When do you want it done?"

"Yesterday!"

Chapter Forty Six

When Alsina and Johnny finally got back to the house Davina was frantic. In the end it fell to Alsina to calm Davina down. Johnny told Stephen their version of events and he listened calmly.

Davina took her up to her room and made Alsina tell her everything. Although Alsina didn't realize it, Davina was giving her someone to worry about in case Alsina was starting to go into shock. So far though, Alsina was coping very well.

"So, did you enjoy the meal?"

Alsina looked at her friend and then broke into hysterical laughter. For a good few minutes she was literally rolling round the bed, howling and crying with laughter.

"Did I have a good meal?" She burst into laughter again and hugged Davina, still crying. Eventually they went back downstairs to a bewildered Johnny, who asked why they were laughing.

That started Alsina off again and Davina joined in. Johnny looked at them as if they had gone mad. They finally calmed down again and explained what Davina had said.

"I thought it went rather well myself." As Johnny stopped speaking the girls started howling with laughter again and this time they all joined in. This was how Jack Fairfax found them.

"Something funny?" He asked and then watched as a fresh wave of laughter went round the kitchen. He waited patiently and after what seemed to him like half an hour, they stopped.

The debriefing went on into the early hours and questions were asked on both sides. What was Jack going to do with the driver? What were the security implications now?

At long last Alsina went up to her room, exhausted. Johnny followed her at dawn and Jack left to go home and change, before heading back into the office to interview the driver.

They charged the driver with attempted murder and got him bound over with no bail before they started questioning him.

He would not say anything and Jack changed the interrogation team several times, before finally agreeing that Johnny could have a crack at him.

Johnny went into the room and sat down. He said nothing to the driver but stared at him the whole time.

"I know what game you're playing. You won't catch me out like that."

Johnny said nothing.

"It's no good, I am not stupid and I won't fall for that."

Still Johnny remained silent.

"There is nothing that you can do to get me to talk. You can lock me up and throw away the key."

"I'm not going to lock you up. I'm going to get you released. And what's more I'm going to make sure that I'm there when you are set free."

The driver suddenly started to sweat. He knew that he would be looked after if he stayed quiet. He had been inside before and he knew how to play the game. It was easy money.

He also knew that if they let him go now, when they had him bang to rights, then his boss would think that he was a grass and that was not good news.

Johnny just stared at him.

The driver was sweating profusely now and feeling distinctly uncomfortable. He looked at his brief, who just shrugged his shoulders.

Johnny got up and walked out of the interview room. He would leave the man to sweat, literally. He walked over to the coffee machine and passed a cup to his boss.

"You did well in there." Jack stated.

"Let's wait and see."

"It won't be long, I can almost smell his fear. Well done!"

Jack told Johnny to go to the house. It was a waiting game now and there was nothing more that Johnny could do there.

Terry drove Johnny back to the house. He nodded to his colleagues as he drove into the driveway.

They had hardly spoken in the car and Terry was starting to worry about Johnny's state of mind again.

As they got out of the car Vincent came bounding up to Johnny who stooped and made a fuss of the big dog. They walked up to the front door which stood open as Alsina made her way towards them.

They hugged each other and kissed lightly. She looked at him and asked how he was. He smiled and nodded and led her back inside the house.

"What will happen now?" Alsina asked.

"I don't really know. It depends on how much the driver can tell us and how far we get with what we already have."

"But having the driver helps?"

"Definitely, that's a nice bonus for us."

"Will he talk?"

Johnny's face went hard again. "Oh yes, he'll talk."

Chapter Forty Seven

Jonathon Pearce was walking out of his flagship pub with his minders. He had spent the evening in a council of war, trying to decide what to do about the new threat to their existence.

Unlike many of the old time criminals, he knew who Frank Underwood was and he and Frank had a history.

Although he had not seen the other man for over ten years, he was not overjoyed to see him come back into his life after all this time.

Jonathon knew that a war was coming. He had seen what had happened in the last few months and correctly surmised that Frank was responsible for Edward Chesney's disappearance and probably Willy Cameron's as well.

While he did not miss Chesney or Cameron, he did object to the way that Frank was gaining power. His own men were loyal to him for now but the lure of Frank's money was powerful for them, maybe too powerful.

He would have to think carefully of how to take Frank down. It needed to be done, of that he was sure. Jonathon knew that he was a threat to Frank and therefore a liability. Jonathon had seen what happened to the other people that Frank thought of as liabilities.

He had just walked towards the open door of his Land Rover Defender as the M203 grenade round hit the vehicle and exploded in a flash of fire and debris.

His minders were killed instantly and he found himself on the ground covered in blood. Fortunately it wasn't his.

He watched as the gunmen walked up to him and one of them chambered another round. Jonathon spat blood from his mouth and looked up at them defiantly.

The gunman took leisurely aim and smiled down at him. "Mr. Underwood sends his regards." The gunshots echoed into the night. And the two men slumped forward towards him.

"Thanks, Tommy." Jonathon coughed.

"Don't mention it and don't say 'I told you so'."

Tommy Rooke helped his friend and boss onto his feet and into the Honda Accord. Earlier in the evening Jonathon had sent Tommy to collect the Mac 10 that Tommy was now placing on the back seat in case things kicked off. Jonathon was glad that he had done so.

"Where to now mate?" Tommy asked.

"Take me to Joseph Stanton's house."

"Are you mad? Has the explosion affected your mind?"

"No, actually it has rather helped to focus my mind. I haven't got the firepower to go up against Frank Underwood, but I know someone who does have." Jonathon replied.

Shaking his head, Tommy pulled away from the pub just as the customers started coming out to see what had happened. Though he did not agree with his boss, he knew that there was no equal to him as a strategist, so he did as he was told.

He drove to Joseph's Stanton's house and parked on the road. Jonathon got out and walked with his hands held high towards the security detail that was rapidly approaching.

"I am unarmed." He stopped and let them search him.

"What do you want?"

"I want to talk to Johnny or Terry Miller."

"They don't live here."

"I know, but they are staying here. Tell them Jonathon Pearce wants to talk to them. Tell them he has some information for them."

Terry had been watching what was happening on the CCTV monitor and came out to talk to him. He walked slowly and deliberately.

"What do you want, Pearce?"

"Hello to you too, Terry me old mate. Long time no see. How are you and the Boy?"

"Piss off, Pearce."

"I have some information that might be helpful to you."

"We don't need your kind of help."

"What, even if it helps you catch Frank Underwood?"

Terry stopped and looked at the other man. He did not like what he saw.

"Seriously Terry, I can help you and perhaps you can help me too."

"Oh, now I get it. You're in the shit aren't you?"

"I should say so. Someone's just tried to blow me up." Jonathon admitted.

"And you think it's Underwood. Why?"

"You must know he is taking over. He's 'Numero Uno' now. He is 'the Man'."

"What are you wittering on about?"

"Oh Fuck! You really don't have a clue do you?"

"Watch your mouth, Pearce!"

"Frank Underwood is taking over everything. He took out the Chesneys, Cameron and every other crime outfit in a one hundred mile radius."

"Says who?"

"Seriously Terry, you need to get Jack down here. I can help you."

Terry got his mobile out and called his boss. He spoke animatedly for five minutes and then shut the phone down. Turning back to Pearce he shook his head.

"You'd better come in and wait. Try anything and I will personally take you apart." With that he stormed off back into the house.

Johnny was talking quietly to Alsina in the kitchen, as first Terry and then Jonathon walked in. He looked up and did a double take. Then he slowly got up and walked towards Jonathon, smiling as he went.

"Well, well. Look what the cat's dragged in."

"How are you, Boy?"

"Better than you from the look of it mate. How you keeping?" Johnny answered.

"I've got to admit, right at this moment I have been better. Aren't you going to introduce me?"

Alsina had been watching things unfold and she was confused. That Terry did not like the man was obvious but Johnny seemed to show him genuine affection.

"Sorry, Jonathon Pearce, may I present my girlfriend Alsina Hauffman."

"I am pleased to meet you. Any friend of Johnny's is a friend of mine." Jonathon smiled.

Terry snorted and walked out of the kitchen. "Johnny, a word please."

Johnny followed him out and asked what was going on. Terry filled him in on his earlier conversation and told him that Jack was on his way. Davina and Stephen entered the kitchen.

When the brothers left the kitchen Alsina invited Jonathon to sit down. She was not sure what to do. She tried to think of something to say but he beat her to it.

"So the boy's finally got a girlfriend and may I say, a lovely one too."

Alsina blushed and looked down at her coffee. She tried to change the subject and offered to make him a coffee.

As she busied herself at the machine, she asked over her shoulder, "Have you known Johnny long?"

"A while, yeah." Jonathon replied.

"How do you know each other?"

"We used to work together, that's how I know Terry too."

"He doesn't look as pleased to see you as Johnny is."

"That's because it wasn't Terry's life he saved, it was mine and Terry should be grateful for that at least, eh Terry? I know I am." Johnny and Terry came back into the room and she turned around to look at them.

"It was his fault your life needed saving in the first place." Terry said as he lent against the worktop.

"Oh, come on! Let's not get into that again. Jonathon's paid for what happened. Let it go!" said Johnny.

"If he had thought before he acted you wouldn't have been shot. He never bloody thinks though, does he?" said Terry.

"Terry, that was over ten years ago, I promise you that I have changed." Jonathon said.

"Then why are you here? If Underwood is after you, why bring it to our door?" Terry asked.

"Because he is after Johnny and you too. I see things and hear things that you don't."

"But you're bent now, aren't you? You must be to have something that Underwood wants." Terry asked.

"I might not declare all my income but I promise you I am still the same person you knew." Jonathon replied.

"Still the same lunatic more likely!" Terry accused.

At that moment Jack arrived and greeted Jonathon warmly. Alsina noticed that Jonathon seemed to stand up straighter when the brothers' boss arrived.

"Jonathon, how are you?"

"I'm fine Sir, thanks for asking and thanks for hearing me out."

"You don't need to call me Sir now. I'm no longer your boss."

"Old habits, Sir, you know."

"Yes, I know it well. So what have you got for us?"

"Well basically, as you probably know, Frank Underwood has taken over both Chesney's and Cameron's patches. I can't prove it but I think he had them and Tony Chesney killed too."

"We have not had it confirmed that Chesney is dead, but we were starting to suspect Frank was up to something." Jack admitted.

"Well, he is now the major trafficker in the U.K. of women, guns and drugs. He's taking over legitimate clubs to put his girls," he paused, "and boys sometimes, to work."

"What proof have you got?" Jack asked.

"Well, he tried to kill me tonight. My car got blown up by a High Explosive round from a 203, just as I was about to get in it."

"I heard something about an explosion. Nobody said it was your car though."

"Well it's not in my name, but I use it all the same. Don't worry, it's totally legit." He added the latter as Terry snorted and started to walk out of the kitchen.

"How do you know it was Underwood?" Jack ignored Terry's outburst.

"They told me he said 'good bye'."

"Was that Tommy Rooke outside?" Jack changed the subject to give himself time to assimilate the information that he had just been given.

"Yes it was, why?"

"You'd better invite him in. I didn't know that, when you went, you would take my best people."

"To be fair Sir, it was only Tommy and you know I would have preferred to stay with you."

"I both know and appreciate it. I am sorry that you had to carry the can." Jack sighed.

"I was to blame Sir, not your problem. I did appreciate what you did for me though."

Fairfax waved his hand in the air to brush away the thanks. He still respected Jonathon and, hell, he still liked him.

Tommy arrived and was introduced to everyone but he seemed embarrassed to be noticed by Jack. In his mind he was still a raw recruit, remembering meeting Jack for the first time. He was in awe of the man.

He smiled shyly as he was introduced to Davina and Alsina. He knew Stephen already as they'd had dealings before over a pub or club, he couldn't remember which.

Terry greeted him with genuine warmth and Alsina thought it strange how he could despise Jonathon and not Tommy. She made a mental note to ask Johnny later. They both seemed like nice people.

They all sat around the kitchen table, Jack asking questions and Jonathon or Tommy answering them as fully as they could. It was obvious they respected one another and they seemed to be able to pre-empt what questions would be asked.

Jonathon gave them chapter and verse on what he knew about Frank's operation and was able to give them more credible leads than they had been able to obtain in the last few months.

He confirmed that Terry was a target too and more worryingly, what Frank had planned for Alsina. That last piece of information drew a hiss from Johnny, who was in on the debriefing. Jack did not ask how he came by the information but noted every last scrap.

The session went on into the night and it was the small hours before Johnny was finally able to join Alsina in bed. She rolled over and asked sleepily, "How did Jonathon save your life and why doesn't Terry like him?"

Johnny rolled onto his back and sighed. He had already decided to tell Alsina the truth about everything.

"About ten years ago we were both working undercover together on a drugs case. It had taken ages but we finally got into the gang. Jonathon was my mentor and at the time Terry's best friend."

Alsina rolled onto her side and stared in surprise at Johnny. He carried on talking, telling her of how the gang had become aware of their identities due to a slip up by Jonathon.

Jonathon had not checked that they were not being overheard when he gave Johnny an update from Jack. The gang they were working with panicked, shot Johnny and left him for dead. Making a run for it, they overlooked Jonathon and he was able to apply pressure to the wound and stop the bleeding. He performed basic first aid checks and called the ambulance, while making sure the gang didn't come back for another go.

"Terry never forgave him. He said he was too cavalier and that he expected better from someone with his experience. He's a bit protective of me."

"What happened to Jonathon?"

"He got booted out of the organization."

"But anyone can make a mistake."

"That is what Jack said at the inquiry but the powers that be decided that someone had to pay for the failure of two years of undercover work. It didn't help that some of the gear that the gang was selling was dodgy and two teenage girls died."

"That's horrible." Alsina gasped.

"I know."

She rolled into his arms and they fell asleep. They slept until late the next morning and when they finally got up only Terry, Mrs. Hoon and the security detail were left at the house.

Johnny walked into the kitchen. "What's up?"

"Thanks to that fuckwit Pearce I'm now stuck here until we can locate Underwood."

"Let it go Terry, at least he warned us. I mean, wouldn't you rather know that you were a target?"

"I know, I know, I just don't like being beholden to him."

"He was your best friend once!" Johnny spoke quietly.

"That seems like another lifetime."

"It's not too late to make amends."

"We'll see."

"Where is he now?" Johnny asked.

"With the boss, they're planning the next moves."

"Let's hope Jonathon is still as good as he used to be." Johnny said hopefully.

"If he's only half as good we will have had a result."

Johnny smiled. His brother was finally acknowledging that Jonathon was good at something. Things could be looking up.

Chapter Forty Eight

"Why am I surrounded by bloody incompetents? Can you tell me that?" Frank Underwood was not impressed when Kevin told him about the botched hit. "How did he survive?"

"I don't know boss. He always was a slippery bugger by all accounts."

"Yeah, he was that." Frank agreed.

"You know him, I mean personally?"

"We used to work together, until he copped the blame for ruining a drugs operation. Ironically enough, Johnny was involved with that too."

Underwood knew that it was not Jonathon's fault. He had not been overheard at all. The reason their cover was blown was because he, Frank Underwood, had told the gang and for a modest twenty grand too.

"Small world." Kevin mused.

"I suppose if you swim in the same pond long enough, you meet the same fish time and again."

"What do we do now boss?"

"We find Pearce and kill him a.s.a.p."

"How?" Kevin asked.

"Put our people into his pubs and clubs, he has to make an appearance soon to prove he is still on top. Pay his guys double to turn him over to us. Money works every time."

"Are you sure they will come over to us?"

"Yes!" Frank stated vehemently.

"How can you be so sure?"

"Because, my old son, once they have seen what happens if they don't, they will come running. It's basic psychology."

"I'll make a start now and let you know when anything turns up."

Chapter Forty Nine

When Jonathon Pearce walked back into his old headquarters it was like coming home.

The older hands nodded or waved. Some looked on in curiosity but there was no animosity.

He followed Jack into his office. Tommy followed on behind. Tommy acknowledged some of the people too but wanted to make sure that there were no hard feelings for Jonathon. After about an hour of rehashing what had been discussed the night before, they got on with planning the operation.

Jack had not forgotten how good Jonathon was at strategic planning. He had been genuinely sad to see him go. He had tried his hardest to keep him but was overruled.

He was pleased to see that nothing of the man's skills had been lost as the session wore on. At last there was light at the end of the tunnel and for once, it did not seem to be a train coming the other way.

With what Jack already knew and the new information supplied by Jonathon, they started mapping out the money trail. Jonathon was evidently very well connected in the criminal underworld but although Jack had kept surreptitious tabs on him, he had no proof that Jonathon himself was anything other than a pub and club owner.

He overlooked the fact that Tommy possessed an illegal firearm, after all, the wealth of information he now possessed more than outweighed that as far as Jack was concerned. They could even prove that Underwood had sold it to them in the first place.

They started chipping away at Underwood without him knowing. Jonathon guessed that all of his clubs and pubs now had Underwood's people in them. Each and every establishment was routinely raided and both Underwood's men and those that had turned on Jonathon were caught up in the net. Because those loyal to Jonathon were also caught up, Underwood did not realize that he was the ultimate target.

Jonathon's rule was that none of his people carried firearms. Although they might now think of tooling up, in case of follow up attacks, they could only get decent weapons quickly if they bought from Underwood and they would only be able to contact Underwood if they were working for him.

Jonathon's own people thought that he was on the run, so they did not know that he was again working with Jack Fairfax. As Underwood's people started talking, more and more of his empire was being unravelled.

It was nearly two weeks after the attempt on Jonathon's life, that Underwood started to get concerned about what was happening.

Chapter Fifty

Johnny, Terry and Alsina had been stuck at the house for the last two weeks and it was starting to show. They had discussed going back to Spain but postponed the idea until they had more information.

They got reports daily and one day Jonathon turned up at the house in person to give them an update. Terry was starting to thaw toward his old friend, but very slowly.

Where Jonathon went, Tommy went and invariably Jack would turn up too. Mrs. Hoon was in her element and the security operation at the house was fast becoming a popular attraction for the rest of the task force. To stave off boredom and also partly to combat the effect of the mountains of food they were now consuming, they all ran and exercised daily, sometimes twice a day.

Alsina was now more than proficient at self-defence. It helped a lot that she did not think of herself as a victim and had not frozen during the various failed attempts at capturing her.

Vincent occasionally ran with them and stayed close to the house when they were inside. The security team were not always happy when he roamed loose but so far there had been no incidents.

Stephen and Davina continued to work at the club and a security team was detailed to follow them and remain in the vicinity to compliment the club security.

They covered every base they could, but boredom and frustration were their main enemies.

Chapter Fifty One

Frank Underwood was starting to feel uneasy. In the last two weeks he had lost nearly half of his men. At first he put it down to being unlucky that they had been caught up at Pearce's clubs but then his own places started to attract attention.

If it had only been one or two people, he would have silenced them himself, or sent Kevin Daniels to do it but this was starting to hurt.

He knew where Johnny was but could not get to him. He had yet to find Pearce, although he was confident that it would not be long.

He called Kevin into the office.

"Any luck with the new recruits?" Frank asked.

"Yeah, I've pulled in some of my old mates, they can be trusted and they are hungry for work. Apparently there is a recession on."

They both laughed at this. If there was a recession, it was not affecting them but that was the way in their business. People with illegal money always needed places to spend it or invest it.

"How are the DVD shops doing?" Kevin asked.

"They are going well. It's early days at the moment but we stand to make a profit within six months and that's without what we put through the till." Frank replied.

Frank had recently invested in a small chain of DVD rental shops to launder his money. The idea was that he could show rentals at maximum, even though they were not. This gave him clean money to put into the bank under his various aliases.

The problem was that, within weeks the shops had started to get popular and he was at over sixty percent of his rental capacity already and there was no sign of it dropping off, which meant he could not put as much through the till as he needed.

He was faced with the happy necessity to expand the DVD shops and look for other businesses that could stand the illicit cash flow.

He was now starting up a scuba diving shop and wholesalers and he was also looking into canal boat sales but that was twofold as he wanted a distribution network that would not draw too much attention.

He knew that the service industry would be a good cover for most things and of course his existing establishments were still raking it in and providing an excellent laundry system already. His small chain of betting shops was a Godsend too.

He had now surpassed all of his goals. He still paid his men extremely well, which kept them loyal, so his day to day problem was how to hide the money and keep it safe.

He was glad of his decision to invest in the new businesses. With his old ones being targeted, he needed somewhere else to hide his cash.

He would have to bring his plans forward to keep pace but that would not be as pressing if he could only get rid of the two biggest thorns in his side, Johnny and Jonathon.

"How is the search for Pearce coming along? Anything I should know about?" Frank asked.

"It's like he's just disappeared. I've got everyone I can spare on the job but no joy."

"Can we bring some more people in?"

"I am but we've got to be careful, some of the youngsters think they're God's gift and can't be trusted on their own. I've already had to slap a couple because they are flashing the cash."

"We thought that might happen. Right, be careful but bring in as many as you can. I want feet on the ground before anyone gets any ideas that we are ripe for a takeover." Frank made sure Kevin understood his orders.

"Will do. Any word on that mortar delivery yet?"

"They reckon by the end of the week. They had to send another one as Customs nicked the last one."

"Coincidence?" Kevin asked.

"I think so. No one knew about it other than us two and the seller. I think it was just luck of the draw. We were due for a tug according to the law of statistics, the amount we have been bringing in lately."

"Maybe we should just retire." Kevin laughed as he said it but he glanced at his boss and was shocked to see him nodding in agreement. "That was a joke!"

"Many a true word spoken in jest and all that bollocks." Frank was conscious of Kevin looking at him strangely as he spoke, not sure what to make of what he said. Then he added, "And that is just what it is, bollocks."

Kevin stopped worrying; he had thought at first that his boss was starting to go soft. He did not even want to think of what the competition would make of it, if they thought that they could muscle in.

"Right, I'll be off to find some more men then. I'll check in with you later." Kevin promised.

Chapter Fifty Two

"Can we please go to the club tonight?" Alsina looked expectantly at Johnny.

"Sweetheart, it's still not safe for us!"

"I know but it is driving me mad staying here. There must be something that we can do. Maybe the cinema or ten pin bowling?" Alsina sighed.

"Why not have people over here instead? We could invite Tommy and Jonathon. Even Jack might be able to come. Also we could see if Davina and Stephen want a night off?" Johnny offered.

"Alright but no shop talk if we can help it, okay?"

They went and found Mrs. Hoon and asked for her help preparing the food, only to be told to leave it all to her. They discussed menus and asked if she wanted to come as well, then they spoke to Davina and Stephen. If they were lucky, then all of their friends would come, though how they would make it through the meal without talking about the current problems was anyone's guess.

Alsina's mood lightened at the prospect of a break from the routine. Now she had tasted a bit of life and was enjoying her work, it was hell for her being cooped up at the house. A five star hell but hell just the same.

To their surprise Jack said he would come and Terry did not grumble, even when he found out that Jonathon was coming.

The food would be good wholesome food, nothing fancy, and there would be quality wines to accompany the meal from Joseph's wine cellar, which had been extensive when he was alive but was now depleting as the year went on.

The festive spirit in Alsina was contagious and even Johnny seemed to lighten up. The change in Johnny affected everyone, up to and including the security teams but they remained vigilant. They had seen what happened when you lost your focus on the job.

They aimed to start around nine p.m. to allow everyone to finish their work. The party atmosphere reminded Alsina of her life in the marina, which now seemed such a long time ago.

The social circuit in the marina had been quite good. Most of the guests then had been friends or acquaintances of her parents but she had enjoyed them just the same. For the first time since coming to England, she felt a little homesick. She had always thought of Spain as her home, because she had spent so much of her life there.

The meal was relaxed, with enough food to feed the off duty security team as well as the actual guests. Not much was said during the meal as they all savoured the food that Mrs. Hoon had spent all day slaving over. It was a beef curry with all the trimmings and a huge chocolate cake for dessert. Then they migrated into the lounge to sprawl on the sofas and generally relax and unwind for the first time in weeks.

They discussed the club, as it was of keen interest to Jonathon. His own clubs were on a much smaller scale to theirs but he had more of them. They talked about what worked and where, new ideas that they had each thought of and Davina's time in Florida.

Then they chatted briefly about Joseph and the influence he had enjoyed in the local area. Both Davina and Stephen were able to talk freely about him without too much sadness, which pleased them both.

Stories about Joseph were new to Alsina, as she had never really known him. Terry told them about when he had first met him and Jonathon chimed in with his recollections of the training course that they had both attended. Everyone who attended the course, already had a background in martial arts or self-defence. Some of the group had decided that there was nothing more that they could learn. It took less than five minutes on the mat with Joseph for all of them to realize that they were in the presence of a true master.

They recalled some of his stories about working in clubs and some of the earlier fights that Joseph had been involved in. Alsina listened and could not believe that they were true. She laughed with the others at the stories of his early days working doors before he had made his money.

Once just after he bought his first Porsche it had been stolen by a couple of kids. Their mistake was to turn up at a nightclub with their girlfriends showing off their new toy. It was rather unfortunate for them that Joseph was working security at the time.

As he checked them at the door he invited them to a drink at the bar and when they left, they found the Police waiting outside for them. The looks on the boys' faces were priceless as their girlfriends started attacking them with their handbags for embarrassing them.

Davina and Stephen knew most of the stories but were impressed with the others' knowledge of Joseph. It brought back happy memories for them and Alsina said it was a shame that she had never really known him, only on the brief visit when they had put the boat in the marina.

Terry was reminded of an operation that he and Jonathon had worked together on and they fell about laughing as they told the others about the target running down the road, stark naked, as he tried to escape. He had been caught in the bath and had left a trail of bubble bath foam streaming after him.

The whole evening was a great success. Everybody enjoyed the stories and were mentally refreshed by the time that they were ready to leave. Nobody had mentioned the reason for being at the house and it was not until Terry checked in with the security team that they let thoughts of the current situation intrude again.

Terry accompanied Jack on a quick circuit of the grounds and they discussed the plans for the next day.

From what they could gather, Frank was finally starting to meet resistance from his competition. They would wait to see what they could gain from the fall out.

They watched as a vehicle's headlights cut through the darkness on the other side of the valley before turning off onto the main road. It was probably the local farmer checking his stock, or a courting couple returning to the real world.

They shook hands and said their goodbyes and then Jack drove off with Jonathon and Tommy in his car. Terry headed back to the house and was overtaken by Vincent who had been out roaming around the grounds. The monotony of waiting would begin again in the morning.

Chapter Fifty Three

One of the remits of Jack's job was to keep abreast of all known gun smuggling raids. To take his mind off the slow progress of his operation, he re-read some of the reports that he had been given in the last few days.

A shipment of explosives and hand grenades had been intercepted at Dover. There was a lot of U.S. gear coming through now, as some of the equipment that had been handed out in Iraq and Afghanistan was sold on the black markets.

One of the other items in the list was an M224 60mm lightweight mortar. That was worrying. Who the hell was planning to use that? With a range of nearly three and a half kilometres, it could cause untold carnage.

He put the thought to the back of his mind to mull it around. Sometimes his subconscious helped him with problems he could not solve. He would give it a try.

If he was not so tied up with the Underwood case he might have been able to divert extra personnel to the matter. It would have to wait for now though.

Jonathon walked into his office looking none the worse for wear for their previous evening's activities. He handed a coffee each to Jack and Tommy, followed up with chocolate biscuits. A good start to the day, if ever there was one, a cuppa and a choccy bickie, you couldn't beat it.

"Anything new overnight?" Jonathon raised his eyebrows as he asked the question. The office never closed as someone was always working.

"Nothing for us, but I was looking at the interception reports for last week and came across a big weapons consignment." Jack replied.

"Anything of interest?"

"Apart from a lightweight mortar, nothing." He watched the shock appear on Jonathon's face as he spoke.

"Fuck, what now? First of all, everybody is using grenade launchers and now they have mortars as well! It's outrageous!" Jonathon could not believe it.

"Well, technically we have them as they confiscated them at Dover. But it was a bold move to try to bring them in." Jack smiled at the look on the other man's face.

"Disgraceful! I'll tell you what. It's a good job that Frank didn't have them when he went for Johnny. Can you imagine the mess?"

"What did you just say?" Jack almost shouted the question.

"I said…" He never got the chance to finish as Jack was already standing up reaching for the phone.

"I want to speak to the officers who intercepted that mortar shipment. Yes, get them to ring me back in the office, straight away."

Jonathon and Tommy watched their old boss warily. They had guessed what Jack was worrying about and thought that he probably had good reason.

They sipped their drinks and waited for the call back. They sat there for twenty minutes and the packet of chocolate digestives slowly disappeared.

At last, the phone rang and Jack nearly pulled it off the desk. Jonathon and Tommy sat patiently as they listened to Jack's half of the conversation. Slowly, he replaced the phone on its base.

"They had a tip off about the shipment. That was how they got the first one. The thing is, that they had another tip off but they haven't found anything yet." Jack repeated what he had been told.

"Do you really think it is down to Frank?" Jonathon was still having trouble believing what he was hearing.

"What do you think?" asked Jack.

"The same as you." Jonathon sighed deeply as he answered.

Picking up the phone, Jack dialled Terry's number at the house. "We have to move you now, a car will pick you up in thirty minutes, okay?" He did not wait for an answer but just hung up the phone.

They all sprinted out of the office. Jack yelled for his driver and two of his men and told them to follow him.

They arrived at the house thirty-five minutes later and went inside. Three minutes later Johnny, Alsina and Terry came out and got into the cars, which left silently and headed back to town. Stephen and Davina watched them go.

"Where do you think they will go?"

"I don't know love. Somewhere safe, hopefully." Stephen answered with sadness in his voice.

"Will it never end?"

"It has to. I don't think I could stand it if anything happened to Alsina or the boys."

"I don't even want to think about that possibility." Davina agreed quietly.

They took Vincent for a final walk before deciding to head over to the club early. They took a change of clothes each, so that they could shower at the club and be ready for the evening. There seemed no point in hanging around the house now that Alsina was gone.

Chapter Fifty Four

Bernie Holt was already at the club when they arrived. He seemed to live there now. They were not complaining but they did try to encourage him to go home every now and then.

They ran through the previous night's incidents to make sure that they had missed nothing on their night off. It had been a fairly good night and relatively incident-free.

Taken up with the mundane matters, the rest of the day flew by. They got changed for the evening and mingled with the clients.

The night seemed to drag on but was broken up by a visit from Jack Fairfax, who just wanted them to know that their friends were safe.

He stayed for an orange juice and then left, leaving them to finish the night and to return home.

They pulled into the drive and saw Vincent running free in the grounds. The security detail must have let him out. They could probably go back to remote CCTV coverage soon, as the others were no longer living there.

They walked through the front door and Vincent ran off to do his final business of the day. They went into the kitchen and started pulling the stew, which Mrs. Hoon had left for them, out of the oven.

Stephen got up to call Vincent in, just as the kitchen exploded in a brilliant flash of high explosive. They never heard the approach of the mortar round. They felt no pain as they died instantly.

The security team reacted as they had been trained to, what was left of them anyway. Instantly alert for a physical assault, the perimeter team stayed on the lookout. The off duty team in the house attempted to rescue Davina and Stephen but the heat and flames from the kitchen drove them back. They searched desperately for hoses and more fire extinguishers, having used up the ones they could find. They desperately wanted to get their hosts out of the fire but could not enter the blazing kitchen.

They watched in awe as they saw movement in the flames, then ran to assist as Vincent materialized pulling the still burning corpse of Davina into the front garden. Then he ran back into the flames and reappeared dragging what was left of Stephen.

The security team attempted CPR but knew as they pushed down on what was left of the couple's chests that it was hopeless. There was no resistance as they pushed and they heard the air escaping through punctured lungs.

They did not see Vincent fall down a little way away, still smouldering from the intense heat, having at long last collapsed with his lungs full of smoke.

That was how Jack Fairfax found them when he arrived a little less than forty minutes later. He was stunned and walked around shaking his head, not realizing that his mobile was ringing in his pocket.

When he finally answered, he told a shocked Terry what had transpired. He told him everything he knew and promised to ring a little later on, when he had found out more.

A flash of light on the other side of the valley made him look in that direction. It was only the farmer again. Or was it?

Quickly he radioed to the Police and security cordon and told them to stop the vehicle. Within minutes he got the message that the car had slipped through the net. He cursed and was tempted to smash the radio unit to the ground.

He started his debrief as soon as the replacement security team appeared. He wanted to know everything before he rang the brothers and Alsina.

Selfishly, he was glad that he would not have to tell Alsina what had happened to her friends. He had grown to like her a lot and did not want that job at all.

When he was finished with the statements, he rang Terry and asked how the news had gone down. He nodded into the phone when Terry told him that Alsina was distraught.

He told Terry that he would be there shortly and then, as an afterthought, he asked about Johnny, fearing what he would be told. His worst suspicions were confirmed. Johnny wanted blood. He shivered, if he was not careful he would be hunting one of his own men and it took a while before he realized that he already was.

Chapter Fifty Five

Frank Underwood was at long last getting some good news. The attack on the house had been a direct hit. He had confirmation from the mortar team that neither Johnny nor Alsina had come out of the house in the aftermath of the explosion.

Finally they were dead. At last he was rid of 'The Boy'. It was too bad about the girl though. She would have made him a lot of money. He hated waste. "Any news on the whereabouts of Pearce yet?"

Kevin Daniels shook his head. "Only a matter of time now boss."

Frank poured them both a drink and handed one to Kevin.

"About fucking time we got some good news. Well done on choosing that mortar team, they really know their stuff."

"Cheers boss."

"No seriously, you did well tonight." He reached into his desk and pulled out a bundle of five hundred euro notes. "Here, you'll need these soon!"

Kevin looked at the fifty thousand Euros that he now had in his hands. He smiled, remembering that he had thought about running just after the botched job in Spain. He was very glad now that he hadn't done a runner.

They sat quietly sipping their drinks and reflecting on what they had achieved tonight. Now Frank knew just how good his guys were with a mortar, he would put them to use against his competition. 'Yes', he thought, 'all in all a good days work'.

Now that Johnny was out of the way, Frank would bring into play some of the plans that had been going through his mind but could not implement.

The mortar would be getting some serious usage. People would soon start to toe the line again.

Chapter Fifty Six

Alsina had not stopped crying since Johnny had broken the news to her. Her normally unshakable life force had all but disappeared.

Johnny sat next to her on the settee and held her in his arms, murmuring to her that everything was going to get better. She was safe at least and that was the main thing.

Terry popped his head in the door and motioned the universal sign for a drink. Johnny nodded and mouthed "Tea with two sugars."

The drink was not for him but for Alsina. He kept hold of her and gently rubbed her back reminding her of the good times, he said nothing about his thoughts, or of her going back to her parents for a while.

Things were bad enough as it was, without upsetting her further by letting her think he was trying to get rid of her. In reality, he knew that he was the best person for the job of keeping her alive. He would keep her really close to him now. He had faith in the other members of his team and he would let them find Frank. Once they found him though, well that would be another matter.

Terry came back into the room with a tray and three steaming cups of tea. He placed them on a little coffee table and spooned in three sugars for each of them. He decided that the extra sugar would be good for them all.

His face was grim as he looked at Johnny and wondered when his brother would start making excuses to get out and join the search.

"You know that you are the best person to stay with Alsina now!" He decided to pre-empt his brother.

"I agree."

"Oh! Right." He was amazed that his brother was agreeing so readily. He had expected a prolonged argument from him and was lining up his verbal armoury for the battle. "What are you going to do with her?"

"Firstly, we stay here, we let the team do their work but until then we go over our options and work out the best plan for us."

Terry was now very worried indeed. This reaction was the last thing he had expected from his brother and he didn't know what to say. He started thinking about what the cause of this miracle could be. Possibly the previous year's events were catching up with Johnny.

You could only deal with so many attempts on the lives of you and your loved ones. Perhaps it was finally hitting home that he was a target. Worse than that, perhaps he had only just realized that Alsina was a real target too.

"I've got to say mate, that was the last thing that I expected to hear from you."

"I'm not happy about being stuck here but what with tonight's events, I can't leave Alsina's safety in anyone else's hands."

"I am still in the room you know!" Alsina looked up as she spoke and sniffed away her tears.

"I know sweetheart." Johnny hugged her.

"I want them as much as you do. I want them caught and put in jail forever. I wish they still had the death penalty." Alsina was trying not to cry.

"I agree with you sweetheart, but hanging is too good for them. They must be made to suffer for what they have done and believe me, they will suffer!"

Both Terry and Alsina turned to stare at Johnny. Terry had expected something like this reaction in the first place but Alsina had only fleetingly seen Johnny anywhere near to this sort of mood before.

She had never picked up on the venom in his voice before, when he was talking about Frank or his gang.

"You know that you can't lose the plot with this one, don't you Boy?" Terry wanted to make sure that he was understood.

"I won't have to, the way this lot are going, they will bring about their own downfall soon enough." Johnny replied.

"Even so mate, you can't go for revenge, no matter how hard it gets."

"Have you forgotten what Joseph, Davina and Stephen have done for us this last year or so?" Johnny looked expectantly at his brother.

"Don't be stupid Johnny, of course I remember but they wouldn't want you to drop yourself in it for them. I mean that would be an insult to all that they have done."

"They deserve justice!"

"And they'll get it. For God's sake Boy, you are my brother. I love you more than anyone else in the world. I thought I'd lost you so many times this last year and I don't want to see you go down for doing something stupid."

"Terry's right Johnny, let it go. Let Jack prosecute them and make Davina's death count for something."

Johnny looked at Alsina with no emotion in his eyes. He knew how much she had cared for Davina and he respected the way she was trying to help him. He hoped that she would never change. She was far too lovely to have her life ruined by what was happening now.

"Alright, I'll try, but I'm not promising anything. If they come for me though, I will defend myself with whatever means possible."

Knowing his brother as he did, Terry decided not to push it. That Johnny had even said he would try was a revelation to him. He looked at Alsina and thanked whatever provenance had placed her in their lives. The effect that she was having on Johnny was the best thing he could have hoped for.

Johnny let the conversation end. He would deal with things in his own way. His main priority now was protecting Alsina. He would worry about the rest when he could, but deal with it he would.

Chapter Fifty Seven

"Right Kevin, you've got a couple of weeks to get things sorted. My solicitor in Spain has your details and he will run through all you need to know."

Kevin nodded silently.

"And make sure that the people you put in place know what will happen to them if they try to tuck me up." Frank added.

Kevin nodded again and went through a mental checklist.

"When you get back, we will sort out the other things that we talked about. Are you happy with all that?" Frank waited for an answer.

"Yeah, sorry I was just thinking about how I'm going to do it. I want to take a couple of the new guys I brought in. I trust them and they are well connected in Spain."

"Whatever you think is good. I'll back you." Frank finally smiled.

"Okay boss, what are you going to do while I'm away?"

"I'm going to keep a low profile. I know we got Johnny but Terry is still around and he will be hunting high and low for me now."

"If you want, I can stay around for a while until we can take care of him." Kevin offered.

"No mate, they can't find me and Johnny was the one I was most worried about. Right then, fuck off and we'll talk when you get back."

Frank watched Kevin walk out of the office and picked up the phone to check on one of his clubs. The resistance that he had been encountering had stopped almost immediately once word got out about how he had dealt with Johnny.

His intention had been to make a statement to let people know what happened if they messed with him and it had worked like a dream.

Hanging up the phone, he called in the two brothers who were standing in for Kevin for the next couple of weeks. They smiled when he told them where he wanted to go. Now, whenever they went anywhere near a brothel, they called it a product test.

Their boss was extremely generous when he was product testing, they would be there for at least the next four hours. Secretly they hoped that Kevin would be away for more than just two weeks, their own quality of life increased tenfold when they stood in for him. Mind you, if anyone had earned the perks then Kevin had, after what he had done in Spain.

Chapter Fifty Eight

As soon as Kevin got to Spain he headed straight to the lawyer's office and collected the keys to the brothel. He travelled everywhere with his two minders and on leaving the lawyer, headed to one of the bars that they knew.

It took a few hours to line up the personnel that he wanted and it would have taken a lot longer without the connections of his men. They turned out to be more of an asset than he had previously realized.

So far, in the last six hours, they had visited twice that many bars and pubs. That his men were well known on the coast was obvious in the way that they had been greeted and the respect that they had been shown by everyone they met.

Kevin was impressed with the fact that although they held the meetings in bars, the men only drank light beers or shandy. They were not out to grandstand or prove anything; they just got on with the job that they had been tasked with.

As the day wore on Kevin discovered that his boss' previous partner had not been as well liked or as well connected as he had led Frank to believe.

Kevin was worried about any reprisals from his previous visit but to his relief, he found that the locals had believed that it had been only a matter of time before someone took the guy out.

By the end of the evening he had garnered a secure contact in the local town hall and for what he thought was a very reasonable price. He would have to wait and see what the boss thought about the deals but he was pretty sure that he would agree.

The lawyer that his boss had used turned out to be connected in the town hall on various levels and the change of ownership of the brothel was done without delay and, more importantly, without too many awkward questions being asked.

From what he could gather, things were changing on the coast, but until they took some of the power away from the local mayors no further problems would be coming their way.

They spent the night in the brothel, which had been cleaned and renovated since the slaying. The solicitor had been as good as gold where that was concerned. Kevin found that his boss had once again picked a winner.

Once he was in control of the premises, he made the call to his boss and was told that the new talent would be arriving the next day. The three men were also given the address of where to arm themselves.

Frank had already had a shipment of small arms delivered to one of his warehouses on a little industrial estate, which, until that last conversation, Kevin had been unaware of.

The next day the three of them checked out the merchandise and invited the contacts that they had made the previous day to an opening night party.

When the girls arrived they checked them over and put them in a villa, which Frank also appeared to own. As the day passed into evening, Kevin realized that he knew virtually nothing of his boss' holdings in this country.

They stayed away from the marina at all costs. They knew that they would not be recognized but decided that it was for the best to give it a miss.

The opening party continued into the next day and by the end of it they had established a distribution line for guns, girls and drugs. The intention had been to slowly ease into the market but as the conversations carried on, Kevin realized that the time to expand was now.

The personnel that they acquired were installed into the brothel and a reliable barman had been found to run the bar. The doormen were supplied by one of his men's contacts and everyone was aware of the penalty involved in crossing Frank, although he was never actually mentioned by name.

At the end of the first week, Kevin thought that he might be able to return to the U.K. earlier than he had expected. If it had not been for the trouble on the Saturday night, he would have left on the Monday morning.

Since the opening night, trade had been brisk. Saturday was busy and he thought about suggesting to Frank that they should get bigger premises if it carried on at the rate things were going.

At six o'clock, when the girls had gone home to change and freshen up, he heard a ruckus at the door, followed by a group of five men pushing his doormen into the bar area. Kevin and his men watched from their table as the newcomers approached the bar and demanded to see the owner.

The barman told them he was in charge and the men produced handguns and pointed them at him. Kevin watched with a bemused expression as the men then informed the barman that he was going to have to pay them "insurance money" of one thousand Euros a week or "accidents" would happen, starting tonight.

As the leader of the group talked to the man behind the bar, the rest of the group were gazing round the bar. They took Kevin and his men to be customers and glared at them, trying to intimidate them into staying out of their affairs.

David, the barman started to argue that he could not pay that sort of money and was told that, if he did not want trouble with the 'Russian Mafia', then he would pay up. At no time in the conversation did the barman give the game away or look at Kevin or his men.

David again said that he did not have that sort of money and the gunman went to hit him with the barrel of his gun. His men turned to watch the fun as he did so and they did not see Kevin pull out the mini Uzi.

As they watched David fall to the ground, they found themselves covered by firepower that more than outweighed their own.

Once they had been disarmed, one of the doormen closed and locked the front doors, while the others tied the group back to back in twos, leaving the leader tied separately.

He started screaming at Kevin, telling him that he did not know who he was dealing with and that the might of the 'Mafia' would come down on him.

Kevin listened quietly to the man as he reached into his pocket and fished out a silencer for his weapon. Slowly and deliberately he attached the piece to the barrel and watched as the men on the floor became more and more agitated.

"My brothers will kill you Englishman!"

"No they won't!" And with that he shot them all in the head.

"Won't that cause us problems with their organisation?" It was one of the men he had brought from England who asked the question.

"What organisation?"

"They are Russian Mafia, organised crime, evil fuckers."

"They might be Russian and evil but they aren't organised. At the moment they trade on the threat of being connected but in reality they don't have any structure here as yet. They are fighting each other as much as anyone else."

"How do you know?"

"The boss deals with real gangsters. He knows where they are and how they operate. Besides if they were real gangsters they would have dealt with it more professionally." Kevin replied.

"How can you be sure?"

"Trust me, I'm right. They didn't even know who we were. We could've been anyone, if they'd done any homework, they would've known that we weren't punters." Kevin shrugged.

A few of his men then proceeded to get rid of the bodies. They backed a van up to the rear doors and loaded the bodies into the cargo area. Then, as two of the locals drove off with them, Kevin and his men set about cleaning up the mess.

Three hours later the men returned, having taken the bodies out to sea and dumped them over the side. They had slashed the corpses and weighed them down with lead weights and rocks from the beach, it lessened the chances of the bodies floating up to the surface once the bacteria started to bloat them.

"Where did you get the lead weights from?" Kevin was curious.

"We're on the coast. There are divers all over the place. Some off them even hide their weights in their boats to save carting them about all the time."

"What happens if they do float?" Kevin asked.

"The bodies shouldn't float, but even if they do, it will look like they got run over by a boat. Anyway, no one knows where they were when they died? If the arseholes were who they said they were, then it could have been any number of enemies. Besides, once the fish have started nibbling, the corpses will be very hard to identify." The local man started smiling.

Kevin listened to the man and realized that he was quite intelligent. He decided to watch him for the rest of his time here and then put him in charge when he left. Initially, he had intended to leave one, or both of the men he had brought with him but now decided that the local knowledge of this guy David would be a better asset.

"Right, let's get started. We open in half an hour, so keep an eye out for any more like that lot!" Kevin ordered.

"What happens if there are any?"

"Play it like we just did, but get them into the rear office first if there are any punters in, understood?"

"Got you boss." David nodded.

The rest of the evening passed uneventfully but Kevin and his men kept on their toes, alert to the slightest trouble. He called Frank and told him in coded English what had transpired. Frank agreed with his assessment and praised his quick thinking.

He stayed the rest of the next week to make sure that there were no repercussions but other than a few drunken stag parties, nothing happened.

At the end of his time there, he called in the workforce and told them who was in charge. David nodded his thanks and later, when he was told privately of his cash bonus, he stated his further appreciation.

Kevin got on the plane a contented man. He relaxed and slept the entire flight while his men sat with him and dozed or read the in-flight magazine.

Chapter Fifty Nine

The plainclothes Guardia Civil officer who had been watching the brothel finished his report for his superiors. He had seen the Russian protection racketeers enter the premises. He had also seen the van backing up to the rear of the building. He called his base for backup, who arrived just in time to follow the van to the local beach and watch the bodies being loaded into the speedboat.

Up until now they had been unaware that the boat was connected in any way to criminal activities. They knew that their bosses would be very happy with the information supplied to them by the Englishman Fairfax.

They had been lucky tonight that only foreign criminals had been involved, or they would have had to blow their cover. As it was, they did not care what the foreign criminals did to one another, as they led them to the organisers of the international drugs and trafficking trade.

Another bonus had been the discovery of the warehouse armoury. When this operation was finished, they would have made a very serious dent in the criminal activities being carried out in their country.

Chapter Sixty

Jonathon watched as Jack got off the phone. Jack was smiling and looking very pleased with himself.

"That was my contact in Spain. They have opened up the brothel again and started what looks to be a distribution line for guns and girls. They might have started a drugs supply too but the jury is still out on that one."

"They're being very friendly to you!" Jonathon commented.

"I worked with José years ago and we still keep in touch. He's a good guy and he was involved with protecting Johnny over there."

"Did Johnny know?" Jonathon looked incredulous at the thought of Johnny needing protection but then thought of whom they were dealing with.

"He knew I was cooperating with the locals but not the full extent. Terry was always in the loop though."

"He must have been frantic when Johnny got injured."

"You know him better than I do, what do you think?" Jack replied.

"Yes I do. Why he didn't go after Frank?"

"I think that Joseph Stanton had a lot to do with that. He persuaded Terry to let me handle things, at least until Johnny was on his feet."

"Did Stanton ever work for you?"

"No, but as you know, he trained most of my men." Jack grinned.

Jack decided to change the subject. "You were always a good analyst. Have you thought anymore about my offer?"

"I don't think even you could swing it for me to come back to work here!"

"If we get Frank, sorry, when we get him, I will be able to do virtually whatever I want to."

"We'll wait and see, that's all I can say at the moment, though Tommy might be interested. I know he misses working here." Jonathon sincerely hoped that Tommy would accept the offer.

"He can come back anytime he wants, he knows that already." Jack confirmed.

"I really don't know that he thinks he can. I think he feels that he let you down when he left."

"Why did he leave with you anyway?" Jack asked.

"I don't know to be honest. I think he thought that I had been treated unfairly. I have asked him several times but he just says we were partners and partners stick together."

"Do you want him to come back, even if you can't or won't?" Jack waited silently for an answer.

"I want him to do what makes him happy. I won't deny that he has literally saved my life a few times, but I can't be responsible for messing up his life by making him stay with me."

"I'll have a word with him." Jack nodded as he spoke.

"Cheers Jack. So, what's the plan now?"

"José is faxing a picture of the guy who started the brothel up again. He thinks he might lead us to Frank."

"That would be a blinding result." Jonathon looked happy.

"I know, let's wait and see what happens. I have men at the airport and they will follow him without showing themselves."

"Are you going to tell Johnny what you know?"

"I'll tell Terry, he can pass the news on."

"How is Johnny taking all of this?" Jonathon asked.

"Actually, quite well, as far as I can gather."

"That's unusual for him!" It was said as an off the cuff statement but both men agreed. It was very unusual. "Can you control him when the time comes?"

"I bloody well hope so, really I do." Jack sighed.

"So do I. I like Johnny and I owe him one. He can't go down for something stupid like a revenge thing. That boy scares me though. Sometimes, he only sees things in black and white."

"That boy scares me too on occasion." Jack agreed.

Chapter Sixty One

Kevin walked into Frank's office and sat down yawning. He had been up all night discussing the events of the trip with his boss. Satisfied that nothing further would come of the attempted extortion, they had called it a night and gone their separate ways.

This afternoon, however, things had taken a turn for the worse.

"What do you mean, Johnny Miller is still alive!" Frank sounded incredulous.

"I only got told today and that was more luck than judgement."

"What exactly were you told?"

"Right, you remember Pete who runs the Nags Head?" He waited for his boss to nod his agreement before carrying on the explanation. "Well I went in there for a late breakfast and he mentioned that one of his punters thought he saw someone who looked like Terry Miller."

"So?" Frank waited for an answer.

"Well apparently he overheard him talking about his brother to the guy that he was with. Do you think the mortar team got it wrong? I know they said that there were no survivors, but could they have been mistaken?" Kevin looked at Frank as he spoke.

"At this point, who the hell knows? What worries me more is the fact that he could still be alive. And if I am being honest, that thought scares me more than I'd like to admit." Frank chastised himself for letting Kevin know that he had a weakness. The saving grace was the fact that Kevin seemed to think that he was scared of having living witnesses, not the fact that he was scared of the boy.

"I mean how hard can it be to actually kill the bloke?" Kevin carried on as if it was the situation, not the person, that scared his boss.

"I know what you mean, I've lost count of the number of times I have tried to kill the bastard and that includes personally."

"I had heard that you had a personal issue with the bloke." Kevin was interested in what Frank would say next.

"It's more like the other way round. He wants payback because I tried to kill him."

"Is he dangerous?" Kevin nodded as Frank confirmed what he had been told.

"Let me put it this way, have you seen the film 'The Terminator'?" When Kevin nodded he continued "Well that is Johnny Miller, once he gets his teeth into something he won't let go."

"He doesn't appear to be looking for you in person."

"Don't let appearances fool you. He is the last man on earth you want after you. It's like he has tunnel vision and only getting to the other end matters."

"What about his brother?" Kevin's interest was sparked.

"He is not quite as bad but if you hurt Johnny, make no mistake, Terry will come for you as sure as night follows day."

"So we take them both then!" It was a statement not a question and Kevin watched his boss nod silently.

"First things first, let's find out what the damage is. Firstly, is Johnny alive?"

"What about the girl?" Kevin asked.

"She's irrelevant at the moment. Johnny will do us the most damage if he is still living. And what is the news on Pearce? It's like he has dropped off the face of the planet."

"I'm still looking though. The boys were on the case while I was away and they had orders to report directly to you in my absence." Kevin suddenly hoped that his orders had been carried out while he was away.

"Right, I need to relax for a bit, I am going for a product test. Find me when you have any news." Frank got up and left the office.

"No bother, as soon as I know, you will."

Chapter Sixty Two

Jonathon stood looking at Johnny across the table. The boy seemed altogether too calm for the events that were happening to him.

"That's all Jack was able to find out at the moment. We know one of the addresses and we're compiling a history of the guy. His passport was a fake but we're letting him run with it until he takes us to Frank." Jonathon shrugged.

"Someone has to know who he is, surely?"

"I'm sure they do but until they tell us, we're in the dark. How's Alsina holding up?"

"Considering her two closest friends were both killed in a horrible way, she's coping very well." Johnny said matter of factly.

"And what about you?"

"Probably about the same. They did an awful lot for me and now I can't even repay them." The regret was obvious in Johnny's voice.

"They didn't seem like the type who would expect to be repaid." Jonathon replied.

"True, they were good people. They didn't deserve to die. How is Mrs. Hoon?"

"From what I gather, she's not good, Terry went over there yesterday to see if she needed anything."

"They've become quite close as it happens." Johnny nodded as he thought about his brother.

"Yeah! Thought so." Jonathon smiled.

"Whatever she needs, she gets, right! If Jack can't arrange it, let me know."

"She's being taken care of, don't worry."

Just then Alsina walked in and sat down next to Johnny. Her whole demeanour had changed from when Jonathon had first met her. Although she smiled at him, it did not reach her eyes. He felt genuinely sorry that someone so innocent had been caught up in their world.

"How are you coping, Alsina?"

"I think I am okay. It is hard for me to take in really. First Amelia, then Davina and Stephen. Even Vincent is gone. I am sorry I didn't get to know the rest of your team who also died."

"Don't even think about being sorry. It's not your fault. I knew most of them well and they loved what they did. If it's possible to die happy, then they did just that." Jonathon tried to assure her.

"It is just such a waste!" Alsina raised her voice slightly.

"I can't argue with you about that but we won't let them die for nothing." Jonathon agreed.

"How is Mrs. Hoon?"

"I was just telling Johnny, Terry saw her yesterday and she's not that good."

"Can we see her? I mean will she see us? Do you think she wants to?" Alsina looked unsure.

"Why don't you ring her and find out. There's no harm in asking." Jonathon suggested.

As Alsina left the room to get her mobile, Johnny nodded briefly at Jonathon. "Thanks for that mate, she needed to hear a kind voice."

"Someone as lovely as her deserves to be happy. You've got a good one there, I hope you can keep hold of her."

"Cheers mate, I'll try, believe me I'll try. How will it work if Mrs. Hoon says she'll see us?" Johnny asked him.

"I don't know. I'll have to ask Jack."

At that moment Alsina came back into the room holding her phone and looking happier than she had for some time.

"She wants to see us as soon as she can. Apparently Terry is due over there later today and she will come over here with him. I didn't know that Terry had seen her."

"Yes, he's been over there quite a lot." Johnny informed her.

"It will do the old bugger good to have someone other than you to care about." Jonathon was smiling. Over the last few weeks his relationship with Terry had been patched up somewhat. Especially when Jack had suggested that Johnny's previous near death experience may not have been Jonathon's fault, in light of what they now knew about Frank.

They would just have to add it to the list of questions that they would ask him when they finally caught him. They were sure that they would catch him now. It was only a matter of time.

Jonathon made his excuses and left them alone, while he headed back to the office. They sat in silence for a while when he had gone and then Alsina jumped up.

"Let's make some food for when Mrs. Hoon arrives."

Smiling, Johnny got up, he liked seeing Alsina this way and thought that anything that could make her smile at the moment was a good thing.

They didn't make anything fancy, although the kitchen was well stocked. The three hours that it had taken for Terry to bring Mrs. Hoon over went quite quickly and for that Johnny was thankful.

He watched as Alsina and Mrs. Hoon hugged in the hallway with tears streaming down both of their faces, sobbing loudly and letting it all out. He raised his eyes to his brother in an unspoken question and got a shy smile in response.

Seeing Mrs. Hoon again Johnny's thoughts flicked briefly to Vincent. He had loved that dog and agreed with Alsina, it was all such a waste.

When she had finished with Alsina, Mrs. Hoon made her way over to Johnny and gave him the same treatment. Then she marched off down the hallway looking for the kitchen.

Before they could stop her she had rearranged the food and put fresh coffee on to boil. They all laughed as she handed her coat to Terry and told him to hang it up. Then she set about the kitchen, looking around and moving things as she went.

All the time chatting with Alsina who followed her around like a lost puppy.

When the kitchen was to her liking, they all sat down at the table and ate the food that Johnny and Alsina had prepared earlier. They did not eat in silence, but talked about what was happening in their lives and how the loss of Davina and Stephen had affected them.

Mrs. Hoon told them that she had felt the same when Joseph had been killed and Alsina heard new stories about Davina's brother, that made her wish even more that she had known him.

They asked about Mrs. Hoon's grandchildren and were updated on what was happening in their lives. The family had tried to get her to retire but she had told them she would make no plans until things had been sorted out for Stephen and Davina.

Finally, after several hours and feeling happier than they had for weeks, Terry took Mrs. Hoon home. Before they left Johnny received a status update, but nothing else had happened since Jonathon had last spoken to them.

They went to bed and slept soundly for the first time in a long while and when they awoke in the morning, Johnny felt a new sense of enlightenment.

He let his subconscious drift and let the problems that they faced swirl around in his brain. Slowly ideas came to him and he made mental notes of what they could try in their hunt for Frank.

He got up to make some breakfast and found, to his pleasant surprise, that Mrs. Hoon was in the kitchen frying eggs and bacon, while the coffee percolator bubbled away in the corner.

"I feel better when I'm working love. Have a seat. Breakfast won't be long."

Johnny sat at the table and turned as Alsina entered the room, having been woken by the smell of bacon.

"I thought I was dreaming." She sat down next to Johnny and they smiled at one another

"I was just saying to Johnny, love, I feel better when I'm working."

"How did you get back here so early?" Alsina asked.

"Oh, Terry brought me over. I love taking care of you, so it's no hardship."

They did not ask the question that was on their minds. What was Terry doing over there at that hour of the morning? They guessed he would tell them when he was good and ready.

Alsina took the cup of coffee that Mrs. Hoon held out to her and sipped at the scalding liquid slowly. It felt like old times, being together again. She thought about Davina and Stephen and felt a little sad.

Time may be a great healer, whether it was or wasn't, she didn't know. What she did know was that she would get stronger with time. Yesterday and this morning had helped to prove that. What was that old cliché that everyone talked about 'Today it the first day of the rest of my life!'

Chapter Sixty Three

"Jonathon, have you got a minute?"

"What's up boss?"

"Have you seen these reports on Frank's suspected income?"

"No. Why?" Jonathon asked.

"According to this lot, he is sitting on a little over one hundred million quid!"

"Fucking hell!" Jonathon exclaimed.

"Exactly. I think we're in the wrong game."

"How accurate are these reports, Jack?"

"Very accurate, I'm afraid. The boys who did these for me rarely make mistakes and if you want to know the best bit, they think he has other aliases as well. He could have at least five times what we can trace so far."

"Can we do anything about this? I mean can we seize any of it?" Jonathon sounded eager.

"Not yet but I can put a block on his accounts. He can still pay in but he won't be able to draw any out."

"I'm not being funny, but is it worth it? He must be cash rich too, from what I know of the business, so I doubt that freezing his accounts will have much effect on him."

"Maybe not, but it starts the ball rolling on the illegal income and then, maybe, we can grab it. God knows we have spent enough on Frank's enterprises already." Jack sighed.

Jonathon sat down at Jack's desk and started to go over the accounts. He had a good idea of how Frank worked and he was absolutely positive that Frank had more money under other aliases.

Jack watched him as he slowly scanned the pages and knew exactly what was going through

Jonathon's mind. That much money was obscene, especially when you knew how Frank had made it in the first place.

He picked up the phone and made the calls to start the suspension of the accounts. It gave him a small amount of pleasure as any advancement he made against Frank was worth it.

"The weapons money is based only on what they have intercepted so far. They've not estimated anything. They've only written what they can prove. Basically what you see is almost certainly only the tip of the iceberg."

"What I wouldn't do for a fraction of that money." Jonathon voiced his thoughts.

"Join the queue mate, join the queue."

"Does the Boy know about this yet?" Jonathon could only guess at Johnny's reaction.

"Actually, it was one of his ideas that started us off in this direction. He hasn't lost his ability to think." Jack was grateful.

"He still worries me though, he is far too calm."

"Terry says the same but thinks that Alsina might be a calming influence on him."

"That would be a result. Bloody hell, can you imagine what would happen if he went off on one?" Jonathon went quiet while he imagined the bloodshed.

"We've seen and dealt with it all before, I swear I'll have a heart attack if I worry about it much more." Jack said flatly.

"Has anyone spoken to Johnny yet? You know, a trick cyclist or whatnot?"

"Briefly, but they will keep trying. They had an informal chat with Alsina too. Impressive girl that one." Jack smiled.

"Yeah, he's had a right result there. I told him so too."

"How are things with you and Terry now?" Jack watched as Jonathon thought about his answer.

"I don't think we will ever be exactly the same as before but at least he doesn't look at me like I was something he picked up on his shoe."

"Give it time Jonathon, he was always protective."

"You definitely do not need to tell me that!" Jonathon laughed.

"What's Tommy up to today?"

"Babysitting Johnny. They always got on and he was a good influence on the Boy."

"What are your plans for the day?" Jack asked.

"I hope to hook up with Johnny and Terry a bit later on and we will have a strategy meeting to see if we can bring the game to us for a bit."

"Right then, keep me in the loop." Jack turned back to his papers.

Jonathon put the reports back on Jack's desk and walked out. He was preoccupied with what he had just read. Not only was the amount of money obscene, it could cause them major problems with the case. With that sort of money, Frank could buy off witnesses, or just eliminate them, full stop. They needed a breakthrough soon, or they were going to have a problem.

Chapter Sixty Four

"It's definitely true! They are both alive!" Kevin waited for an answer.

"Bollocks!" Frank exploded.

"I know what you mean. Will that boy ever bloody die?"

"Yes, of course he will, of that I have no doubt, but we will need something a bit more sophisticated than we have tried before." Frank started to think.

"What have you got in mind?"

"I'm bouncing a few things around at the moment. I'll let you know more when I've given it some more thought."

"Okay, where does that leave us for the moment?" Kevin asked.

"We'll carry on as planned and take out the rest of the competition. The mortar team knows how to play it and once we start with that shit again, the rest will crumble and come begging to us."

"Fair play. What do you want me to do now?"

"Keep looking for Pearce, oh, and Kevin, make sure you find him!"

"It won't be long now. It can't be long now. He has to surface sooner or later and then we'll nail him." Kevin tried to sound confident.

Frank nodded. Things were going far too slowly for his liking and he wanted it to be finished sooner, rather than later. Enough was enough where Johnny was concerned.

"What news on Spain?" Frank asked.

"It's all good, no more funny business from anyone and the money is flying through the doors."

"Good, where are we up to in France?" Frank continued with hardly a pause.

"Going from strength to strength on that score. We have our guys working the ports and they are very good."

"What about the new ventures, any problems there?"

"Nothing at all and the DVD shops are still going brilliantly." Kevin was glad of the change of subject.

"Good, good. We are going up north later in the week. It should only be an overnighter but make sure you are available. Don't tell the lads yet, they don't need to know." With that Frank got up and left the room.

He walked into the loading bay of the premises that he was currently using as his base of operations. As he looked around the warehouse, he wondered in which direction his life was taking him. He certainly had enough funds to just walk away, but what would he do?

He didn't fancy the prospect of looking over his shoulder every five minutes. He could afford good security but that would mean putting down roots. Plastic surgery was always an option but he didn't want to go down that route just yet.

His thoughts turned to Johnny again, that boy would be the death of him if he wasn't careful.

Chapter Sixty Five

Jack walked into the safe house that Johnny and Alsina were staying in for the time being. He had been on the phone all morning and pulled in a few favours, which had been easier than he had hoped for.

Alsina greeted him warmly and they went into the kitchen. Terry, Johnny and Mrs. Hoon were already there, talking to Jonathon and Tommy.

"I don't have much time I'm afraid, so forgive me for being blunt. I have been talking to Davina and Stephen's solicitor this morning and he asked me to make arrangements with you for the reading of their respective wills."

"What has it got to do with us?" Alsina was curious as to why they were being summoned, as surely it was a private matter for the heirs alone.

"Basically, you are the heirs!"

"What?" Alsina gasped.

"You, Alsina get the house, club, cars and all of the assets except the boat and a small sum of money, which goes to Johnny and Terry."

"That can't be right!" They all said it at once and Jack waved down their protests.

"I can tell you virtually word for word what the wills say and, having spoken to their solicitor for most of the morning, it is a done deal."

"That cannot be right!" Alsina was shocked "Why?"

"I'll give you the condensed version but they both thought of you as the sister they never had. As for the boat, they told their brief that, as the boys had got more use out of it than they had, their instruction to him was that they might as well keep it."

"But surely there are family members who deserve to get something." Terry argued.

"No, actually, there aren't." Jack replied.

"Seriously boss, this can't be right. Me and Johnny don't deserve the boat."

"They left a list of instructions with the solicitor, suggestions of who gets what if you want to share it around a bit. There aren't many, but you will understand why when you see them." Jack told them what he knew.

"It's true, child. Since the trouble started, they had made sure that all of their affairs were in order. I have to confess I knew what their intentions were and I have to say I wholeheartedly agreed with them, although we didn't expect it to happen quite so soon." Mrs. Hoon was gently rubbing Alsina's shoulders as she spoke. "They loved you more than you will ever know."

"But why me?" Alsina was totally shocked.

"They said you would say that and that is exactly why it is you. Accept what they have given you. They felt partially responsible for your problems and felt, too, that you deserved a bit of luck." Mrs. Hoon answered.

"I have also been on the phone to the licensing people and they have no objection to you taking over." Jack opened his arms wide in a 'what else could I do' gesture. "If you get any problems whatsoever, then refer them to me, but as from now you are the proud owner of one of the best night clubs in the country."

"But I haven't finished learning the trade yet." Alsina said weakly.

"That's alright sweetheart, Tommy and I will help you, or if you prefer, Bernie will." Jonathon had also known what the meeting was about and Jack had asked if he would help the girl.

Alsina looked from Jonathon to Tommy and then back again. Then she looked at Johnny and Terry. She opened her mouth to speak and then closed it without saying anything. She was truly speechless. She turned to Mrs. Hoon, who opened her arms and gathered her into them.

"But…"

"I know child, I know. You have to accept what you cannot change."

Jack told them the details for the reading and then made his excuses and told Jonathon that he would speak to him later at the office. Tommy accompanied him to the front door and then returned to the kitchen in time to catch the conversation between Alsina and Jonathon.

"Um, thank you for your kind offer Jonathon. Did you mean it? I mean, can you spare the time?" Alsina asked.

"Of course I did love. I will always make time for you. In fairness there isn't a lot that you need to know now and Bernie will be on site all the time. I'm sure Johnny will help you as well if he's not too busy with his new yacht." Jonathon smiled.

"Piss off mate, I still haven't taken it in yet." Johnny looked at Terry and then added, "What the bloody hell are we gonna do with a boat?"

"Enjoy it I suppose. It will make it easier for you two when you visit Alsina's parents. I'll let you use it for the honeymoon too if you want." Terry laughed.

Both Alsina and Johnny turned deep crimson and looked at each other. Of course Alsina had entertained thoughts of marriage to Johnny, when she had first got to know him, but having them aired in front of her friends embarrassed the life out of her.

"Oi! Leave it out mate." Johnny was still a deep shade of red but his brother's words had struck a chord. He had actually dared to hope that, if this trouble finally ended, maybe he could settle down with Alsina, but that bridge would be crossed in the distant future.

Jonathon started humming 'here comes the bride' and Terry started laughing. Tommy tried to pretend he wasn't there but could not help smiling.

"I think I preferred it when you two didn't like each other." Johnny frowned at Terry and Jonathon, then turned to Alsina and said "Sorry about that sweetheart, some people just never grow up."

Alsina was still speechless, but her face was slowly returning to its original colour. Given another couple of minutes she would have been over her initial shock, but it wasn't to be.

"Oh goody, a wedding! You have to let me help with the arrangements." Mrs. Hoon clapped her hands together with glee and hugged Alsina to her again.

Alsina started to protest, but could not articulate the words that were running through her mind. Tommy finally took pity on them and saved her by saying, "I think we had all best wait until this thing is over before we start to plan anything, don't you? Besides, I don't think he's asked her yet!"

"Cheers mate, finally some sense at last." Neither Jonathon nor Terry pushed the point and Johnny nodded to his friend for coming to his rescue.

Alsina mumbled something about agreeing and then fled from the kitchen thinking that she was going to die of embarrassment. Her colour was fading back to normal again but the start of a smile was forming on her lips.

"Tossers!" Johnny followed her from the room, but in his heart he could not be upset with his brother. He had seen the smile on Alsina's face and decided that he would have to have that conversation sooner, rather than later.

As they left the room, Mrs. Hoon chided Terry and Jonathon, who were not in the least bit repentant. She had to agree though, that nothing would please her more than to see Alsina and Johnny tie the knot.

"Oh mate, that was fun. Did you see the looks on their faces?" Jonathon laughed.

"That was quick with the wedding march tune. I'd forgotten how funny you could be." Terry agreed.

"They need some happiness in their lives and, if nothing else, it will take Alsina's mind off the current situation, Johnny's too, for that matter. Anyway you started it." Jonathon replied.

"True enough mate, true enough. Do you want to come for a spin on my boat, by the way?"

They both fell about laughing and tears were streaming down their faces. Tommy just shook his head and turned to Mrs. Hoon who was also shaking her head.

They were all glad of the light relief and were in no hurry to think about the real world for the moment.

Jonathon's phone started to ring and he reached into his pocket to answer it. He listened to the message and stopped laughing immediately, then said, "See you there" before hanging up.

"There's been a mortar attack on a pub just north of the river. Jack wants us down there."

"What about me and the Boy?" Terry asked.

"You can come, but Johnny has to stay with Alsina."

"Okay, I'll let them know." Terry nodded.

They grabbed their coats and left the house, explaining to Johnny as they went. He told them to keep him in the loop and then went back into the bedroom that he shared with Alsina. Terry could not believe how easily Johnny had taken the news.

Johnny was smiling as he re-entered the room. He would have to thank Terry and Jonathon later, because Alsina had just agreed to be his wife, when this was all over. If they had not made the joke in the first place, he may never have asked her.

They spent the afternoon in bed together and, for the first time, Johnny was not chomping at the bit to get on with the hunt.

Mrs. Hoon decided not to disturb them until it was time for dinner. Then she shouted her goodbyes as she left and told them where to find their food. She too was happier than she had been in a very long time.

Chapter Sixty Six

It was a bombsite. Jonathon and Terry were allowed access behind the Police tape and sought out their boss.

Jack was talking to various members of his own task force as well as several heads of other departments. This attack stepped on so many toes it was unreal.

Jack enjoyed a good working relationship with nearly all the government departments and he did not want to foul them up because of Frank Underwood. He needed all of their cooperation to catch Frank.

His minions were in constant contact with headquarters and emails were being sent to everyone who had an interest. He had already decided to step up the operation but this had forced his hand. Frank needed stopping and needed stopping quickly.

"What's happening boss?" Terry asked the question while Jonathon talked to some of their colleagues.

"Bloody Underwood is at it again! Is there no end to the weapons that that man can get hold of?"

"It does seem to be getting a bit serious." Terry agreed.

"Worst of all is I have just had a report of another one, south of the river this time." Jack told him.

"What's the body count?"

"Not sure yet, at least thirty, but we don't know if they are players or just collateral damage." Jack shook his head.

"Do you think there will be anymore tonight?" Terry asked him.

"I sincerely hope not."

"What do you want me to do?"

"Talk to the eyewitnesses here and then you and Jonathon come with me to the other site. We are rounding them up and I want some answers, pronto." Jack started to turn away.

"Jonathon's on it now, I'll catch up with him."

"Can you get a wriggle on? I want to get to the office later and have a quick team briefing." Jack said over his shoulder.

"Looks like you have most of the team here already, and some hangers on by the looks of it." Terry countered. "Are we looking at two mortar teams or just one?"

"One, I think, why?" Jack turned back to look at Terry.

"I just wanted to make sure that they had left the area. I don't fancy a rocket up my arse while I'm making enquiries."

"Bloody hell, I hadn't thought of that. Fuck, you're a target yourself. I should never have brought you over here." Jack was looking around anxiously for the Police Commander. Finding him he pulled him to one side and made sure that they were confident that the area was safe.

"Change of plan Terry, go back to Johnny and stay with him. I'll send an escort part of the way to make sure that you are not followed." Jack ordered.

"Is there a problem boss?" Terry looked around.

"Not yet, but I don't want to take any chances. And make sure that Johnny doesn't get any ideas about joining in the search."

"I think that is the last thing on his mind at the moment." As Terry walked away he was looking for Jonathon. Tommy would take him back and then head directly to the other site. It was probably for the best, as there were way too many feet on the ground at the moment.

Chapter Sixty Seven

"You are not going to believe this Frank, but Jonathon Pearce is working with Fairfax." Kevin was breathing loudly into the phone as he spoke.

"What?"

"Just what I said, he's working with Fairfax." Kevin repeated.

Frank started thinking. Had it all been an elaborate hoax? Had Fairfax already known then that he was playing for the other side? Had Pearce been undercover for all this time? No, it couldn't be.

"Are you sure it's him?"

"I'm looking at him now. He arrived with Terry Miller and Tommy Rooke."

"Fuck, can they see you?"

"I'm not *that* stupid boss. Besides, they have other things on their minds."

"Is Terry still there?" Frank thought quickly.

"No, he left just now, why?"

"I was just wondering if we could get the mortar team back to finish them both off, Pearce *and* Miller."

"Won't that provoke Johnny?"

"It's too late to worry about that now. If Pearce is working with them, we have to have a contingency plan."

"Pearce is a muppet, isn't he?" Kevin said.

"No, he isn't. He used to work with me years ago, as I told you. The thing is that he's almost as good as me at planning." Frank answered.

"I didn't know that."

"No reason for you to know, it was a long time ago."

"Will he be a problem for us?" Kevin asked.

"Not now I know where he is and what he's doing. Now I think about it, it might actually work in our favour. Can we get someone to follow him?"

"Leave it with me." Kevin was nodding into the telephone.

"Make sure whoever you choose is good though Kevin. Tommy is one of the best counter surveillance operators that I know and though I hate to say it, Pearce is no slouch either."

"As I said boss, leave it with me."

"I don't suppose you've got anyone on Terry?" Frank sounded hopeful.

"Fuck me boss, give me a break, he was only there five minutes and then he was off. I think Tommy took him somewhere."

"If he crosses your path again, put someone on him. He could lead us to the Boy." Frank was almost shouting.

"I'll let you know as soon as it happens Frank, okay?"

"I suppose it will have to be. Come back to the office when you're done there and I will let you know what I've decided."

Frank lowered the phone gently on the hook and then placed his head in his hands, exhaling loudly. He did not know what to make of the recent turn of events. In the background his paranoia was at work.

He breathed slowly, in and out and started thinking through his problems. Ironically, Pearce had taught him this technique years ago and he found himself still using it because it worked.

After about fifteen minutes he thought that he had it figured out. Pearce had only hooked up with Fairfax to save his skin. It made sense and he would do the same if he was in Pearce's shoes.

Yes, that was definitely it. This was a strategic alliance. Now that he knew what was happening he could plan for the consequences.

Certainly, it was a shock, but it really didn't change his plans. He needed them all dead and that was still on the cards. Again he thought of the possibilities of finishing them off in one big group.

Ideas came to him slowly and he considered them and rejected them one by one until he had a viable list of options. He still had not completely made up his mind when Kevin Daniels returned with the latest information.

Kevin had put someone onto Jonathon, but had pulled him off when he thought that Jonathon had spotted him. In any event, he was headed for the second attack site so it was a moot point. Better safe than sorry where those boys were concerned.

Chapter Sixty Eight

"If you don't mind me asking boss, why did you pull me off the site and leave Jonathon there? From what we know he is just as much a target as me." Terry asked.

"I know, but although Johnny likes and cares for him, he is not as likely to go off half-cocked if something happens to Jonathon. If something happened to you on the other hand… I don't think I need to explain myself."

"Fair comment, it didn't occur to me why Jonathon was still there until I was on the way back and by then it was too late to do anything about it." Terry admitted.

"How is Johnny coping with being stuck here?" Jack asked.

"Actually, he's good at the moment. He has other things on his mind."

"What can he possibly be thinking about that is more important than someone trying to kill him?"

"He's going to marry Alsina."

"What? When?" Jack's face was a mixture of disbelief and relief.

"After all this is over." Terry answered.

"I thank God that he met her. You know, can you imagine what he would be like without her? It just doesn't bear thinking about."

Terry nodded. He knew that this was what anyone who knew Johnny thought. Alsina had a lot to answer for but in a positive way. "Right, what did the crime scenes tell us?"

"We're looking at one mortar team. We're fairly definite about that. The length of time between the attacks is about right for the team to get from one site to the other."

"They must be bloody good too!" Terry was thinking out loud.

"That's what's worrying us. We're convinced that they are the same team who hit the Stanton house and so far they have not missed their targets." Jack agreed.

"Are we checking Regular Army and TA records to see if anyone that good has been discharged recently?" Terry suggested.

"It may not be one of ours, there are enough foreign operators floating around who will do something like this for the right money."

"I would like to hope it was a foreign team, I don't like the thought that we trained the bastards who did this."

"My sentiments exactly, Terry." Jack nodded.

"Where are we up to with finding Frank?"

"We're following the paper trails, it's slow, but with some of his people gradually coming around to our way of thinking, I believe that we might crack this wide open very soon."

"I hope you're right Jack, this is getting bloody tedious."

"What's getting tedious?" Johnny was actually smiling as he entered the kitchen.

"This whole situation son. Congratulations by the way."

"Bloody Hell, that got out quick." Johnny replied.

"Terry had to explain to me what exactly was more important to you than finding Frank. I must say that I understand entirely, she's a cracking girl."

"Thanks boss, I haven't given up on Frank though. She's not safe while he's at large."

"You're not safe either Boy, remember that if you can. You're not immortal." Jack retorted.

"I seem to be doing alright at the moment, but I will be careful. I don't want anything messing up my chances of meeting old Frank again."

The temperature in the room seemed to drop about ten degrees as he spoke. Terry glanced at Jack and then they both looked at Johnny.

"I'm warning you Boy. Let justice take its course." Jack commanded.

"That's just what I intend to do."

"Why is it that I don't think you're talking about the same thing as me?" Jack asked.

"I don't know what you mean boss, I really don't."

"Just make sure that you don't do anything stupid. There's no point making Alsina a prison widow just because you can't control your temper."

"I don't have a temper boss."

"You know exactly what I mean. Just be good, please."

"I promise you, I will not do anything stupid. Frank is going down, one way or the other. I really don't care how it happens, but I sure as hell don't want to be looking over my shoulder for the rest of my life." Johnny stated.

Jack let the matter drop as Alsina entered the room and sat on Johnny's lap. He was not at all convinced that the boy would behave, but he could do little about it until nearer the time.

"Congratulations Alsina! I hope you will be very happy."

"How did you know, we were not going to tell anyone." Alsina looked puzzled.

"Just look at his face, it's written all over it. I've known this boy for too many years not to realize when something this important has happened." Jack told her.

"I see. Can I ask you a favour? Please do not let anything slip to my parents. I want to tell them myself."

"My lips are sealed, but I suggest you tell them soon because anyone who knows him will spot that something is different." Jack suggested.

"You make it sound as if I'm a miserable bugger normally, boss."

"I would never call you miserable Johnny, but you have to admit that you don't normally walk around with a smile from ear to ear."

"Fair play, boss. I think he's right sweetheart, perhaps you should tell your mother sooner rather than later." He had changed the direction of his gaze half way through the conversation and now only had eyes for Alsina.

"It might have to wait, as I want to tell her face to face."

"Why don't you both go back to Spain for a bit? In fact you could go too Terry, that would get you out of the way for a while." Jack suggested.

"I don't want to run away from Frank, it sets a bad precedent." Terry shook his head.

"Don't think of it as running away, more of a tactical relocation for personal reasons. I promise to keep you informed of what's happening."

"Will it cause any logistical problems with us keep jetting over there? I have to admit I am starting to feel a bit like a yoyo." Terry asked.

"Don't worry about a thing."

Johnny looked at Alsina. He had already given up on any chance of her staying in Spain and being out of the way for a reasonable length of time. Also, he thought that it would be good for her to spend some time with her parents. He hoped that her parents would give them their blessing. The sooner they told them, the sooner he would know.

"I will do whatever Alsina wants. What do you think sweetheart?"

"I would like to tell them face to face, so I suppose it would be for the best, sweet heart." She had not quite grasped the familiarity with the term sweetheart. Whenever she said it Johnny thought that she meant it literally. He loved the sound of it and was endeared to her even more.

"Right then, sweetheart, we go to Spain."

"One thing though, do you think we're safe from Frank over there? If he has weapons of this calibre over here, wouldn't it stand to reason that he has more on the continent? I don't think that it's worth the risk to Alsina and the Boy if there's any chance of a repeat attack over there."

"Trust me Terry, José is taking care of things over there for you. He will not let you down."

"That's a fair point. He hasn't failed us so far." Terry agreed.

"In that case, I suppose we are going then." Johnny confirmed.

Chapter Sixty Nine

"Any news for me yet?" asked Frank.

"No boss, they've all gone to ground at the moment, but I have an idea." Kevin replied.

"Oh yeah, what's that then?"

"We attack another competitor. They came out for the last two so I am guessing that they will come out for the next one. After that we can just follow them to see where they take us. If they are all together, then we can sort out all of our problems in one go."

"I like your style Kevin. Yes, sort it but don't take too long. I want this finished with soon!"

"It will be done tonight!"

"And let me know what you find out."

As Kevin drove away to sort out the arrangements for that evening, Frank checked his accounts for a final time. Whatever happened he was financially secure and currently had two avenues of escape open to him, should the need arise.

He looked around his temporary headquarters. Through necessity he had been forced to change locations on an almost daily basis. He had even stayed in a Travel Lodge for a few days. He found the anonymity refreshing.

So far this week he had changed his arrangements three times and had had to postpone his intended trip up north. He was getting frustrated because the northern trip would secure a larger power base but he couldn't do anything about it at the moment.

Another growing problem was that his clubs were being raided. He was losing personnel and girls in a way that was becoming increasingly difficult to provide quick replacements.

At the moment he was okay. His competition would not make a move against him after the mortar attacks and were content to wait and see in which direction he would go next.

Jack Fairfax was becoming a problem, but he would deal with him later. Hopefully his problems would lessen with Johnny and Jonathon out of the way. Also, his rivals were waiting to see how he handled things with Jack and, if he came out on top, then he would be the undisputed chief of their world.

Wandering back to his desk he poured himself a drink and savoured it as he waited for the phone to ring. He knew that it would not ring for hours yet but he silently hoped that Kevin would get a move on.

He dozed in his chair for the best part of an hour and then made the effort to get up and take a shower. The last few days had been so up and down that he didn't know whether he was on his arse or his elbow.

Still the phone hadn't rung and he poured himself another drink. He switched on the radio and tuned it to a news station. Nothing had been reported, so far, about any pub bombings. He switched the station to a music programme.

Amy Macdonald came on singing 'This is the life' and he listened to the beat. He had heard somewhere that this song was one of the most downloaded songs of all time. It was strange what one picked up without really listening. He couldn't even tell you where he had heard it.

It must have been an all time hits programme because after about ten more songs, the most requested song ever was played. He sang along to 'Stairway to Heaven' and closed his eyes. He tried to remember where he was when he had first heard it, but he couldn't concentrate and gave up.

All in all, this was not a bad station. He noted the name and frequency for future reference and listened to a few more songs. Finally, he turned off the radio and stalked back to his desk.

He was just about to call Kevin when the phone rang.

"What?"

"Sorted. We're waiting around the corner and I'll let you know when they arrive."

"Make sure the men know that they have to be careful." Frank said.

"Will do. I'm using the same lot as before and they know how to play the game."

"Game… I wish it was that simple." Frank replied.

"Figure of speech boss, you know what I mean."

"Get back to me as soon as!"

"I just wanted to check in with you and to let you know that it had started." Kevin replied.

"Let's hope that we get some movement soon, yeah?"

"Okay Frank, leave it with me."

He hung up the phone and let out a sigh of relief. "At last", he thought, but they had been here before, so he wasn't about to count his chickens.

Chapter Seventy

Walking through Gatwick Airport, Alsina had seen an engagement ring that she liked. Trying to keep his mind from mulling his problems around, Johnny made an impulse buy and Alsina put it on her finger.

Once he was sure that it fitted, he got down on one knee in the shop and formally asked Alsina if she would marry him. Terry started to laugh as Alsina started blushing furiously and tried to pull Johnny up from the floor before anyone noticed.

Johnny refused to get up until she had answered and when she finally said "of course" a little too loudly, he rose in one fluid motion. There was a spontaneous round of applause from the assistants and Alsina went red again.

Pushing him out of the shop she punched his shoulder threatening all manner of punishment and torture. Terry followed them slowly and winked at the assistants as he left, still laughing.

"You old romantic, you."

"Thanks, Terry." Johnny answered.

"Don't encourage him, please. I thought I was going to die of embarrassment in there." Alsina laughed.

"Are you ashamed of me?" Johnny asked.

"Of course I am not. I just was not expecting you to do anything so silly." Alsina was still laughing.

"Neither was I, to be honest. It sort of caught me by surprise too." Johnny said.

"I was impressed anyway little brother. I think you'll make a cracking couple."

"So do I." Johnny and Alsina said it at the same time and all three of them started laughing.

Alsina looked at the people around her and noticed that they too were smiling. More people had seen them than she had first thought, but it did not worry her now that she was over the worst of her embarrassment.

"Ever get the feeling of *déjà vu?*" Terry asked them.

"I know what you mean Terry." Johnny agreed. "How many more times are we going to go back and forth?"

"Well there are at least another two or three flights that I know of." Terry answered.

"Eh, d'you know something that I don't?" Johnny looked enquiringly at his brother.

"Well, you've got the honeymoon for a start." Terry quipped.

Terry ducked as Alsina threw a magazine at him and he started laughing again. This was going better than he had hoped, although secretly, it was what he wanted.

They had not told her parents that they were coming, as Alsina wanted it to be a surprise. She was still not sure what her parents would say, but she hoped that they would be happy.

They reached the boarding gate and queued for the plane. Even the ground stewards and stewardesses now recognized them as frequent flyers.

Once they were seated they settled in to read or sleep and had an uneventful flight. They retrieved the Range Rover again and drove at a leisurely pace to the marina.

The old gate guard smiled warmly at them and lifted the barrier for them to pass through. They stopped and spoke briefly to him and asked if there was any news. Apparently nothing much had happened, so there was nothing to report.

Terry drove up to the back of the Hauffmans' boat and Johnny followed Alsina onto the rear deck. She called out for her mother and watched as the shock was replaced with worry that something bad had happened.

Alsina moved her hand as she spoke to allay her mother's fears and the sun caught her ring and glinted off of the diamond set in its centre.

Her mother's eyes were drawn to the stone and it took a while to take in the meaning of it. When she realized what the ring signified, she cried out in delight and threw her arms around her daughter.

Werner finally came onto the deck and asked what all the noise was about. Alsina proudly held up her hand and her father inspected the ring, smiling.

Johnny walked up to her father and formally asked for his daughter's hand in marriage, which started Alsina blushing again.

"He started doing this today when we bought the ring. He got down on his knee right in front of everybody."

"You must tell me all about it my child. Get the champagne, we are celebrating." Sabine replied.

Terry had been unloading the cases onto the 'Jodast', his boat as it was now. He still could not get used to the fact and thought of all it meant to him and his brother. When he was finished he strolled over to the increasing sounds of festivity on the Hauffmans' boat. They welcomed him with open arms and forced a champagne flute into his empty hand.

They spent the next few hours catching up with what had happened and filling in the gaps for Alsina's parents. They grew solemn for a while when the conversation got around to Davina and Stephen, but her father broke the silence by declaring that he wanted a tour of their new boat.

A Guardia Civil patrol stopped to say hello, but refused the offer of champagne. Five minutes later they were on their way, smiling at the good news.

Both Terry and Johnny knew that there was a security detail nearby, but as yet had not spotted them. They assumed that José was using his own people more now and hoped that he would make contact.

They carried the party on to the restaurant in the marina. Nobody wanted to cook, so it had been an easy choice. Yet another bottle of champagne appeared courtesy of the house and they ordered while they sipped it.

They noticed a lone woman sitting at a table a few down from theirs and invited her to join the celebration. Being new to the area, she accepted and her accent gave her away immediately to the brothers.

"Whereabouts in Liverpool are you from, love?"

"Knowsley. How could you tell?"

"I think it might have had something to do with your accent, not sure though."

"That would be southern humour would it?"

"What did she say Terry? Does she come with subtitles?" Johnny asked.

They laughed and toasted Johnny and Alsina.

"Where are you staying?" Terry asked her.

"My partner and I have just bought a place above the marina, although we've had a place down the coast for years."

"That's nice, is he coming down as well?"

"No, he's working in England at the moment, so I'm on me tod."

"You're welcome to eat with us if you like. It can't be much fun on your own here." Johnny offered.

"Thanks, that would be great, I'll pay my own way though." The woman offered.

"Whatever you're happy with."

They ordered food and chatted as though they had been friends for years. Her name was Sandra and Alsina hoped to see more of her in the time that she was here, as she seemed really lovely.

After the meal, Sandra said goodbye and walked to her taxi. She had imbibed a little more than she had expected to and decided that walking the five hundred metres to her house was beyond her at that moment. The others carried on celebrating and eventually headed for home at just after midnight.

Alsina hugged her parents tightly as they said goodnight and her mother kissed Johnny goodnight too. Then they walked back to the 'Jodast' and headed for their cabins. They had drunk enough to forego a nightcap and all expected to sleep soundly.

Terry received a message from Jack saying that he hoped they had enjoyed the meal and that security was in place. He also mentioned that Sandra's story checked out and there would be no problems there.

Terry asked for an update on the situation and then asked again, when his boss went silent.

"They hit another pub tonight. Fifteen dead and nearly as many wounded."

"Do you want us back?" Terry asked.

"No, stay there, there's nothing you can do. Jonathon is sorting it out for me. I'll let you know more in the morning."

"Are you sure you don't need me back?" Terry was keen to get back in the action.

"Goodnight Terry, sleep well."

"Goodnight."

Terry turned swiftly around when he heard the soft footfall behind him, reaching for his gun at the same time.

"You okay Terry? You're a bit jumpy." Johnny eyed the pistol as his brother put it away again.

"Yeah, that was Jack, they hit another one tonight."

"Are we going back?" It was Johnny's turn to ask.

"Not yet, Jonathon's sorting it."

"Are they sure?" Johnny continued.

"He just said 'goodnight' and hung up."

"Nothing we can do then. Goodnight." With that he turned and walked away, leaving Terry silently thanking Alsina again for coming into his brother's life.

Chapter Seventy One

"Right, Jonathon Pearce is here but that is all. No sign of Fairfax, Terry or Tommy Rooke." Kevin spoke quietly into the phone.

"Has Pearce left yet?" Frank demanded.

"Not yet but we have him covered when he does." Kevin replied.

"Just make sure they don't show themselves."

"Trust me, boss."

"Maybe Pearce will lead us to the others." Frank said more to himself than to Kevin.

"Let's hope so, boss. I'll let you know when I have something more."

"You do that!"

"Gotta go, Tommy has just turned up." Kevin started to close his phone.

"Ring me later."

Kevin cut the connection and concentrated on the arrival of Tommy Rooke. He made doubly certain that he wasn't seen.

He watched as Tommy walked over to Jonathon and started talking. Then Tommy waited while Jonathon spoke into his phone, nodding as Jonathon repeated what he was hearing.

Kevin wished that he could hear that conversation or at least this half of it. He was pretty sure that it was Fairfax on the other end and any information would be welcome now.

After about an hour, Tommy drove Jonathon back to headquarters and they remained there for the rest of the night. Kevin didn't know it but Jonathon had fallen asleep at his desk in the early hours of the morning.

Both Tommy and Jonathon now had a change of clothes at the office and they used these the next day as they moved around the town, heading back to the crime scene and then returning to the office.

Kevin had to change his men out four times to make sure that they did not stand out to Jonathon and Tommy. They settled down to wait late into the afternoon and realized that it was going to be a long one when the pizza delivery moped turned up.

Kevin had been to see Frank briefly during the day and kept him abreast of the situation as it unfolded. Both he and his boss had now not slept for nearly forty-eight hours and it was starting to show.

Kevin hoped that they would get a break soon, as he tried to catch a couple of hours of shut eye in the back of the small family saloon that they were currently using to follow Jonathon. He had had better days.

Chapter Seventy Two

The following morning the brothers and Alsina went out for a jog. Alsina assumed that the other people out exercising were part of the security team but the brothers knew this for a fact.

They got back to the boat and showered before changing for the day ahead. Alsina's mother wanted to take her shopping today, so they piled into the Range Rover and headed for the nearest retail park.

They hit the cafés first for a late breakfast and as much coffee as they could stomach. They laughed and joked and Johnny smiled when he saw Alsina's mother try to slip her fifty Euros spending money.

"I have my own money now Mama."

"I am sorry. I forget that you work now. You have a good job." Sabine still held the money.

"I haven't told you everything that happened in England yet." Alsina had to think about what she was going to say.

"Why?" Her mother's tone sounded cautious as if more bad news was coming.

"Davina and Stephen named me in their will."

"That was nice of them. Did they leave you a lot?" Sabine asked.

"I think they left me pretty much everything, except the boat." Alsina replied.

"What?" Sabine looked incredulous.

"That is what we all thought." Alsina added.

"How much is everything?"

"I think at the moment it is close to four… maybe five million pounds."

The colour drained from her mother's face as she listened to her daughter. She knew that Davina had liked Alsina a lot but to do this for her was incredible.

"What are you going to do with all that money? I mean, I hope that you are going to talk to someone about savings and things." Sabine's maternal mode cut in.

"They have a great accountant at the club and their solicitor will handle everything for me, he is really nice Mama."

"Just make sure they know what they are doing!" Sabine did not know what to say.

"Yes… um… do you and Papa need anything? I mean, you don't need any bills paid or anything like that?"

"My darling, it is a lovely offer, but you do not need to worry about us. It is your money. Use it wisely. We still want to pay for the wedding though, I think it is important for your father."

Alsina rolled her eyes up into her forehead. She had forgotten how old-fashioned her father could be. Of course he would want to pay for the wedding. If she couldn't stop him, then she would make sure that it was a small affair.

They finished their breakfast and wandered aimlessly around the boutiques. Well, to Johnny and Terry it appeared aimless. To the girls it was exactly how they used to shop when Alsina still lived in the marina.

After a couple of hours, the party broke for lunch at one of the bistro type affairs in the food court. There was plenty to choose from and something of a holiday atmosphere descended on them for a few hours.

Later, they headed home and met up with Werner to have a drink. Alsina finally got to tell him about the money and they argued briefly about the wedding costs. Alsina was not too worried either way, as it seemed likely it would be a long way off and so she would have time to work on her father.

Terry was in regular contact with his boss, but there was nothing earth shattering to report.

They headed back to the restaurant for the evening meal, but it was a rather subdued affair compared with the previous evening. There was no sign of Sandra, but Alsina was sure they would see her again.

They laughed and joked with the waitresses, who had known them all for some time now and nodded at fellow customers. Although Johnny seemed relaxed enough, there was a tension about him that Terry and Alsina picked up on.

They finished earlier than the previous night and headed back to the boats. Marina life could be both glamorous and dull at the same time.

Chapter Seventy Three

In stark contrast to the brothers, Jonathon had spent the day sifting through rubble with forensics and searching for clues. They already knew that Frank was targeting the competition, but they did not know that this attack had been brought forward with the sole intention of flushing him and Johnny into the line of fire.

They had left the office and headed for the crime scene early. Jonathon decided that he would keep Tommy close to him for a while, so they asked a colleague to collect some things from their homes so that they could keep on top of things at the office.

Jonathon spent the night working in the office comparing evidence and trying to link the events together as best he could. Tommy was chasing the errands that Jonathon needed in the office. Tommy didn't mind, as they worked well together.

The next day was spent mostly on the phone, liaising with different departments. Having seen the devastating effects of the mortar, they prioritised finding out who supplied it and who was operating it. Hopefully they could kill two birds with one stone, if the seller supplied the operators as well.

The day ticked over smoothly, but agonizingly slowly. Tommy took advantage of the shooting range in the cellar to hone his skills. As time wore on he realized just how much he had missed working there.

After a few hours Jonathon joined him and blew the cobwebs out of his system. It was very tempting to return to work here. Running his small empire was nowhere near as exhilarating as chasing down criminals.

The fact that Jonathon and Tommy were good at their jobs was evident and it didn't take long for personnel on other cases to ask their thoughts on different matters. In the old days it had been a toss-up who would eventually replace Jack when or if he retired. The only two candidates were Terry and Jonathon.

Jonathon and Terry's friendship was not marred by the competition but enhanced by it. The only thing that had destroyed their relationship was the incident with Johnny. When Jonathon had been fired Terry became the only runner. Most of the department now looked up to him and his leadership skills were excellent.

Some of the staff weren't sure what would happen if Jonathon came back. They were not to know that Terry had already asked Jonathon if he would come back or that Terry had told him that he would gladly work as second in command to him. Terry had confidence in himself, but he was honest enough to admit that Jonathon was better.

All this was of course hypothetical, as Jack did not look to be retiring anytime in the near future. The rate things were going, Johnny would be the next boss of the department but in the way distant future.

Frustrated with getting seemingly nowhere, Jonathon called Terry and gave him an update. "Thing is mate, I can't see why they needed to bomb the place. Things were turning their way and it wouldn't have been long until they had it all sewn up."

"There has to be another reason that we aren't seeing. What could they gain from mindless killing?" Terry thought the problem through as he answered.

"Nothing really, other than to see how they responded, or to see how we responded."

"But we did nothing out of the ordinary, did we?" Terry asked.

"Not really. The only change we made was not letting you stay to investigate the sites." Jonathon replied.

"Yeah… but that was only a precaution."

"Yeah, nothing came of it. There were no attacks on you or Johnny."

"Nothing at all, unless…" Terry went quiet.

"What?"

"Supposing we were seen at the attack site. We know they are looking for you and us, perhaps they saw us, but I left too quickly?"

"Thin, but plausible. Actually, now I think about it, I did get the idea that I was being followed the other night." Jonathon conceded.

"What? You never said anything."

Jonathon sighed, "Well I had already found out that I wasn't. I took some counter measures but no one fell for them. After that I was especially aware of what was behind me at all times and unless they had a multi-vehicle tail running, I am sure there was no one there."

"What made you think that you were being tailed in the first place?" Terry asked him.

"You know… the usual. A gut feeling, something was not quite right. I don't know."

"Might be an idea to use Tommy as a blocker. There aren't many better than him, or has he lost his edge?"

"Don't you worry about Tommy mate, he can still hold his own." Jonathon had a touch of pride in his voice.

"Will he come back to us do you think?"

"I don't know. I hope so."

"What, you don't mind that you would be on your own, or are you coming back as well?" Terry hoped he knew the answer.

"The jury is still out on that one mate. I really don't know what will happen. Let's get this mess sorted first and then I will see."

"Fair play." Terry yawned.

"Anything new with you lot?"

"We went shopping." Terry yawned again.

"Nice."

"Exactly."

"No, seriously, what have you been up to?"

"No, *seriously*, we went shopping."

"What all day?" Jonathon sounded amazed. "I've been shopping with you before and it takes less than ten minutes, that's if you stop to use the loo or something."

"Let me put it this way, I now know more about ladies fashion than I knew before, in fact I now know more than I ever wanted to know."

"Oh right, you went with Alsina."

"And her mum." Terry added.

"Nice."

"Actually it wasn't too bad. Food was good too and Alsina is a sweet kid."

"The Boy has done well for himself there." Jonathon grinned.

"You know what? I think he finally realizes that."

"Always was a bit slow on the uptake that one... a bit like his brother." Jonathon waited for the answer that he knew was coming.

"Piss off and do some work."

"I'll call you when I know something more."

"Good luck mate." Terry was still laughing.

"And you. See you mate."

"And Jonathon, don't forget to use Tommy tomorrow. If there is a problem, he will find it. At least we'll know that we aren't paranoid."

"Even paranoids have enemies." Jonathon hung up the phone and laughed out loud to himself just as Tommy walked in.

"Second sign of madness that, mate." Tommy joked.

"What's the first?"

"Telling yourself the joke in the first place."

"Very funny Tommy. I was just talking to Terry. He thinks that you should shadow me around tomorrow to see if I am being followed."

"No problem. Do you think that you are?"

"Not certain, maybe. It can't hurt to be sure though, eh?"

"What do I do if you are?" Tommy asked.

"Let me know and then follow them when they get off."

"If you're right it might speed things up, funny, but I thought the same thing today myself."

"Why didn't you say anything?" Jonathon looked interested.

"I was going to check it out tomorrow." Tommy smiled.

Chapter Seventy Four

"Nothing, absolutely nothing." Kevin sighed as he gave Frank the news.

"What, you spent all day tailing him and we are no closer to finding out where they are?"

"Sorry boss!"

"Do you think that he sussed the tail?" Frank sounded concerned.

"No, I am pretty sure we are okay. I think it was just a busy day for him."

"No sign of Terry or Johnny?" Frank asked half-heartedly. Already knowing that he'd have been told if there was.

"Not a thing."

"Have you got anyone watching the office, perhaps they are stuck there."

"Can't do a lot without drawing too much attention. You know the set up there."

"Fair enough. Any ideas?" Frank waited for some good news.

"I think that they have gone to ground. Perhaps they realized that Terry was too high profile."

"What worries me more is where the hell Johnny has been!"

"Yeah, from what you said I would have imagined that he would be hunting you high and low at the moment." Kevin nodded slowly.

"He should be. Unless he's radically changed and I can't see that personally."

"Don't worry boss, we'll find them soon enough."

"Not soon enough for my liking."

"Anything happen while I've been out of the loop?" Kevin wanted to know.

"Nothing for you to worry about. Do me a favour and stay focused. I have to know where they are."

"At the risk of repeating myself, leave it with me."

"Right then, call me when you have news."

Frank looked around his office. He had moved premises, yet again. He was thinking of his misfortune, or rather his mistake at not realizing that Terry and Jonathon would be at the original bombsite. He should have planned for that contingency. That was a major slip up.

He started theorizing again, going through the 'what ifs'. If he killed Terry first, then he was sure to get Johnny's attention, but did he really need that kind of trouble.

He thought again about what happened when he had stabbed Johnny. Surely he should have died. It could only have been luck that he was not a corpse now. Had he made a mistake with his knife work? Maybe he was getting too old for this. All he knew for sure was that he must get it right this time.

Johnny's behaviour was worrying though. Johnny ought to be hunting high and low for him by now. He needed information and he needed it quickly. He liked to know all the moves on the board before committing his pawns.

He couldn't risk trying to contact any of his people in Jack Fairfax's organisation. It had taken a while, but he now realized that Jack was aware of the informants.

The false intelligence was now too obvious to miss. He had thought that his people were well hidden. Those people had been loyal to Jack in the past but the money he had thrown around had worked wonders. This had allowed him to stay one step ahead, up until now.

Someone in his crew had talked. It was inevitable really, but he had hoped that it would have happened later rather than sooner. He needed to find out who was grassing and stop them. He could not rule out anyone, whether they had been pulled in for questioning or not, but it stood to reason that someone had been offered a deal.

He made a telephone call and arranged to have one of the new girls brought over. He would product test here tonight, so that he was on top of things. Kevin would hopefully be ringing with the good news any time now, so he might as well enjoy himself.

If the worst came to the worst, he could always take Jonathon out first and then have a go at the others. Surely Terry would need to return if Jonathon was taken out of play. The question now was how he would do it? Should it be a big grandstand play or something a bit subtler that would make Jack think before coming after him?

The arrival of the girl distracted him and he let his thoughts wander as she slowly undressed first herself and then him. This should be a good night. So far he had said nothing to her and she had used her initiative. She would go far.

Chapter Seventy Five

Terry walked into the galley and put the small coffee machine to work. Johnny walked in about five minutes later and they each sat silently contemplating the situation while they sipped their coffee.

"Any thoughts, Terry?"

"None to speak of."

"What did Jonathon have to say?"

"Too much and nothing relevant." Terry finally answered.

"You spent all that time on the phone for nothing?"

"He thinks he is being followed and I have to admit, from what he said, that he could be right. We will know more about what's going on later today."

"Tommy?"

"Yep." Terry nodded.

"He *is* the best. Do you think he will come back to us?"

"Who knows, Jonathon wants him to."

"What will he do if Tommy does come back?"

"Hopefully Jonathon will come back too."

"Are you happy with that Terry?" Johnny was curious.

"Actually, yes. It helps to know that it probably wasn't his fault that you got shot and that I might have overreacted a bit."

"Understandable, I suppose. You were very hard on him and he did save my life."

"I know, what can I say? I was out of order." Terry shrugged.

"Have you told him?"

"Not in so many words but he knows how I feel."

"Will he work for you?"

"I'll work for him, he's better at planning than me." Terry said flatly.

"Bloody hell mate! I never believed that I would see the day when you thought that."

"Got to be honest Boy, it might just keep us alive."

Alsina walked in and they set the machine to go again. They toyed with the idea of cooking, but decided against it. They would go to the restaurant and get something there. It wasn't the cheapest, but the food was superb and none of them needed to worry about money now.

They headed back to their cabins to change into their running gear. A short blast before breakfast would see them right. Alsina popped across to her parents' boat to see if they wanted to join them for a change, but her offer was declined.

They warmed up and headed for the beach. It had turned out nice again, but then it normally did. That was one of the lovely things about living in Spain. They nodded to the runners that had loosely followed them before. They blended in well, but now she knew what to look for, Alsina could see them for what they really were, bodyguards.

The run went uneventfully and they quickly showered and changed again for breakfast. They ran into Sandra in the restaurant and had a brief chat. They agreed to take her out on the boat at some stage, as she had lived on the coast for a while and had never been out on a boat. Then they made their way back to the 'Jodast'.

Alsina rang Bernie Holt to check on the club. They had reopened and he was managing it for her. Actually he was now a twenty percent owner, as one of the suggestions that Davina had made in the list she had left with the solicitor was that he should get something.

Johnny had been in agreement, as he thought the club was in very safe hands. He liked Bernie and he knew also that his boss respected Bernie and that was good enough for him.

"The club is doing well and Bernie says to say hello to you two."

"How is he? Any trouble while we've been away?" Johnny asked her.

"Nothing that he spoke of, I suppose that you could ring next time just to be sure though, Johnny."

"If there was anything wrong, then he would have told you. I know that he respects you, so don't worry." Johnny said firmly.

"Do you think the rest of the staff do? I mean, most of them have been there for years and now I come along and take over."

"Sweetheart, they love you. Everybody loves you. You are lovely."

"But do they think that I will be good for the club?" Alsina wanted to know.

"Of course, you did the best thing possible when you made Bernie a partner, and have any of them said that they want to leave?"

"Well, no, but still…"

"Just stop worrying about it, you are doing fine!"

"Oh!" Alsina could not think of anything else to say.

"What are the plans for the rest of the day?"

"I thought we could go shopping again." She laughed as she watched his face drop and then added "Ten Pin Bowling."

"That will make a change, we can try and get your Mum and Dad to come and see if Sandra can make up a partner for Terry."

"I hope Mrs. Hoon won't get jealous." They both laughed at that. Terry had still not openly told them anything about his relationship with Mrs. Hoon. They were still laughing when he came in.

"Do you fancy a bit of bowling mate?" Johnny asked.

"Blinding, who's going?"

"We thought the three of us, Mum, Dad and Sandra." Alsina had spent so much time with

Johnny now, that some of his mannerisms were washing off on her. Though she still spoke quite formally on occasion, at other times she spoke like a Londoner. "That's if it won't upset Mrs. Hoon?"

"Don't you worry about that love, you just make the invitations."

"Okay, how are we going to get there? There are too many of us to fit in the car."

"We can take your parent's car too and maybe Sandra can ride with them." Terry replied.

"Right, I will go and ask them now, I won't be a minute."

Alsina came back looking slightly unhappy. Johnny looked up and wondered what could be wrong.

"My parents have to go to Germany today, my aunt is very ill."

"That's a shame sweetheart. Are you going with them?" Johnny gave her a hug.

"No, I do not really know her."

"Anything we can do? We don't have to go bowling if you don't fancy it now." Terry offered.

"No, it is fine. It will probably help to take my mind off of things."

"Did you get hold of Sandra?" Johnny asked.

"Yes, she can't come either."

"Then it is just us sweetheart, don't worry I'll go easy on you." Johnny laughed.

Alsina smiled as she remembered the ten nil thrashing that she had given him on their last outing to the bowling centre. He had said the same thing to her then, not realizing that there were only a few things that interested her over here and bowling was one of them. Consequentially she played a lot and was very good at it.

"Don't hold back on my account, sweet heart." She retorted.

Terry laughed as he too remembered the thrashing that his brother had received. They took their time getting ready and checked to see if Alsina's parents were leaving straight away, or whether they would still be there when they got back.

Werner and Sabine were leaving within the next couple of hours so they said their goodbyes. Johnny offered to drive them to the airport, but they decided to leave their car there, as they did not know when they would be coming back.

Johnny, Terry and Alsina drove out of the marina and the security team slotted in behind them. They were like an ever-present shadow now and it was a comforting thought for Alsina.

The drive to the bowling alley took no time at all and they spent the afternoon having fun and generally getting beaten by Alsina.

"It's a good thing you don't shoot like you bowl, Boy."

"You can talk Terry, I've seen a two year old bowl better than you did today." Johnny grinned back.

After bowling they headed for a DVD shop to rent a film for the evening and it wasn't until they got back to the boat, that Alsina found out that Johnny had swapped 'Save the last dance for me' for 'Jaws'. She groaned and shook her head slowly.

"Sweet heart, that is so childish. You know I want to go diving this week." Alsina pouted.

"You have nothing to fear, they kill the shark at the end of the film. Oh! Sorry, I spoiled the ending for you." Johnny grinned.

"Very funny."

"Seriously, they are more scared of us than we are of them." Johnny informed her.

"You speak for yourself, if I saw a shark I would walk on water to get away."

"We aren't lucky enough to get any sharks close in to the shore." Johnny said quietly.

"You know that you actually sound sad about that!" Alsina said in disbelief.

"I suppose I am really, they are wonderful creatures and even though I love the film, it did a lot of harm to their reputation."

"Johnny, I am sure that they don't make good pets and I really do not want to be bitten on my bottom."

"I wouldn't blame a shark for doing that, I'd like to." Johnny smirked.

Alsina laughed and slapped him playfully around the head. Having gone straight to the galley when they got back, Terry shouted out that dinner was ready.

They sat down to eat and Alsina asked if it was one of Mrs. Hoon's recipes.

"Actually it is. That woman is the best cook I have ever met." Terry admitted.

"Why don't you invite her over?" Alsina suggested.

"Actually, I might just do that. It's boring playing third wheel to you two sometimes, love you dearly though I do." Terry replied.

"Great, it will be fantastic to have her over, what do you think, Johnny?" Alsina looked at him expectantly.

"Yeah! Fantastic, we can eat properly at last." Johnny sounded delighted.

"That is not what I meant and you know it." Alsina chided him.

Johnny smiled and swallowed a mouthful of shepherd's pie. Though both he and his brother could cook, he relished the idea of Mrs. Hoon coming over.

"Does anyone fancy a quick drink before we watch the film?" Terry asked.

"Yes, please Terry, have we still got that rum left?" Johnny enquired.

"That sounds like a nice idea, thanks Terry. I will have the same as Johnny." Alsina noticed that Terry was still not that forthcoming about his relationship with Mrs. Hoon.

They finished the meal and poured out a generous measure of rum. Then they settled in for the film. Because they had all seen the film before, they talked over it in places and compared diving styles and then dive sites with sharks.

Alsina was amazed that the brothers had actually dived with sharks before and more so that they liked the experience.

"It's true what I say sweetheart, they are actually more scared of us than we are of them. Most attacks are mistakes."

"I will take your word for it." Alsina still sounded doubtful.

They continued watching the film and then caught up with the Spanish television news. The situation in England had made the international news. Mortar bombs in Mainland U.K. were big news any day.

Terry rang Jack and was told that there were no new leads. Tommy had not checked in, but they were not worried about that too much. Terry hoped that Tommy would report soon, as he sensed that something had changed, but couldn't put his finger on what exactly.

They all sat around the boat sipping their rum and waited for a follow up call from Jack. When the phone rang it was Jonathon, not Jack, who was on the other end.

"It was a good call to use Tommy."

"What did he find?" Terry asked.

"I am being followed and he was able to follow them undetected. At the moment we have a warehouse under observation and we are awaiting developments, as they say."

"Any sign of Frank?" Terry sounded hopeful.

"Not yet, but this looks very promising indeed. We did see the bloke who the Spanish put us on to."

"What, that Daniels character?"

"That's what it said on the passport, but we think it's a fake."

"Still… he must be high up in the organisation or something, surely." Terry said thoughtfully.

"We'll have to wait and see. Tommy swapped out with an overnight team and they are logging everything that moves." Jonathon replied.

"Will they stand out?"

"No, they are in a warehouse down the street. It's empty, but has great 'eyes on' so we should be good."

"What does Tommy think?"

"He says that they are very good, and from him, that's high praise indeed."

"He actually used those words?" Terry was impressed.

"Yes."

"Fuck, they must be good then."

"Precisely." Jonathon agreed.

"Anything else going on, any leads?"

"Nothing much but it's looking like this attack was intended to draw us out, well you in particular."

"Well it worked to a point, they know you are working with us now." Terry said calmly.

"That's the shame of it. I should have thought of that."

"You can't think of everything mate." Terry consoled Jonathon.

"I used to be better than this."

"Mate, you are still the best in the business, whether you work for us or not."

"Cheers, mate. I appreciate that. Doesn't stop me thinking I fucked up though." The regret in Jonathon's voice was obvious.

"You recovered it well, you found the warehouse, so let it go."

"Hmmm. How are the Boy and the 'beautiful one'?"

"They're good. They bring out the best in one another." Terry told him.

"You can't help but like her. Shame she hasn't got any sisters."

"They say 'hi,' by the way. Do you want to speak to them? They're right next to me."

"Hint taken. No, just say 'hi' back and I'll let you know as soon as anything happens over here."

"Anytime, day or night. We want to know as soon as you know." Terry said firmly.

"No problem, speak to you soon mate."

"Yeah, bye."

Although they had heard most of the call, Terry went over the important bits for the benefit of the other two.

"Do you really think they killed those people just to bring you out in the open?" Alsina could not believe it.

"It looks that way sweetheart. At least something good has come out of it though, we have a strong lead."

"But will it be enough? I don't like feeling that people are getting hurt because of us." Alsina added.

"Nothing we can do about it though. If we were dead, they would still be hurting or killing people. It's the nature of the business." Terry took a deep breath and let it out slowly.

"It's horrible." She buried her face in Johnny's chest and he absently stroked her hair while he whispered that it was all going to work out.

Terry caught Johnny's eye and mouthed, "Is she alright?"

Johnny only nodded and smiled so as not to disturb her. Everyone in his organisation was impressed with how well Alsina was coping. Men or women, some people couldn't cope well with being a target.

"Let's have an early night. We'll all be fresher in the morning. Sleep well both of you." Terry walked to his cabin.

"Yeah, why not. How about a dive tomorrow sweetheart?" Johnny gave Alsina a huge smile.

"Oh, very funny." Alsina was not impressed.

"It was only a thought."

"Do you want me to sleep on my parents' boat?" Alsina smiled back at Johnny.

"Only joking sweetheart, let's not be too hasty." Johnny tried to backtrack.

"Anyway if a huge man eating shark attacks in the marina tonight and sinks your parents' boat, we won't be able to save you." Terry added from the doorway.

"Shut up Terry. He was only joking sweetheart, don't listen to him." Johnny retorted.

"Sweet dreams." Terry said over his shoulder.

"Good night Terry. You are not funny by the way." Alsina couldn't help but smile as she spoke. Terry winked at her and entered his cabin.

"I promise you can choose the film tomorrow." Johnny offered.

"You don't get off the hook that easily sweet heart." Alsina whispered.

"Come to bed and I'll make it up to you." Smiled Johnny

"Hmmm." She allowed Johnny to lead her into their cabin and closed the door.

The next few days blurred into each other again and her parents returned after a week. They had a meal on the 'Jodast' to celebrate the return to good health of her aunt. After the meal, they fell into the routine that they had been following on and off since returning to Spain. They watched the latest film releases and sipped rum and coke, as they gently relaxed and hoped for more news from Jack or Jonathon.

One night after watching yet another newly released film, they went to bed and it seemed like they had only just dropped off when the phone rang in Terry's cabin.

Yawning loudly they knocked on his door and looked expectantly at Terry. He nodded and spoke into the phone before ending the call.

"They've got Frank. They saw him briefly and they are planning to hit him in the morning."

"Are they sure?"

"Oh yes, Jack was there when they saw him. There's absolutely no mistake."

"Finally!" Johnny punched the air.

"They go in at 06.00 so we should know fairly soon."

"What happens if he leaves beforehand?" Johnny asked.

"Tommy is back there now. Nothing can go wrong. He won't get away."

"Not long to go now. No point in going back to bed is there?" Johnny said.

"No, put the coffee machine on. We may as well be comfortable."

Chapter Seventy Six

"Any news Kevin?"

"We followed him all day. It was a repeat of yesterday. Crime scene, office and then crime scene."

"Fuck it! Take him out tomorrow. Let's see if we can bring Terry out in the open." Frank had had enough.

"How do you want to do it boss?"

"Same way we tried last time, 203."

"Won't he be expecting that?"

"Not this soon. Tell whoever you choose to do it, in the morning. I don't want any chance of this slipping out tonight."

"Consider it done. Right then, where do you want it done?" Kevin waited for an answer.

"When he surfaces from the office tomorrow morning. I want to make a statement to Jack Fairfax and put the fear of God into his people. Terry won't be able to resist coming out for that."

"I like your style, boss, but that's a bit risky, isn't it?"

"Not really. Pump a shed load of 203 rounds into the office at the same time. Might as well make the most of the opportunity, eh?" Frank smiled.

"Fair enough. You sure you don't want me to do it?"

"No, just in case it goes tits up."

"They left the office at ten this morning, so assuming they'll be following the same routine, I will be in at eight o'clock to prepare the men."

"Stay here tonight, it'll be easier." Frank told him.

"You're the boss."

"Yes, I am. Get the girls back in, we may as well enjoy ourselves."

"It's a hard life."

"Not after tomorrow it's not." Frank smiled.

They decided to keep most of their crew at the warehouse that night. They told nobody what they had planned, so they weren't worried about a leak, but it made sense to have everyone ready for the morning.

Unbeknown to them, Jack's people recorded the arrival of the girls, as well as the arrival of the rest of their men. Frank's men didn't get much sleep that night, but the girls proved a pleasant distraction.

The little industrial estate was a hive of activity. Frank's people were used to the estate working through the night so didn't pay too much attention, which was a shame for them, as the same could not be said of Jack's people, who took note of everything.

Chapter Seventy Seven

The sights and sounds of daily life started filtering through to those in the warehouse. Lorries started their engines and warmed up while the drivers collected the day's worksheets from the dispatch offices.

The breakfast van pulled up and started selling fried egg rolls and coffee like it was going out of fashion. There were always new faces in the queue so the increase in sales, which, by the end of the day, would amount to nearly double the normal day's takings, was not readily noticeable.

At two warehouses, small minibuses and people carriers were being warmed up. Breakfast rolls were passed around and everyone ate their fill. Coffee was passed around following the food and was warmly received.

Similar actions were taking place at both sites. Weapons were being checked and rechecked. One site differed in the equipment being checked.

Body armour was being strapped into place and ballistic shields were being carried.

Police firearms units were in place and out of sight, waiting for the call to action. Dog units were around the periphery waiting for their final orders.

Kevin Daniels called over to two of his men. They followed him into the boss' office and looked at the grenade launchers on the desk and then at Frank and Kevin.

"Got a special job for you two." Kevin looked at them.

"What do you need us to do?"

"It's quite simple really. Take out Jonathon Pearce as he leaves his office this morning. Then, when you are sure that you got him, hammer the fucking place until you run out of ammo."

"Are you serious?" The two men thought he had gone mad.

Frank watched in silence.

"Always." Kevin replied.

"Fucking hell Kevin, if we get caught…"

"Well don't get fucking caught!"

The two men remained silent. They were not happy with their assignment for the day. They didn't mind bombing a pub, but to go to war with Jack Fairfax was another thing entirely.

"Are you alright with this or do I have to get someone else?"

"No, we're good." They finally agreed.

"Well fuck off then and don't come back until it's done, you hear me?"

"Yeah."

"Good, tell the others to start packing the place up, we're moving later this morning. Ring me when it's done and I'll tell you where we'll be." Kevin told them.

"You need anything else?"

Kevin looked at the men to see if they were being sarcastic, before answering in the negative.

The two men collected the weapons from the desk and checked to see if they were loaded. Finding that they were, they carefully carried them to their vehicle and shouted to one of the others to open the gates. As they passed a small group of their colleagues, they told them to start packing up.

They were just closing the rear doors of the Toyota Corolla when the gates started to open. Before they were halfway open, a Police Land Rover crashed into them and sent them flying towards the loading bay.

Armed response units and mini buses, both marked and unmarked, followed the Land Rover into the yard and armed officers jumped out of them.

"Armed Police, stay where you are!"

All hell broke loose as Frank's people went for their weapons and opened fire. The Police returned fire with a devastating success rate.

Frank's people ran for cover in the warehouse and held out for as long as they could.

Taser guns were deployed as well as live ammunition. The two men tasked with killing Jonathon Pearce reached for their weapons. Seeing the 203 launchers the Police had no option but to shoot to kill.

"It's Fairfax, boss. I don't know how but he found us." Kevin was anxious.

"Impossible!" Frank shouted.

"You have to face facts boss. It can't be coincidence can it?"

"Right get the two brothers that replaced you when you were in Spain, we're out of here." Frank had calmed down a little.

"What about the rest of them?"

"Fuck them. There won't be any left at this rate and we can't take them all."

"What are we taking with us?" Kevin almost shouted the question.

"Just personal weapons and the four of us. Chuck a couple of grenades at the fuel pump when we go. That should get their attention and keep them busy while we have it away."

"What about the papers and weapons that we have here? What about the money?" Kevin could not believe that Frank would leave any money in the warehouse.

"Leave it, I can get more. The fire will destroy most of it and I haven't got anything too incriminating here. Come on, you're wasting time and I really don't want to be here when Fairfax comes waltzing through the front doors."

Kevin searched for the brothers, but found them already engaged in a gun battle. Running back to his boss, he shook his head and pulled the pins on the grenades.

He threw two towards the fuel pumps and a third towards the office. He had thought about letting the fuel take care of the office, but decided against it. The explosions followed rapidly and he threw another high explosive grenade towards the fuel pumps, just to make sure.

Frank was already waiting in the little access tunnel they had carved out into the next warehouse. He owned both properties, but nobody knew this other than Kevin.

They had set up a stack of tyres to cover their escape route. When the flames caught hold of them it would be hours before it was cool enough to search for bodies.

Breathing heavily and sweating in the close confines of the tunnel, he and Kevin ran to the exit and hurried to the waiting Ford Fiesta. Frank drove while Kevin constantly searched for some sign of pursuit, but he could find none.

Their luck held as they negotiated the covered alley into yet another warehouse. Frank owned this one too, under yet another alias.

Chapter Seventy Eight

Jack was walking towards the warehouse building, dodging bullets that ricocheted off the vehicles surrounding him. He felt a slight tug and looked down at his chest. He was thankful that he had put on his body armour this morning, as he looked at the small hole that had just appeared in his Puffa Jacket.

Sporadic fire was being returned from various approaches to the warehouse and from the warehouse itself.

The Police were shouting commands to surrender and some of the men did, which was a bonus for Jack. There was still a sustained barrage of fire from inside the building and Jack kept his head down while he waited for it to be dealt with.

Jonathon looked over at him and grinned as he and Tommy crouched down behind one of the armed response units. Jack heard the muffled explosions inside the building and started to get concerned with what sort of firepower they were up against. His line of thought lasted about four seconds as the cloud of petrol gas, which had been released when the first explosions occurred, suddenly ignited due to the high explosive charge.

The men in the building were decimated and all the remaining windows blew out at once. Police officers outside the building were thrown to the floor as the blast wave took out the warehouse doors. The vehicles that Jack and Jonathon were hiding behind rocked on their springs from the violent backlash.

What was left of the contents of the warehouse was now burning fiercely, emitting a dense black smoke. Jack couldn't be sure but he thought that he smelled rubber burning.

The Police were pulled back and the wounded treated while the fire brigade arrived and dealt with the conflagration. Jack cursed his luck as he waited for the confirmation that Frank Underwood was among the dead or injured. As the fire burnt on, he called Terry to give him an update.

He knew that Terry wanted to know that Frank was under arrest or dead but he had to admit that nothing could be confirmed. He told him that he would call him as soon as he knew something definite and beckoned Jonathon over to him as he ended the call on his mobile.

"Anything they can tell us?" He indicated the survivors of Frank's little band.

"Nothing boss, we are questioning all of the survivors, but nobody knows anything for sure."

"When can we get inside to verify things?"

"Not for a good few hours yet. After the fire service have finished the bomb squad have to go in to make sure there are no little surprises." Jonathon was constantly looking around as he spoke.

"What about thermal imaging? Have the heli's got anything at all for us?"

"All they can say for sure is that there were people inside when it kicked off. They lost the trace as soon as the bombs went off." Jonathon had kept abreast of developments as they unfolded.

"Bombs?"

"Probably grenades. The last one must have been high explosive and acted as a daisy cutter when the fuel caught."

"Fucking hell! They didn't stand a chance in there." Jack shook his head.

"Absolutely, they got exactly what they deserved."

"That wasn't what I meant."

"I know, but I did." Jonathon said firmly.

"Have you got no compassion left?"

"Not since they have tried to kill me and my friends, no, not really."

"You've changed, Jonathon!" Jack looked at the man in front of him.

"Don't you want me back now?"

"I didn't say that."

"If I want to come back, will I be welcome?" Jonathon persisted.

"Always." Jack sighed, "Why, have you decided?"

"Yes, I want to come back. I've decided that I miss the action too much."

"Well it took you bloody long enough." Jack smiled warmly.

"I was undecided until today, but seeing what just happened made me realize that people like Frank Underwood need to be stopped."

"Well, let's hope that he finally has been."

"I bloody well hope so boss."

"You can call me 'Sir', now you work for me officially again."

"Yes Sir, boss." He smiled and went to talk to Tommy who smiled when he found out that his friend was joining Jack again.

The industrial estate was all but shut down for the rest of the day. Although the food vans did a roaring trade as fire fighters and Police ate around the clock, enabling them to carry on.

Jonathon returned to the warehouse they had staged the assault from, for a few hours' sleep and awoke to find half of his team sleeping around him. It looked like everybody was in for the long haul. It was this type of commitment that he had missed the most.

Chapter Seventy Nine

Terry relayed the news to Johnny and Alsina as the day wore on but they could not celebrate until they knew for sure that Frank was dead.

They knew that he wasn't among the living prisoners, but they would not believe that he was dead until they saw the body.

"What do you want to do today sweetheart?" Johnny tried to distract her.

"Nothing really, I want to be here when you get any news."

"You can go across to your mum and dad if you want. You can catch up on their trip. I promise to come and get you as soon as we know something."

"Why don't you both come with me? You can bring the phone and the change of scenery might take our minds off of things for a while." Alsina suggested.

Johnny was just about to decline when his brother interrupted him.

"Actually that sounds like a blinding idea love."

Bowing to his brother's sentiments, they locked the boat and walked over to Alsina's parents, who were delighted with the company.

None of them had eaten anything that morning so Sabine provided a pretty fair imitation of a full English breakfast. She nodded approvingly as even her daughter accepted the offer of second helpings.

They sat and waited, with the occasional call to or from Jack or Jonathon. Once, they even got hold of Tommy, who told them about his friend's plans to re-join their organization.

This bit of information pleased Johnny immensely and he was happy when he saw Terry smiling at the news too. Alsina liked most of Johnny's friends but had become especially attached to Tommy since she had been introduced to him.

When they were hungry again, they walked to the restaurant to have a spot of lunch, as the breakfast had cleaned Alsina's parents out of food. They ate quietly and slowly and every time a mobile phone rang they looked at Terry.

They ran into Sandra and had a drink with her, but even her constantly upbeat attitude couldn't change the mood of the others. She didn't know the story of what was happening, but could tell something was badly affecting them.

After she had left for a business meeting, they returned to the boats and resumed their wait.

Terry called Jonathon for an update and they talked about his return to the organization. He told him that they were all very happy to have him back.

Jonathon told him what had happened in more detail and they all shook their heads when he repeated it for the others. Johnny had seen the effects of a daisy cutter and could only imagine what devastation was left at the warehouse.

His friends had been lucky that they had a barrier between them and the explosion. He was thankful for that, as he had got used to having Jonathon and Tommy around again.

They swapped back to the 'Jodast' for a couple of hours to shower and change, before heading back to the restaurant for an evening meal.

It was a frustrating day for all and they were still hanging on every phone call. They didn't get an update until well after the meal and by that time they were having a drink on Alsina's parents' boat.

"It doesn't look encouraging, Terry." Jack waited on the other end of the line.

"Why not?" His heart was sinking as he waited for the news from his boss.

"We don't think the remains we found can be Frank Underwood."

"Bollocks!" He didn't speak loudly so as not to offend Alsina's mother.

"I know what you mean." Jack agreed.

"You think Johnny is still a target?"

"Until we can prove otherwise, we have to assume that nothing has changed."

"Have you got any idea at all where he is?"

"Nothing as yet. We notified the ports and airports. Jonathon and Tommy are at the Eurostar terminal, just in case he tries to leave the country that way."

"Nothing we can do here then." Terry said numbly.

"No, just go to bed and try to sleep, if you can."

"Great, I'll tell the Boy."

"Good luck. I'll call you directly I get anything."

"Cheers boss. Ring anytime, even if it's the middle of the night."

"Will do, mate. Hang in there."

"Good night, Alsina sends her love and says to be careful." Terry watched Alsina smile as he passed on her message.

"Tell her thanks. Try to get some sleep." Jack ended the call.

Chapter Eighty

The Ford Fiesta was now parked in the secluded front garden of a suburban house with substantial grounds.

Frank Underwood was pacing up and down in the lounge with the phone permanently glued to his ear. He nodded occasionally and stopped pacing as reports flooded in from what was left of his empire.

Everyone seemed to be turning on him now as if they could sense his demise. What was left of any local and national competition made their moves against him and within twenty four hours of the initial raid on his base of operations, most of his clubs and pubs were either closed or under new management.

Damage limitation was the name of the game now. Strangely, he was not that upset. Kevin seemed to be more incensed than he was. The mere fact that anyone would dare to oppose them was anathema to Kevin.

"Don't worry Kevin, it has probably done me a favour in the long run, mate."

"Cheeky fuckers. Have they forgotten where all their newly earned money came from? Turncoats the lot of them."

"It really doesn't matter. I have enough for both of us to start again somewhere far away. If you want to come with me, great, but I'll understand if you want to stay. Call it a severance bonus. I will look after you."

"Don't talk like that boss, we can still make a comeback from this." Kevin was still angry.

"I really don't know if I want to, mate. Look at what we've achieved and the money we've made. We don't need to work again and I certainly don't need the respect, or the aggravation." Frank sounded relaxed.

"I don't like people taking liberties, that's all." Kevin grumbled.

Of the hundred or so employees and associates that they had on the payroll the previous day, they would be lucky if they could round up ten. Most were either dead, or had been arrested and those that were left were making their own futures at his expense.

"Look at it this way, the power struggle that we leave will stop anyone coming after us from our side. As for Fairfax, that may still be a problem, but nothing that can't be sorted."

"I've got to admit that the free for all that you'll create by leaving will be something to see."

"And if nobody takes complete control, we can always come back when the dust settles. Hell, even if I don't want to return, the least I can do is back you in a takeover bid."

"I'm not as creative as you boss, that's why I'm so good at what I do now. I always stick to what I know I can achieve and then I can't fuck it up." Although Kevin declined the offer there was pride in his voice.

"Then come with me and we start somewhere else. With any luck they'll think we're dead and it will give us a little bit of breathing space."

"Don't you want to get even with anybody, anybody at all?" Kevin asked.

"No, although we *will* have to deal with Johnny fairly sharpish. We can't afford to have him coming after us."

"I know I've asked before, but is he really that much of a problem?" Kevin was sceptical.

"Yes, he is and from your question, do I take it that you are thinking of coming with me?"

"What else can I do? If you don't want to fight, what's the use of me staying?"

"Good lad. Right let's make a few more calls and grab what we can. No point leaving too much cash to go to waste."

"How safe do you think it is to go collecting?" Kevin asked.

"Depending on how we do it, quite safe."

Frank outlined his plans for a final collection of his funds. They would move quickly and get what they could without causing a fuss. Then they could cross to the continent and make the final plans for dealing with Johnny.

"What about Pearce?" Kevin looked at Frank with open curiosity.

"Fuck him, he isn't like Johnny. He may hold a grudge for a bit but he isn't as relentless as Johnny, or Terry for that matter."

"What about Fairfax, surely he is going to be more of a problem?"

"That could be true. We will have to play that by ear." Frank was eager to move on.

The phone rang again and Frank answered it, said "thanks" and then hung up.

"That was David. Johnny is back in Spain."

"When do we go?"

"Soon as I can get organised."

As they left the house, they switched vehicles to a nondescript white Transit van. Leaving the Fiesta in the garage with the door securely bolted, they drove out of the house and headed for the pick of Frank's remaining businesses.

Within a few hours they had collected millions in cash and jewels, some from his numerous hiding places and others from the daily cash rich businesses that he had operated.

Most of his people were unaware that he had been in and out. Those that did know had stayed loyal and he signed over deeds to properties, occasionally backdating the contracts. They didn't know his immediate plans and expected to have to give the businesses back when he took the reins again.

Everything went into the back of the van and then got transferred onto a medium sized fishing trawler. They toyed with the idea of heading to La Rochelle in France, but decided to take a direct route to Spain.

La Coruña was their ultimate destination and from there they could travel overland to the south of Spain. Once there, they could finalize their plans.

The boat trip was leisurely and the only problems were heavy seas encountered in the Bay of Biscay. They didn't get seasick which was a bonus. It did get a bit crowded though when they joined the host of serious pleasure craft sitting out the worst of the weather out to sea, before making a late run into land.

They were in no particular hurry and were working on the principle that nobody was looking for them, or so they hoped. They made no contact with David while they were on the ship and played things very close to their chests. The skipper and crew could be relied upon to keep their mouths shut, but it really didn't matter. Once they had completed this little bit of business, they were history.

The trip took just under two weeks, with the trawler acting as though it was actually a working boat. Nothing was said when they docked in La Coruña. They stayed in a small hotel outside the port while they bought a car and got the papers registered under yet another alias.

Kevin could see from the meticulous attention to detail that his boss had been planning something like this for a long time. When he commented on it, he was told that it never hurt to have contingency plans.

Finally, when the car was prepared and everything else was ready to go, they loaded up their gear and headed off towards Madrid. They then went south to the coast, where they arrived in the little town that housed his brothel and other business interests. Frank made no move to approach any of his holdings.

Yet again they stayed in a small hotel with secure parking and did a quick reconnaissance of the surrounding area.

It was three weeks after the devastating raid on his base when Frank was ready to carry out his latest plans. They had rented a small farmhouse and set about preparing it for what they intended.

Chapter Eighty One

Neither Terry nor Johnny got much sleep over the next few days. They desperately wanted to return to England to help with the search. All of Frank's known premises were under surveillance and even some of the suspected ones where they only thought that he had an interest.

Moves were made to seize assets, but some were foiled by the back dated contracts. As it was, they could only hope to seize those in the name of Frank Underwood, few as they were. They followed the paper trails towards his other aliases, but it could take years before they finally unwound the lines of deception that he had put in place.

They hit lucky on some of the premises, seizing large sums of money that couldn't be explained away. One warehouse alone held over a million in cash that was just sitting in a large safe. It was old, but still did its job, and it took them some time to open.

Alsina stayed at Johnny's side as much as she could. None of them left the marina and they sent Alsina's parents out for what they needed. They got a little light relief when Sandra shouted out from the quayside a couple of times and they invited her onto the boat for drinks.

She could tell that they were preoccupied and didn't outstay her welcome. Alsina was especially glad of these interruptions, as it helped her keep her sanity.

Terry was constantly on his mobile and the restaurant started doing takeaways especially for them. They discussed moving out of the marina to a better defensive position, but overruled the thought in the hope that it might encourage Frank to make a move.

Johnny was not happy about Alsina being in the line of fire again, but accepted that he could do nothing to make her leave him for even a little while.

One morning, after days of not leaving the boat, they decided to walk to the restaurant. It was as much for the change of scenery as for the food.

As they approached the restaurant, they noticed that it was full of fit men in their thirties. They wondered if Frank had found them until the owner waved them over and invited them for a drink. Terry guessed it must be safe for them to approach, as there was no interception from the security team.

"What's going on?" Terry asked the question although they all wanted to know.

"I am having a reunion for my old army unit." The owner told them.

"I didn't know you had served." The interest was plain on Terry's face.

"It was a long time ago and we don't get to see each other much, so I try not to dwell on the old days." The owner explained.

"You must have been close." Terry observed.

"All men who fight in a war together bond in a special way, but you know what I'm talking about, surely, I've seen you with your friends."

"We were never soldiers, we haven't fought in a war." Terry became wary.

"But you have risked your lives together for a common cause. I can see it in the way you interact."

"That's an interesting theory, but we just work in admin." Terry was getting a little worried about breaking his cover. When they had first arrived at the marina it was for Johnny's recovery and they thought the story about the outboard accident had been accepted.

Maybe it was time for them to move on. He had not realized how perceptive the owner was and, although he trusted him and he had been cleared by the security team, the less people knew, the better it was for all concerned.

"Forgive me, it's none of my business. I don't mean to pry, I'm the soul of discretion but you really don't need to pretend for my benefit." The man smiled at Terry.

"Thanks, I think."

"Don't worry, I have spoken to nobody about this and my staff are not as observant as me, but if you ever need help you only have to ask." The owner walked back to the bar to talk with one of the waiters. They were in for a busy day.

Johnny had been listening to the conversation, but he was not overly concerned about it. He smiled at Alsina who was trying not to catch anyone's eye, but they were all staring at her. He thought again how lucky he was to have her.

The restaurant owner, whose name was Marcus, came to her rescue and put his arm around Alsina. "This is Alsina, she and her boyfriend Johnny are my friends. Behave people."

"Lucky bugger!" One of the group shouted.

"Thank you. May we join you?" Johnny answered the man.

There was a rush as nearly everyone stood and offered their seats to Alsina. In the end, Marcus waved them down and produced two chairs from the surrounding tables. Terry found his own seat and they ordered drinks.

"Today everything is on the house, so order whatever you like. Today I'm in a good mood." Marcus told them.

His friends all cheered and ordered jugs of beer to start with. They would change over to spirits a little later, but wanted to go easy for the first couple of hours.

Strangely, they all drank copious amounts of water with their beer. Johnny began to realize that they were not your average punter just out to get drunk. Some serious thought had been put into this session.

Everyone took part in the toast to Marcus and Johnny looked over to his brother, who was deep in thought. It worried Terry that Marcus had noticed how they interacted. If he had, then someone else could as well.

Coming up behind Terry, Marcus bent down and whispered in his ear.

"I can see that what I've said has upset you. Please don't worry on my account. I shouldn't have said anything, but, what with your last few trips here, I couldn't help but notice."

"It's not you Marcus, but if you noticed then others might as well."

"Is this to do with the club bombings in England?"

"What made you think that?" Terry looked surprised.

"I knew Joseph Stanton."

"Of course, he has had the boat here a while." Terry felt a little better.

"I knew him before that. When you first came over he asked me to keep an eye out for you, you know, to make sure you were left alone."

Terry looked at Marcus with fresh admiration. In all the time he had been here he would never have guessed that there had been any connection to Joseph.

"He never said anything to me about it." Terry answered.

"Joseph thought that you had enough on your plate worrying about Johnny."

"Is there anyone he didn't know?"

"I think there might be a few people in Australia, but I couldn't swear to it." Marcus joked.

Terry laughed and Marcus clapped him on the shoulder as he walked away to talk to his friends. A more relieved Terry looked over to Johnny and smiled. Alsina looked up at that moment and smiled at them both. He had lost count by now of how many times he had thought what a lovely smile she had.

Terry joined in the laughter as one of Marcus' friends finished telling a tale about Marcus in a desert with a bag of scorpions. He eventually started to relax as the tales slowly got more and more outrageous.

After a few hours it was time for everyone to go for a short siesta. Terry offered some money, but Marcus declined, insisting it was his treat. He was himself overruled as his old unit threw a wad of money on the table to a chorus of "let us know when you need more."

Terry found out that Marcus owned a few apartments in the marina and that his friends were staying in them for a week or so. He had spoken to Marcus on many occasions and was still amazed to realize that he actually knew very little about him. It wasn't that Terry hadn't been interested, but more that Marcus had skilfully dodged the questions without raising suspicion on Terry's part.

Terry was impressed anew, as it took a very special person to do that to him. A large part of his training had been focused on him collecting information from people, but he realized that he was in the presence of a master in the art of counter intelligence.

It also surprised him that he was not upset by the thought. He felt strangely honoured that Marcus had shared his secret with him. At some time in the future he would like to spend an afternoon just chatting to Marcus, apart from anything else, he was good company.

Terry decided to strike while the iron was hot and chose to go back for dinner that evening. It might do him some good to throw a few ideas and questions at Marcus. After all, Marcus was in the marina full time and might have good information on Frank's operations over here.

They slept for a few hours on the boat and then went over to invite Alsina's parents. Johnny was happy that they were so near, as he didn't think it fair that Alsina should have to be exiled from her friends or family.

Looking around at the boats in the marina and thinking back to his earlier conversation with Marcus, Terry wondered how many other people around him had similar stories and, more to the point, how many had Joseph Stanton known? For all he knew, he could be in the middle of an army of people, friendly to his cause, of which he knew absolutely nothing.

It was a shame that Stephen and Davina were dead, because he realized now that they would have known who everybody was. Of course, Terry had known that Marcus had served in the army, even though he had told Marcus otherwise, from the intelligence report on the marina done before they had first come over. He had not known about Marcus' friendship with Joseph, though. He cursed Frank Underwood for doing this to them.

Alsina asked if he was still with them and interrupted his train of thought. He smiled at her and apologized for not being with it. Johnny was watching him with a look of curiosity and he knew he would have to tell his brother about Marcus soon. That way if something did happen over here, then at least Johnny would know he could rely on someone.

They returned to the 'Jodast' and lounged around for a bit. Terry was onto Macbeth in his book now and Johnny flicked through the English and Spanish news, as Alsina gave him a shoulder massage.

Alsina was already at her parents' boat when the brothers arrived to collect them. They strolled over in the direction of the restaurant and pointed out new arrivals and the renovations that seemed to be an ongoing theme in the marina.

When they arrived at the restaurant, they found some of Marcus' friends already there and accepted an offer to join them for a meal.

Marcus' friends seemed none the worse for wear after their mammoth drinking session earlier and Marcus broke the habit of a lifetime and joined them for a meal.

Alsina's parents were accepted into the group and her father came out with a few army stories of his own. The meal was noisy and enjoyable and Terry got Johnny and Marcus together to ask about the state of affairs on the coast.

Johnny was interested to hear that Marcus had known Joseph, but decided Terry could fill him in on the blanks later so as not to make Marcus have to repeat himself.

It came as no surprise that Marcus knew about the brothel, as bar and restaurant owners who catered to the English abroad were some of the best-informed people on the coast.

The amount of information a tourist or resident will give up to a bar worker is incredible. Although it is always a favourite trick for some people to reinvent themselves, you can learn a lot by listening to what people talk about while they are drinking.

A classic example of reinventing was that, to Marcus' knowledge, there were two thousand members of the 'SAS' living on the coast and most of them had come into his restaurant at some stage.

He knew thousands of 'Quality' builders and electricians, boat skippers who knew absolutely nothing about boats and divers who knew 'Everything' about any subject.

Most people got confused with their lies and Marcus was able to put together a fairly comprehensive list of criminals, players and faces in his area.

He told them about the rumours of an alleged protection racket aimed at the brothel and he listed a number of people who could be called upon to side with the brothel workers if they needed it.

Some of Marcus' old friends chimed in with their take on the state of play on the coast. They knew some of the players by reputation and in some cases actually had dealings with them. Of course, they didn't know anything about why Terry was asking, but they were content to talk to him about things.

Terry started thinking about the six degrees of separation theory, that said that you were no more than six people away from knowing someone famous or infamous. For instance you might know a customer in a bar who was an ex-Policeman, he in turn might know someone on the royal protection squad and they in turn might know the Queen.

This could be said for the people around him. Some of them knew minders or security personnel in the U.K., who in turn knew people working in Spain as bodyguards, who might actually work for Frank Underwood.

Some of the men even offered to visit the brothel, but Terry doubted that this was an altruistic offer in a number of cases, especially when it was suggested that he might pay the bill for the visits.

He made light of the suggestions and headed the conversations in the direction of the Costa Criminals and what they were up to. This started another wave of outrageous stories about who had worked for whom and what had happened when certain rich individuals came over to party.

Talk turned towards nightlife in the U.K. and the gangster scene and Terry was more than a little relieved when Alsina's nightclub was mentioned only in passing. He did notice the way that her ears pricked up when they mentioned how good it was.

The conversation naturally turned to the current situation in the gangland community and Terry and Johnny listened raptly to any mention of Frank Underwood.

It was apparently no secret that Frank was high up the pecking order, or that he was now a target for both Jack Fairfax and for Frank's criminal competition.

Terry listened intently to mention of Jonathon Pearce and was happy to learn that he was to all intents and purposes, clean. Some of the men around the table had worked for him and only had good things to say about him. Nobody guessed that Terry and Johnny had anything to do with the situation.

Terry was surprised to learn that they knew Jonathon's history and knew of the story about when he and Johnny had been discovered while working undercover. None of the group realized that the Johnny they spoke of was the same man sitting quietly listening to their stories. He felt a twinge of guilt when he heard that they thought that Jonathon's bosses had treated him unfairly.

Terry was more than happy with the way the conversation was going and only slightly unhappy that none of the group knew for sure where Frank was now. Rumours were circulating that he was in Europe now, but Terry knew from his conversations with Jack that nothing had been confirmed. He kept his own counsel on this piece of information, though.

They ended the evening with a promise to join Marcus for breakfast the following morning. Terry was beginning to wish that he had known who Marcus was from the start. However, he was thankful that Joseph had been thoughtful enough to worry about him in the first place.

Again, he thought about the affect that Joseph Stanton had had on his life and Johnny's for that matter. He would be eternally grateful to him and wished that he could have done more for his three friends before they had died.

He sat in the rear of the 'Jodast' and drank a silent toast to Joseph, Davina and Stephen. He promised himself that they would get justice, if it was the last thing he ever did.

Chapter Eighty Two

The men in the brothel still did not know that their boss was nearby. They paid the takings into his accounts religiously and both Frank and Kevin were able to ascertain that the men were loyal.

Eventually they made their presence known, but in a very discreet way. They didn't approach the club, in case it was under observation. If the authorities hadn't known about it before, then it was a good bet that some of the men captured at the warehouse would have let the information slip.

They spoke to David, the man that Kevin had left in charge, and he was surprisingly forthcoming. He told them that some of the employees had talked about going it alone without Frank and that they had decided against it. Kevin guessed correctly that it was probably due to this man that they still had any loyal employees in Spain.

Frank offered the same deal to David as he had with the people who still remained loyal to him in the U.K. After this trip, the brothel would be turned over in its entirety to David for him to do whatever he wanted with it.

David was very pleased with the idea and enthusiastically filled them in on the recent events of the coast. He told them what he knew of the happenings in England, but also told them that he was not as well connected as he once had been.

David agreed to source the manpower for whatever they had in mind and suggested that they use some of the girls in the brothel as an alibi. He also proved that he had been the correct choice for the management role, when he supplied up to date intelligence on Johnny and Terry in the marina.

"Don't worry, I used a new face and he won't be recognized."

Neither Frank nor Kevin insulted David by asking if he was sure that nobody had spotted his man.

"It won't be easy though. If you go after them you will probably have to attack them in the marina. I have not seen any overt security measures, but I think we can safely assume that there is a security presence in the marina after what happened the last time. They wouldn't be stupid enough to leave them unprotected."

"I tend to agree with you on that, eh Kevin?" Frank said thoughtfully.

"I agree. There has to be some security, it will just be a question of finding a way around it. Any way to get at them on the boat?"

"I think the security guards and the marineros are too vigilant for that, to be honest, Kevin." David admitted.

"What about the restaurant or the shower block?" Kevin continued.

"The restaurant is the best bet. The staff have been working there forever, so there aren't any undercover security working there. I suppose if you have to move on them in the marina, that would be as good a place as any."

"You don't sound that happy about going after them in the marina, David." Frank observed.

"If it has to be, it has to be, I suppose, but there's only one way in and out. That's if you use cars. Mind you, a water attack would be the same, there is only one entrance for that approach too."

"What about walking in and out." Frank continued.

"Once it kicks off you would be running, not walking, out. There are more ways out of the marina on foot and I suppose you could leave a vehicle just outside the marina in one of the parking spaces."

"Right, leave it with me for a bit and I'll work something out. I want as many exit options as possible and that includes both on land and water." Frank went silent.

"If I think of anything, I'll let you know. Are you coming out to the brothel, while you're here?" David asked them.

"No, go and see my solicitor and he will organise the change of ownership papers. Don't tell anyone that I'm here, not even if you trust them completely."

"No problem."

"Right, thanks for that David. I'll be in touch." Frank went silent again.

David stood up, knowing that he had been dismissed. He was still extremely happy with the turn of events, but was trying not to show it. He would let everyone think that Frank still owned the brothel, as that would give him more security from outside influences. Even though most people thought his boss was on the ropes, they would not have the balls to try to take him on, not after the

Russian fiasco. After that it would be too late, as he would already be established.

He walked into the bar and picked up the phone to make an appointment with the solicitor. He might as well get the ball rolling, in that direction at least.

After he had made the appointment, he called in all of his employees. They had all heard about Frank's problems in the U.K. and were not surprised to be put on standby. They hadn't guessed that Frank was in the country but were happy to stay close to the brothel in case they were needed, especially when they were told that they were on double time until further notice.

Chapter Eighty Three

Terry decided to go and see Marcus, he didn't want to bug the guy, but the wealth of information he had at his fingertips was second to none and very good quality.

Alsina and Johnny went with him, as much for a change of scenery as anything else. When they reached the restaurant they found that Marcus wasn't there. On being told that he was expected back from one of his suppliers within the hour, they decided to wait.

A few of Marcus' old friends walked into the bar and selected tables next to the three of them. The coffee machine roared in the background as it tried to keep pace with demand. Everyone was drinking copious amounts of water to stay hydrated, although occasionally one of them ordered a beer.

It was obvious that they both liked and respected Marcus and Terry got the idea that it wasn't that easy to gain their respect. He knew the type well and smiled to himself. He had worked with similar guys for many years and liked what he saw.

He would ask Marcus if any of them were looking for work, as he was sure that his boss would be interested in some of them to replace his lost team members.

He thought for the umpteenth time that Frank had a lot to answer for. He casually opened his phone and called Jonathon, to ask if anything important was happening at the office.

"Hello mate, what's up?" Jonathon answered quickly.

"Nothing, just called to see if you have anything new?"

"Nothing as yet, we are keeping tabs on his place over there, but at the moment there is just no sign of him."

"You think he could be over here?" Terry asked.

"Don't know. Anything's possible."

"Fair enough. How's Jack?"

"He needs to take some time out. He won't admit it of course but you know what he's like."

"He feels responsible for the team." Terry agreed and nodded into the phone.

"Yep."

"I feel so useless over here."

"Honestly mate, there is nothing you can do here except put yourself up as a target and the boss won't let you do that." Jonathon understood what Terry was going through.

"Any chance you can get him to come over here?"

"What do you think, Terry?"

"Silly question."

"How is the Boy, he must be climbing the walls now." Jonathon changed the subject slightly.

"Funnily enough, he isn't."

"You're having a laugh."

"No seriously, I really think he is doing fine and I think I know why too."

"Alsina?" Jonathon hoped the girl was the answer to Johnny's behaviour recently.

"Got it in one."

"How is she, still as lovely as ever?"

"You want a word?" Terry laughed.

"Yeah, why not. It'll bug the hell out of Johnny."

Terry passed the phone to a confused looking Alsina who listened and then burst out laughing. Johnny looked on bemused and then looked at Terry who just shrugged his shoulders. Alsina closed the phone and passed it back to Terry, smiling.

"What did he have to say for himself?" Johnny enquired.

"He said that, if I get tired of you, he would love to be considered for your replacement." There was a twinkle in her eye as she spoke.

One of Marcus' friends was walking back from the toilet as she spoke. "If there's a queue, can I join?"

"Bollocks to the lot of you." Johnny was laughing as he spoke and Alsina put her hand on his leg and gave it a squeeze.

"As your older brother and practically family, for Alsina anyway, I think I should get first refusal." Terry added solemnly.

Alsina and Johnny rolled their eyes and laughed together.

"What would I say to Mrs. Hoon?" asked Alsina.

"Fair point, it was only a thought." Terry laughed.

Marcus arrived at that moment carrying a case of rum. Everyone stood up and offered him a hand and he told them where his car was parked, so they could go and get the rest. He placed the crate in his storeroom and grabbed a coffee as he came back.

Sitting with Alsina, he waited while the brothers and his friends came back in with their loads. When they had all finished unloading, they all ordered another drink before joining Marcus and Alsina at which point the conversation became quite noisy. Everyone was talking over everyone else and generally making fun of each other.

Terry decided not to try to talk to Marcus now but invited him over to the boat later for a drink. Marcus agreed and said he would try to get over in a couple of hours, after he had satisfied his friends' demands for attention.

Alsina and the brothers left the restaurant and slowly wandered back round to their berth.

Johnny waved at Alsina's mother, who invited them onto her boat. She offered them tea. She had bought PG tips, as her daughter had developed a taste for it in her time at the club. Johnny was secretly pleased that it was not the normal rubbish they served in Spain as English tea. Johnny smiled as she waved a packet of chocolate digestives at his brother. Even if Terry was full to bursting, he would always find room for a chocolate digestive.

While they were drinking, Sabine told them that she and her husband would be returning to Germany again as Alsina's aunt had relapsed.

Terry was secretly happy that they would be away from the marina. If Frank was in the vicinity then the less people they had to worry about, the better they could deal with things.

"Do you need a lift to the airport?"

"No thank you Terry, we will leave the car in the long term parking again, but I do appreciate the offer."

"It really is no trouble. Let me know if you change your minds."

"Thank you. What are you and Johnny going to do with my daughter while we are away?" Sabine asked him.

"You know, the usual, clubbing every night and maybe the odd rave on your boat."

"You are very funny Terry. I am surprised nobody has told you this."

Terry smiled at the older woman. He had developed a deep affection for both of Alsina's parents. They were good people and it was great that they had been here for Alsina, as the stress she was under at the moment was immense.

"Actually, we might go bowling with a few of Marcus' friends. They are getting bored and Marcus might even take a little time off." Terry smiled.

"You must try to let someone else win this time my darling." Sabine joked.

Alsina smiled and nodded. "I will try this time Mama, but it is so hard to play that badly."

"Just remind me again why I love you sweetheart." Johnny playfully punched her on the arm.

"It's because I bowl so well sweet heart."

Her mother laughed at their conversation and thought again how lucky her daughter was to have found someone so devoted to her. She already loved Johnny like a son and she knew that her husband felt the same way.

"Will you look after the boat while we are gone?"

"Of course, it will be as good as new when you come back." Alsina promised.

"We will come and say goodbye when we leave." Sabine continued.

They got up and walked to the rail at the rear of the boat. Johnny watched as Alsina skipped lightly onto the quayside then followed her off the boat.

Terry was the last to leave and landed lightly on the quay. They waved at Alsina's mother and jumped onto the 'Jodast'. They still had a little time before Marcus was expected, so they busied themselves with tidying up a little.

"Do you think we should ring the boss or Jonathon?"

"No Boy, they will ring us, if there's any news. We just have to trust them."

"Fair play, what shall we do now?" Johnny looked around the boat.

"Why don't you ring Mrs. Hoon, Terry? I can't wait to see her again. Nor can Johnny, even if it is just for her cooking." Alsina said smiling.

Terry nodded as he watched his brother feigning outrage. Yes, it would be nice to invite Mrs. Hoon over, but he wasn't sure if it was safe.

"I'm not sure if that is such a good idea at the moment. It may not be safe for her." Terry voiced his thoughts.

"Why don't you ask her? It's her decision after all." Alsina continued.

"Sod it, why not." He dug his phone out of his pocket and dialled the number. He spoke into the phone and voiced his fears after making the invitation, then he smiled and hung up the phone.

"She will ring me when she's booked the flight."

Two cries of "excellent" sounded at the same time. Johnny walked to the small refrigerator and passed small bottles of water to the other two. They were sitting on the fly deck sipping their drinks when Marcus finally arrived.

Filing down the small stairway, they settled onto the rear cushions. Johnny grabbed another bottle of water for their guest and asked if he wanted anything else. On being told "maybe later", he settled down next to Alsina.

They chatted for a few hours, going over what Marcus knew and what he thought he knew. His old friends had visited the brothel in passing and reported back that nothing out of the ordinary was happening there. Although they did make a comment on the amount of security that they saw around the place.

Marcus said that, if he knew that his old friends were visiting a brothel, then he would have put on extra security too. Everyone laughed at this.

Chapter Eighty Four

"Terry? It's Jack. How are you coping?"

"I'm good boss, we all are, I think. Any news?"

"Just a recap really, Frank is definitely alive and has gone underground, possibly in Spain. I have alerted the security team over there and I am considering sending Jonathon out to you."

"Why don't you come as well boss, you can even stay on the boat for a while, after we catch him."

"I like your confidence, Terry."

"Seriously boss, come on over."

"Am I being paranoid, or have you and Jonathon been talking about me. He used a similar phrase this afternoon."

"You might well be paranoid, but in this case you assume correctly. You need a break! It's not your fault that the team got killed. You know that, right?"

"I appreciate you saying that, but I sent them in." Jack spoke quietly.

"We can take some of that blame too boss. If he wasn't after us, then none of this would have happened."

"If I hadn't put Johnny on the case in the first place, a lot of this wouldn't have happened."

"That's a lot of 'ifs' there, boss." Terry countered.

"Listen, just be extra vigilant."

"Sure thing. Are you sure we can't tempt you over?"

"We'll see."

"Fair enough. Do you want to talk to the Boy?"

"No that's fine, but tell Alsina that, if she needs to go to her parents in Germany, I will sort it out for her."

"You sure you don't want to tell her that yourself. She'll be pleased."

"No mate, just let her know and tell her that I'm thinking of her and her parents." Jack hung up.

After the phone call, Terry gave the news to Alsina. This was one of the reasons that everyone liked working for Jack, he paid attention to detail and cared for the people he worked with.

"Any chance he will come over?" Johnny gently stroked Alsina's back as he spoke to his brother.

"I'm not sure, but at least he's thinking about it."

"It would be nice to see him, especially after what he has offered." Alsina was indeed pleased with the offer of help. Although she was more than capable of booking flights for herself, her aunt lived in the middle of nowhere and any assistance in getting there was a bonus.

"I'll keep on at him, don't worry." Terry promised.

"Have you had any thoughts on how Frank is going to come for us?"

"To be honest Boy, there are lots of ways that he could do it."

"Do you think he knows we are here?"

"I wouldn't put it past him. As much as I hate to say it, he's very good at his job."

"Yeah, good job his close quarter fighting skills weren't up to scratch when he stabbed me."

"I'm very pleased for whatever mistakes he made that day." Terry said happily.

"Me too mate, me too."

"And me, although if he had not stabbed you, then we would never have met." Alsina looked at Johnny with a wistful smile.

"I suppose I will just have to thank him when we next meet then, sweetheart." Johnny smiled.

Alsina looked at Johnny as he said the words and a slight chill ran down her spine. She did not want him to meet Frank again. She never wanted to meet Frank again either, but she was a realist and knew that it was inevitable that one day soon they all would.

Terry looked at his brother and knew that, for all his calm exterior, it wouldn't take much to set him off. He would have to keep a close eye on him if he could. Alsina was a great influence on him, but he doubted that even she could control Johnny if Frank came at them again, especially if Alsina was in the line of fire.

Unaware of the concern that he was causing, Johnny continued stroking Alsina's back and gently squeezed her shoulder. The girl sitting next to him meant the world to him and that had never happened to him before. He had gone out with girls before, but none of them had ever made him feel as he did now about her.

They headed over to the restaurant to eat and have another chat with Marcus. Terry wanted to give him the heads up that Frank might be in the area and if anyone could find out for sure it was Marcus.

Marcus was talking to some of his friends as they walked in and he smiled and waved at them, then pointed to a table and signalled that he would be two minutes.

A few of his friends looked up and smiled. A couple of them wolf whistled Alsina, who shyly smiled back and blushed slightly. Marcus told them to leave the girl alone and, when he finally came over to them was all smiles.

"Don't judge them too harshly, they mean no harm." Marcus advised.

"I don't, I know that they are only teasing me. They are nice people." Alsina replied.

"I wouldn't go that far love." He was laughing as he said it and Alsina knew Marcus cared deeply for his friends. "What can I get you?"

"We all fancy the pasta tonight and a little bit of a chat if you have time?" Terry answered.

"What's up?" The note of concern in his voice was touching and Terry worked quickly to allay his fears.

"Nothing really mate, but there is a whisper that Frank might be over here and we just wondered if you'd heard anything, or you knew anyone who could verify it?" Terry asked.

"I've heard nothing yet, but when I know, you'll know, I promise you that. What makes you think that he's over here?" Marcus responded.

"Jack Fairfax." Terry said quietly.

"Back in a minute. Let me make some phone calls."

"Listen Marcus, we don't want to cause you any grief."

"I'm not worried about Frank. I've been over here a long time and I'm well established."

"Even so, he's a nasty piece of work." Terry persisted.

"I appreciate your concern. Right, back in a bit."

The food came before Marcus returned and they ate slowly as they watched him on his mobile phone. He smiled a lot and waved his hands around as he spoke. One of the calls made him frown and the call after that made him look over at them and smile.

They were onto their coffee by the time he made it back to their table. He pulled a chair over and sat down.

"There might be some truth to it. There is a possible sighting, but it is as yet unconfirmed."

"Where? When?" Terry asked quickly.

"This morning as it goes, at a petrol station."

"Anyone with him?"

"Only one person that I know of."

"Is it one of his U.K. guys or someone from over here d'you think?"

"I don't know any more than what I was told. They think they saw him and they think he was with one other person, sorry." Marcus shrugged.

"Don't worry Marcus, I'm only running through possibilities at the moment. I have to tell the boss though." Terry got his phone out and rang Jack, whose mobile, unusually, went straight to voice mail. He left a quick message summing up what he had been told and then dialled another number.

"Jonathon? It's me mate. I have just been told of a possible sighting of Frank over here. Apparently, he was at a petrol station, we're waiting on confirmation." Terry listened to the voice on the other end of the phone.

"No mate, it was one of Marcus' contacts." Nodding his head Terry added, "I've left a message for Jack but he hasn't rung me back yet, mate." He listened again and then said, "Right, bye."

Terry marshalled his thoughts, before telling the others what was happening. "They have nothing concrete over there, but there are persistent rumours that Frank is over here. With any luck,

Jack is coming over with Jonathon and Tommy to liaise with José."

"When are they coming?"

"Jonathon doesn't know, but the reason I can't get hold of Jack is because he's sorting out someone to cover for him until he gets back. So it looks like he's definitely coming over."

"Great, they will be handy to have around. I suppose Jack will have to work closely with José, but Jonathon and Tommy will definitely come in useful over here."

"That's not Tommy Rooke by any chance, is it?" Marcus leaned forward as he spoke. Evidently his interest had been stoked.

"Yes, do you know him?"

"Like a brother, albeit a long lost one, but a brother just the same."

Everyone at the table looked at Marcus now, waiting for him to expand on what he had just said. He smiled as he saw the open curiosity on their faces.

"Me and Tommy go way back, we grew up together. We joined up together, but I lost track of him after he went into your line of work."

"It's a small world, I'll give you that." Terry didn't know what else to say.

"I suppose when you do the things we did for a living, it isn't really that small, if you think about it. The lads will be pleased to know he's coming over, he never makes it to our little reunions." The wistful look on his face was further evidence that he missed his old friend.

"Tommy never says much about his army time." It was Johnny's turn to speak now as he was close to Tommy.

"He never did dwell in the past much, did our Tommy." Marcus nodded.

"I am glad he is on our side. I like him." Alsina hadn't had much to say for most of the conversation but she could relate to Tommy.

"Yep, he always was one for the ladies." Marcus winked at Alsina.

"I always thought he was a bit shy around them, he never talked about girlfriends when we worked together." Johnny was a little confused about the statement.

"He never used to be, but just before he got out, he had a bad experience. Did you know he was married?"

"What?" Three faces listened intently to Marcus' next words.

"She was a lovely girl, Bethany was her name. She was the world to Tommy, but she was killed in a car crash. I don't think I am talking out of turn, but he'd probably not have told you. He sort of withdrew into himself after Bethany, so much so that most people thought he was gay when they met him."

"That explains a lot, now that I think about it. When I first met him people used to wind him up about it. He took it in good part, but some of the guys could be a little close to the bone. Jonathon put a stop to that though. He never told me why." Terry smiled as he remembered how Jonathon had put a stop to it.

"Jonathon Pearce?" Marcus looked incredulous.

"Fuck! Do you know him too?" It was Terry's turn to be incredulous now.

"Bethany was Jonathon Pearce's sister!"

The table went silent as both Johnny and Terry contemplated what they had just heard. Everything now fell into place, with regards to what they knew about Jonathon and Tommy. Alsina felt a great sadness for her friend, even though she hadn't known him for that long.

"Did you know about any of this Terry?" Johnny was aware that Terry had to keep some things to himself, but he was sure that he would have told him something of this magnitude.

"Of course I didn't Boy." He gave his brother a contemptuous look.

"But you and Jonathon were best friends." Johnny insisted.

"Perhaps he couldn't talk about it back then and after my appalling behaviour over your little fiasco, we sort of lost touch."

"Fair comment, I suppose." Johnny said thoughtfully.

Marcus looked at the brothers and wondered if it would have been better if he hadn't told them about the marriage. He knew that Tommy would never have said anything, but he still felt the need to protect him. He knew the rumours that had gone round about his friend and he was still touchy about it on his behalf. He changed the topic slightly, "So you work with Jonathon as well as Tommy. Jonathon's a good bloke."

"Yes, he is, although the Boy always knew that, it was only me that acted like a prat." Terry admitted.

"If you don't mind me asking, what happened?"

"The Boy there got shot and I believed it was Jonathon's fault. So did Jonathon actually, but that's no excuse. I behaved very badly and I'm quite ashamed of myself. Jonathon was good enough to accept my apology."

"What made you all think it was Jonathon's fault?"

"Actually it was Frank Underwood. We didn't know that he was playing for the other side and had informed them about our operation. He blamed Jonathon."

"Are there any issues with me knowing all this?" Marcus asked them.

"I suppose there are, technically, but with all the help you've been, I think it only fair to be honest with you. My boss knows that you know some of it and he doesn't seem to mind."

"Jack Fairfax is a good man."

"Oh, don't tell me you know him too. Is there anything else that I need to know?" Terry shook his head in disbelief.

Marcus just smiled and took a swig of his drink. Alsina laughed and snuggled into Johnny. Having seen this, but not heard the conversation, Marcus' friends made ribald comments from the surrounding tables and smiled at them. Terry looked bemused and tried to make sense of everything he now knew.

Marcus called a waiter over and ordered drinks for everyone at the table. He sighed and waved his hand at his friends when they shouted their requests too. The waiter smiled as he took the orders from them.

Terry's mobile rang, he pressed connect and listened to the person on the other end, before smiling and saying "see you then, bye."

"When are they coming?" Johnny still had his arm around Alsina.

"Mrs. Hoon is coming tomorrow lunchtime."

Alsina's face lit up with happiness as she realized who had called. Johnny still looked puzzled for a moment, before he too smiled.

"Decent food at last!" Johnny joked.

"What's wrong with my food?" Marcus looked quite hurt.

"Sorry Marcus, his food, not yours." He indicated his brother. "As a chef Terry makes a good Policeman."

Marcus still didn't fully understand, so Alsina told him about Mrs. Hoon. He watched the animated looks on their faces before asking, "So, you are bringing a cook out from England. Wouldn't it just be cheaper to eat here? I can give you a bit of a discount if the money is a problem."

Johnny laughed with Alsina as Terry turned a deep shade of crimson. "Oh, just spit it out Terry. Are you a couple or not?"

Terry said nothing, but the penny finally dropped for Marcus, who tried to be tactful. "Where are those drinks then?"

Terry nodded his thanks at Marcus and glared at his brother. Alsina caught his eye and his gaze softened.

"We are just good friends okay." Terry finally admitted.

"That's good. Shall I make up the guest room?" Johnny asked innocently.

Terry went a deeper shade of red and walked off towards the toilets, smacking his brother on the head as he passed by him. He could still hear Johnny chuckling and Alsina reprimanding him, saying that he deserved all he got, when he reached the door.

By the time Terry returned to the table, he was no longer the topic of conversation. Alsina had phoned her parents for an update and been told that they would be away for a while longer.

Marcus brought a coffee over for Terry, saying that if he was driving he should not drink anymore. Terry accepted the offer graciously and then paid the bill for the evening, without Alsina knowing.

He signalled to Johnny that it was time to go and they stood up, with Alsina reaching for her purse. She caught Terry's smile as she straightened up and sighed.

"Next time you have to let me pay, Terry."

"Right you are then! Breakfast is on you."

They said their goodbyes to Marcus and his friends, who seemed to be settling in for the night. Johnny didn't relish Marcus' job, a session like that could go on until breakfast. He put his arm around Alsina and they followed Terry back to the boat. It was the first time his brother had looked happy in a while.

Chapter Eighty Five

Frank decided to assemble his men away from the brothel, just in case anyone was keeping it under observation. As far as he was concerned, it was history anyway. Once his men had carried out his orders, they would go their separate ways.

David decided to keep the normal personnel on the door, so that nothing would arouse suspicion. He pulled in a few friends and acquaintances from further down the coast, giving them only the basic information about the job, leaving out the names of the targets and who was really in charge.

The more experienced players knew what the score was, as soon as Kevin Daniels opened the gates of the villa for them. Nothing happened in the U.K. without word filtering through to them on the Continent.

None of the men had a problem. They would follow their orders and then wait and see who finally came out on top before jumping ship, if it became necessary.

David had managed to bring fourteen people, including himself, for the afternoon's activities. From what Kevin and Frank saw of them, they seemed more than capable. They knew that Johnny and Terry usually had lunch at the restaurant in the marina now and had made their plans accordingly.

Frank had provided weapons from a different source than his usual armoury. As far as he was concerned, until the situation was settled once and for all, nothing from his previous business assets was useable.

He decided to arm the men with semi-automatic, nine millimetre pistols and pump action shotguns. He wanted his men to control the situation from the start and shotguns seemed the most effective means of achieving what he wanted.

Making sure that each man had a fully loaded shotgun and spare cartridges for them, he then began to distribute the spare shells for the nine millimetres.

The lookout was ready to go to his position, in one of the adjoining bars. Frank would wait until mid-afternoon before sending him in, as they knew that their targets spent most of the afternoon enjoying their mealtime, chatting in between courses.

The lookout man didn't have a shotgun, but he was armed with a nine millimetre. None of the men drank alcohol while they waited, but there was an endless supply of soft drinks and tea or coffee if the men required it.

Most of the men had been around firearms before, but nearly half of them were not that proficient in their use. That was another deciding factor in Frank's choice of primary weapon. He was working on the principal that even the worst shot would have a chance of hitting his target, if the shotgun was pointing in even vaguely the right direction.

The plan was simple and he ran through it again and again in his mind, to make sure that he had covered all eventualities. He was confident that he had enough men to deal with the fallout, if there was a large security team in place. He knew that there must be one, but his spies had not been able to pinpoint any of them.

Frank was aware of the group of men who were frequenting the restaurant on a daily basis, but was fairly confident from their attire that they were punters and nothing more. After all, Speedos didn't leave a lot of room for hiding a weapon, not the sort he was worried about anyway.

The lookout was now in place and Frank was waiting for the call to let him know that he could move his men in. Everyone looked up expectantly as the phone trilled in his hand and began gathering up their weapons when he closed the connection and got to his feet.

They climbed into the vehicles and made the slow journey over to the marina. One way or another this was going to end today. He knew he couldn't start a new life with Johnny still alive and hunting for him. Now it was time to settle things, once and for all.

Chapter Eighty Six

Terry was up early to prepare the Range Rover for the trip to the airport. He checked that the fluid levels were all topped up and that he had enough fuel for the trip. He also made sure that he had enough space for Mrs. Hoon's luggage in the boot.

Alsina and Johnny walked to the car from the boat, having decided that the trip to the airport would break the monotony for them. Besides that, the fact was that they had all missed Mrs. Hoon very much.

Terry fired up the big engine and slowly eased the car out of the marina, he looked around for the security vehicle that he knew would be following, but unless they had opted for a bus, it was nowhere in sight.

He was nearly at the airport before he, at long last, found his hidden escort. Smiling, he continued driving without acknowledging them and made his way onto the one-way system leading up to the car parks, just outside the departures building.

He pushed the button and waited while the camera recorded his number plate, before printing it on the ticket. The whole operation took a matter of seconds.

The barrier lifted and he slipped his sunglasses off, so he could negotiate the twists and turns of the covered multi storey car park. He found a space fairly easily, which was surprising, and they locked the car before they headed for the lifts and then on to the arrivals area.

The air conditioning in the huge arrivals area was working overtime. The temperature chilled down very quickly from the ambient heat outside. They walked over to the arrivals board and checked on the progress of the flight, which was on time.

Making their way over to the coffee bar they ordered drinks and sat down, while they waited for their friend to come through the entryway into the arrivals hall.

They had just finished their drinks when they saw Mrs. Hoon coming through the clear glass doors into the reception area. Alsina ran to greet her, while Terry and Johnny followed at a more sedate pace. They were never more than five metres from Alsina the whole time.

There were tears in both the women's eyes as they hugged each other, almost jumping up and down. Releasing Alsina she reached over and kissed

Johnny on the cheek, slowly running her eyes over his body to see how he was bearing up.

Terry smiled at her and she kissed him full on the lips, while Alsina and Johnny exchanged knowing glances. The body language between the two of them told the younger pair everything they wanted to know about the relationship. Everyone was smiling.

"Do you want to freshen up before we head back, or have a coffee or anything?" Alsina offered.

"No thanks love, I would prefer to get back and settled if that's okay with you lot?"

Everyone was happy enough with the decision and Alsina and Mrs. Hoon walked arm in arm in front of the brothers while Terry pushed the fully laden baggage trolley. They stopped at the machine to pay for the ticket and then continued on back to the car.

The girls got in the back as Terry fired up the engine to get the air conditioning working, while Johnny returned the trolley to a retrieval point. Mrs. Hoon was glad of the air conditioning, as her blood was thicker than theirs due to her staying in the U.K. while the others had acclimatized slowly over the past few weeks.

She took off her jacket and Alsina placed it in the boot to give them more room. Then she reached over and took the older woman's hand in her own and happily gave it a squeeze.

"We have all missed you so much!" Alsina beamed.

"The feeling's mutual darling. Nothing to do while you were away but fret and wonder what I was going to do with myself."

"Don't worry about a thing while you are here. Enjoy yourself. Have you ever been on the boat before?"

"No love, Joseph and Stephen kept inviting me, but they didn't need me cramping their style over here. Plus, who would have looked after Vincent if I wasn't there?"

The reminder of Vincent caused the conversation to drop off a little and it was a while before anyone spoke again.

"Have you been to Spain before?" This time it was Terry who spoke as he glanced back at her in the mirror.

"Not the mainland, the islands, but that was many moons ago."

"I think you will enjoy it here. There is lots to do and see." Terry informed her.

"As long as I am with you all, that will be good enough for me. What's my kitchen like?"

Alsina groaned and Johnny flashed a cheeky smile at her and mouthed the word 'Yes!' to her.

"You are not spending all your time in the kitchen. We didn't invite you here to wait on us, that just isn't fair." Alsina said firmly.

"You know me love, never happy unless I'm cooking." She patted Alsina on the knee and smiled at Johnny. "You need feeding up my boy." She handed him a tub of her homemade biscuits. "That should start you off."

"No arguments here Mrs. H." Johnny replied, eagerly opening the container.

"I mean it. When we get back to the marina, we are going out to eat or you are getting right back on the plane." Alsina tried to look stern but couldn't carry it off.

"Well, my lovely, I'll go out to eat with you just this once, but that is only because I have been up since dawn and you probably haven't got half of the ingredients I'll want anyway."

Alsina seemed placated and spent the rest of the journey pointing out landmarks and places of interest. Malaga was an interesting city and she knew it quite well having spent a lot of her youth there.

The hour it took for the return journey seemed to fly by and they were entering the marina before they knew it. Mrs. Hoon gasped at how pretty it was and smiled at the security guard as he opened the barrier for them.

They drove slowly around to the boat and parked up. Mrs. Hoon was speechless and Alsina led her onto the boat while Johnny and Terry followed at the rear, carrying the luggage.

Terry took her cases directly to his cabin and glared at Johnny, daring him to make a comment. Johnny wisely said nothing.

Alsina gave her friend a guided tour of the whole boat, before finally showing her the galley. Mrs Hoon started opening cupboards straight away to see what she had to work with and realized that she would need to make a shopping trip very soon.

Terry led her to the cabin and showed her the small shower room and then left her to settle in, before they headed to the restaurant for lunch. He wanted to introduce her to Marcus too, because, as he now knew, he had been friendly with Joseph.

It didn't take Mrs. Hoon long to get ready and they had a leisurely walk around the marina in the direction of the restaurant. Alsina introduced her to the various people they met and when they arrived at the restaurant, they found the outside terrace tables taken up by Marcus' old friends.

The men immediately offered Mrs Hoon their seats, after she had been introduced to them, but she declined politely stating that she would prefer to be out of the sun for the time being.

Marcus came out of the kitchen as they walked into the restaurant and greeted her warmly. He had heard a lot about this lady from Joseph and Stephen and it was great to finally put a face to the name.

"So, at long last I get to meet the legend that is Mrs. Hoon."

Alsina and Johnny laughed as she blushed to her roots and Terry put his arm around her shoulders. "Oh, stop that nonsense at once." Mrs. Hoon blustered.

"I've heard so much about you over the years. It really is nice to have the chance to meet you in person." Marcus persisted.

"I'm sure you are exaggerating, young man."

"I haven't been called young in a fair few years. You've just made my day." Marcus was beaming from ear to ear.

"She left her glasses on the plane mate, she'll be alright when the airline send them on." Johnny ducked as Mrs. Hoon aimed a slap at his head and held up his hands in mock surrender. "Only joking, honestly, Mrs. H."

"I should think so. I see you've lost your manners while you've been away my boy."

Marcus showed them to their seats and told them what the special of the day was. He took their orders and then headed off into the kitchen to make sure that everything was perfect when the meal was served. It felt funny, but having Mrs. Hoon in his restaurant made him feel like he was being inspected for a Michelin star. If what he had been told about the woman was true, he could learn a lot from her.

The meal was a success and he followed it up with a special dessert that was a particular favourite of his. He watched as Mrs. Hoon took a mouthful and was happy with the appreciative look on her face.

"You have cinnamon in this?" It was a statement more than a question.

"Don't you like it?"

"I love it, I've never used it like this before. I'll have to give it a try when I make this for the boys and Alsina."

"If you need to use my kitchen, please feel free. The only condition is that I get to try what you make too."

"You're on."

Chapter Eighty Seven

Jack Fairfax, Jonathon Pearce and Tommy Rooke were due to catch the later flight for their journey to Spain. Everything was arranged and they would be met by José at the airport and brought to the Marina to check in with the brothers.

Jack had spent the morning at the office, tying up loose ends and making sure that his people knew every number that they could contact him on, if the need arose.

Jonathon and Tommy didn't really have a great deal to do, so they tidied up their desks and chased down any outstanding leads that they thought would be of interest. Although they were now fairly sure that their target was in Spain, they still wanted to make sure that every effort was being made to find his exact location.

Some of the day was spent being congratulated about their return to the fold by those who had been out of the office when the news was first broken.

Jonathon watched the curious looks of some of the older hands as they realized that Terry had some competition when he went for Jack's job. Jonathon, who already knew that Terry would step aside for him, smiled at the shock that was coming for the troops when they found out too.

He knew that Terry had been number two here for so long and hoped that people wouldn't make too much of it. Terry had already promised to help him ease into the position. It was this quality that made Terry so very good at what he did, because he was just as happy taking orders as giving them and that was a very rare thing with some of the men they knew.

Jack didn't mind either way, as, in his opinion, either man was more than up to the job. He was just pleased that Jonathon and Tommy had come back to the job, as they were both worth their weight in gold to his operation.

They finished what needed to be done and were then driven to the airport in Jack's car. They breezed through Passport Control and were seated in a private room up until the moment when their flight was called. In their time with Jack, they had both passed through airports regularly, but it seemed that there were definitely more privileges when they travelled with their boss.

The only drawback was being out of touch with the office while they were in the air, but the flight time was minimal and they would be updated as soon as they touched down on the other side.

The service on the flight was excellent. When they arrived at Malaga airport, a member of José's squad whisked them away from the plane. They tried to engage the man in conversation as they were all fluent in Spanish, but he seemed to be reluctant to answer any of their questions, including why his boss was not there to meet them, as had been previously arranged.

The man's mobile phone rang and he answered it before passing it on to Jack, who took it and conversed briefly with José on the other end. His face went white as he ended the call and faced his two men.

"It all kicked off while we were in the air. Terry's in a coma!"

"What about the Boy and Alsina?" Neither Jonathon nor Tommy could conceal their anxiety.

"I don't know, apparently it all happened so fast. José is ringing me back, as soon as he gets some news."

"Bloody Hell, what the fuck happened?" Both Jack and Jonathon stared at Tommy as he spoke, he had never sworn in front of his boss before, ever!

Chapter Eighty Eight

The two minibuses arrived at the barrier to the marina and the guard stepped forward to ask where they wanted to go. The deeply tinted windows and the three rows of seats prevented him seeing exactly who was in the back of the buses.

Even if he could have seen inside properly he probably would not have been able to connect the face of the man in the rear of the first minibus to the faded picture that still hung on the wall of his security hut, from so many months before.

He waved the vehicles through, when the driver in the lead vehicle pointed to the diving mask and snorkel that was sitting on the top of his dashboard.

The only thought that passed through his mind was that the dive centre owner was going to be very happy with the amount of money he made today. He wished that there had been some women in the vans, as it never hurt to have women in wetsuits walking around the marina to brighten up his afternoon.

The two minibuses stopped in the middle of the road that separated the quayside terrace from the restaurant. They left the engines idling as the doors opened to expel the passengers.

The only sound was the noise of the engines and the chambering of shells in the shotguns. Then the screaming started and all hell broke loose.

Chapter Eighty Nine

The meal was finished and the group were just getting to their feet to leave, when Terry casually took in the arrival of the two dive buses.

Perhaps it was because he was used to seeing minibuses full of divers coming and going, or perhaps it was because he was happy with the arrival of Mrs. Hoon. Whatever the reason, he wasn't worried when they stopped and he turned to say good-bye to Marcus.

The familiar sound of a cartridge being loaded into a shotgun brought him whirling back round in a crouch as he faced the men and tried to protect Mrs. Hoon, at the same time as pulling his pistol.

Some of the people at the nearby tables started screaming as the first shotgun blast took him in the shoulder, knocking him back into Mrs. Hoon and they both fell over the back of a chair. Terry's gun flew from his hand and he tried weakly to recover it. The adrenaline rush keeping him conscious for a few seconds, before the pain of the wound took him into unconsciousness.

Johnny reacted instantly to the sound and pushed Alsina to the floor, pulling a table over to try to give them some protection from the lethal hail of pellets. He drew his Sig Sauer as the table came to rest between him and the gunmen.

The sound of the shotguns kept on coming and Johnny tried to keep Alsina's head down as he returned fire. His actions drew the attentions of the rest of the group and Johnny was glad of the heavy iron table that stood between him and the enemy. He briefly wondered why Marcus used garden furniture inside his establishment and then thought that he really didn't care, so long as it gave him some protection from the deadly pellets.

Johnny emptied his magazine and was replacing it when he heard the sound of nine-millimetre fire mixing in with the shotgun blasts. He had seen Terry go down and hoped that his wound was not bad. As he looked over he saw Marcus dragging his brother behind another table, as he fired Terry's gun at the advancing men.

"Marcus, how bad is he?" Johnny shouted.

"Losing a lot of blood, concentrate on the rest of them, or we will never get out of here."

Marcus heard Johnny firing at the approaching men as more shotgun pellets ripped through the air around him. Mrs. Hoon was trying to stem the bleeding from Terry's shoulder with napkins and Marcus threw a tablecloth in her direction.

"Keep direct pressure on the wound and try to stop the blood as much as you can." Marcus ordered.

"Don't worry about me. Shoot them!"

Marcus smiled at her instructions and returned fire. He glanced at Alsina and saw her trying to get to Mrs. Hoon to help Terry, while Johnny was trying to push Alsina down behind the cover of the solid metal tables. He started worrying about how he was going to get another magazine for Terry's weapon, when the attack started to falter.

Peering around the table, Marcus saw his friends attacking the gunmen with his terrace furniture. The attacking men were not expecting any trouble from the rest of the customers in the restaurant, hoping the sight of the shotguns would scare them into submission.

The first of the attacking group to be assaulted from behind, dropped their weapons and some of Marcus' friends grabbed them and turned them back on their initial owners.

Marcus saw more men running to the scene, this time armed with sub machine guns and he desperately looked around for another clip for his weapon.

Johnny saw the approaching group as well, but he knew who they were. He recognized some of them and their weapons and body armour would have given them away to him even if he hadn't known them. The security team was kicking into gear and Frank's men now had to divide their fire.

Marcus' old friends worked well together as a unit and slowly the tide turned in their favour. Fortunately for them the security team had seen them over the previous days and were able to recognize them as friends and not part of the threat.

Johnny started to stand up when he suddenly came under a barrage of fire. The table stopped most of the pellets, but he was suddenly aware that some of the shotgun cartridges were not just loaded with lead shot from the way the table reacted and sounded each time it was hit.

He risked a look over the table to try to get a line on whoever was shooting at him and his world suddenly went black, as a solid projectile glanced off the side of his head knocking him unconscious.

Frank Underwood roared with glee when he saw Johnny go down and he ran across, dragged Alsina from the floor and started backing out of the restaurant. As they went, he aimed at Johnny to make sure that this time he had actually killed the boy.

Alsina stamped her heel down the inside of his calf as he pulled the trigger and he saw Johnny's shirt puff up as the bullet entered him. Frank had seen enough and called to Kevin to help him into the vehicle. Alsina screamed at him and fought all the way.

Once they were in the minibus they sped off backwards, abandoning their men. They reversed towards the exit of the marina at full speed, before screeching around in a one hundred and eighty degree turn, wheels spinning and sliding as they collided with the barrier and smashed through it.

Kevin was looking in the mirror to check for any pursuit, when he crashed into the bus that was coming toward them, round one of the many corners of the access road to the marina.

The minibus bounced off the larger vehicle and crashed into the garden wall of one of the expensive properties that surrounded the port, killing Kevin instantly.

Frank was in a state of shock, but managed to drag the nearly unconscious form of Alsina out of the wreckage. He still carried his shotgun and he blew the lock off the nearest gate and entered the property. Repeating the action on the front door, he dragged Alsina into the house and threw her onto the settee.

He dug his hands into his pockets, looking for fresh cartridges for his shotgun. Finding none, he threw the now empty weapon across the room and checked his pistol. The magazine was still fully loaded, so he returned it to his pocket and then looked around at his surroundings.

Chapter Ninety

Johnny was aware of pain and a lot of noise as someone tapped on his collarbone in a hard repetitive motion. His eyes fluttered open and closed a few times, before remaining open.

Marcus was looking down at him and anxiously checking to see if he was okay.

Johnny groaned as he put his hand to his head and felt the blood congealing there. He looked around as Marcus asked if he was alright.

"How's Terry?" He asked. "Where's Alsina?"

"Underwood's got her, I'm sorry."

"What?" Johnny tried to stand up and Marcus supported him as a wave of nausea hit him and he nearly collapsed again. He waved the security team medics away who then went to tend to Terry and stumbled out of the restaurant followed by Marcus. "Which way did she go?"

Johnny saw Mrs. Hoon administering first aid to Terry and checked to see if she was hurt. She was unhurt and Terry was breathing, so he was thankful for that at least.

"They drove out of the marina." Marcus looked crestfallen. "I am so sorry, Johnny."

Johnny wasn't listening to him though and jumped into the remaining minibus. Reversing as quickly as he could manage, he swung the vehicle around until it faced the right way. His head was spinning and going backwards was too hard for him to concentrate.

He accelerated out of the marina and noticed that the security guard was pointing in the direction of an accident involving a bus. Recognising the other vehicle involved, he pulled over and ran to the minibus.

He could only find one person in it and he was dead, so he quickly spun around, instantly regretting it. He put his hand on the minibus to steady himself and waited for the fresh wave of nausea to leave him.

As he waited, he noticed the shotgun damage to a nearby gate and decided to check it out. He waved off the bus driver, who tried to stop him, pointing up the hill towards the sound of the approaching sirens.

Johnny had just made it through the gate when an ambulance came flying round the corner and slammed on its brakes, followed closely by a Guardia Civil 4x4.

Chapter Ninety One

Alsina was brought out of her semi-conscious state by a vicious slap to her face. As she struggled to open her eyes, she felt her shirt being ripped from her body. She regained her focus quickly now and found herself looking into the enraged face of the man she had last seen driving the car during the failed kidnapping attempt on the beach.

Frank Underwood was now trying to rip off her jeans and undo his own trousers at the same time. She struggled to hide her nakedness and simultaneously tried to stop him. She suddenly remembered something Johnny had taught her and started screaming and kicking out at Underwood.

"Do you know that I had it all planned out for you, Bitch? You were going to go the way of the rest of the drug-craving, little junkie whores, doing anything for a hit."

Alsina tried to get her knee between his legs, but couldn't quite manage it. Frank attempted to scare her into submission by playing the psychological card, trying to make her envisage a horrific future.

"Yeah, once you were hooked on Smack, you would do absolutely anything. I even had a buyer lined up, Bitch. But now I'm not going to bother with the drugs. I don't want you numb and senseless. I want you to feel every last little bit of pain, every last sensation. Do you hear me, Bitch?"

Her struggles increased, as did her screams. Johnny had once told her that it would distract her attacker and also help to bring her to the attention of any would-be helpers. She bit and fought and screamed, as though her life depended on it, which it probably did. As she lashed out with her open hands, she clawed her nails down Underwood's face. She was deeply satisfied to see blood start to flow almost immediately.

"Good, good, keep it up girlie, I like a bit of a fight."

"That's handy, so do I!"

Alsina stopped struggling and her heart leapt with joy as Underwood's body tensed. He recognized the voice of the person behind him and he exhaled slowly.

"Why can't you fucking die? I saw the bullets hit you, for fucks sake. I saw the blood!" Frank was incredulous.

"You of all people know how much blood you get from a head wound, Frank."

"But I made sure of it this time. I saw the second bullet go into your body."

"You mean you saw the second bullet go into my shirt. You *are* slipping."

Frank turned to look at Johnny and, as he did he slipped his hand down towards the pistol that was sticking out of his pocket, out of sight of Johnny.

"Maybe Boy, maybe, but not as badly as you." He swung the gun up to line on Johnny and eased the safety catch off. "Coming in unarmed for fuck's sake."

"Give it up Frank, it's all over! You won't get away from here."

"It's over for you, I can assure you of that. And when I'm done with you, I'll finish your little girlie off too, eventually." He leered at Alsina.

Johnny watched as Frank's finger tightened on the trigger and started to move. He was halfway across the room when Frank's aim suddenly wavered and he screeched in pain. The gun went off, but the bullet passed harmlessly by Johnny and embedded in the wall.

Johnny crashed into Frank, who screeched again and let go of the gun, which jerked out of his hand and landed against the wall. Johnny couldn't understand what was happening, but he was happy enough to take advantage of it, whatever it was.

Frank's hands flew to his groin and Johnny followed the move with his eyes. Alsina's bloody hand came away from Frank's open fly, having ripped the flesh with her fingernails and Johnny remembered one of the moves he had taught her, but it now seemed like such a long time ago'.

Frank rolled off Alsina and she rushed into Johnny's arms.

"I knew you'd come my darling. I just knew it."

"I have to admit it was pretty touch and go there for a minute. Did he hurt you?"

"Nothing I won't get over. You stopped him before he could go too far. I love you my darling." Alsina hugged Johnny tightly to her and his head started spinning again. He slumped against her and Alsina quickly released him to see what was wrong.

While she focused all of her attention on Johnny, she hadn't noticed Frank crawling over to the other side of the room.

As Johnny's head cleared, he noticed a movement at the outside edge of his vision and turned to see Frank reaching for the pistol. Johnny looked around frantically and his eyes focused on the discarded shotgun, so he grabbed it.

Not knowing if it was loaded or not, he thrust the end of the shotgun into Frank's Adams apple and crushed his windpipe. Frank's hands flew to his throat, dropping the pistol as his air supply was cut off and he clawed at his throat ineffectually.

All thoughts of shooting Johnny left Frank's mind as he struggled to get air into his tortured lungs. His movements slowed and his lips slowly turned blue, as his hands continued to tear at his throat.

Johnny vaguely thought about trying to help the man, but just then another wave of nausea hit him and he passed out. He came round to Alsina's gentle touch and she helped him to stand. He looked at her torn shirt. She had been able to save her jeans, but the shirt was a wreck.

He slowly shrugged his shirt off and handed it to her, in between waves of nausea. She put it on and buttoned it up, but it was way too big for her. She started heading towards the door with him, but he stopped and went back to the body, as he had to make sure that Frank Underwood was really dead.

Johnny checked the carotid artery and could find no pulse. He then placed the back of his hand just in front of Frank's open mouth, but felt no breath either. When he was finally convinced that Frank was *not* going to come back from the dead, he let Alsina lead him from the house.

Johnny and Alsina walked back to the marina slowly and as they passed the gate, the security guard ran out to help them. As he reached them the guard saw Johnny's scars, on display for the whole world to see now that Alsina had his shirt on and he flinched automatically. That young man had led a very painful life. He guided them to his hut and called the Guardia Civil over to them and an ambulance. He pointed to the blood on Alsina's shirt and she shook her head and pointed at Johnny.

Marcus arrived at the same time as the ambulance and told Johnny that Terry was in a coma and on his way to hospital, accompanied by Mrs. Hoon. Johnny thanked Marcus, who helped him into the back of the ambulance, before they were driven out of the marina with a Police escort. Johnny drifted in and out of consciousness several times on the journey to the hospital. Although she was still worried, Alsina wasn't as afraid as when it had first happened.

Marcus walked back to his restaurant, which now resembled a war zone. His friends called him over to ask how Johnny was. Miraculously, none of them were badly hurt. They had been trained professionals once and that training had never left them.

"What are you putting on for us next year then Marcus? You will have to go some to beat this you know?"

Marcus looked at his friends and then roared with laughter. They told the officer in charge that they would be in the bar next door if they were needed and then headed off to get a well-earned drink.

Chapter Ninety Two

José called Jack back when they were halfway to the marina, to divert him straight to the hospital. He updated him on the condition of both Johnny and Terry, much to the relief of the men in the back of the car.

"It's a shame he had to kill him, I suppose we'll never find the rest of his traitors in our group now, or the rest of his assets."

"Cheer up boss, we might get lucky at some of his sites and I have a few ideas about how we can track some of his aliases. Me and Tommy have been thinking about how best to do it and we might be lucky."

"How do you mean?" Jack was curious.

"Well, it's like this, I don't suppose he trusted anyone enough to give them his account numbers and there would have been a ton of cash coming in. So, if he is dead, those accounts won't be getting any more income, therefore, if we look for similar paying in patterns of the accounts that we do know about, we can freeze any that look the same."

"That's not really that precise though, is it?"

"That's the beauty of it. If the money is dodgy, no one will come forward and say, 'I want my money back', now will they? And if we do mistakenly freeze a legal account, then we can always unfreeze it, once they have proved without a doubt that the money is legit. It's a win, win situation." Jonathon was insistent.

"I'm still not sure." Jack was still sceptical.

"Oh, come on boss, how many accounts will be taking the amount of money that Frank's businesses did per day? I'm telling you, it won't be that many and we'll only stop the ones that have suddenly stopped receiving income."

"You should have been in the Inland Revenue, you know that."

"I'm not that heartless boss, honest."

"What do you say Tommy? You're very quiet." Jack looked at Tommy.

"I agree with Jonathon, boss, I think we have to try at least."

"Right, I'll kick it upstairs, the revenue people will be delighted to get their hands on it anyway."

"Boss, I know you told us what José said, but is there a prognosis on Terry or the Boy?"

"I don't know Tommy, Terry is still in a coma and they are pumping fluids into him. Johnny is in and out of consciousness, but more in than out at the moment. The women are worried, but they'll cope well enough from what I've already seen."

"Women?"

"Alsina and Mrs. Hoon, she was visiting them. Poor lady had only arrived today, as well."

"The crafty bugger." Jonathon smiled at Tommy. "Did you know about this?"

"No mate. Good luck to him, though. It's about time he settled down and, man, can she cook?" Tommy smiled.

"No arguments there." Jonathon was unconsciously rubbing his stomach as they spoke and even Jack laughed at that.

"How long to the hospital do you think?" Tommy asked the driver in Spanish, but was answered in perfect English. The driver thought that it would be twenty minutes, more or less.

"Do you think that Alsina will be okay? She's suffered such a great deal in so short a space of time."

"I think she will be fine, Tommy. From what José can gather, Johnny stopped Frank doing anything nasty to her. Just a few light cuts and bruises from the sound of it."

"He was lucky he died quickly, I don't want to think about what Johnny would have done if that bastard had hurt the girl."

"I have to agree Tommy. As I said to Jonathon the other day, that girl is a good influence on the Boy. Although, I think it had more to do with the fact that he was injured and close to passing out again, he just wanted to make sure they were safe."

"He had a lucky escape then, eh Jonathon?" Tommy turned to his friend.

They all nodded. In their minds Frank Underwood had got off lightly. What with Terry shot and Alsina intended for the sex trade, none of them would have blamed Johnny for making the man suffer.

"It's saved us the expense of a trial at least. You've got to hand it to the Boy, he certainly took that economy drive memo. to heart."

"Very funny." Jack rolled his eyes as Jonathon spoke of the latest memos. from the powers that be. The whole operation had cost a small fortune and looked like it would carry on for a while longer.

Both Jonathon and Tommy had been in the room when Jack had called his immediate superior and pointed out that the money they recovered alone would put them in profit, and that was without the sale of the confiscated assets.

"If my plan works out, can we get a bit of commission on what we recover?" Jonathon asked cheekily.

"Of course you can, it will be in the form of my eternal gratitude." Jack laughed.

"That will be handy down the pub, when I send Tommy to get a round in, I don't think."

"It'll be a first for you to put your hand in your pocket to buy a round anyway. Isn't that right Tommy?"

Tommy nodded sagely as Jonathon tried to look indignant.

Chapter Ninety Three

Johnny drifted off to sleep again and Alsina sat at his bedside holding his hand. Mrs. Hoon had just walked in to check on both her and Johnny.

"How is Terry?" Alsina asked as soon as she saw the older woman.

"Same as before love. Johnny?"

"He is in and out of consciousness all the time. I think that he is more conscious than not now though."

"That's good, I just wanted to check. I'll go back and sit with Terry now. Do you want anything from the machine love?"

"No thank you, give Terry a kiss from me when he wakes up please." Alsina told her.

"I will. Be sure to tell Johnny that Terry is getting better when *he* wakes up, too."

"Of course. I will try to come and see Terry when Johnny is awake again. I know that he is worried."

"Okay, that bloke José said that Mr. Fairfax is on his way in now."

"Oh good. That means Jonathon and Tommy will be here too."

"If you say so. Give Johnny a kiss from me." With that Mrs. Hoon walked out of the ward and headed for the vending machines.

Alsina sat staring at Johnny while he slept. It was strange, but she thought that he looked more peaceful now than she had ever seen him. She herself was still struggling with the fact that it was finally over.

Underwood had been confirmed dead and that was all she needed to know at the moment. His number two was also dead and it looked like most of Frank's men were either dead or dying as well.

It seemed that Underwood's men had preferred to die rather than go to a Spanish prison. Either that or they had been too fired up to notice the reinforcements arrive. Trading shots with people who trained with guns day in and day out was just suicidal.

About half an hour later, Alsina heard hurried footsteps approaching the room and looked up into the anxious faces of Jack, Jonathon and Tommy.

"How is Johnny, love?" It was Tommy who beat the other two to the question.

"He is getting better, I think."

"And how are you?"

"Nothing to worry about, but thank you for asking."

"Do you know how Terry is, love?" Jonathon joined the conversation.

"I think he is still the same, but Mrs. Hoon can tell you more. She is with him."

"Thanks, we'll be back in a minute. Do you want anything to drink or eat?" Jack asked her.

"No thank you. Go and check on Terry, Johnny will want to know when he wakes up again."

"Right then, back soon." Jack said kindly.

The three men left to find Terry and Mrs. Hoon. On the way they ran into José, who gave them the latest on Terry's condition.

"They are keeping him in a coma. His body will heal quicker that way. There are no foreign bodies or shrapnel inside him now, so we will have to wait and see what happens when they bring him out of the coma."

"José, my friend, I cannot thank you enough for your help on this. I mean it. I really appreciate it." Jack shook his hand warmly.

"Jack, it is no problem. Just keeping this scum out of my country is reward enough and you know that you only have to ask me if you need anything else."

"Thanks mate. What's the latest on Johnny?" Jack knew that José had spoken to the doctors.

"They are checking to make sure there is no swelling on the brain. His head took quite a pounding when the bullet hit him."

"But he will be alright, though?" Tommy sounded anxious.

"The doctors think so. I have an apartment close to here so if you want to go and relax after the flight and things. Feel free to use it, all of you. I should be able to tell you more when you return."

"If it's alright with you we'll wait until Johnny is up to talking. We just want to make sure that he is okay for now." Jack replied.

José shrugged his shoulders. "Of course. No problem, Jack."

"Right, thanks. You remember Jonathon?"

"It's good to see you working with Jack again." José reached over and gripped Jonathon by the hand.

"I had an offer I couldn't refuse."

"And you Tommy, it is good to see you again, my friend." José smiled warmly.

Tommy shook hands and smiled at José. He was the same around everybody, until he got used to people, slightly nervous and tongue tied, even if he'd met them before, but he liked José so added, "It's good to see you too, José. I'm just sorry that it's not under better circumstances."

"I agree. Come. First we see to Terry and then to Johnny, yes?"

They all traipsed into the room where Terry was lying in bed. The other beds were being kept empty for security reasons, so he had the room to himself. Mrs. Hoon looked up and started to stand, but Jack put a gentle hand on her shoulder. "It's okay, stay seated, please. Has there been any change?"

"Nothing." She spoke shyly and made little eye contact with Terry's boss.

"Right then, if he comes to or there is any change, we will be with Johnny. Could you tell him that we are all here wishing him a speedy recovery when he wakes up, please?"

"I will Sir, thank you."

"Do you need anything? Toilet break, food or drink?"

"No that's fine thanks. I'm good, really."

They made their way to Johnny's room and Alsina rose before they could say anything. Tommy went to her and hugged her to him and she relaxed in his arms.

Both Jack and Jonathon leaned over to kiss her on the top of her head, but they were interrupted.

"Oi! Put her down, she's spoken for."

Tommy smiled down at his friend and Johnny smiled weakly back up at him, before nodding slowly at Jack and Jonathon.

"Are you alright Boy?" Jonathon spoke before Jack could articulate the same question.

"As good as I can be, under the circumstances. Sorry Frank died boss. I know you had questions for him."

"Don't worry about that now. It's no great loss, just concentrate on getting yourself better. You put Alsina through quite a scare."

"I put myself through quite a scare." Johnny said ruefully.

"Impossible, I don't believe it!" laughed Jack.

Johnny smiled and said nothing. Instead he reached for Alsina's hand and held it gently.

"How is Terry?"

"Still in a coma, but they're waiting to see if he can heal a bit more before they try to bring him out of it. He will pull through though, so try not to worry."

"Thanks boss. You guys missed all the fun." Johnny smiled weakly.

"So we heard. You did well though, it looks like you owe your friend Marcus a big thank you." Jack reminded him.

"I don't think I would still be here if it weren't for him and his friends, you know."

"I think he will be over later, so you can thank him then."

"Are you staying on the boat, boss?"

"Not yet. José has a place for us until you two are up on your feet."

"Oh, right. You are welcome on the boat you know."

"As soon as you are out of here, deal?"

"Deal!" Johnny's smile was stronger now.

"Right, well as you seem to be fine for now, we'll go and settle in and come back later."

"It's fine boss, go. Can you get them to let me know when Terry's condition changes?"

"Of course. See you a bit later."

"Yeah, Tommy and I will come and see you if Jack gets tied up. You know what he's like." Jonathon added.

"That's cool mate. Thanks for coming."

"See you soon Boy, Alsina." Johnny smiled at Alsina as Jonathon said goodbye.

Alsina smiled back at them.

Chapter Ninety Four

Jonathon walked out of the shower while Jack was still on the phone. Moves had been started to claim the known assets of Frank Underwood, both in Spain and the U.K.

José had raided the brothel and, with no owner present, decided to close it down and wait for someone to come and complain. Although they didn't yet know it, the owner was not Frank, but he would not be coming to complain, as he lay dead in the mortuary with most of Frank's men.

The girls turned up for work to find the doors locked and sealed with Police tape. One or two of the more experienced girls decided to hang out in the nearby bar, hoping that any trade would come their way.

The bar owner was only too pleased with this turn of events, as he benefited from the increase in trade taken from the premises next door. He decided to make enquiries about the current ownership of the brothel. You never knew when a profitable business opportunity would present itself.

Concurrent raids were carried out on all Frank's known properties in the area and significant sums of arms and cash had been seized. Large amounts of drugs were confiscated and, although a major narcotic supply chain had been neutralized, a smaller crime wave was started as a direct consequence.

With little or no drugs available in the local area, junkies were forced to pay inflated prices, which they could not meet. More robberies were committed on easy to medium security targets. Farmers' fields and farm equipment, building supplies and heavy equipment all fell victims to the need to get a fix.

The local Police were not too upset by the robberies. Some of the thieves were so stupid that they tried to sell the stolen goods back to the original owners, thus giving the Police the excuse they needed to search private homes and residences.

Older crimes were uncovered, which helped to tip the balance in the new crime wave. The fallout from Jack Fairfax's operation ranged far and wide. Old vendettas were settled as people saw an excuse to get rid of their competition and settle family feuds with one simple telephone call.

José was surprised at the amount and quality of the arms that were seized. To his knowledge some of the weapons should not have been readily available on the open market at this time.

José took the three Englishmen to dinner and they chatted contentedly while they waited for their food.

"I should really thank you guys for what you have done for me and my country."

"To be fair José, it wasn't us. Do you think any of Marcus' friends will be in trouble?" said Jack.

"Don't worry, it has already been 'sorted' as Jonathon loves to say."

"The boys were lucky really, no disrespect to your guys on scene, but the extra bodies really made the difference."

"I am not disputing that and neither are my colleagues, who will get most of the credit for it, as we cannot have it widely reported that we condone foreigners fighting criminals on our shores."

Tommy smiled at that. It would make good headlines if the truth was reported in full, but the reality of the situation was not lost on him. It made everyone feel good to think that their tax money was being well spent on the Police forces.

"We are also working as quickly as we can to get Marcus open again as soon as possible." José added.

"I think he will appreciate that. He might even pick up a bit more trade once people realize that a big gun battle happened there." Jack watched as the waiter served the food with an almost reverential service. "Do you come here a lot José?"

"You could say that, my uncle is the owner."

"It's a nice place. How come you didn't work for your uncle? It looks busy enough."

"There is not enough excitement for me in a restaurant."

"There certainly was in Marcus' place today." They all laughed as Jonathon made this comment and then José raised his glass.

"A toast gentlemen, to absent friends!"

They all raised a toast to their fallen comrades. Jack thought of Joseph Stanton and funnily enough he thought of Frank Underwood too. Frank had been good at his job but he had turned and Jack felt slightly saddened.

"Any news on Terry or Johnny?" They now looked to José as Tommy asked the question that was on all their minds. Although they had all been at the hospital earlier that day, they all cared deeply for the brothers, and hoped for an update.

"Nothing as yet Tommy but as soon as there is a change, I will be notified."

Chapter Ninety Five

Johnny was now wide-awake having slept or been unconscious most of the day. He watched Alsina sleeping lightly by his side. She had started off in the companions' chair, but had moved onto his bed after about an hour of tossing and turning.

The nurses came and checked on Johnny, but said nothing about the beautiful girl asleep by his side. One or two of the younger ones winked as they left and he grinned back at them.

Johnny was absently stroking her hair, when he saw Mrs. Hoon standing at the door.

"Is there any change with Terry?" He knew the situation hadn't changed over the last couple of days, but he still asked.

"None as yet, but as soon as he does, I'll come and tell you."

"Thanks for that. How are you? You look tired."

"Johnny love, you know you're not supposed to say something like that to someone of my advanced years. We are liable to get a complex." She smiled at him.

"You aren't as old as you make out. Thanks for what you are doing for Terry. I know he will appreciate it."

"It's nothing lad, he would do the same for me, he already has in a way."

"Oh, how so?" Johnny looked curious.

"Oh, it's nothing, he was just a shoulder to cry on when I was down, you know?"

Johnny nodded, he did know. His brother was a great listener. This he knew from personal experience. Terry had been his anchor after Frank had stabbed him. He had always been there for him.

He knew that Terry was expected to pull through, but it didn't stop him worrying all the same. He didn't know what he would do if he lost Terry as well as all the rest of his friends. That just didn't bear thinking about.

"Do you need anything? Are they looking after you Mrs. H?"

"Don't worry, Johnny love, all I need is for you and your brother to get better. That will do for me. And make sure you look after that girl of yours too."

"I will, she means the world to me."

"I know she does and you mean the world to her too. So make sure you get well soon, you hear?"

Johnny did a mock salute and the action made Alsina open her eyes. She looked around uncertainly for a moment, before she remembered where she was. Looking from Johnny to Mrs. Hoon, she raised her eyebrows in a silent question.

"No change, my lovely, he's still asleep or, as the doctors keep insisting, in a coma."

"Can you stay and talk for a while?"

"No my lovely, I have to get back to make sure I'm there when he wakes up."

"I will come and see you later. Maybe I can keep you company for a while."

"That would be nice, child, I'd like that."

"You can both go now, if you want." Johnny was eager to learn of any change in his brother's condition and, if Alsina was there when it happened, she could report to him straight away, without bothering Mrs. Hoon. He could see how much Mrs Hoon cared for his brother and could not believe that he had missed this relationship starting. In fairness though, he had been concentrating on other things at the time.

Alsina looked at him, as if reluctant to leave him. He nodded and kissed her on the forehead. "Go, it's alright sweetheart."

He watched as the two women walked out of the room and then picked his mobile phone up from the bedside cabinet.

"Jonathon? It's me, any news?"

Chapter Ninety Six

Jonathon laughed as he received the call from Johnny. He had guessed that the boy would call. He knew him almost better than he knew himself.

"Nothing much to report. I've lost count of the amount of money we've recovered, both here and at home. I tell you Boy, we are in the wrong line of work. That was a joke boss." He added the latter for the benefit of Jack who was scowling at him.

"Not funny!" Jack did not need another one of his team following Frank Underwood's example and heading for the high life. He listened to Jonathon's end of the conversation, adding comments where he thought necessary and nodding when either Jonathon or Tommy said something relevant.

When Jonathon had finished the conversation, he put his phone on the table and looked at his boss and Tommy. "That boy is like a machine, all business, business, business."

"You can't blame him for taking an interest I suppose, you know him as well as I do, probably better." Jack looked lost in thought as he spoke.

"I suppose he just wants to make sense of it all. All those lives lost, some good, some bad, but lost all the same and all for money."

"Lots of money." Tommy interjected.

"Agreed, lots of money, but where did it get anyone? No-one is any better off, that's for sure." Jonathon sighed.

"That's quite profound coming from you Jonathon. Something on your mind?" asked Jack.

"No, just alcohol. This has been one of the longest years of my life!" replied Jonathon.

"We know that feeling, eh Tommy?" Jack watched as Tommy nodded silently.

"Time for a quick one before we go to the hospital?" Jonathon looked hopeful.

"It would be rude not to." Again Tommy nodded in agreement with his boss' answer.

Chapter Ninety Seven

Terry came out of the coma after four days. The first thing he saw was Mrs. Hoon smiling back at him. He was weak after his ordeal, but now at least he was on the road to recovery.

"Don't try to speak love, you're safe now."

"How are Johnny and Alsina?" His throat was dry and his voice cracked.

"They're fine and Underwood is dead. Johnny killed him."

Terry lay back and sighed deeply. It was over, at last. He closed his eyes and fought to stay awake. He lost the battle and a little while later he was snoring, deeply and evenly.

Mrs. Hoon waited for a few minutes to make sure he was fully asleep, before going to find Johnny, leaving the medical staff to make their checks.

She walked slowly through the hospital, having had very little sleep for the past few days. The most she had been able to grab was about three hours.

She walked into Johnny's room to find Johnny awake and Alsina asleep in his arms. He looked up at her when she entered and she smiled, nodding happily at him.

"Terry came to a few minutes ago, he asked after you. I told him you were fine and that Underwood was dead. He's sleeping peacefully now."

"Thank you so much, I'll come and see him now." Johnny started to get up.

"No, wait until he wakes up again, he will probably be stronger then and I know he will want to talk to you."

Alsina opened her eyes, having been woken up by the conversation and Johnny's sudden movement on learning that his brother was awake.

"Terry is awake sweetheart." He answered her unasked question.

"Oh, that is great news." She leaned over, kissed him hard on the lips and then got off the bed. "I will get a wheel chair for you."

"Hush child, leave him be. Terry is asleep now and we had best wait until the doctors have seen to him."

"It's alright love. We will see him when he wakes up again. Will you call Jack for me please?" Johnny asked her.

Alsina made the call and Johnny overheard his boss shout "Yes" on the other end of the phone. She ended the call and handed the phone back to Johnny.

"They are coming over." Alsina said simply.

"Great, now let's see about me getting out of here."

"I'll leave you to it and get back to Terry now, if that's okay?" said Mrs Hoon.

"Thank you, that's great. If you see my doctor on the way, can you send him in please?"

Chapter Ninety Eight

In the days following Terry's voyage back to the land of the living, several strange and unaccountable things happened. Johnny was released the same day as Terry came to, much to his surprise, but to his great delight.

Johnny stayed in a hotel near to the hospital to be nearby, in case his brother needed anything. Alsina stayed with him and she was finally able to coax Mrs. Hoon over for a decent sleep and luxurious soak in the huge en-suite bath.

Johnny stayed with Terry while she bathed, that being the only way that she would leave his hospital room. Johnny and Terry spoke at length about the case and subsequent accomplishments, their future plans which had previously been on hold, and whether they could assist the asset recovery operation that was currently underway.

Terry, at long last, opened up about his feelings for Mrs. Hoon and spoke of her reciprocal feelings. Johnny was ecstatic that Terry was finally happy and Terry was elated that his brother was still alive. It was unusual to see Johnny without Alsina at his side and Terry broached the subject that had been bothering him for a while now.

"Why don't you quit, Boy? You have a lovely girl there and it's obvious she thinks the world of you. Why risk putting her through any of this again, eh?"

"I suppose the same could be said of you, Terry."

"I'm too old to change, but you aren't. Alsina has the club and I bet she would just love to have you working with her."

"Has she said anything to you?" Johnny watched his brother carefully.

"You know she hasn't. She hardly ever leaves your side. I thought I was hallucinating when I didn't see her this morning."

"You know me Terry, better than anyone else. You know I wouldn't be happy to live off her earnings."

"We can sell the boat. That should give you a bit of money. Perhaps she could make you a junior partner."

"To tell the truth mate, I think she might be looking to offload the club. Too many bad memories."

"Well, she has enough money to do whatever she wants now. Go for a voyage around the world. Take the boat if you want to, at least you will have contributed something."

"I don't really know what we will do, to be honest. I like what I do and Alsina doesn't seem to mind."

"Why not take extended leave for a bit. Heaven knows we have earned a bit of time off."

"Are you trying to get rid of me?"

"Far from it mate. I realized when it all kicked off just how much I love you Boy. I don't want to watch you get yourself killed."

"Thanks for the vote of confidence, I don't think."

"You know what I mean. Frank was probably the best we have come up against. His training saw to that, but we were lucky in so many ways. I do not doubt your abilities, I never have, but if anyone else with our level of training goes bad, it will be the same again and we definitely lost our edge with Frank."

"You've really given this some thought, haven't you mate."

"Yes. I nearly lost you so many times in the last year and in the process I lost some good mates.

On a purely selfish note, I don't think I would cope very well, if something did happen to you or Alsina. She could be a target, as this case proved."

"I hear what you're saying mate, I really do, but I just don't know what to say."

"Just say that you will give it some thought, that's all. Deal?"

"I promise that I will talk to Alsina about it and see what she wants. I couldn't live with myself if something happened to her because of me. I couldn't live with myself if something happened to you, come to think of it. Perhaps you should give it up too."

"I've already told you Boy, I'm too old for change now. I'm happy with the way things are, but you have different priorities now."

"What about Mrs. H?"

"I've already spoken with her and she is content to go along with whatever I decide. She has lived alone for so long now, I think it would kill our relationship stone dead if I was at home, under her feet all day."

"Listen, I'm going nowhere until you are up and out of hospital, so there is no need to be having this conversation right now, is there?"

"The sooner you make a decision, the easier it will be." Terry insisted.

"Like I said, I will talk to Alsina."

"I can't ask much more than that, I suppose."

Jack Fairfax walked in just then and they both looked at him to find out if there was any news.

"Not a lot has happened today. We raided a warehouse near that little industrial estate where he escaped and recovered two million quid in cash. There were some cars there too. They weren't new, but they must come to nearly a million quid on their own."

"Not a bad days work, eh Boy. What else did you find?" grunted Terry.

"Same as the other sites so far, but we did find some notebooks with what we think are dates and delivery times. We are trying to match up possible venues and cargoes, but that may take a while."

"What d'you think the shipments could be?"

"Who knows, drugs, guns, girls, boys? It could be flowers for his mum's birthday for all we know."

"He must have put something down on paper somewhere. He couldn't keep track of that lot without writing it down. No-one is that good." Terry replied.

"We live in hope. I wish sometimes we could work the way José does. He just shuts everything down until they prove they are innocent."

"The perfect world Guv, the perfect world. When d'you want me and the Boy back at work?"

"How about we wait for you to get out of hospital first, Terry?"

"It won't be long now, boss."

"I know, but there's no hurry. Listen, we're leaving tomorrow. You two stay out here and get well. Jonathon and Tommy will come with me to sort things out at home."

"Are they coming in to say goodbye?" Terry asked hopefully.

"You've changed your tune. Not so long ago you couldn't stand to be in the same room as them."

"Not true boss, I never had anything against Tommy."

Jack shook his head and laughed. He knew how badly Terry felt about his behaviour and knew that Jonathon didn't hold a grudge. He was pleased with the way things had turned out for

Terry and Jonathon, but sometimes he wished that Frank was still alive. It would have made his life a lot easier, or so he liked to kid himself.

He knew José would keep him in the loop with what was happening over here when he was back in the U.K. He didn't share his boss' views that all the assets they recovered were the property of the Crown. José had been as good as gold where Terry and Johnny were concerned, also Marcus come to that, the Spanish government deserved their share of the spoils.

"How do you think the recovery is going, honestly, boss?" Terry asked.

"I have to say I'm surprised and frustrated at the same time. I had no idea how much he was making just in arms sales alone. His men were loyal until near the end and, to be honest, who wouldn't grass him up if they saw he was on the ropes and they were headed off to jail for a stretch?"

"I hate to say it boss, but he had some bloody good ideas."

"I know and it doesn't help that I think we gave him some of them on his training courses." Jack added sadly.

"Got to admit it, that sucks." Terry agreed.

"Where is your lovely lady Terry? I thought she was a permanent fixture in your room." Jack changed the subject.

"She's getting some rest at Johnny's hotel. The room service in here is not up to much, though I have to say, I'm becoming addicted to their steamed fish."

"Once you are strong enough, the doctors say that they will let you go back to the boat. There's a private clinic not far away and they can cater to all your medical needs, courtesy of José's people."

"That's really nice of them. He has really pulled through for us. I must remember to thank him when I next see him."

"I think he wants to thank you two actually Terry. He got a promotion this week."

"Why thank us? We didn't do much."

"This is the biggest case of its kind over here. If there is anything even vaguely related to Frank Underwood then the Spanish authorities are going to seize it. The weapons alone have given them something to think about. José's bosses just love the pair of you."

"I have to say that Terry and I did have rather a vested interest in catching Frank. I think it's fairly safe to say that our lives depended on it."

"Even so lad, you have given them a great deal both in monetary gain and positive Press. You have even impacted on the national drug problem as well. You two are heroes, you really are."

"We're nobody special boss, we were just doing our jobs." Johnny answered.

"You're wrong there lad, you just need time to see it."

"Right, changing the subject rapidly, what time are you off tomorrow?"

"You never change, do you Johnny?"

"Don't know what you're talking about, boss."

"Alright, I'll let it go for now. However, you'll have to get used to it when you get your official commendations."

He laughed at the look of horror on the brothers' faces and waved down their pleas for pity. "Don't worry, they will be done in private. I wasn't joking when I said they love you two here."

Chapter Ninety Nine

Alsina dozed on the bed, while Mrs. Hoon lay in the bath. The adjoining door was open and they carried on a haphazard conversation. The quiet spells in between were interspersed with light snores as the events of the last days finally caught up with the two women.

The bond between them strengthened as they chatted about their relationships with the brothers. Alsina already knew that she would marry Johnny, but she was surprised and saddened to hear that neither Mrs. Hoon nor Terry were interested in marriage.

"It's like this lovey, when you get to our age there isn't really any point. I've already done the marriage thing before anyway."

"Rubbish, you are never too old!"

"We aren't missing out on anything love, honestly."

"I will talk to Terry about this." Alsina informed the older woman.

"He will tell you the same as me love. Just be happy that you and Johnny are getting married. At least you can plan that now."

"I was starting to worry that Underwood would never be caught."

"There is always hope love. Terry taught me that and there is no way on earth Johnny was going to let anything happen to you. He would die first."

"He nearly did."

"Is that a problem?" Mrs. Hoon was starting to worry.

"No, well yes, a bit. Oh, I just don't know."

"You know that Terry wants him to give up work."

"Since when?" Alsina asked.

"He has been thinking a lot about what happened. He doesn't want to risk losing Johnny. What do you think love?" she asked Alsina.

"That has to be Johnny's decision. I cannot make up his mind for him."

"He would do anything for you love, if you asked."

"That is not going to happen. If he wants to talk to me about it, then I will listen. If he does not, I will do whatever he wants. The most important thing to me is that we are together." Alsina replied.

"That's what Terry wants for you too. He just thinks that you have more of a chance if Johnny is not in this line of work anymore, but you have to think about what you really want too, love."

"I will wait and see what Johnny says. It has to be his decision." Alsina repeated.

"Okay love, I don't want to upset you but you should consider the options."

"Don't worry, you will be the first to know, I promise."

Chapter One Hundred

Alsina, Mrs. Hoon and the brothers walked onto the 'Jodast'. Practically every unit available had checked the boat over. Dogs, electronic and manual searches were all utilized and they were only allowed onto the boat once everyone was completely sure it was clean of any type of malicious devices. Water samples had been taken from the fresh water supply and they had even run the engines to make sure that there were no nasty little surprises.

A schedule had been set for Terry to follow at the local clinic and they had familiarized themselves with the layout of the place. One bonus was that, after the initial visits the medical staff would make house calls.

Marcus arrived within an hour of them settling in. He had been a regular visitor at the hospital during their confinement, but found it increasingly difficult when his restaurant was given the green light to reopen.

The brothers thanked him again for his help and watched as he tried to shrug it off as nothing.

"If you ever find that you need help in any way, you only have to ask and we will be there for you Marcus, that goes for the both of us."

"Thanks Terry, but I hope I never have to call in that favour."

"I think you and your mates deserve a drink at the very least. If I'm up to moving about later we will put in an appearance at your place. Are any of the lads still here?"

"Not now mate, but they told me to tell you that they were glad to be of service. How much of that was down to Alsina's pretty face I couldn't say though." Marcus watched Alsina go crimson before sticking her tongue out at him. "They also said to say thanks for making their stay so entertaining."

"We'll try not to be around for your next reunion, God knows what they will expect if we are. Maybe an invasion of a small country or something?" Terry joked.

"I think they'll be happy enough with just getting pissed to be honest, but I will pass on your offer."

Terry's smile turned into a grimace as he moved too quickly for his damaged shoulder. Johnny looked at him with concern, but Terry waved him away when Johnny moved to help his brother.

"We may not make it tonight Marcus. The old boy needs to take things slowly if he wants to make a full recovery." Johnny grinned.

"No rush mate. It's not as if we're busy at the moment, anyway. Although there does seem to be a bit of a macabre interest from several of the locals and a few of the more informed tourists." Marcus answered.

"Costa del Crime mate, it still draws the crowds." Johnny declared.

"Hmm. Oh well, I might see you later then, or I might not. Let me know if you want something sent over."

"That won't be necessary thanks, I'll see to them tonight. Terry shouldn't move about too much anyway." As Mrs. Hoon spoke, a look of pure pleasure broke out on Johnny's face.

"The offer's still there if you need to use my kitchen Mrs. Hoon."

"I'll let you know if, or when that's necessary, thanks Marcus."

Marcus left and they all lounged about on the boat for a while, lost in their own personal thoughts. Johnny moved around the cabin topping up drinks and Mrs. Hoon made a start on preparing the food for their meal.

"Why did they need to check the boat again, Johnny?" Alsina enquired.

"Nothing like being thorough, is there sweetheart. I know Frank is dead, but it's better to be sure that he didn't leave us any little surprises." He kissed Alsina as he answered her, before settling down next to her, placing his arm over her shoulder and pulling her gently towards him.

"But it is over isn't it?"

"Yes. I don't think we need to fear any of his organisations now. We can cause them trouble, but they don't know how much we know about them, or even if we know about them, yet. I'm sure they will just leave us alone and try to stay under the radar."

"Is the security team still in place?"

"If it is, it's not one of ours, maybe José has something on the go, but it has been a while since Frank died now so there's no need."

"Why do you still call him Frank?"

"He was a friend and colleague for a long time love, old habits die hard." Johnny replied.

"He tried to kill you!"

"He didn't succeed."

"I don't know how you can forgive him."

"I haven't forgiven him, especially after what he had planned for you." Johnny stated.

Alsina shuddered at the thought. She couldn't imagine herself in the role Frank Underwood had planned for her. In truth she didn't want to. She saw that dangerous look on Johnny's face again as he spoke and she was glad it was over.

She flipped open her phone and called Bernie Holt for an update on things in the club. She seemed satisfied when she ended the call.

"Anything new?" Johnny asked.

"Everything is excellent, he can't wait for us to get back, but there are no problems to report."

"Have you heard from your parents yet?"

"They should be back soon, I think my mother is a little worried about me." Alsina answered.

"How much does she know?"

"Only that he is dead. I don't want her to know what he had planned for me!"

"I won't say a word sweetheart, neither will the others." Johnny said confidently.

"Thank you." She snuggled into him and they listened to the sound of Mrs. Hoon preparing their food. She drifted off to sleep and only woke up when the food was ready.

Johnny was talking to Jonathon and smiling. They received daily progress reports on how much of Frank's assets they had recovered. It seemed there was no end to his creativity in hiding his wealth.

Chapter One Hundred And One

Jonathon turned from the phone to speak to Tommy, who had listened to only one side of the conversation.

"They are on the boat. No dramas there. Terry is still a bit sore."

"It's good that they are out of hospital, but a pity that he's in pain." Tommy felt sympathy for his friend.

"Yeah, but as long as he takes it easy, he should be alright."

"What did Johnny say when you told him about today."

"Well as you can imagine Tommy, they were surprised."

"I can't say that I wasn't, I mean, an old people's home, for fuck's sake."

"There is serious money to be made with the old coffin dodgers mate." Jonathon nodded wisely.

"But was there no depth that he wouldn't stoop to?"

"I'm sure that it's just the tip of the iceberg, Tommy lad."

"Did they say any more about jacking it in?"

"Johnny is still undecided. Terry is staying with us though. He is adamant about that. Jack is pleased, but he is undecided about Johnny. One part of him wants him back tomorrow and the other part thinks that he is being selfish for thinking like that and that it is up to Johnny to decide what is best for Johnny."

"What does Alsina say?" Tommy was curious.

"She is happy with whatever the Boy decides. Don't forget she still has the club."

"She deserves it too. She is such a nice kid."

"Are you getting all broody on me Tommy? Do you think it's time to settle down and have kids of your own?" He watched the sadness return to Tommy as he thought again about Bethany. "She wouldn't want you to mourn her forever mate. She loved you too much for that, you know."

"I just look at the two of them and think they were made for each other. Why put themselves in harm's way?"

"You know Johnny as well as I do, he lives to be put in harm's way."

"But that was before he had Alsina. Is it fair to her?" Tommy sighed.

"Only they can tell that, mate. Come on, let's go down the pub. Jack can join us later. He owes us a pint for today anyway."

"Where is he?" Tommy asked.

"You know Jack, some meeting or other. Everyone wants a piece of him now the money trail is being followed."

"I wouldn't do his job if you paid me."

"No offence mate, but I don't think they will ever offer it to you." Jonathon chuckled.

"Piss off and bring your wallet, tosser."

Jack joined them in due course, when they were three pints each into the session. He had a smug look on his face, which immediately caught the other two's attention.

"What news, boss?" Tommy asked.

"Good news. The company are springing for the repair on Joseph Stanton's place."

"How the fuck did you manage that?" Jonathon asked in surprise.

"I just pointed out how much of a factor they were in bringing in all Frank's money."

"It can't have been that easy surely." Jonathon probed.

"No it wasn't, but I think they are owed something. Alsina is at least."

"Have you told them yet?" Jonathon asked.

"I'll let that be a surprise for when they come home."

"Will they come?"

"I think so."

Chapter One Hundred And Two

The days flew past in the marina; Terry was up and about in very little time at all. Alsina was able to show her parents that she was unhurt and they, in turn, showed their appreciation to Johnny for keeping their daughter safe from further harm.

"That is a lovely watch, mate."

"I know. I still can't believe they bought it for me."

"They like you, even more since you saved Alsina's life again." Terry added as an afterthought.

"I would have done that anyway and they know it."

"Accept it mate. They are happy for you to be part of their family." Terry smiled.

"I know. It's all going quite fast to be honest. I'll have to go to the U.K. soon to finalize the details."

"Are you sure you don't want the wedding here, Marcus is happy to provide the venue."

"It's easier for all the people we know in England, plus Alsina wants the wedding at the club. She thinks Davina would have liked that."

"I know she would." Terry agreed.

"I'll get on to Jack to sort out the flights and stuff. I wonder what he's been up to recently. Jonathon doesn't seem to know."

"Nor does Tommy. He just grumbles about never wanting to be a boss."

"Good news about Jonathon's pubs and stuff."

"Yeah, I think he will offload them to be honest. He doesn't want to divert his energy from work at the moment."

Now the threat from Frank had been eradicated, Jonathon's holdings had been restored to him and reopened. It had provided a pleasant diversion for a couple of days and relieved a bit of stress, but now he was content to get back to work. He seemed to have made it his life's mission to recover as much of Frank's hidden assets as was humanly possible.

Terry eyed the Rolex Submariner on his brother's wrist as he dug his phone out of his pocket. It was a lovely watch indeed.

Chapter One Hundred And Three

This time, Alsina and the brothers' passage through the airport was not the usual standing in line and checking of passports. José whisked them past all the queues and wished them a fond farewell.

When they reached Gatwick, they were met by no less than Jack Fairfax and Tommy Rooke, Jonathon having been left in charge of the office. Not that he really minded. He was obsessed with his job now and took it as a personal affront if he did not find at least a million pounds a day.

When they reached the car park, Tommy got the car, while Jack chatted with them until he returned. They got in and Jack turned around in the front seat.

"We have to make a pit stop on the way to the office. I need to clear something up. Sorry if you were expecting to go straight home, I know you are looking forward to meeting up with Mrs. Hoon again."

Mrs. Hoon had returned to England a week previously, on the pretext of making a start on Terry's flat, getting it ready for him in his diminished capacity as his arm was not fully healed and wouldn't be for some time to come. Terry knew what she was really up to, as did Johnny. That much had been necessary to enable Jack to get Mrs. Hoon in place for Alsina's impending surprise.

As they turned onto the familiar roads leading to Davina's house, which was how Alsina still thought of it, she looked around in alarm.

"I really do not think I want to go to the house if it's alright with you. Can you drop me off at the end of the road and I will wait for you there, Jack?" She had made no plans for repairing the lovely house and in truth she had been putting off making any decisions.

"I'm sorry about this Alsina, but I don't want to leave you unprotected for a while. Don't worry, the house doesn't look as bad as it did when you left."

"Jack's right sweetheart, don't worry, I'm here. You have to see it sooner or later anyway."

"I don't know Johnny, I just have so many sad memories of the place now."

"Don't forget, there are also a lot of happy memories, d'you remember when you first saw the house? Also, remember when I brought the Mini to you? There are tons of happy memories here. Davina and Stephen wouldn't want you to be unhappy here."

As they talked Tommy continued to drive in to the property. He went as fast as was comfortable for his passengers, so as to allow as little time as possible for Alsina to come up with more excuses not to see the house. As the car swept up the drive Alsina sighed as she made a physical effort to open her eyes. She gazed at the place that she held so dear and yet harboured such powerfully sad memories for her. Then she cried out loud and burst into tears.

The sight that greeted her was not at all what she had been expecting. Far from being the bombed out shell that she remembered, she was now looking at a fully restored and improved property. It was essentially the same as it had been before in looks, but even in her emotionally charged state, she could see subtle differences.

"There are more gadgets on the roof!"

"If you feel up to a guided tour, I think you'll find that there is a lot more of everything and not just on the roof." Jack replied.

As they approached the front door it swung open and Mrs. Hoon walked out pulling off a pair of rubber gloves. Alsina looked from the older woman to Terry and then Johnny before saying accusingly, "You knew!"

They remained silent, but Johnny gently stroked her back and head, running his fingers through her hair. She looked again at the house and saw a little black and brown shape emerge behind her friend.

"Oh, it's a little Vincent." She started crying again.

"It didn't seem right to have the place up and running again without him. As it happens it is a blood relation of Vincent. Joseph was very good friends with the breeder." Jack got out of the car and opened the door for Alsina to climb out too.

Alsina walked into the open arms of Mrs. Hoon who was also crying as she whispered into the younger girl's ear. "It's all yours now my lovely, I'll stay on if you want me too."

"I didn't know... I didn't know anything about this." Tears were still streaming down Alsina's cheeks.

"We know you didn't sweetheart, but it's what Davina and Stephen would have wanted. Everything's brand new and the kitchen is slightly different, I had to tell them what was best for me to work with."

"How long have you known?"

"A while now. Come and meet your little one."

"What is he called?"

"Well, that's up to you." Mrs. Hoon replied.

"Hello little one. I think you are a… Dominic!" Alsina bent down to stroke the young dog, who promptly licked her face and then ran off to jump up at Johnny.

"He has a thing with animals." Terry smiled as he spoke and then he too bent down, gingerly, to stroke the little Rottweiler.

The whole of the inside of the house had been gutted and remodelled. Alsina's new room was where Joseph's old room had been and everything was fresh and new.

The latest up to date and energy efficient lighting and heating systems had been installed. A huge T.V. had been installed in the lounge and a smaller one, albeit only slightly smaller, had been installed in the kitchen.

"We seem to spend so much time in there anyway." Johnny said by way of an explanation.

The windows were bombproof and the external doors were now much more secure than before. She found that she now had a permanent security suite and control centre and more state of the art security gadgets and cameras.

"What do I need all this for?"

"Well. You are going to marry Johnny, so we thought we might as well put it all in now, rather than later. You know what he's like for attracting trouble." Jack said confidently.

"Thanks boss." Johnny responded.

"But seriously, do you think we will ever need to use it all?" Alsina continued.

"It's better to be safe than sorry." Jack, Terry and Johnny all said at the same time.

Alsina shook her head and Johnny gathered her up in his arms. "Don't worry about it sweetheart, at least you know the takings will be safe if you ever have to bring them home from the club."

Mrs. Hoon called them down to the kitchen and handed out cups of tea and an open packet of biscuits to Tommy, who proceeded to pass them round. They all leaned against the work surfaces and drank slowly, in almost total silence. Alsina couldn't quite take it all in, but was happy that they thought enough of her to surprise her like this.

"Right, we have to get off now, I hope you don't mind, but we thought Terry could stay with you two for a while, just until we have everything sorted."

"Of course, you do not need to ask."

"Always a gentleman, that's our Jack." smirked Johnny.

"Unlike that boy of yours, Alsina. Right, Tommy, let's go. We will ring you later or Jonathon can brief you in person when he comes over later."

Alsina took her bags from the hallway, where Tommy had left them while she was being shown the improvements and headed to her new room. Johnny followed with his and Terry's bags and Mrs. Hoon showed him which room to put them in.

"Are you sure that you are okay with this sweetheart?"

"Oh Johnny, it is the best thing that you could have done."

"But it isn't too soon, is it love?"

"Of course not. I love it. I was trying to pretend that I would not have to come back here and that would have been a big mistake."

"As long as you are happy my love. Are you tired?" Johnny asked.

"No, not really."

"Oh that's a shame."

"Oh right!" Yawn. "Yes, now you come to mention it I am rather tired."

"Oh good." Johnny shut the door and scooped up his fiancé before placing her very gently on the huge bed.

Terry followed Mrs. Hoon down the stairs, grinning, having heard the last part of the conversation between his brother and Alsina.

"Are you tired Mrs. H?"

"Enough with you Terry, we're too old for those sort of games."

"You are never too old for *those* sort of games."

She laughed and pulled him down the stairs after her. He settled into one of the chairs around the table as she went about making the dinner. He watched her deft preparations knowing that he would never be as good as her in the kitchen.

She looked up and smiled at him. Things would not be back to normal in this house for a while, but they were well on their way now to some sort of normality.

Chapter One Hundred And Four

Jonathon walked through the front door of Alsina's freshly refurbished home. Although he had been involved in some of the planning he hadn't actually seen the final result, being far more engrossed in hunting hidden money. He looked around and nodded appreciatively. He liked what he saw.

"This place is just great!"

"I know. I really wasn't looking forward to coming back here." Alsina confessed.

"I can appreciate that, sweetheart, but you did. That's great."

"I can't describe it. It is like the best of everything with the worst taken away."

"They were special people, from what I remember."

"Yes, they were." Alsina sounded wistful.

Jonathon thought that it was to be expected, that it would be hard for Alsina to acclimatize to the new-look house. He knew what lay underneath the façade of the house and it would take a heavy ordinance blast to do anywhere near the damage that the last attack had achieved.

"Where are the boys?" Jonathon asked.

"Where do you think? They are in the kitchen."

"Oh good, is there any tea on the go?"

"You English and your obsession with tea. I will never understand it."

"It's like you Germans and your obsession with beer, I will never understand that." joked Jonathon.

Alsina gave him a withering look. She knew that Jonathon was fond of a pint of beer or two. "Ah yes, the famous English irony."

They walked through to the kitchen, where the brothers looked up and smiled a greeting. As if by magic, a cup of tea appeared in his hand and Mrs. Hoon wandered off in search of biscuits or cake. He sat down at the table. He hadn't eaten properly for a while now and was quite looking forward to sampling Mrs. Hoon's cooking again.

"What have you recovered so far then mate?" Johnny looked at Jonathon as Terry asked the question. They were both keen to know the current total of ill-gotten gains that had so far been recovered.

"I'm glad you're both sitting down, the last tally was nearly five hundred million pounds."

"Fucking hell!" The two men spoke at the same time so their voices seemed as one.

"I know! You wouldn't believe that he could get that much so quickly."

"We're in the wrong jobs, you know that?"

"You wouldn't change sides for the world, Boy." Jonathon stated.

"Even so, that is a lot of money." Johnny confessed.

"And there is still more out there."

"What the hell was he into?" This time Terry took charge of the conversation.

"Well that's just it. It wasn't just the illegal stuff. The fronts that he set up were making serious money. He bought everything for cash without loans or mortgage and they started bringing in huge returns. I think he had to set up so many to try and share the illegal income in a more efficient way."

"Money goes to money, as they always say." Terry mused.

"Fortunately, they say crime doesn't pay too."

"Well it certainly didn't pay for Frank, well not for long anyway," added Johnny.

"I tell you what. If we left his legitimate businesses alone, I reckon they could pay off the national debt in a couple of years."

They all laughed at that. They liked the idea of Frank Underwood's money being used for something constructive, rather than causing misery to so many people.

"Do you think that you have all of his men now?" Johnny continued.

"We can't really be sure, one or two may have slipped through the net, but hopefully they will lay low."

"When do you think that Jack will let us come back to work?"

"I honestly don't know. That was one of the reasons he got this place sorted. At least you will be safe here."

"But we'll be climbing the walls soon mate." Johnny moaned.

"No you won't. You've got your new business to set up."

"What new business?" Neither Terry nor Johnny understood the comment.

"Wedding planners. I assume you will be helping Alsina with the arrangements."

"Piss off!" Terry chuckled.

"No gratitude, that's your problem boys."

Alsina came over to stand behind Johnny. She had been listening to the conversation and it suddenly occurred to her that Jonathon was right. She would need help arranging her wedding.

"I'll help you love, don't worry." Mrs. Hoon had seen the look of distress on Alsina's face and correctly interpreted it.

"Thank you and I hope that I can count on both of you." She looked at the brothers. Jonathon sniggered, earning a glare from Terry.

"We'll go over to the club tomorrow love, don't worry. I think Bernie has had some experience of this sort of thing before." Johnny had become quite close to Bernie when his cover story needed him to work at the club. He seemed to remember that Bernie had told him once that he never wanted to plan another wedding, as long as he lived.

"That's a great idea." Alsina's smile faltered as she looked at Jonathon. "We will be allowed to go to the club, won't we?"

"Of course love, Tommy will drive you. It's as safe there as it is here."

"Do you think Tommy will drive me on my wedding day?"

"Why don't you ask him love, I think he would be thrilled."

"Do you think I should invite my parents over to help too? I know they don't know a lot about things over here, but it might be nice for my mother at least." This question was directed at Johnny who nodded enthusiastically.

"I think that's a great idea. They can stay here with us and we will have someone else to talk to. I think they will be impressed with the house too."

"I hope so. I am becoming more attached to it with every hour that passes."

Jonathon watched Alsina as she spoke to Johnny. He was glad that she liked the house. He liked the girl a lot and was glad that she and Johnny were planning ahead. He thought of Johnny like his own brother and was glad that he was in his life again.

"Are you staying for dinner Jonathon, there's plenty." Mrs. Hoon started laying the table.

"If it's not too much trouble, then, thank you, I will."

"You're more than welcome mate, she lives to cook." Terry winked at his lover and she smiled back at him.

"And you can tell us what businesses Alsina should invest in, while we eat. Any that Frank was making money with would be a good start." They laughed at Johnny's suggestion, but it gave Jonathon a couple of things to think about.

"Actually Boy, that's not a bad idea. I might even take my own advice and expand my own holdings."

"Do you want a junior partner? We aren't all marrying into money." Terry turned his head as he spoke and winked at his old friend so that Johnny couldn't see him. He needn't have bothered.

"I know you're trying to wind me up Terry. It won't work. Alsina knows how much I love her." Johnny retorted.

"Do you love the girl, I'd never noticed." Terry retorted.

"Piss off." Johnny laughed.

"That's quite enough of that sort of language at the dinner table thank you." Mrs Hoon smiled at Johnny and tried not to laugh as she spoke.

"Yeah, that's enough talk about love for one night." Jonathon joined in with the laughter. It was nice to relax for a while, after the times they had been through.

Chapter One Hundred And Five

The next morning saw Jonathon at work bright and early, as usual. Tommy was not far behind him and found there was a message from Jack waiting on Jonathon's desk, telling him he would be back in the office by midday at the latest.

Jonathon looked up as Tommy placed a fresh mug of coffee on his desk. It had become something of a ritual for them now. Jonathon seemed to spend less and less time away from the office and, no matter what time Tommy returned to it, Jonathon was already there.

"How goes it, this fine morning?" Tommy inquired.

"I'm just checking something out on the inventory of weapons that we recovered."

"And?"

"And, we haven't recovered the mortar yet." Jonathon said with a note of concern.

"But it's only a matter of time, right? There have been no further attacks, so the operators must be dead."

"You know better than that Tommy. Until we see it with our own eyes it still exists."

"Are any of the surviving members of his crew talking yet? Could they shed some light on the situation?"

"Most of them didn't know the mortar team and those that did don't want to admit that they do. Multiple murder charges are something they seem very keen to avoid."

"What about the rest of his empire?"

"There is a definite shortage of drugs in the area. I think the lads from up north are making a move on supplying the shortfall." Jonathon answered.

"And the girls and boys?" Tommy continued.

"That is a more specialized market. Someone will no doubt take over the reins of that little enterprise quick enough." Jonathon was a realist.

"Have we turned up any more shipments or staging houses?"

"Not since the last one you were on. Why?"

"Just curious, I suppose. I got to thinking that there may be some loose ends out there and we should do something about them. Other than the money that is." He added the last bit when Jonathon arched his eyebrows at his statement.

"I'm not just concentrating on the money. I'm looking at the whole picture."

"That's good mate, I just worry about the state of their minds. I mean if they haven't been started on any sort of drugs yet, they must be shit scared."

"I agree, but they just haven't shown up in any of the paperwork that we have recovered so far." Jonathon said reassuringly.

"But you are still looking right?"

"Yes, don't worry." Jonathon sighed. Tommy was always looking out for the welfare of the human victims. He would probably never change and, deep down, Jonathon didn't want him to.

"What made you think of the mortars anyway?" That was the thing about Tommy, once he was satisfied that he had made his point, he just moved on to another aspect of the operation.

"They caused too much carnage to be forgotten about."

"Fair enough. You want me to ask around?" Tommy gave Jonathon a questioning look.

"I would appreciate it, mate. Don't forget, if they are still operational, then Alsina and the Boy could still be targets."

"That's a long shot though. You're just being overprotective right?" Tommy asked.

"Who knows? As I said, until I see them here in this office, they still pose a threat."

"Fine, leave it with me. I'll go over some of the ground that we've already covered, just to be sure and then move on to new avenues."

"Are you getting any stick from our old competitors yet? They must know that you are working with me and therefore Jack."

"Jonathon, mate, look at me. Do you really think that anyone is going to slag me off to my face?"

"Fair comment. Even I wouldn't want to meet you down a dark alley at night."

"Cheers mate, I love you too."

"Talking of people that I wouldn't want to meet down a dark alley, Johnny sends his best." Jonathon said with a smile.

"I'll pop over there later, see how they are and what they're up to."

"Good, I think Alsina wants to ask a favour."

"What is it? Do you know?"

"Yes I do, as it happens, but I promised I would let her ask you. Don't worry. It's nothing bad. In fact I think that you actually might like it."

"Fair play." Tommy shrugged. "I'll pop round there on my way out."

"That would be good, I told them that you would drive them to the club."

"What did the Boy say to that?"

"He's cool about it. He knows it's for the best." Jonathon showed his surprise as he spoke.

"I have to say that I admire the way he has handled himself over this whole operation. I thought that he might go off the plot a little."

"Me too, he has surprised us all. Maybe all your teaching has had some effect on him after all."

"Our teaching, mate and I learned a lot from him too." Tommy replied.

"We all did mate, even Jack learned some things, and I thought he knew it all."

"Kind of you to say so Jonathon." Jack walked into the office and dragged a chair over from an empty desk. He placed a brown paper bag on the end of Jonathon's already crowded desk and the smell of egg and bacon rolls filled the air. "Pull up a chair Tommy, there's enough for you too mate."

Tommy looked at his watch, before reaching around behind him and pulling his own chair from his desk. Jack handed him a roll and Jonathon searched his desk for serviettes or tissues or something similar.

"What's new, boss?" Jonathon spoke just before he poked a piece of his roll into his mouth.

"The top brass are happy with the way things are going. They like your suggestion, however unworkable it is, about running Frank's business to earn an income. It has given them some ideas about undercover operations for the future, so they asked me to convey their thanks."

"I should bloody well hope they are happy with the progress we've made so far, the amount of money they are getting in."

"They are, Jonathon. I'm just letting you know how things are at the moment."

"Still, at least they listened to my idea." He pretended to preen himself in front of the others.

"Don't let it go to your head, son. There is nothing we can do about it, not at the moment anyway." Jack laughed.

"Anything else, boss?" This time it was Tommy who spoke. He was becoming more comfortable with the amount of attention that his superior was giving him. He was starting to relax around him and was therefore able to contribute ideas that he had floating around in his mind.

"They are concerned about the possibility of informants in our set up. They think that maybe this should be a priority now."

"What about the human trafficking?"

"That's still a high priority. Don't worry Tommy, we will do what we can as soon as possible."

Tommy nodded and took another mouthful of food, washing it down with what was left of his coffee. He wiped his mouth and returned his chair to its original position, then checked his watch again.

"I'm off to see Terry and Johnny. I'll check back in with you later, unless you have anything else for me boss?"

"No, that's fine Tommy. Give them my regards and tell them I'll try to see them later on in the day."

"I'm driving them to the club a little later. Will that be a problem?"

"No, I'll check in with you to see where they are before I leave the office."

"Okay, see you both." He turned and walked out of the office, nodding to the few early birds who had also come in to get a head start on the day. None of them were surprised to see him already on his way out. That too had become a ritual for them.

"Is it me, or does Tommy seem more confident to you, Jonathon?"

"It's not you boss, he was a bit unsure of himself before when we last worked for you, but I think our time away has helped him a lot."

"So he's happy to be back at work then?"

"Definitely!"

Chapter One Hundred And Six

Tommy arrived at Alsina's house and was greeted by Dominic. He was just bending down to pat him when he heard footsteps on the gravel driveway. Standing up, he looked around for the source of the noise, while involuntarily reaching for his gun.

"You know that would have looked great on a report "I was shot while I was playing with a cuddly Rottweiler puppy", yeah that would have been just fabulous."

"Piss off, Johnny."

"How are you, mate?"

"Yeah good, I think, Johnny."

"Any news?"

"Jonathon has a bee up his backside about the missing mortar. He thinks there is a slim possibility that you two may still be targets."

"I suppose I have to agree with his assessment. He's normally bang on target about this sort of thing." Johnny replied.

"The top brass want the moles in our lot weeded out quickly. They are embarrassed and worried about further leaks, or worse, another Frank Underwood."

"The money seems to be there to be made, Tommy. It must be tempting for a few of them at least."

"I reckon we should be searching for the human traffic victims. That would be more important in my view."

"I have to agree with you. If Frank had succeeded with his plans for Alsina, it would be her we were looking for now and I don't even want to think about that scenario."

"You've changed, Johnny, you appear to have calmed down a bit. You're not as hot headed as you used to be. Is it something to do with the stabbing, or just a bit of everything?"

"I don't know, mate. I had a lot of time to think things through after the stabbing and I have to admit, I think Alsina has helped a lot."

"I can see that. She's a very special person, Johnny. You need to make sure that you keep hold of her."

"You don't need to worry on that score. I plan to try very hard. Though I have to admit, I sometimes wonder what I did to deserve someone like her."

"Don't put yourself down lad, you do deserve her."

"Yes, he does. Though I don't know if I deserve him." Neither of the men had seen or heard Alsina approach and Johnny looked a bit embarrassed, partly because Alsina had heard what he said and partly because he had just committed the same error that Tommy had made on his arrival, not being aware of his environment.

"Hello, sweetheart, I didn't see you there." Johnny tried to hide his discomfort.

"So I noticed. Hello, Tommy." She walked over and kissed him lightly on the cheek. Tommy smiled down at her.

"Hi, Alsina, how are you?"

"I am fine thank you, have you had breakfast?"

"I had a roll at the office."

"We have food if you want some. Mrs. Hoon always cooks enough to feed an army."

"I'll take a coffee thanks. Jonathon said that you need me to drive you to the club today."

"Yes, and I have another matter that I would like to discuss."

Tommy looked across to Johnny to try to get a line on what he would be asked, but Johnny just winked at him and put his arm around his fiancé. Dominic trotted along behind them.

They entered the kitchen and Mrs. Hoon gave Tommy a hug before handing him a cup of coffee and a plate of bacon and eggs. She waved away his protests and ushered him into a chair to eat his meal.

Alsina sipped her own coffee and waited while he ate. She chatted with Mrs. Hoon about things in general, until Tommy had finished his meal and refused another helping.

"I would like to ask you a favour and I hope you don't feel that I am being too forward."

"What's that then, Alsina?"

"I wondered if you would drive me to the club on my wedding day? I hope you don't think that this is 'taking a liberty', is that how Johnny says it?"

"I would be honoured sweetheart and of course you're not taking any liberties."

Alsina relaxed visibly as the tension left her. Tommy could not think why she would be so worked up over asking such a small favour, so he asked her.

"Why so serious sweetheart?"

"I didn't know if you would think it was a misuse of your skills. Johnny and Terry say you are the best person behind a wheel that they have ever seen."

Now it was Johnny's turn to look embarrassed. Tommy had been his hero, after Terry of course, for many years.

"They said that, did they?" Tommy was smiling in a bemused manner.

"What I actually said was, that it would be nice to give the old fart something to do that didn't involve too much effort."

"He did not. Johnny I cannot see why you do not tell Tommy how you feel." Alsina threw her hands up in the air and looked at Johnny, waiting for an answer.

Realizing that he would not be let off the hook, Johnny sighed and gave in. "Alright, Tommy I would really appreciate it if you drove my fiancé to the ceremony, as I would like her to get there on time and in one piece. She means an awful lot to me and you are the only person other than myself or Terry whom I trust to look after her."

"Well if you put it like that, of course I will, but I've already said that. Don't you listen to anything I say Boy?"

"Not if I can help it, no." He would have said more but Alsina chose that moment to kiss him hard on the lips and thus end any further, silly statements.

Tommy took pity on Johnny. "What time do you want to go to the club today, Alsina?"

"Whenever we are all ready, if that is agreeable with you?"

"Your wish is my command, my lady."

Alsina laughed. She did not know why she had been so worried about asking Tommy to drive her, but now that he had agreed it seemed like a great weight had been lifted from her shoulders.

They took their time sorting things out in the house and Tommy found out that Terry would not be coming with them. Instead he would stay and keep an eye on things at the house until one of their colleagues arrived to take over.

Terry had used a practical argument with Jack. Until they could prove there was a viable threat to their lives, why tie up unnecessary manpower when they could do some of the easy stuff themselves?

It also gave him and Mrs. Hoon some quality time alone, having been cooped up with Johnny and Alsina for what seemed like a lifetime now. Tommy watched how Terry looked at the housekeeper and realized that he had never seen Terry look like that at anyone else. He thought about Bethany, as he did at various times of the day or night, but strangely this time, he was not disheartened. It had been a long time since her death, but perhaps at long last, he would be able to move on.

They left Dominic with Terry and drove out of the grounds. Alsina watched Tommy as he drove and realized that Johnny had not been exaggerating about his skills. She had been driven by Tommy before, but had not paid that much attention. Now she watched him closely as he headed in the direction of the club.

Tommy was aware of every vehicle in his vicinity. He registered the pursuit car that Jack had arranged for him, although he made no sign of recognition. The trip proved uneventful, but he was never sorry for his vigilance.

He parked in front of the main entrance to the club and Bernie Holt greeted them. He hugged his business partner warmly and shook hands with Johnny and Tommy before leading the way into the club.

Both Johnny and Tommy nodded as they noticed the extra protection that was now subtly in place. Bernie didn't mind the expense and the club was thriving, so it could easily afford it.

Johnny wondered again about the effect Alsina seemed to have on people. He smiled as he followed them into the foyer and then into the dance hall. Alsina had decided that she wanted to see the club again in its entirety, before sequestering herself in the office.

Alsina looked towards the bar with a pang of regret. She still missed Amelia deeply and it hurt her physically to think of the wasteful loss of lives that Underwood had caused.

They walked into the office and Johnny and Tommy sat on the settee while Alsina and Bernie sat around the desk.

"Why are the security costs so high, Bernie?" Alsina asked.

"We're on a high state of alert at the moment. Until I get the all clear from Jack, I think it would be best to continue like that."

"You know best in that department, so whatever you say goes."

Bernie nodded his thanks and looked across to Johnny who was smiling back at him. Alsina had learnt her lessons well. She was tactful and let the people who were more knowledgeable or more experienced deal with the situations that she knew little about.

"These figures look good, Bernie, we are making improvements every week. You have done well."

"I can't take too much of the credit for that. I just implemented what Davina and Stephen had planned to put into operation. Some of the themes were your idea though, I believe."

"I remember that Joseph had a master plan. I think we all just followed his outlines." Alsina declared.

"You do yourself a discourtesy, Alsina. I know you did more than that." Bernie chided her.

Alsina blushed and changed the subject. "Has there been any more trouble since I left?"

"Nothing big, just run of the mill things. I have a log of any incidents and actions that we took." He threw a small book to Johnny who read it and in turn passed it on to Tommy. Both were nodding silently when they had finished.

"Right then, I have a favour to ask you. Can we hold my wedding here please? It would mean that we had to shut to the public for an afternoon and evening. Would you have any objection to that? It is only for one day."

"Of course, I have no objections. I can't think of a better venue and it will make it so much easier to police the whole event."

"I am so sorry that we have to worry about things like security. I really thought that we were finished with all of that nonsense." Alsina suddenly looked very sad.

Bernie smiled at her use of colloquial English. It was evident that she spent a lot of time with

Johnny. Even some of her mannerisms were the same.

"It's not for you to worry about Alsina. We're all happy to do it until we are sure that it is truly finished, eh Tommy?"

"You'll get no argument from me, Bernie. It's just like the old days, looking after the Boy here." He leaned over slightly to avoid a punch that Johnny directed at his shoulder.

"Don't worry about what the staff think, sweetheart. They work for you, just tell them what to do." Johnny tried and failed to keep a straight face as he said this.

"Oh piss off, Johnny." Three heads turned as one, to stare at Alsina as she said the words and watched as she turned a deep shade of crimson. Then they all fell about laughing.

"Oh mate, that girl definitely spends too much time with you, she really does."

"I have to agree with you on that one, Tommy. Sweetheart, language please, I have to apologize boys. It's because she is a foreigner, she has no manners."

Even Alsina laughed now and stuck her tongue out at Johnny.

"See what I mean?" He ducked as Alsina picked up a stress ball and threw it at him. They talked about more mundane matters for another hour or so, before Tommy received a phone call from his boss.

"Jack wants to know where you will be in about another hour."

"I think, that if we are all finished here," Alsina looked at them and everyone nodded "then we will be at the house."

"He says "Right then", he will see you there later." Tommy put his phone back in his pocket. "Should we tell Terry he is on his way?"

"I think that might be an idea." They all nodded agreement to Johnny's answer.

Chapter One Hundred And Seven

Terry greeted Jack at the front door. He was freshly showered and relaxed. Tommy drove in about two minutes after Jack and found them still talking in the hallway, with the front door wide open. They all traipsed into the kitchen and hunted for chairs before accepting the obligatory mug of tea.

"I don't have much time, but I thought that I should let you know the latest."

"Fire away boss."

"Thanks Johnny. Firstly, thank you all for being patient. I know this is hard and perhaps harder still for you two." He indicated the brothers. "I can't begin to understand how you are coping, not having been through anything like this myself."

"Thanks boss. It means a lot to the Boy and me to know that you are trying to get it sorted."

"As I said, patience is the key here. I assume Tommy has told you of the official thinking. I agree with them, but think that finding the mortar is also a priority, as is locating the human victims." Jack smiled at Tommy, who nodded.

Tommy accepted that, once his boss said he would do something, it would be done. Jack didn't make idle promises, which was what made him as well liked amongst his team as he was. Both Johnny and Terry knew he had a sincere empathy with the human traffic victims and Johnny was still trying hard not to think of Alsina as a potential victim.

"We are turning the pressure up on the hunt for moles in the organization. It is still early, but things look promising. The same applies to the human traffic. Sorry boys and girls," Jack gestured towards Alsina and Mrs. Hoon, "but we still haven't located the mortar."

"D'you want me and Terry to help find it?"

"I think the only way you could do that would be as a target and, before you volunteer Johnny, I am *not* prepared to let that happen."

"I would prefer that, too." All eyes went to Alsina and Johnny nodded his acceptance of her wishes. The others marvelled at his acquiescence and mulled over the changes that the girl had brought about in him.

"I know I don't have a lot of say, but I would prefer it if *you* weren't a target either Terry." Now Mrs. Hoon became the centre of attention.

"You have as much right to an opinion as any of us love." Terry spoke quietly but nobody doubted his sincerity, least of all Mrs. Hoon.

"Right, now we have got that notion out of the way, I will move on." Jack took charge of the meeting again. "I'm trying to allow you as much freedom as I can. Top brass agree that you may still be targets. I know you think it only a small possibility, but it's still a possibility. That said, I am happy for you to leave the grounds as long as you have security with you. At the moment, that is Tommy, but if Jonathon needs him then I will find someone equally up to the task."

Everyone gave Jack their full attention. Nobody queried his thinking. He had not lasted as long as he had through making foolish decisions.

"Also, the club is a safe haven, so you can move about freely in there. I have briefed Bernie about my concerns and he will do whatever is necessary. Members of our team will take it in turns to supply your provisions, if Mrs. Hoon would be so kind as to supply a list of your needs."

"Is that really necessary boss? Is that not wasting valuable manpower that could be utilized elsewhere?"

"The team have already volunteered to do it in their own time Johnny. Accept their help. They wouldn't offer it if they didn't mean it. Though I dare say in some cases it's a ploy to get hold of some of Mrs. Hoon's delightful cooking once again."

"Once tasted never forgotten." Tommy nodded his head vigorously. Mrs. Hoon beamed with pleasure at the words.

"Also Alsina, I know you are planning your wedding. I can foresee no problems with this, given the choice of venue, so please carry on as you are doing. A break from the monotony will do us all good. And Tommy will be available on the day." Jack was watching Tommy who was obviously curious as to how he knew. "Jonathon mentioned it to me."

Tommy nodded slowly. It was obvious really, but he was still surprised. Jack had a way of finding things out that he still didn't understand. He supposed that was what made Jack the man he was.

"Right, if there are no questions, then I'll have to be off."

"Only one."

"Yes Alsina?"

"Are you coming to the wedding?"

"I wouldn't miss it for the world."

"Good, that is all I wanted to know." Her smile lit up the room and it was infectious.

"Right, thanks for your time. Let me know if you need anything, or ring Jonathon. He's probably still in the office. Actually Terry, could you do me a favour please?"

"What's that boss?"

"Tell him to go home and get some sleep. Or at least come and spend an evening over here with you lot."

"I'll do what I can, boss." Terry promised.

"So will I, boss. I'll bring him here in handcuffs if necessary."

"Thanks, Tommy. Right I'm off. Talk to you tomorrow."

Terry and Tommy escorted him out. When they returned to the kitchen, Mrs. Hoon gave them their orders. "Tommy you go and collect Jonathon and Terry you call him now and tell him that Tommy is on his way. If he gives you any trouble then tell him I will get Tommy to take me over there to collect him myself."

They all laughed and were not surprised that five minutes later Tommy was on his way to the office to collect him. That gave Johnny and Alsina time to freshen up and Mrs. Hoon time to sort out the menu for the evening and the snacks for later.

Jonathon and Tommy spent the night at the house, having eaten their fill and drunk far too much to legally drive. Mrs. Hoon stayed over too and the next morning saw her in the kitchen frying mountains of bacon and trying out a pancake recipe.

Jonathon felt totally relaxed as he let Tommy drive him to the office. Johnny and Terry had decided to hammer out the plans for the wedding with Alsina, who had rung her parents to invite them over for a holiday of sorts.

Chapter One Hundred And Eight

Alsina's parents arrived and the wedding arrangements proceeded without many problems. They shopped for the dress with heavy but subtle security and Alsina found out that she had friends in places that she didn't even know about.

When she tried to pay for the dress, she found the account already settled. When she queried this, she found out what one of her favourite clients at the club actually did for a living. He did not run a dress shop as she had once understood. He actually had his own fashion label, which, although only small, was still unique and prestigious in its own right.

Catering was handled by their club's own caterers and provided as a courtesy. Jack and his team handled the flights, mainly from Spain and Germany, and the accommodation for all of the guests. Jack pointed out that it was in his best interests to coordinate all of the security issues. José had to decline his invitation due to work issues.

To Alsina's delight, the wedding preparations were going like a dream. Bernie, contrary to his earlier misgivings, excelled in his role and the big day approached with startling speed and surprisingly little stress.

Alsina and her mother spent a lot of time with Mrs. Hoon. After a few days, Sabine helped in the kitchen at Mrs. Hoon's invitation and, unexpectedly, the two women worked extremely well together.

Johnny and Terry ran every morning, sometimes with Alsina and sometimes with Jonathon, who had taken to coming over most mornings to clear his head and indulge in a decent breakfast. Tommy normally came over just for the breakfasts.

They had had a break through with the human trafficking investigation, which had effectively ended Frank Underwood's old supply line. They knew that someone else would start up soon enough, but they were content that it would not be as large or complex a set up as Frank's had been and therefore easier to find and dismantle.

While Tommy had been making enquiries about the mortar team, he had uncovered an arms cache, which brought the team huge kudos with their masters. Also included in the find were two lightweight mortar units with ammunition.

Satisfied that the mortar team posed no threat now, Jack terminated the security detail and the whole house breathed a sigh of relief. Marcus and friends arrived a few days early for the ceremony and were put up at the house, which was full to overflowing.

They now had three people cooking and preparing meals and a fairly joyous mood prevailed on everyone concerned. A mixed stag and hen party was held at the club in separate sections before eventually joining together at the end of the evening.

The final preparations were made and the big day arrived at last. Tommy arrived early to take Johnny and Terry away before Alsina started dressing, with the assistance of both her mother and Mrs. Hoon.

The club was a hive of well-organised activity and all the staff had been put on short shifts so as to be able to attend if they wished. The security staff were immaculate in highly polished shoes and dinner jackets and fell to their duties with zeal.

All the guests were in place when Tommy arrived with Alsina and the 'Wedding March' began. A collective gasp went through the assembled company when they saw the creation that Alsina was wearing.

The dress itself was simple to emphasise the wearer's natural beauty. The train was fairly short and flowed behind effortlessly. She looked quite simply, stunning.

Alsina shone with a radiating beauty. She was smiling shyly as she walked down the aisle on her father's arm, staring at Johnny who, in turn, had eyes only for her. When she arrived at the altar he mumbled, "You are beautiful" and she beamed happily at him.

Johnny's ring was plain and subtle, hinting at an understated style. Alsina's ring was very special to her, as Tommy had given it to her. It had been Bethany's ring and Alsina had wept when he offered it to her.

The ceremony took on a dreamlike quality to Alsina, who followed her cues from the minister faultlessly. A loud cheer went up when Johnny was told he could kiss the bride and he kissed her passionately, for what seemed like a short time to him.

The polite coughing from the minister and the not so subtle "Alright Boy, that's enough," from his brother brought them back to the rest of the congregation, who were still cheering.

The chairs were moved and tables brought in and everybody lent a hand in setting up the dinner tables for the wedding breakfast. The atmosphere was electric and Alsina thought that this was the happiest day of her life. She compared this day with the day that Johnny had first come into her life and she was happy. She looked at her parents, who also seemed to share her mood.

Johnny put his arm around her waist and pulled her to him, kissing her once again. "You have made me the happiest person on the planet, my love, thank you."

"You are mistaken, sweet heart. I am the happiest person on the planet."

He stroked her face and then kissed her lightly again, before leading the way to the top table. Alsina looked about her and noticed that all her staff had attended, which pleased her immensely. She smiled at them and returned waved acknowledgements. She never wanted this feeling to end.

The speeches went off without a hitch. Bernie, who was the Master of Ceremonies, called their attention to Jack, who toasted 'absent friends' and they all thought of the people they had lost in the last few months.

Johnny and Alsina led the first dance, as is customary and then Alsina danced with all of her friends. Marcus was dancing with her when Johnny tapped him on the shoulder and cut in. Marcus' friends had been on their best behaviour all day, as they had promised Marcus they would be. They also danced with the bride, who thanked them all for their help in the marina.

The party increased in pace and everyone enjoyed themselves. Tommy danced with Alsina and she then introduced him to some of her friends from the club. She cared deeply for this man and she hoped that she would never experience what he had, when Bethany died.

Jonathon replaced Tommy, who in turn was replaced by a smiling Jack Fairfax. Terry and her father also jumped in when they could, but they all backed out gracefully whenever Johnny appeared at her side.

Jonathon pulled Terry to one side. "D'you know, I don't think I've ever seen the Boy smile so much?"

"You're not wrong, mate. She's a good girl that one."

"Lovely!" Jonathon said.

"Right, let's grab Tommy and have a drink at the bar."

"You're on Terry, mate. How was it, being Best Man?"

"Terrifying."

"I know what you mean. I was Tommy's best man."

"You never actually talked about that, Jonathon."

"It was a difficult time for us both. I think he's over the worst of it now, well, I hope he is."

"You really care for him."

"Like a brother." Jonathon admitted.

"Where does Marcus fit in?" Terry asked.

"Grab a bottle, that is a bloody long story."

"Best grab two then, he's coming over, or three if Tommy's joining us."

"Better make his a soft drink, he's driving again later."

Chapter One Hundred And Nine

The party ended at three o'clock in the morning. Surprisingly, most of the guests had remained fairly sober, but one or two were fading fast.

Taxis, limousines and minibuses had been laid on to return the guests to their various residences. Most of them waited outside for Alsina and

Johnny to leave before starting out on their own homeward journeys.

Security was on the ball. Apart from the Bride and Groom there were many potential targets for an opportunist. Bernie's security personnel mixed well with Jack's people, who would have worked for free, such was the respect they had for the happy couple. As always, attention was being given to even the smallest detail. Both bosses were tremendously proud of their people.

The teams were relaxed, but alert. It would take a very lucky move to even get close to any potential targets, with the current arrangements. Johnny led Alsina out through the main doors to be showered with confetti from their friends and the other well-wishers. Still the security teams stayed at their posts, their only concession to the day was that they were all wearing huge smiles.

Tommy was waiting at the rear of the vehicle that would take them back to the house for what was left of the weekend, before picking them up on Monday morning to transport them to the airport to start their honeymoon.

Fireworks exploded in the air and the guests looked skywards, surprised by their sudden appearance. The security teams too, glanced skywards before radioing to their controls. Nobody had told them to expect this, was it planned? If it was, it was a major security cock up.

Tensions rose among the security personnel, as the word came that the light show was not authorised. Johnny picked up on the change in atmosphere and hastened his bride to the Range Rover. He caught Tommy's eye as he approached and the big man searched the surrounding area to make sure that there was no imminent attack.

Another brilliant flash split the sky and as it faded Tommy's eyes were drawn to an object that appeared to be falling in his direction.

"Incoming!" He shouted to make sure that he was heard over the percussion sounds of the fireworks. He made sure that Johnny was moving to cover his new wife as he himself moved to cover Johnny.

The explosion was deafening. The Range Rover disintegrated behind Tommy and he was flung unconscious through the air towards the young couple.

The shock wave knocked Johnny from his feet and he fell onto Alsina who clung to him with amazing strength before relaxing her grip as they hit the ground. Johnny heard a dull crack as her head hit the ground next to his and saw Alsina's eyes start to glaze over as blood started to spurt out of the gash in the back of her head.

Terry launched himself off the top step and simultaneously pushed Mrs. Hoon into Alsina's parents. Jack Fairfax moved to shield them from any blast wave and Jonathon followed Terry down the steps towards his fallen friends. He gave Johnny a cursory glance as he passed a now kneeling Terry, who was frantically trying to stem the flow of blood coming from Alsina's head.

Jonathon stopped abruptly when he reached Tommy and dropped to the ground to check on his friend. He slapped Tommy's face and tapped on his clavicle, which he knew from experience would elicit a response from his friend if he was anywhere near to being conscious.

The security teams sprang into action. Vehicles flew from all directions towards the exit to try to find the launch site. It could not be too near, as all the danger points had been secured earlier in the day. Armed men rushed around in synchronized movements, searching the car park and grounds, hunting for their attackers.

Mortars were still falling as Marcus and his friends went to Bernie to render assistance if necessary and were waved towards the doors. "Get the people into the club, they will be safer inside." Marcus guided his friends into action and then looked for some other way to help.

Tommy's body spasmed and he murmured something that Jonathon couldn't quite catch.

He shouted at his friend and shook him to try to wake him up. Tommy was starting to rouse himself now and Jonathon gasped out loud as his friend finally spoke.

"Alsina?"

"Terry and the Boy are with her now, mate. Don't worry yourself, just rest!" Jonathon realized with a shock that he hadn't seen the girl moving or talking. So great had been his hurry to reach Tommy that he only now realized his mistake. He looked over at the brothers and saw Terry start to rise.

Johnny lifted Alsina from the ground as if she weighed nothing at all and made his way into the safety of the club. It was only now that he realized that mortars were still falling. It all felt surreal as he carried the unconscious girl into the building. As he walked, his experienced mind thought that the mortars must be being fired from the very extreme of their range. Every precaution had been taken to ensure the safety of this wedding. It should not be happening.

Sabine was screaming as Johnny approached her carrying Alsina and he watched Werner hold her tightly to him, which allowed Johnny to take their daughter safely into the club. Bernie Holt rushed towards Johnny and took Alsina from him while Terry pried his brother's arms from around her body.

"Let him work Boy. Leave them be. She will be alright."

Gunfire erupted from somewhere outside the grounds. The mortars stopped falling, but return fire sounded in response to the initial bursts. Johnny's eyes never left the still form of his wife. He didn't hear Terry's words or the gunfire from outside, which was starting to subside. Terry guided him to a seat.

Sirens screamed in the night and flashing blue lights lit the darkness not covered by the club's brilliant security lighting. Johnny watched as the club's first aid kit was brought to Bernie and he ripped off the sterile protection from various dressings. Iodine solution mixed with the blood that pulsed from Alsina's head only to be covered up by the bandages and dressings.

Paramedics were bounding up the stairs from the newly arrived ambulance and Johnny realized that they must have been very close at the time of the attack, for which he would always be eternally grateful. He watched as the freshly gloved hands gently pushed Bernie out of the way and took over the life saving procedure.

The blood started pumping through his veins and arteries again and Johnny looked around for the first time. He took in Alsina's parents and Mrs. Hoon, all standing as close as they could without getting in the way.

Terry's words finally started to penetrate his brain and he looked at his brother, whose face now showed visible relief. "She will be alright Boy, let them work, okay?"

"Where's Tommy?"

"He's still outside, another team is working on him. He blocked you from most of the blast."

"Is he badly hurt?" Johnny started to stand up again and Terry pushed him back down.

"Sit there Boy, Jonathon is with him. I think he will be okay."

"Did they catch them?"

"I don't know yet, I wanted to make sure you were alright."

"I'm fine. Just go and find them Terry, please. Make the fuckers pay!"

"I'm on my way." With that Terry stood up and headed for the doors on the run. Jack thrust a pistol in his hand as he ran past him and he headed for Jonathon and Tommy, the latter who was now just starting to rise.

"Are you alright, mate?"

"I think so. Johnny? Alsina?" Tommy asked.

"Johnny's good, but Alsina is out for the count. The paramedics are working on her. Jonathon, which way did the others go?" He swapped his attention to his old friend, knowing that Tommy would not be able to tell him what he needed to know.

"Turn right out of the gate, they are about half a mile up the road, I think the gunfire's stopped, but be careful. The idiots used a pick-up truck to give them a better chance of escape, but they turned the wrong way, towards the club and it's pretty hard to disguise a mortar unit. I'll follow you as soon as I make sure this one's alright."

"Don't worry about me mate, just go with Terry."

Jonathon handed his friend over to the waiting paramedics and sprinted after Terry, who had not waited for the outcome of the conversation.

Announcing his presence before coming up behind Terry, he moved to his friend's side and they looked around at the returning security teams.

"Where are they?" Terry asked.

"Some of them are back there on the road. We think two of them escaped. Sorry."

"Any survivors talking?" Jonathon asked.

"Not yet."

"They will be." Jonathon growled and they strode off to find their attackers.

The security team looked the other way as Jonathon grabbed an injured man and shouted into his face. "Where are they going? Who are they?"

"Fuck off. Arghhhh…" The latter came as Terry jerked the man's head back. Any further questions were cut off as their attacker lost consciousness. Jack Fairfax appeared at their side and took control of the situation.

"Go back inside and look after Tommy and Johnny. Go now!"

They thought about arguing, but decided against it. They knew Jack cared about Johnny and Alsina as much as they did, so they let it go. He would get the information they needed. That was for sure.

They walked into the brightly lit area around the club and passed through the ring of Police guards.

Their friends all watched them approach and nodded encouragement to them. They would do all that was in their power to help the young couple that meant so much to them. Terry and Jonathon acknowledged the looks and gestures and caught Johnny just before he climbed into the back of an ambulance with Alsina.

"Go to the hospital, we will follow you. Jack is trying to locate the whereabouts of the last of the attackers."

Johnny looked up at his brother. "They got away?" He sounded incredulous.

"Only two Boy and not for long, trust me on that."

Johnny shook his head and climbed into the ambulance to sit with Alsina. He saw Tommy being loaded into another ambulance before the doors closed and the blues and twos started, signalling their departure.

Terry checked on Mrs. Hoon and Alsina's parents. Her mother was in a state of shock, but her father was as calm as he normally was. He trusted the brothers implicitly and his military training was paying him back in spades.

Telling Bernie where they were going, they all got into Jonathon's car and headed out after the ambulances. It didn't take long to get to the hospital and they were admitted without any fuss.

Chapter One Hundred And Ten

Jonathon stayed with the family in the relatives' room and Terry sought out his brother. When he found him he was standing next to Alsina's bed. The casualty staff were working around her, having made sure that she was stable and they did not seem too alarmed by the readings on the monitors.

"How is she Boy?"

"Stable. She should be as good as new."

"And you?"

"I'll live. Any news on the last two?"

"Not yet, Johnny. We're in the relatives' room when you're finished here. We can talk there. I know Sabine and Werner want to know how she is."

"Can you send Sabine in?"

"I'll check." Terry replied.

Five minutes later Sabine walked into the room and hugged Johnny. She looked at her daughter, who was looking so fragile at the moment.

"Jack has arrived. I think he has news."

"Will you stay with her for a minute?" Johnny asked.

"Of course. I will get you when she wakes up."

Johnny walked into the relatives' room and Jack repeated what he had just told the others. "We followed them to a pub, 'The Bugle', on the other side of town."

"I'm coming with you."

"No you're not. Alsina needs you here."

"You're having a laugh if you think that I can stay here." Johnny hissed.

"Please Johnny. It wouldn't do anybody any good for you to be there."

"I need to see this finished, tonight!"

"And it will be, but let Terry and Jonathon handle it." Jack pleaded.

The three men looked at Johnny. Mrs. Hoon and Alsina's father looked up from where they sat as, slowly, Johnny regained his composure. Then he turned and left the room, without saying another word, heading for Alsina's room again.

There was an audible sigh of relief as he left. Jonathon and Terry listened as Jack outlined his plan. Nodding, they said good-bye to Mrs. Hoon and Werner and followed their boss from the room.

Chapter One Hundred And Eleven

Jack pulled up at the staging point near 'The Bugle'. As he walked up to the van that was being used as the base of operations, his men made room for him.

"Anything new to report? Are they still in there?'

"Nothing new boss, they're still in there and we've managed to get eyes inside the pub. They're at a table by the far wall and there aren't that many punters in the way. The observation team are returning now."

The two women who made up the observation team seemed a bit agitated. Jack knew them to be very cool under fire and couldn't understand why they should be acting this way.

"What have you got for me, are they still in there?"

"Johnny just walked in there, boss, we didn't see him coming."

"What?" Jack looked furious.

"Oh shit!" Both Terry and Jonathon spoke at the same time and started to run towards the pub.

"Is he armed?" Jack shouted as he ran to keep up.

"I don't know. I don't think so." It was Terry who spoke, as neither he nor Johnny had been carrying weapons all day, up until the point when Jack gave him the pistol outside the club.

"Thank fuck for that! Stop here and wait!"

Jack called all of his men to order and laid out his plan. It had just been changed, thanks to Johnny, but if the attackers were still armed he gave them authority to shoot to kill.

"On three, go."

They burst into the pub from all entrances and were in time to witness Johnny landing a blow from a pool cue onto the head of one of the attackers.

The man fell to the ground unconscious as his companion started to rise, his hand reaching for his pocket.

Johnny effortlessly altered the direction of the pool cue and caught the man's hand in mid-flight. The man let out a screech of pain and his hand fell to his side. Johnny dropped the pool cue and seized the man by his shirtfront and hauled him bodily over the heavy pub table.

The man hit the floor with a loud thud and Johnny landed on his chest. He held the man to the floor with his left hand, crushing the man's throat. With his right hand he made a fist and smashed it into the man's face.

"If you *ever* fucking come for me or mine again, I'll fucking *kill* you." Spittle flew from Johnny's mouth as he shouted and punched at the same time. At long last he was able to release his frustrations of the past year and he hit the man again and again.

Strong hands pulled Johnny off his victim and he struggled to get at his prey once more.

"Leave it alone Boy, for fucks sake, let it go."

"Stay out of this Terry."

"Do as your brother says, Boy. This scum isn't worth it. It's over mate. Let it go." Jonathon suggested.

Slowly the anger ebbed from Johnny and he sagged against his brother. Terry and Jonathon were still alert for a resumption of hostilities and carefully led Johnny away from his victims.

They met Jack halfway across the floor and Johnny hung his head. "Sorry, boss."

"Take him back to the hospital you two," Jack said to Terry and Jonathon and then, to Johnny, "We will discuss this later."

They took him out of the pub and got him into the back of Jonathon's car. They didn't speak as they drove back to the hospital, but, as they pulled up, Johnny said. "Sorry!"

"Forget it. We would have done the same. Terry would not have let you down, nor would I."

"I know, sorry."

They walked into the hospital and Johnny left the others to re-join Alsina and her mother. He smiled as he saw his wife's eyes open.

"Where have you been?" Her voice was very weak.

"It's over. We got the last of them."

"Are you hurt?"

"No, I'm well. How are you, sweetheart?"

She smiled at him and turned her gaze to the monitors. "I will live. Now kiss me, Mr. Miller."

"Certainly, Mrs. Miller."

Chapter One Hundred And Twelve

The television news carried the story of the attack the next day. Late editions of the morning papers also ran what little was known so far. Jack was reading over his copies when Johnny walked into his office.

"I thought you would still be at the hospital, Johnny." There was not any trace of anger in Jack's voice.

"I thought I should come and apologize to you, boss. Alsina understands why I'm not there."

"I don't like my orders being ignored, Johnny. I don't speak just because I like the sound of my own voice."

"I know that boss. I wasn't thinking clearly last night, though I understand if you feel the need for a disciplinary hearing."

"I agree with you."

"What, you want a disciplinary hearing for me?"

"No, you weren't thinking clearly last night. In fact you were *clearly* not thinking at all. Do you realize what would have happened if you had killed them?"

"Yes boss, I think so."

"Well as I said, I don't *think* you were thinking properly. The explosion had clearly affected you. On this one occasion, I am prepared to overlook the fact that you deliberately ignored my orders, but if you ever do that again it won't just be a disciplinary that you have to worry about. Do you understand?"

"Yes boss, thank you. It won't happen again."

"How is Alsina this morning?"

"She's much better. She has a fractured skull, but there should be no long-term damage. As you know, head wounds bleed a lot and look much worse than they usually are. I'm not saying that she isn't poorly, but it could have been a good deal worse."

"Well I'm glad for you both. Now, go back to the hospital. You are officially on sick leave. Spend it with your wife."

"Thanks, boss. Do you think there are any more of Frank's people left to worry about?"

"No, I talked to your victims from last night. Frank told them what to do before he left for Spain and they did it. After they heard he was dead they didn't know what else to do and thought that it would give them a chance to take over some of his operation, besides they were well paid beforehand."

"I don't think that anyone could really take over *that* operation." Johnny stated.

"Only if it was one of our people, but I'm making moves to ensure that it doesn't happen again on my watch. We caused that problem, we trained him and we put him in the path of temptation."

"We can't blame ourselves boss, it was his choice."

"It doesn't make me feel any happier. Now go and see your lovely wife. Tell her I'll be over later if I can."

"Thanks again, boss."

Johnny walked out as Terry walked in. "I wondered if there was anything I could say that would influence your decision on the Boy?"

"No, he has nothing to answer for."

Terry didn't comprehend at first and then he understood that his boss was giving his brother a second chance. He backed out of the office smiling and followed his brother out of the office.

"You are bloody lucky. You know that don't you, Boy?"

"Yes, he's a good man." Johnny replied.

"What on earth did you think you were playing at? You went in alone. Why didn't you wait for me?"

Johnny looked at his brother, as he fully understood what he had just been told. Deep down he knew that his brother would have helped him, even if it cost him his job. He nodded his thanks to Terry and looked out of the window, trying to put some order to his thoughts.

They reached the hospital and Johnny went straight to Alsina. Terry went to check on Tommy and found Jonathon already there. Tommy was sitting up and they were chatting quietly.

"How are you, mate?"

"Good, thanks Terry. How's Alsina?"

"She will be fine and I think that is down to you mostly. You blocked most of the explosive force!"

"Tell me about it. Not one of my better actions." He pointedly rubbed his back and groaned. "How did the Boy get on with Jack?"

"Got a reprieve, lucky bugger. I tell you, I could quite cheerfully have murdered him last night."

"Oh well, it ended up alright in the end, eh Terry?" Tommy shrugged.

"I'm glad you can be so bloody philosophical about it."

"It's all over mate. Jonathon just told me that they were the last of Frank's men. Alsina will get better and will bounce back. Look at what she has already been through. She's tough, that one."

"No arguments from me there." Terry said.

"Or me. I was just telling Tommy about the Boy last night. I'm not sure if I wouldn't have done the same myself in his shoes."

They all contemplated that thought. All of them cared deeply for Johnny and Alsina. If they were honest they probably would have acted in the same way. Just then Johnny walked in.

"Hello all. How are you Tommy?"

"I'm good ta, though not as good as you, I see. Why aren't you with your wife?"

"She'll be alright. Alsina wants to know how you are, so I volunteered to find out. She would have made my life hell if I hadn't."

"I'm good, Boy and so is she, that's the main thing."

"Thank you. Thank you for caring and thank you for shielding us last night. We both appreciate it."

Tommy looked a little uneasy. "I really didn't do that much. It just comes easy when you have an arse the size of mine."

"Well thanks anyway. When are they letting you out?"

"Today I think." Tommy replied.

"Can I ask you a favour, mate?" Johnny asked.

"What's that then?"

"Will you pop in and see Alsina to show her you are well. I don't want her worrying unnecessarily."

"No problem Boy, it'll be my pleasure. Now piss off and tell her I'll see her later."

Johnny left the room and Terry stood up to follow him. "Thank you both for what you've done for us. Some people wouldn't have done what you two did."

"Piss off Terry before you have me and Tommy blushing. That's what mates do."

"If either of you two ever needs anything, just ask."

Both men stared at Terry silently. The offer was in the open now. That was enough for all of them.

Chapter One Hundred And Thirteen

"Did you see him sweet heart?"

"Yes love, he's coming to see you later."

"He must not rush things too quickly. Let him get better first."

Johnny snorted. "This is Tommy we are talking about. He's built like a bear."

"Even so, he must not overreach himself."

"He's fine love. That is why he's coming to see you, so he can actually show you how good he is." Johnny rolled his eyes.

"Was anyone else hurt at the club?"

"Miraculously, no. Jack thinks the car was just a lucky hit. Apparently, when they bombed the house, they never expected it to be as good as it turned out. They just aimed for the kitchen because they had seen us congregating there. They were good, but luck was on their side."

"Can you tell Bernie that I'll call him later."

"No need. I've already spoken to him and he's coming over in a while."

"Surely he has enough to do at the club."

"Nothing is more important than you, my lovely. He's coming over, end of story."

Terry and Mrs. Hoon entered the room, closely followed by Alsina's parents. Her mother was back in control of herself now she knew that her child was going to make a full recovery. After looking her over once more, they left her and Johnny alone, then they headed off to give their own thanks to Tommy.

"I do love you. You know that don't you?"

"Not as much as I love you, Johnny. If anything ever happened to you, I think that I would die."

"Nothing will ever happen to me sweetheart. I'm lucky."

"How can you say that, after all you have been through?"

"Because I have you." Johnny grinned.

She smiled at him and yawned. He eased onto the edge of her bed and lay down next to her. "Sleep now, my angel, you need to get better."

Alsina stared at Johnny and slowly her eyes started to close. He watched her sleep for a while, before he himself succumbed to the powerful call. The nursing staff worked around them in as near to silence as they could manage. The young couple had become something of celebrities among the staff. Most of the men thought Johnny was a hero. Most of the women wished that they could find someone like him for themselves.

A bit later, when Jack walked in, he found them asleep in each other's arms and decided not to wake them. Instead he sought out Tommy and gave him an update on what was happening. Just then Jonathon walked in with two vending machine coffees, passed one to Tommy and gave his to Jack, before leaving to get another one for himself.

After nearly an hour, Jack tried Alsina's room again and found them awake. He chatted with them for a while and then returned to the office. He still had much that he wanted to achieve.

Chapter One Hundred And Fourteen

The front door was open and Dominic came bounding out onto the drive. Johnny helped Alsina out of the car and then crouched down to give Dominic some fuss. Alsina went to bend down but Johnny stopped her.

"Let's not push things too soon, love."

"Johnny, I am not fragile. I won't break."

"You are only just out of hospital. Dominic will understand."

"I have missed him."

Johnny sighed and let her have her way. Dominic jumped up once and then turned his attention back to Johnny. It was as if he sensed that he could not to take liberties with his mistress.

Mrs. Hoon hurried to meet them as they entered the house, on their way to the lounge. Alsina was initially aiming for the kitchen as normal, but Johnny steered her to the settee.

A few minutes later Jack Fairfax arrived with Tommy and Jonathon. They exchanged warm and sincere greetings and the spacious lounge was more than enough to accommodate them all.

"I'm downsizing the operation as of Monday. You are no longer targets and now it's more a question of following the paper trail for the money. Jonathon will be concentrating on that for me until I need him for more pressing matters."

"What do you want us to do, boss?" Terry asked.

"I want you to take a holiday, a proper one, you and Johnny. I know we've talked about it before, but your time abroad was not really relaxing was it?" Jack replied.

"What would we do with more time off boss? The Boy was champing at the bit the whole time we were away." Terry countered.

"Right, don't misunderstand me, I don't want you to go, but I want you to think long and hard about your positions. I'll understand if you want to leave after all of this." Jack responded.

"What on earth gave you that idea boss?" Johnny was incredulous.

"You've given so much of yourselves up until now, Johnny, you most of all. Maybe you need to rethink your priorities now that you are married." Jack answered.

"He's right though Boy, you have to think about Alsina now." Terry suggested.

"So you are going to leave as well then, Terry?" Johnny asked.

"You know I won't. Mrs Hoon and I have talked about it and we're happy the way things are and too set in our ways to change now, but you aren't." Terry grimaced.

"You know I love doing what we do." Johnny stated passionately.

"I do Boy, but what about Alsina?" Terry raised his eyebrows.

"I have already said that I will back Johnny with whatever he decides to do." Alsina replied.

"But wouldn't you prefer to know he is safe?" Terry asked.

"No Terry. I cannot see him being happy doing a nine to five job, can you?"

"But he can work in the club with you." Terry argued.

"He won't be happy with that and you know it." Alsina almost shouted.

"Can I say something?" Tommy finally joined the conversation.

"What is it Tommy?" Alsina smiled warmly at the man she grew fonder of every day.

"Why don't you just take a holiday? Relax properly and think of your options. Bernie can run the club and we'll be here if there are any issues."

"But the result would be the same, I don't want to leave the job!" Johnny said stubbornly.

"Just take some time out, Boy, that's all that they're saying." Tommy said in a placating manner.

"And do what exactly?"

"Whatever you bloody want Boy. Just give yourself some time. If you still feel the same when you get back, then so be it. I will say no more about it." Tommy promised.

"Are you okay with that too, boss? If I want to come back I can?" Johnny asked.

"All I want is for you to spend some time with your lovely wife. You've had a tough time of it and you still haven't had a proper honeymoon." Jack responded.

Seeing that Jack and the others were ganging up on him, Johnny finally gave in. He knew in his heart of hearts that he would be back, but the thought of quality time with Alsina was becoming more and more appealing.

Alsina put her arm around him and he squeezed her gently in return. If she had really wanted him to quit, he would have considered it. He would have done it for her and she knew he would, but she would never ask him to.

"Where are you going on honeymoon, by the way, Boy?" Jonathon enquired.

"I don't know. I thought we could just take the boat and head out somewhere, if that's alright with Alsina?"

"As long as I am with you, I don't care where we go."

Just then Jack's mobile rang and he walked out of the room to answer it. Jonathon looked up as he walked back into the room.

"Right, no rest for the wicked. Jonathon, Tommy, we're out of here. Terry and Johnny, have a good holiday."

"But boss, I don't need one."

"Terry, for once in your life, just enjoy yourself!" Jack instructed. With that the three men left the house and drove away.

They all looked around, at a loss for something to do. For the first time in months they could finally relax.

"So what are we going to do then?" Johnny looked around for inspiration.

"I think I want to go to bed." Alsina started to get to her feet.

"Why, aren't you feeling too good, sweetheart?"

"I will be when I have been to bed." She held out her hand and waited for Johnny to realize what she meant. Smiling he winked at his brother and led Alsina out of the room.

Terry watched them go and his gaze fell on Mrs. Hoon. "What should we do?" He raised his eyebrows hopefully.

She put out her hand and he stood up to take it. "You can help me make the supper." They walked towards the kitchen. "Seriously though, do you really think it's all over? I mean how can we ever be sure?"

"We can't love, but life must go on and living like we have been is not life." Terry answered.

"But what about the kids? Can't they move somewhere with a new identity, or is that just in the movies?"

"You know Johnny wants to get back to work. He would never agree to that."

"Even so, it just seems so unfair." Mrs Hoon sighed.

"He chose this life. We both did." Terry added.

"But Alsina didn't, did she!"

"No love, not initially, but she has now, by accepting what the Boy wants."

"Will he change his mind? Do you think there is any chance at all?" Mrs Hoon asked.

"We will just have to wait and see." Terry replied.

Thank you for reading my book. If you enjoyed it please feel free to write a review on whichever site you bought it from. Alternatively you could email me at dids@didshall.co.uk to let me know what you think.

Printed in Great Britain
by Amazon